Praise for *How to Lose a Lord in 10 Days or Less*

"Plenty of scintillating romance and simmering intrigue."

—*Publishers Weekly*

"A richly emotional, wonderfully engaging romance."

—*Booklist Online*

"The author snagged me with likeable characters, a good plot, and a concern that things would turn out well. I need not have worried; she finished this up with a perfect ending."

—*Long and Short Reviews*

"Michels deftly combines banter with touches of poignancy."

—*RT Book Reviews*

"Elizabeth Michels has become one of my go-to authors for a fun and sweet historical romance!"

—*Under the Covers*

"If you are looking for a terrific story packed with life, laughter, and love, *How to Lose a Lord in 10 Days or Less* is the book for you!"

—*Romance Junkies*

# The INFAMOUS HEIR

# ELIZABETH MICHELS

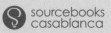

sourcebooks
casablanca

Published by Sourcebooks Casablanca, an imprint of Sourcebooks, Inc.
P.O. Box 4410, Naperville, Illinois 60567-4410
(630) 961-3900
Fax: (630) 961-2168
www.sourcebooks.com

Printed and bound in Canada.
MBP 10 9 8 7 6 5 4 3 2 1

*For my dad. Thank you for reading me tales of rabbit gentlemen and sinister foxes every night before I fell asleep, for encouraging me to reach for my dreams, and for entertaining me with stories of your youth over bad coffee in countless hospital waiting rooms. You inspire me.*

# *One*

ANOTHER PUNCH SKIMMED PAST ETHAN'S EAR. THE rush of air and cheers of the other men closed in on him as the blow sailed by. He put his weight behind his next swing, his knuckles colliding with his opponent's jaw. He watched as the man toppled to the floor with an echoing thud, and he waited.

Ethan stretched his swollen fingers out one by one, flexing through the pain before curling them back into place. Havering, the unfortunate gentleman he was determined to best today, could still get up. If that happened, Ethan would be ready.

He shifted his weight from foot to foot, impatience bubbling through him. A cool trickle of sweat rolled down his temple, falling to his bare shoulder. The man still made no move to rise. Taking a step forward, Ethan leaned over to see if Havering's eyes were open and if he was breathing—a caution Ethan had acquired of late.

"Get up, Havering! Come on, chap! Get up, damn you!" the man's second bellowed above the din.

Meanwhile, cheers were already sounding before the count could be made. Ethan threw a quick glance to the side, not daring to remove his gaze from his opponent for more than a second. The open space around him closed tighter. Murmurs rumbled through the crowd as everyone waited for the end of the match to be called.

"I knew the bastard would go down in the first round. Drunken arse," Lord Cladhart said, sidling up to stare down at the man with him.

Ethan's mouth tugged into a lopsided grin. He was glad to have a friendly face with him today after so long on his own. Besides, Cladhart, his father's long-time business partner and friend, was dead-on with his assessment. "You're only relieved you didn't have to fulfill your duty as second and step in to bloody your own knuckles."

"My knuckles have been bloodied plenty, I'll have you know."

"In the last twenty years?" Ethan nudged Cladhart. "Not likely, old man."

"You might be surprised. I may not be able to pummel every gentleman here without resting as you're apt to do, but I could still put you on the floor, Ethan Moore," Cladhart grumbled. An uneasy moment of silence passed before he began to laugh.

Ethan released the breath he'd been holding and chuckled, relieved he hadn't offended his only ally. When one arrived unannounced at the door of one's father's business partner with nowhere else to turn, it generally wasn't advisable to annoy the man. Ethan required a place to sleep tonight, after all. "You had me readying for another blow to the eye there, Cladhart."

"I should blacken both eyes for calling me old. I've aged the same eight years you have since you left." He nodded toward Havering still lying on the floor. "I'd wager I'd stand a better chance than he did."

"A schoolgirl would stand a better chance than he did." Ethan wiped his brow with the back of his hand.

It was true that Havering hadn't been much of a challenge. In a perfect world, Ethan's opponents would put up a bit of a fight before falling to their knees, but that didn't happen often. There had been that time in France, but in hindsight he'd been a bit too foxed to stop the drubbing he'd received that day. He touched his now slightly crooked nose, the ever-present reminder of that fight. Spain, on the other hand—no, he would not think about Spain. This was his new life. He was here now, back in England, close enough to his childhood home to recognize the sights and smells in the streets, yet far enough away to maintain his distance.

He'd grown used to fighting for his food and his rent over the last eight years. Most saw the sport as entertainment, but for him it had been a means of survival. Eight years ago, he'd thought it might be a skill that could finally put his life back to rights. He'd been wrong about that last bit. But at least fighting had allowed him to eat and have a warm bed at night. After being booted from his home by his father, he couldn't be particular about such things. He curled his fingers back into fists as he watched the man on the floor.

Cheers were sounding all around them as the count continued. "Seven and twenty! Eight and twenty! Nine and twenty! Thirty!"

"Mr. Moore wins!" a man near the back of the room bellowed. The answering chaos of money changing hands, gloating, and disappointed grumbles filled the small boxing establishment off Whitby's High Street.

Ethan smiled thinly as he moved closer to his opponent, gazing down into the defeated man's bloody, swollen face. The man had been bested to be sure, but he would live to fight another day. Cladhart followed him to the center of the floor, clapping a hand on his shoulder.

"Ethan, now that he is thoroughly beaten, we should gather our winnings and leave. I'm aware it's a sore subject, but I told your father I would meet with him this evening to review the week's reports. If I had known you were coming to town, I would have made other arrangements... Though you could accompany me. There's no reason to wait any longer. You've been away long enough as it is."

"Have I?" A moment passed between the two men, both knowing what Ethan was asking. He'd had good reason to leave home at nineteen. That reason began and ended with his father.

Cladhart remained silent on the subject, his sharp gaze never leaving Ethan. As ever, his calm face revealed nothing.

"Or you could accompany *me*. Instead of reviewing dull paperwork, we could use our winnings to buy a round of drinks and our way into a high-stakes card game." Ethan moved to the far side of the room where his belongings were piled in the corner.

"The last time you said those words, you ended the evening half naked at the Swan's Leg while I tried to fend off that barmaid."

"How was I to know Green wasn't bluffing? My play has improved, I'll have you know."

"Nevertheless…" Cladhart ran a hand over his chin in thought as he followed Ethan. "You can't turn up on my doorstep unannounced and expect me to change my calendar."

Ethan slipped his shirt back on, the fabric sticking to his hot skin. He pointedly ignored the man's last comment. "The mining reports won't go anywhere before tomorrow. You might even be able to convince me to approach my father and beg his forgiveness by the end of the night. It isn't likely, but you could try."

"Indeed." Cladhart's face lit briefly with a grin. "Perhaps we can increase our take for the day." One eyebrow raised in the same manner Ethan recalled from when he was a child.

He could remember practicing the expression in the mirror as a boy. There was plenty else crooked about his face these days, but he had finally mastered the raised brow. It was a pleasant change to be back home. His old life on the Continent faded away and his future stretched out in front of him. Escaping danger could be enjoyable after all. He could have a life here without eyeing every shadow, and waiting. Ethan had been right to come back to bury the past and start anew. He wasn't with family, but this was damn close. Cladhart was twelve years younger than Ethan's father and had always been more of an older brother to Ethan than his father's business associate.

Ethan shrugged back into his coat, shaking it into place. Glancing down at the fabric in his hand, he sighed at the prospect of knotting it into anything resembling a cravat. Nevertheless, he tossed it around his neck and began tying it in a crooked knot. "As long as we end the day with money in our pockets, all will be fine. I could use a little excitement to break the monotony."

"Pugilism isn't enough to hold your interest anymore?"

"It's lost a bit of its shine for me recently, as a matter of fact," Ethan said. He patted the finished cravat and looked up.

"Perhaps it's time to raise the stakes from fisticuffs to dueling at dawn."

"I wouldn't go that far. I don't want to kill anyone or be shot at, to be honest." He glanced at the man being revived with smelling salts and swallowed down the memory that had followed him across the waters to England.

"Still. There's nothing like the crack of a pistol piercing the morning air."

Ethan chuckled at the wistful tone of Cladhart's voice. "While you watch from the safety of the nearby street, perhaps."

A silence fell between them. After a moment, Ethan looked up from the buttons on his coat.

Cladhart's eyes were narrowed on a point across the room. "What's your brother doing here?"

"Trevor?" Ethan turned, following Cladhart's gaze

until he spotted his brother just inside the door, dread already gathering in his stomach. "This hardly seems the type of establishment he would frequent. We're a full day's ride from the estate."

Time may have passed since the last time Ethan had laid eyes on his older brother, but he hadn't changed. He was still Trevor, perfect Trevor. As usual, he was so polished in his appearance that the rest of the room seemed soiled in comparison. "Out of place" was the first phrase that came to mind. What would drive his brother from whatever local society event was occurring this afternoon to this dank saloon that smelled of sweat and spilled blood? Trevor spotted Ethan looking in his direction and made his way toward them through the dissipating crowd.

"Good of you to come see the show, Brother," Ethan said. Every muscle in his body tensed for another fight.

"I see the news is true—you have returned. I wanted to see for myself." His dark red head dipped for a second as he took in Ethan's appearance. "News of such things travels quickly, you know. I take it you've decided to return to the family and beg Father's forgiveness. After you hit the local gentry in the face, I mean. We will have to host a celebration to commemorate such a *joyous occasion*." His voice was flat, not matching his happy words.

"I wasn't planning to return home."

Trevor glanced from Ethan to Cladhart and back again. "Father will discover you're back in the area and learn of your…hobbies." The glimmer in his brother's dark brown eyes made it clear that a lecture on Ethan's behavior loomed in the future. It would always be the same between them, no matter their age or how long they'd been apart.

"Is that why you came here? To warn me about Father? He made his thoughts regarding me known long ago, Trevor."

"I'm seeing to a business matter this afternoon. I was simply curious…"

"And here I thought you'd stumbled through the door mistaking this establishment for your tailor's. You can never have too many waistcoats the color of a peacock, I always say." Ethan delivered the barb knowing it would hit its mark.

His brother's eyes narrowed on Ethan's black attire before he tugged on the lapels of his grass-green coat. "Cladhart, I wasn't aware you would be spending the day in the pursuit of entertainment with my long-lost younger brother."

"And yet I am."

"I can see that." Trevor's lips pursed.

An oddly tense moment ticked past before Cladhart asked after some business with the jet mine, which was the exact moment Ethan ceased listening. The resemblance between his brother and his father was remarkable, especially when they talked about the account books. He shook his head to clear it of the thought.

Just then they were joined by the referee. "Mr. Moore, what a victory, eh?" He gave Ethan a toothy grin, then turned to Trevor. "Lord Ayton, jolly good show of strength, am I right? You must be quite proud of your brother here."

"Indeed," Trevor replied. However, his attention

was held somewhere across the room. "Will you excuse me? I see someone I must speak with."

"Very well." The referee turned to Ethan, dropping a pile of coins into his hand with a smile. "Your winnings, Mr. Moore."

He'd won. He may be weary of boxing, but it was the one thing he was skilled at, his one claim to success. And he wasn't about to relinquish that small thrill of achievement, no matter what had happened in Spain. Not yet, and perhaps not ever. "Thank you. Money always eases the pain of the bruises," Ethan said, accepting his prize.

"That it does."

Ethan turned back to Cladhart as the referee moved away from them. His father's business partner was watching Trevor across the room again, a frown etching his face before he shot a sidelong glance at Ethan. "How much did we win?" Cladhart asked, his gaze drawn back to Ethan's brother like a magnet to the north.

Ethan followed Cladhart's gaze across the room to where Trevor was speaking to a man Ethan didn't recognize. Trevor lacked his usual cool superiority as he listened to the stranger. "Who is that man?" Ethan finally asked after a moment.

Cladhart didn't respond or look away from the exchange. A pack of papers bound in red ribbon was shoved into Trevor's hands with enough force to push him backward a step before the man fled the room without a backward glance.

"Will you excuse me, Ethan? I need to speak with that man as well." He was gone before Ethan could reply.

Trevor turned, watching as Cladhart charged out

the door. The papers bound in the red ribbon trembled in Trevor's grasp. Stuffing the packet into the pocket of his coat, he looked back at Ethan. In that short glance, Ethan recognized an all-too-familiar feeling reflected in his brother's gaze. Fear.

Maybe it was time to consider going home after all.

❧

"Oh, posh. Your curls are lovely, dear." The Dowager Duchess of Thornwood spoke over the squelching plod of the horse's hooves down the muddy road. "This damp North Yorkshire weather may entice them to be a little grander than they would be on a sunny afternoon, but you'll still be the most beautiful lady at the party." Her mother's warm smile almost made Roselyn believe her words. Almost.

"I appreciate the sentiment, Mama. But I can't be seen with hair so large it will scarcely fit within the doorway to Ormesby Place! What will Lord Ayton think? What if my hair is the reason my entire future falls apart?" she asked in wide-eyed horror, gripping the seat of the carriage as they rounded a bend.

"Dear, it's never as terrible as you believe it to be. Lord Ayton will admire your dark tresses as I do. He's already fond of you—enough to be considering marriage if rumors can be counted as fact. Fret not, my beautiful child. Your hair will not be your downfall. You know you have your father's wild curls." The dowager duchess's smile faded into thoughtfulness as her gray eyes traced the strands of Roselyn's hair curling around her face. She pulled her gaze from Roselyn, staring out the carriage window into the misty day. "He always looked so fierce on rainy days such as these." She took a steadying breath. "But that was long ago. Wasn't it, dear?" The dowager duchess donned a brave smile as she pinched color into her cheeks.

"Fierce is not the look I'm trying to achieve today, Mama," Roselyn complained. She didn't wish to have anything in common with the man who'd chosen his own mad dreams over his own family's welfare, least of all his awful hair. Years later and the thought of his betrayal still held a held a sharp sting. Fierce? Was that how she looked? She turned to look at the rain-streaked carriage window, trying to catch a glimpse of her reflection. Her reckless curls remained—as they always did—tightly contained in an elaborate style of twirling braids secured by what felt like thousands of pins atop her head. Her yellow hat covered the mass of it and matched her dress to perfection, yet she brushed her fingers across the brim anyway to ensure its placement.

"What gentleman would want to wed a lady who arrives at parties looking fierce? Must we arrive at Ormesby Place just now, in this downpour? Let's cry off. We could be fashionably late…by a day. No one will notice with the focus of the festivities centered on the return of Lord Ayton's younger brother."

She found it odd that the younger Moore brother was to be welcomed back to the family at all. Years ago, he'd been tossed from the estate in the midst of scandalous talk about their mother's abandonment. It had seemed the time to stand together to face enemies, but clearly not for the Moores.

Roselyn had spent almost every afternoon in support of her friend Katie Moore. She'd assisted her in any way she could, even if that was simply offering her friend company on overly quiet days at home. However, only so much could be done when one's family was falling to pieces. She'd had to watch as the bright-eyed girl she knew so well pulled away from everyone in her home. Even now, she lived in a cottage on the estate and was more at home in the stables than any parlor. Katie claimed she preferred a life lived on the edge of the woods that separated their estates, but Roselyn could still see the hurt behind her eyes every time she spoke of her family.

Did her brother know how he'd added to Katie's pain at such a time? Of course Roselyn didn't know the full story, but it was rumored that he'd punched his father in a fit of rage. It was no wonder he'd been disowned. The image was the opposite of the laughing boy she remembered from years ago. But then again, people did change as they left childhood behind. She certainly had. Roselyn gave a small shake of her head.

Now, in the blink of an eye, the man was back and being celebrated with such fanfare as a party in his honor. Poor Katie, to have all of these unfortunate memories brought back to mind. Her friend claimed to be pleased with her brother's return, even though she'd admitted to Roselyn only yesterday that she'd had to ride to Whitby to convince him to finally return.

Roselyn, of course, would continue to keep her thoughts private because Mr. Moore's return did seem to please Katie and Lord Ayton. Lord Ayton had organized the gathering, after all. And with his lordship at the helm of activities, she was sure it would be a lovely event. She took a calming breath and turned her attention back to her mother, who was still discussing the damp weather.

"I don't wish to make my entrance with a sodden dress and disheveled hair either." Her mother touched the silver-streaked hair beneath her hat as if the very idea of rain might entice her curls to fall flat. "But this is a drizzle at best." Arranging her skirts around her on the seat opposite Roselyn, she asked, "Is this blue too dark for my coloring?"

"You look perfectly respectable, Mama."

Her mother smiled. "Do you like these gloves with this ensemble?" she asked, holding out cream-colored gloves with tiny blue bows tied at the wrist.

"Aren't those my gloves?" Roselyn reached out and inspected the ribbon detailing. "They are! Those are the gloves that match my blue day dress, and now they'll be stretched and misshapen." Her nose scrunched up in dismay.

Her mother pulled her hand from Roselyn's grasp. "You make my hands sound as if I've been behind a plow tilling fields." She smoothed her skirts again and lifted her chin. "I'm sure your gloves will survive the day."

"I hope you're right. Everything must be carried out to plan." And with Lord Ayton's attention to precise detail, she didn't wish her future to fall to pieces over a pair of ill-fitting gloves. Nothing could be left to chance. Roselyn bit her bottom lip in worry, watching the blur of green trees streak past the window. They would arrive soon.

Ormesby lands bordered Thornwood properties. It seemed odd to be traveling only a few minutes down the road to stay for the week, but her mother had insisted they stay for every moment of the party, and despite her momentary lapse, Roselyn wasn't about to disagree. It would allow Trevor Moore, Lord Ayton, more time in her company to extend the offer of marriage—just as she had planned. With every turn of the carriage wheels, her future came closer. She could see everything falling into place, just beyond her reach.

"I'll be at ease once he asks for my hand and the announcement is made. Then everything will be official. Until then it's only Lily's word that Devon spoke with Lord Ayton in private last week. She could have misunderstood the situation entirely. Perhaps they talked of ships or some other dreadful topic only my brother would find entertaining."

"I trust Lily's word on the matter. And Devon has been far too pleased about something these past few days, even for such a happily married man," her mother said. "I suspect he is under the impression he won't be required to attend balls this season if you are engaged before it begins."

"He and Lily aren't coming to London with us?"

"Of course they are, dear. Sometimes it's best to allow a man to believe what he wishes to believe so that we might have a pleasant day, free of complaint."

"Even when that man is known in society as the Mad Duke of Thornwood?"

"Especially when dealing with Thornwood," her mother grumbled.

"Everything is still only suspicion. I can't plan my

future on suspicion. If only Lily had more information, we could—" She was cut off by the jolts of the slowing carriage accompanied by her mother's announcement.

"Oh look, we've arrived."

The impressive stone house outside the carriage window seemed to fade into the surrounding mist of the soggy afternoon. It rather reflected Roselyn's mood at the moment. The house was not light and confident in cream-colored limestone, nor was it dark and foreboding like the black jet of her necklace. Instead, Ormesby Place rested somewhere in the middle in a state of elegant, gray uncertainty. And soon it could be her home.

She straightened her spine and allowed her much-rehearsed party smile to lift her face. The carriage door opened and a footman handed her mother down, then Roselyn. The light mist sifted down from the sky like the powdered sugar she'd seen their cook shake onto the top of cakes. As a child she had actually preferred the frequent rains of the North Yorkshire moors. Of course, that had been before she cared about her appearance, when she'd run wild across the terrain without thought.

"Do carry my embroidery bag inside," the dowager duchess commanded the footman. She shoved the tapestry bag into the man's arms and beckoned to Roselyn to hurry along.

She watched as her mother scurried to the door of the home, fleeing the moist air. "Mama, what of our other luggage?" Roselyn called after her retreating form as the coachman unloaded their trunks to the drive, clearly anxious to be in the dry stables. "My gowns cannot become damp. They'll be ruined!"

"Get a footman to bring them in, dear, as I have done, and do hurry in out of that weather," her mother called out as she disappeared inside.

Roselyn heard the carriage roll away toward the stables, leaving her alone to guard her trunks from the rain. She glanced around in search of anyone who might be of assistance. She couldn't abandon her belongings in the drive. Her life's plans hinged upon looking presentable during this gathering, and that wasn't likely with water-marked gowns.

She turned, her eyes clinging to a tall, broad-shouldered figure walking toward her from the direction of the stables. Very good. He would take her things inside and she could get out of this hair-murdering drizzle.

The man wore all black. Shouldn't a footman be in livery? She shielded her face from the water, her eyes narrowed on his dark breeches, black lawn shirt, and the coat that hung open from his broad shoulders. How indecent! Perhaps he worked in the stables. What she did know was that he moved with a nonchalance that announced his lack of respect for anyone whose eyes might fall on him. His neck was exposed, for goodness' sake! Was this the way servants dressed at Ormesby Place? Thornwood's livery always looked so polished and friendly. This man looked neither.

Although the corner of his mouth quirked up in a hint of a smile, an underlying warning of danger seemed to be etched into his tanned skin. His dark hair fell in disarray around his angular face, threatening to obscure his vision, yet he did nothing to brush it away. She had never seen a servant show such disregard for his appearance. She knew from spending so much time with Katie that there was no such thing as formality on Ormesby grounds, but this was taking that a bit too far. If she became lady of the house one day, she would certainly have to do something about the servants' attire and presentation to guests. *When* she became lady, she corrected, feeling more confident about her future already. She smiled, this time with genuine feeling behind it—the feeling of determination.

As he drew near, his head dipped in a slight nod before he continued on his path. He was leaving! Where was he going when guests were arriving?

She turned after him, calling, "Pardon me, haven't you come to take my things inside?"

His steps slowed. He turned, taking another backward step away from her as he called in return, "No. Why? Are you ill?"

"Why would you ask…" She broke off in confusion as she fought the urge to chase after him.

"Crippled, then. You're crippled?" His lips pursed in consideration as he gazed at her.

Her head fell to the side as she tried to understand the man before her. "Do I look infirm?"

"Actually you look quite…" His words ceased as he looked over her body and her increasingly wet dress. His gaze remained on her neckline for a moment too long before returning to her face, his lips quirking up into something resembling a crooked smile. "…quite firm, my lady."

She could feel warmth spreading up her exposed neck, heating her cheeks until they burned. A stable hand discussing her body in such terms and daring to look at her with such unconcealed heat in his eyes? The nerve! "Make no mistake, sir. Lord Ormesby will hear of this. If you value your position in life, you will have my bags taken in the house at once." Her spine stiffened in a manner that would have made any one of her governesses proud. Something about this man got under her skin and irritated her to no end.

A grin spread across his face, exposing white teeth and crinkling the corners of his eyes. "Lord Ormesby can't be rid of me that easily, princess." He paused to chuckle in a deep, rich voice that somehow managed to annoy her further. "He's already tried and failed at it once."

"I pity Lord Ormesby then, for having such an impudent man in his employ!"

"Did I say I was in his employ?" he asked, laughing.

"Clearly, you belong in the stables, sir." But her confidence began to crumble with his laughter. Her brows drew together as she asked, "Who are you then?"

"Haven't you heard? This is my party." He bowed with an excessive flourish and a roguish grin. "The newly returned Mr. Ethan Moore at your service, my lady."

Ethan Moore! Then he was indeed back from his travels. Roselyn studied his face for a moment, looking for some shred of the boy she'd once known. They'd been friends when she was a child, but no shred of the man before her seemed at all like the gangly youth who had climbed trees with her and, on one occasion, put a snake in her chair. She hadn't been fond of him that day with the snake when she was six, and she certainly wasn't fond of him now.

"Oh, but you are most assuredly not at my service. For here we stand, Mr. Moore, in this damp weather with no footman to take my belongings inside."

"The servants are all busy taking Lady Farnsworth's luggage to her suite, so you may as well enjoy the rain." He shrugged and lifted his face to the gray clouds. *He* seemed to enjoy the rain that splashed on his face well enough.

She did not agree with him on that score. "I suppose I don't have a choice. I'm not going to abandon my possessions in your muddy drive."

"There's a fresh layer of rock here," he countered. "You'd have to dig down for a half hour to find mud. I think an enclosed trunk or two will survive."

"Mud or no mud, I will need assistance with my things. Thank you very much."

"You're welcome. Happy to offer a lady sound advice when I can." He began to turn and leave her there.

"Sound advice?" she asked, both angry and confused by his actions.

He turned back and looked her in the eye as he spoke with slow, deliberate words. "When I said your belongings would weather the rain without issue?"

He truly wasn't planning on assisting her or even calling for someone else to carry her things? She looked down at the gathering moisture on the top of the nearest trunk. "My trunks are made of the finest leather and embossed with my name. See?"

He took another step toward her, gazing down at the name stamped in script on the lid beside her. "Ahh, Lady Roselyn Grey of Thornwood Manor.

You've changed," he mused, his eyes lifting to meet hers. There was something hidden beneath his gaze, a riddle that tickled at the edge of her brain—or perhaps it was simply more of the tripe that was on the surface of the man. Either way, she needed to understand what he was about and how he'd grown from the boy she claimed as a friend into the arrogant individual who stood before her.

Curiosity, that's what was crawling through her limbs with such warmth. That's what held her still as rain poured all around them. For a moment she was trapped there against her will, waiting for him to look away and end the connection between them. His nose had been broken at some point since he'd left home because there was a small bump where it twisted to the left, and his eyes were not pure green but peppered with flecks of gold and rimmed with brown. Somehow the imperfection pulled her in, which was something she'd never experienced before. Eye color, like all things in life, should be sortable into categories. Yet, his eyes refused to be filed under green, brown, or hazel. Instead they resided in an indefinable place that left her singed as if she'd stepped too close to a fire—a fire she couldn't recall existing when she'd last seen Mr. Moore.

Finally he offered, "Right fine they are, too."

What was fine? His eyes like moss on tree trunks caught in a brief ray of sun? "Fine" wouldn't be the word she would use to describe them.

She shook her head to free herself of whatever spell he'd cast on her. What were they speaking of? Her trunks! Yes! "You can't spare a footman to haul my trunks and valise inside?"

"I'm afraid not."

"Not a single servant to assist your guests as they arrive? And I thought Ormesby Place to be a welcoming, organized home. The devil it is." She muttered the last bit under her breath, sure he hadn't heard her.

"What was that, my lady?" he asked, leaning in.

"Oh, nothing." How had he heard her comment? She always tried to be so careful of such things. It was as if the ugly habits she'd worked so diligently to eliminate from her life were rising to the surface against her will. And she blamed Mr. Ethan Moore for every bit of it.

"If your precious possessions mean so much to you, princess, I will personally assist you with your things."

Finally he was going to see reason. She smiled in relief. "Well, that was all I required. Thank you."

He bent and lifted the small valise from the top of the pile of trunks, slinging it over his shoulder with a grin. "That trunk looks light enough. You should be able to manage it." With those careless words, he turned and began to stroll away toward the door.

Was he whistling? What an infuriating man!

Roselyn stood rooted to the ground in shock for a moment, watching him walk away through the rain. Then, something snapped within her. The gently bred lady she tried to portray was stripped away, leaving behind the young, reckless girl she thought she'd outgrown years ago. He couldn't walk away from her in such a manner.

She took two steps to the edge of a flower bed, scooped up a fistful of fresh soil within her white-gloved hand and flung it as hard as she could at Mr.

Moore's back. Watching as it splattered across his upper arm, slinging droplets onto his cheek, she felt a moment of visceral triumph. Then she gaped at him.

What had she done? She hadn't even considered doing anything so childish in years—not since that summer when she'd set a trap to trip him as he crossed one of the fields, then laughed as he tugged her down into the dirt with him. The memory of her laughter faded as reality set in. Her plans! What had she been thinking? But, of course, she *hadn't* been thinking.

He turned, an affronted look crossing his face as he stared at her.

In that moment, in spite of their current ages, he was the boy next door again, chasing Katie and her through the woods as they cackled with glee. She bit her lip to keep from laughing.

He glanced down at his arm in disbelief, dropped her valise to the ground, and began prowling toward her. Oh. Perhaps this had been a mistake. A challenging gleam filled his eyes, turning them as dark as black water in a cold lake.

Oh dear. She blinked once, twice, then turned and ran.

She'd made it to the corner of the house where the edge of the lush gardens overlooked the moors when she felt a large hand wrap around her upper arm, dragging her to a halt. She could feel the heat of him behind her. She had never been so close to a man before. Her heart hammered within her body. Even Lord Ayton had never dared touch her like this. She'd never felt a gentleman's body pressed into hers as Mr. Moore's was now.

"Leaving so soon?" he murmured, his lips almost grazing the rim of her ear.

"No." It wasn't the most intelligent response, but stringing words together into thought seemed impossible at the moment. Not when a very solid chest hovered at her back. How had she gotten herself into this mess? He didn't seem like the boy who grew up on the neighboring estate at all now.

"Glad to hear it. Because someone is slinging mud out here, and I wouldn't want you to get covered with it as you wander the grounds." His hand slid down her arm with a deliberate slowness until her hand rested inside his. He lifted her gloved fingers for his inspection. "It seems you're already covered in mud. Well, then. This won't do any further damage."

When she turned to protest, she was met with a cold mound of mud dripping from her shoulder. Her eyes flared and she retaliated without thinking, bending to grasp a handful of earth and slinging it across Mr. Moore's shirt. A second later, a scoop hit the front of her dress just as she slung another fistful, hitting his shoulder.

He stepped closer as she threw her head back with a gleeful laugh that felt as if it had been bound within her for years. Had it been so long? Years without laughter in her life? The loss was a worthy sacrifice for the future she wanted—of course it was. She'd worked so long to tame any touch of madness that ran wild in her veins, only to allow a few minutes in Mr. Moore's company to transform her back into the girl she thought she'd banished long ago. But it was only a stolen moment in the garden, a single laugh.

His hand came to her cheek, stilling her movements. The smile slipped from her face as she watched
him. She couldn't breathe. He was standing too close.
His bare, mud-roughened fingers slid down the side of
her neck in a slow whisper of touch.

She looked up into his face as he towered over her,
her gaze landing on his lips. His fingers slipped into her
hair and she found herself leaning into his touch. She
placed her hand on his chest even as he shifted closer,
his mouth promising far more than shared laughter
with every lingering second. What were they doing?
What was *she* doing? She'd never felt such a longing
to surrender to someone's touch as she did now, to
experience what his lips would feel like pressed against
hers, to live in this moment and this moment alone.
But she shouldn't do this…this…whatever this was. It
wasn't right.

Roselyn broke their connection, pulling her eyes
from his to focus on the rolling hills of green in front
of the house. She dropped her hand from his chest,
curling her fingers together as if she could hold the
warmth of his body there in her palm. She was practically engaged to his brother. This man would likely
be her brother-in-law soon. There should certainly be
a kinship between them, but no good could come of
their current unexpected closeness. His hand fell away
from her, making her suddenly aware of the cold rain
that had soaked through her clothing. Turning back
toward him, she saw the same loss and resignation that
surged through her reflected in his eyes.

"My lady, I believe we should go inside now." He
held his arm out to escort her into the house.

She cleared her throat, forcing her thoughts back to Lord Ayton, her imminent engagement, and the house party, where they should have remained. "Yes, I suppose we should." Linking her muddy glove through his arm, she allowed him to lead her back to the front of the house, past her sodden luggage, and into Ormesby Place.

As they stepped through the front door they were greeted by a wide-eyed stare from the butler, yet he only offered his welcome to the house. Behind him an oak stairway swept the corners of the room, leading to the upper floors of the house. The home was charming in a neglected sort of fashion. That had never bothered Roselyn on her visits, but after the wedding things would need an update. She was torn from her investigation of the large chandelier hanging above the hall when she heard a clump of mud splat against the polished wooden floor at her feet. Oh, this was not a good way to enter the party. In hindsight, fierce would have been preferable to sodden and dripping with mud. Just then, the dowager duchess rounded the corner from the drawing room, stopping when her eyes landed on Roselyn.

"Roselyn, dear! Gracious!" she exclaimed in greeting. "I came to check on you… What's happened?" Her cool gray eyes swept over Roselyn, then narrowed on the gentleman at her side.

"Pardon me, Your Grace," Mr. Moore offered with a slight bow. "Your daughter slipped on the wet drive outside."

"She slipped?" her mother clarified.

"Yes, you know how artless I can be at times, Mama. Mr. Moore was kind enough to offer me assistance." She dropped his arm, realizing too late she was still clinging to it.

"Are you injured?"

"No, Mama. I'm not infirm at all." She looked to the mud-covered man at her side. "Mr. Moore already questioned me on that score and found me quite... How did you put it, Mr. Moore?"

"Well. Quite well, my lady." He gazed down into her face. A grin was pulling at one corner of his mouth as he continued, "Will you excuse me? I seem to be covered in mud, and I wouldn't want the house to seem *disorganized and unwelcoming* to our guests." He nodded in farewell and bounded up the stairs, taking them two at a time until he disappeared around the corner.

"Roselyn, we must get you changed out of these wet clothes. You look as if you've rolled here in the dirt instead of arriving by carriage."

"My apologies, Mama. I'll be cleaned up and ready for the day in a few minutes." She could feel the heat rising in her cheeks the longer she stood there shrinking under the dowager duchess's scrutiny.

"Very well, dear. We are at the top of the stairs to the left. The blue room. Here, this maid will assist you." Her mother beckoned to a passing maid as she shooed Roselyn up the stairs so no one would witness her state of dress. "And do have our trunks brought in from the rain," she added as the maid passed on her way to follow Roselyn upstairs.

"Yes, Your Grace." The maid dipped into a curtsy, then shot a telling look to the butler where he stood near the door. Roselyn paused, watching the exchange before climbing another step. That had been so simple.

She looked down at her destroyed yellow day dress, the result of her attempt at the same outcome, and chuckled. Perhaps her mother's methods were more efficient, but she was having difficulty regretting the events outside. It was odd—she couldn't recall a single time in her grown life when her fingers had touched dirt. Or laughing quite so much in years.

"I must look my best today," Roselyn said as she entered the room with the maid.

"Yes, m'lady. If I might say so, m'lady, I think we might start by removing the dirt from your face."

Roselyn glanced to the mirror, finally under-standing her mother's shock as well as the maid's. "Goodness!" Her hair had already begun escaping its confinement under her water-marked yellow hat. Dark ringlets sprang forth around her soil-stained face, creating a halo of curls and giving the illusion that she was the official deity of dirt. Meanwhile, streaks of black earth trailed their way down her neck in the pattern of Ethan Moore's fingers.

Her cheeks flushed as she traced the smudges that covered one cheek where his hand had been only a few minutes ago. She couldn't allow such a dangerous association again. No matter what pleasant and long-ago memories that man brought to mind, she must keep to the course she had planned for her future. And that future was with Lord Ayton, not his brother.

Dropping her hand to her side in determination, she turned to the maid. "How quickly can you remove mud?"

# Two

A QUARTER OF AN HOUR LATER, ROSELYN DESCENDED the stairs, attempting to look as if she hadn't just been scrubbed head to toe before running down the hall to rejoin the party. Carefully, she placed each foot on the next step and lifted her chin high. *Breathe. You are Lady Roselyn Grey. You are sought after for your delightful company, and you do not have mud behind your ears.* She had just affixed her party grin to her face in preparation for what lay before her when Lord Ayton started up the stairs.

Her breath caught, but she recovered while he nodded in greeting to someone in the hall below. Lord Ayton was dressed appropriately for the gathering in his home, his tailored and pressed suit hanging to perfection on his lean frame. His dark auburn hair had been freshly trimmed for the occasion, giving him a polished appearance she appreciated. He was so unlike his brother, whom she really shouldn't be thinking of at all. Lord Ayton shifted the papers neatly stacked in his hand and glanced up, catching sight of her for the first time.

"Lady Roselyn," he offered with a nod and a hint of

a pleasant smile. "I was informed of your arrival. I trust the ride here from Thornwood was without incident."

"My arrival was quite uneventful, my lord," she lied, hoping he wouldn't read the truth on her face. It would benefit no one for him to know about his brother and the incident with the mud.

He took a few steps toward her, his brows drawn together as he studied her face. "I would like to speak with you, but later perhaps."

"Oh? We can speak now. I mean to say, I'm not terribly busy if you have time now."

He pulled a pocket watch from his waistcoat and grimaced at the time. "I have business to attend to before dinner and after. The world doesn't stop simply because my brother decides to return to the country, nor for your visit, enjoyable as it is to see you." He said the last bit almost as a forced afterthought as he turned away to continue up the stairs.

"Don't let me keep you," Roselyn said to his back. She was trying not to be offended by his businesslike nature, which seemed to be a common occurrence between them. He did have a house full of guests and an estate to run. She would most likely feel the same in his position, wouldn't she?

Turning back to her, he added, "I can meet with you tomorrow evening in the drawing room. I should have one hour. That should be plenty of time."

"Certainly. Tomorrow evening," she squeaked in response.

He considered her for a moment before lowering his voice to say, "Lady Roselyn, I believe we both know why I wish to speak with you."

"Yes." Her heart began to race.

"If you would put together a list of what you will require of me moving forward, I believe we can have a fine arrangement. I mentioned this to your brother and he thought it a rather organized manner of things, but I thought you might…"

"I appreciate your forthright thought on the matter, my lord. Above all else in life, we should be prepared and organized about our futures."

"I'm pleased we're in agreement on such matters." He reached into his pocket, removed a folded piece of paper, and handed it to her. "Here are my expectations of you. Review them. We shall speak tomorrow evening and proceed from there."

At her smile, he turned and ascended the stairs. She waited until he was out of sight before tearing into the folded paper. She slid her fingers over the crisp edges of the document as her gaze flew to the neat lines written there.

*Manage household staff and make Ormesby Place a pleasing environment.*

Well, certainly. And she would begin by increasing the number of footmen available to visitors.

*Host local gentry who call in a manner befitting the station of Lady Ayton.*

Lady Ayton. She mouthed the title with a grin. It was a lovely title, although, as Ayton was only a courtesy title, she would one day bid it farewell to become Lady Ormesby. She would be well settled in life, which was what she'd wanted for some time.

*Provide two male offspring resulting from biannual couplings.*

…Biannual couplings. That sounded…agreeable, if a bit shocking to have been put to paper. The remaining three hundred and sixty-three nights of the year would be hers to enjoy alone. It was kind of him, really it was. She regained her wits to continue reading his list.

*Dress appropriately with funds placed in the personal account for the lady of the estate.*

*Dine with Lord Ormesby when you do not wish to take your dinner in your suite of rooms.*

Dine with Lord Ayton's father when she grew lonely in her rooms? That almost sounded as if he didn't intend to dine with her. In fact, where in his list of requirements for a wife was time spent together? There were the two nights every year, but surely there was more. She flipped the paper over to see if their time was listed on the back, yet she saw nothing. Five requirements. Had her life been boiled down to this list? Or would anyone's life look this dismal when written on paper? This was everything she wanted—an orderly life with none of the rumors that plagued her family.

But it was also a sharp reminder that she was entering into a bargain with a man she barely knew. At two evenings a year, it didn't seem likely they'd ever learn much about each other.

She was still staring at the list when she heard someone approach. Glancing up, she came eye to eye with Lady Smeltings. The woman always had a fond smile for Roselyn. She was a matron of the *ton* who held the highest of standards and an even higher arrangement of white hair atop her head.

"Lady Roselyn, what a lovely party this is becoming. So good to see you. How long has it been? Oh, who can keep track of these things?"

"It's good to see you here as well, Lady Smeltings."

The woman stepped closer, her eyes bright with excitement. "Might there be an exciting event in your future? I saw you with Lord Ayton a moment ago."

"Yes, he was…here." She folded the note she still held in her hand and stuffed it into the edge of her glove at the wrist.

"Just between us, everyone is quite pleased at this potential union. Oh, now I know nothing is official and all is quiet for now, but seeing you two here together on the stairs…I couldn't resist offering you my felicitations." Lady Smeltings dropped her voice to a whisper to finish, "In advance, of course."

"Thank you, but we were simply…"

"Oh, no need to be modest now, Lady Roselyn. I can't imagine anyone being more perfectly suited for marital bliss than the two of you."

"Perfectly suited," Roselyn repeated, her voice as flat as the muddy drive. Her gaze drifted over the woman's shoulder to the man with the tousled dark hair as he moved through the hall below with the same arrogance he'd embodied outside. Roselyn swallowed and stared until Ethan Moore disappeared from view.

"When I heard this match might occur, I was so happy. We are all quite happy. Aren't you happy? I can't imagine anyone not being happy about this."

"Of course," Roselyn replied, her opinion of Lady Smeltings eroding the longer their conversation continued. Why did the woman's happiness over her future with Lord Ayton irritate her so? She craned her neck to catch another glimpse of the man in the hall below the stairs.

Lady Smeltings reached out and grasped her hand as she spoke, regaining Roselyn's attention. "Isn't it wonderful how everything works out?"

"Indeed. It's wonderful." *Just blasted wonderful*, she finished to herself.

❧

Ethan strolled out onto the south lawn. The soft grass shifted under his boots, the only evidence left of yesterday's rain. He blinked into the weak morning sun for a moment, thankful it was knocking the chill from the air, before a yelp of alarm caught his attention. One of the gardeners was fleeing his work of pruning the hedgerow that bordered the lawn as a lady called out after him, "My apologies. That arrow must have been warped."

Lady Roselyn Grey. Was she trying to wound the servants now? She shook her head as she laid the bow at her feet and glanced around, a blush creeping into her cheeks at her blunder. Everyone's gaze was averted from the spectacle except for his younger sister's. Katie was bent over in laughter. She hadn't changed in eight years. She'd grown, certainly, but she hadn't changed. There were some parts of his unexpected return home that he enjoyed, like seeing Katie…and yesterday's muddy adventure had been altogether entertaining.

He chuckled as he watched Roselyn make a show of testing out another bow while the other ladies and gentlemen continued launching arrows across the open lawn. At least all the other guests seemed to land their arrows in the vicinity of the targets.

He turned, looking at the hedgerow and abandoned gardening tools not far from where he stood. How had her arrow gone so far afield? He walked a few paces away to retrieve the arrow from the base of the shrubbery.

Smoothing the feathers at one end as he walked, he moved toward Roselyn. Clearly someone must keep an eye on her. No one else seemed to be stepping up to the job this morning, so he supposed the responsibility fell on him.

"I'm glad I'm not the gardener this morning," he offered as he strolled up behind her.

Roselyn swung around with her arrow still nocked. "Why is that?"

He leaned away from the point of her weapon, guiding it from harm with a gentle push of his hand. "Because he won't survive the day with you shooting arrows all over the property."

"Oh, that? It was a faulty arrow. I have a new one now, so it won't happen again."

"I'm sure you're correct," he lied as he inspected the perfect arrow he held in his hand.

"Are you going to stand there watching me? You're making it difficult to concentrate on the target with that glare of yours."

"I'm not glaring at you, princess. I'm ensuring the safety of the guests gathered here on the lawn."

"I'm not that misguided in my aim! Certainly no lives are in danger."

"Tell that to the gardener you tried to skewer."

"I was distracted and my equipment was damaged."

Ethan lifted the bow from her hands and inspected it. "Clearly."

"If you're so talented, let's see you try then." She stepped back and motioned for him to proceed.

"My pleasure. You can see how it should be done."

Ethan lifted the arrow in his hand and laid it against the bow. He hadn't tried his hand at archery in quite a few years—target practice didn't fit into the life he'd built for himself. His days had been spent training for the night's fight, finding opponents, and placing wagers so that he could survive to repeat the process the next day. This was different. He released the arrow and watched as it sank with a thud near the center of the target.

"That shot was pure luck," she blustered.

"Luck?" He raised one eyebrow in disbelief.

But the challenge he saw in her eyes had him reaching for another arrow. A moment later he breathed a sigh of relief as his arrow found one of the outer rings of the target. It wasn't a bad shot considering the time that had passed since he'd last tried this hobby. Turning back to Lady Roselyn Grey, he flashed a smile made of more confidence than he felt. "Let's see you try to best that."

"Very well." She pulled the arrow back from far too low to have decent aim and sent it soaring into the grass in front of the target. "My fingers slipped. That doesn't count."

"You need to lift your arms higher and look down the arrow."

"I don't need your assistance. I'm quite practiced

at archery, I'll have you know. I even dressed for the occasion." She smiled down at the tiny print of her dress to point out the arrow-point design.

"Yes, your skill level is astounding."

"Are you jesting?" She drew back in outrage.

"Perhaps." He chuckled.

"Hmph."

"Are you aiming for the target or that tree in the distance?" He pointed to the far side of the open lawn.

"I can't very well aim for anything at all with you breathing down my neck every time I make an attempt."

Ethan threw his hands up in surrender and took a large step backward, gesturing for her to continue. As her next arrow shot across the crowd and caused the guests to gasp in fear, he stepped to her side once again.

"Please allow me." He caught her gaze for a moment, and just like yesterday, her gray wolflike eyes held him captive in their depths. Silence fell; only the distant sounds of the other partygoers crept in on their connection.

Had she always possessed the sort of beauty that hit a man like a punch to the gut, leaving him breathless? He'd never noticed her eyes when they were children, but now he found that when she looked at him, it was all he could do to maintain his wits. Perhaps returning home was the best course of action after all.

Finally, she looked away, breaking the spell. "Very well."

"Raise your bow. Higher. Straighten your arm, but loosely. No, like this." He stepped around her to grasp her elbow, guiding it into the correct position. "Turn your body this way." His hands slipped around her waist to pull her back into the proper stance. It was a reflexive move from years of training for boxing, but it pulled her into his embrace at the same time.

Her hair smelled of flowers growing wild in the heat of summer. He wasn't certain how long he'd been standing there with his hand splayed over the curve of her waist. How long was too long? She fit perfectly within his arms, her muscles tight beneath his touch as shallow breaths made her almost tremble.

She turned her head to look up at him from the corner of her eye. It should have been a questioning expression—after all, he was questioning the appropriate nature of his actions as well—but there wasn't a hint of reproach in her gaze. There was only his own longing mirrored back at him, a desire to be alone in the garden covered in mud together just as they had been yesterday. He tightened his hold on her and saw the bow in her hands dip toward the ground in her inattention to their archery lesson.

He needed to let her go. Someone would notice if he continued on this path. Pulling his hand from about her, he guided her arm back into position and nudged her jaw with a brush of his fingers until her eyes left his. He should step away from her. He should, but he didn't, instead leaning close to her ear, the same way that he had yesterday in the garden, and speaking in a quiet tone only she could hear. "Now pull the string tight. Look down the arrow. Do you see the target?"

"Yes," she said in a breathless whisper.

"Release the arrow, but only when you're ready." The smell of her wildflower-scented hair tickled at his senses as he spoke.

Her grip released as the arrow pierced through the air and landed on an outer ring of the target. "I did it!" she exclaimed, twisting to look over her shoulder at him with a smile brighter than a thousand stars and a twinkle in her light gray eyes. It was the sort of smile he thought he would never grow weary of seeing.

Before he could stop himself, his hand was resting on her shoulder, squeezing her in congratulations. And now that it was there, he'd be damned if he could pull it away. Instead he ran his fingers down her arm under the guise of checking her hold of the bow.

"Mr. Moore…" she began.

"It's Ethan. It's always been Ethan with you. We're neighbors, after all, even if I have been away for some time."

"All right then. Ethan…" She broke off as a blush of pink swept up her cheeks.

"Yes?"

"Ethan, I don't know what…"

"Well done, Lady Roselyn," Trevor's dry tone called from behind them, ending any revelation Roselyn had been about to share.

What unfortunate timing. Ethan's hand fell from her arm as he turned to greet his brother. "Trevor, you finished your business early then?"

"Yes, I did. I was informed I'd left Lady Roselyn alone too long." His eyes narrowed on Ethan. "Although, it seems you've been keeping her company in my absence. You have my thanks, Brother."

There was something almost menacing in Trevor's gaze. Did he have an interest in Roselyn? She hadn't mentioned Trevor once in conversation, and yet

Trevor's words had sounded possessive. Ethan glanced back and forth between the two in search of a telling glance or a sly smile, but only saw Roselyn's surprise and Trevor's glare in his direction. It was hard to believe his brother would be involved with anything beyond the numbers in his precious ledgers, let alone a lady who was inclined to throw mud at gentlemen. Ethan had been gone from home some time, but Trevor and Roselyn? He swallowed the sudden desire to hit Trevor.

Roselyn took a small step away from him as she turned her gaze on Trevor. "Your brother was showing me the proper way to shoot an arrow." She smiled at Ethan, yet it was a practiced smile that left him empty. "He's an excellent teacher."

"It was nothing," Ethan replied.

Trevor cast his version of a charming smile on Roselyn, making Ethan slightly nauseous. "Your aim seems quite on the spot. I'm glad the fresh air agrees with you this morning."

"It does. I enjoy the outdoors."

"Do you?" Trevor's head tilted in thought as he studied Roselyn.

Of course she did—she always had. Did Trevor not know the lady before him? Ethan watched but remained silent.

"I suppose I must take you for a walk about the property tomorrow," Trevor proclaimed. "Your mother will have words with me if I neglect to show you all that Ormesby lands have to offer."

"That would be lovely. I often walk the paths at Thornwood and would love to see the different vantages offered here," Roselyn replied just as any practiced princess would, but somehow it didn't match what he knew of her. Roselyn didn't simply walk paths—she took them at a run…or she had years ago, before he'd left home.

How often did she rehearse such lines about vantages offered on the chance she would be asked about her walking habits? Her ploy was so clear and yet Trevor was believing every word she said. Ethan shook his head, trying not to laugh.

"You know there are jet mines here at Ormesby," Trevor hedged, his discomfort with how their family profited from their lands evident. "The views aren't quite what you're used to, I'm sure. However, we find them pleasant just the same."

"I find your family's interest in mining fascinating. I've never seen any mines in person. That area was considered quite out of bounds when I was young and exploring the area with your sister. Do people really crawl into the earth to harvest wealth from the ground for you?"

"Mining is a dangerous business, Lady Roselyn," Trevor reprimanded. "We can look from afar, but a mine is no place for a refined lady such as yourself."

Ethan had to cough to disguise his laughter. The little Ethan knew of this now-grown woman told him that his brother was as far off target with his assumption as Roselyn's arrows had been—although she was making a valiant effort at refinement this morning.

Roselyn looked around at his laughter. "Do you have as much objection to my seeing a working mine as your brother does, Mr. Moore?"

"No, quite the contrary. I think your curiosity could be safely satisfied." He grinned before adding, "A muddy mine may just suit you."

Trevor stepped between them before she could retort. "I would prefer a quiet walk through the moors, if you don't mind, my lady."

Roselyn looked around Trevor to continue the conversation, ignoring Trevor's obvious desire for Ethan to leave them. "Mr. Moore, you believe the mines to be safe?"

"He's been away for years. What does he know of the mines?" Trevor interjected.

Ethan ignored the comment. Although he'd never taken an interest in the family jet mining business, he'd always liked visiting the mines on their property. He found it interesting to see stones pulled from the earth and then transformed into polished black jewelry. "They're safe. As long as you watch your step…"

"You should come with us tomorrow. That way Lord Ayton can talk freely while you keep a wary eye out for danger."

"That isn't exactly what I had in mind, Lady Roselyn," Trevor cut in.

"Oh, don't you see? This is the perfect plan." She nodded in vigorous agreement with herself. "We'll all meet in the hall at nine in the morning?"

Ethan ran a hand through his hair. It was one thing to help her with archery when he thought her unattached, but it was another matter altogether to tag along on his brother's walk with a lady he was interested in. "I believe I'm busy."

Trevor's jaw tightened. "Yes, I recall you making plans for that same time, Brother."

Then again, Ethan had always been fond of morning walks about the estate—especially when they served to irritate Trevor. But at the challenging gleam that must have shown in his eyes, Trevor stepped closer. "Will you excuse us for a moment, Lady Roselyn?"

"Is something the matter, Trevor?" Ethan asked.

"Why do you wish to come with us tomorrow?" Trevor asked through teeth gritted into a grin as he pulled Ethan away from Roselyn.

"This is my celebration," Ethan replied with a shrug. "I find walks on the property to be quite entertaining."

"Claim a previous engagement, and you shall have my allowance from Father for this month for your troubles," Trevor stated. He could always be counted on to throw their father's funds around to his benefit.

Yet, a morning with Roselyn was worth much more than what Trevor was offering. Did he not realize this lady's worth? Ethan bristled. "No. I find I'm attached to the idea of a walk. Fresh air is worth more than coin—especially Father's coin."

"Ethan," Trevor ground out in warning.

"Yes, Brother?" Ethan tossed a quick smile back to Roselyn, who was waiting only a few steps away and attempting not to listen to their whispered conversation.

Trevor clenched his teeth together before answering. "The prior engagement you are about to recall having is *triple* the importance of a walk outside."

"Is it?" Ethan watched Trevor for a moment before giving in to his brother's wishes. With three months of his brother's allowance from their father, he could take time away from boxing, perhaps learn what options he had in life outside of beating men to the ground. It was the rational decision. Damn. Only a week in his brother's company and he was already compromising himself. The thought made him a bit nauseated, but he turned back to Roselyn nonetheless. He needed the funds, and it was only a morning walk with his brother. What could possibly happen in his absence? "I'm afraid I'm otherwise engaged tomorrow, Lady Roselyn. My apologies."

"I understand. I was hoping you would join us, but if you're busy…" She broke off, gazing with a sullen expression at her hands.

Trevor attempted to charm her as he always had with the proper ladies in town. "Lady Roselyn, with your enjoyment of the outdoors, have you seen our gardens?"

"Only briefly, yesterday when I arrived. But I was a little distracted at the time." Her gray eyes cut to Ethan, slicing him open with their sincerity.

He felt like a complete arse. Perhaps he was better suited to a life of wagers and fights. After all, for the past eight years, there had been no ladies to deal with. Amorous barmaids perhaps, but certainly no ladies.

"I have a few minutes to spare. Come. I'll show you the prizewinning roses we grow here at Ormesby," Trevor said as he offered her his arm. "Brother, I will see you at luncheon."

"I'd be honored, Lord Ayton," Roselyn replied. Turning to Ethan, she smiled as she offered, "Thank you again for the assistance with archery. With any luck I won't wound anyone now."

"The pleasure was all mine, m'lady."

With a smile and a swish of her green dress, she was gone on the arm of his brother. How had Trevor been fortunate enough to catch the interest of a lady like Roselyn Grey? Title, inheritance...it came down to birth order, which in their case was only fourteen months' difference. For the first time in his life, he felt the pang of jealousy. He and his brother had always been at odds as children, different as the summer sun and winter snow, but without any envy on either part. They'd always competed for the largest fish or the farthest jump on horseback, but without the bite of longing for anything the other possessed—until today. Perhaps stepping away from the lady causing this turmoil within him was for the best.

He shrugged and turned to walk back to the house.

"Sir," the butler called out as Ethan neared the terrace.

"Yes, Celersworth?"

"Do you know where Lord Ayton has gone? He has a visitor who says it's quite urgent he speak with him."

"A visitor? Who is it?"

"He elected not to provide his name, sir."

"How odd," Ethan mused. "Well, tell him he'll have to come back another time. Trevor is escorting Lady Roselyn through the gardens, and given his mood, I wouldn't recommend disturbing him."

"Should I inform him to return tomorrow morning, sir?"

"No. Trevor will be out for a walk by the mines, at Roseberry Topping I believe, and will be unavailable. I can speak with the visitor if you'd like."

"That won't be necessary. I'll deliver the news."

Ethan continued on across the terrace, following Celersworth back into the house.

A visitor who refused to give his name was odd. What business was his brother involved with of late? Ethan might have been away from home for years, but he could still see that something had Trevor out of his normal routine. And so Ethan had watched this past week. Secret meetings, whispered conversations, and disappearing for entire afternoons with no explanation added up to one solid fact—Trevor was planning something.

As Ethan rounded the corner into the main hall, intending to slip back upstairs and change into something suitable for fight practice in his suite of rooms, he caught sight of a man leaning against the parlor door frame. The visitor was dressed well enough in a dark coat and clean white shirt, his round face sitting atop a knotted band of cravat that only served to emphasize the width of his neck. Yet, something about the gruff set of his jaw or the mulish stance of his shoulders pronounced his lesser standing in society. What brought him here seeking a meeting with Trevor?

Ethan shrugged, continuing up the stairs. Whatever his brother's business, he was ignoring it to spend time with Roselyn. Somehow that fact ate at him more than the presence of a stranger in their home.

～⁂～

Roselyn set her tea aside and smiled across the sitting area. It was her second best smile, the one she offered children in the park, ladies she passed on Bond Street, and this evening, a room full of matrons shooting her knowing glances every few seconds. She'd told her mother of Lord Ayton's intentions this evening, so naturally every eye was upon her.

She smoothed her pale-green skirts around her legs. Her dress achieved the ideal look of cascading flowers she had hoped for, with the embroidery of hundreds of tiny pink blossoms trailing down the thin overskirt that skimmed the floor around her feet. It was perfect, but even flowers made of thread would wilt at the tedious conversation in the drawing room this evening. She turned her smile on Katie to hiss, "It's been over an hour since dinner. Where's your brother?"

Beside her on the settee, Katie's boot swung under the hem of her simple beige dress with unladylike vigor, much like the rest of Lady Katie Moore. "I haven't seen him since this morning," Katie returned around a mouthful of lemon cake. "I worked with my new horse this afternoon."

"He should be here by now, shouldn't he? I mean, what does one talk about for an hour after dinner? I feel it's thoroughly discussed by now, whatever it is."

"I've heard all I care to hear of Lady Smeltings's talented, sought-after, and excessively attractive children, I know that much for certain."

"Shhh," Roselyn hissed so they wouldn't be overheard. But by the small grin on her mother's face across the room, she was too late.

"He kicked me, you know. Would you like to see the bruise?" Katie shifted as if she was going to lift her dress in the middle of the drawing room. "It's quite impressive. Half my leg is black."

Roselyn stopped her with an elbow in her arm. "Your

brother kicked you? Why? I can hardly believe..." Roselyn paused at the lost look in her friend's soft green eyes. "We're speaking of your new horse, aren't we."

It wasn't a question. Conversations with Katie often turned on a moment from stylish gowns, jewelry, and marriageable gentlemen to wild terrains, stable cats, and trainable horses.

"Yes. I'm having a devil of a time bringing this one under rein."

Someone gasped from the vicinity of the card table by the windows.

Roselyn's gaze darted around to see if anyone else had heard her friend speak in such a fashion. "Katie, we're hardly alone in your cottage. I don't think these ladies will appreciate your use of the word *devil* the way I do." She whispered the d-word so no one would hear such things from her lips.

"You don't think Lady Smeltings's perfect children have a devil of a time with anything?"

Roselyn suppressed her giggle and made work of adjusting one of her gloves. She enjoyed chatting with Katie, but she needed to remain focused on her task this evening. It was too important to chance with overheard oaths.

The last thing she needed now was to have talk of less-than-ladylike behavior spread before her engagement became official. Many guests were already leaving to return to town, and she was ever so close to having all of her own preparations in order. Perhaps other ladies had need of the London season to find a husband, but other ladies didn't have things planned to perfection as she did.

She'd found an entirely acceptable match next door to the estate where she lived. Trevor Moore, Lord Ayton, would be her husband. His brother would leave again as quickly as he'd arrived. And she would no longer be Lady Roselyn Grey, daughter of a madman and sister to the Mad Duke of Thornwood. No, she would be Lady Ayton, and the future Lady Ormesby once Lord Ayton's father passed and the courtesy title was no longer needed. Her life would be well run and perfect in every way. Predictable and glorious!

She'd been repeating different versions of these same words to herself all afternoon. That silly list of his didn't matter. It was only a list. And, his brother... He certainly didn't matter, not one bit. Lord Ayton and London—that's what she should be dwelling on.

She took a breath and let it out slowly. "We'll arrive in London next week. Can you believe it's almost time for us to enjoy the season?"

Katie exhaled with a puff of exasperation, scrunching her nose as if some foul smell had invaded all of Ormesby Place. "I loathe the London season. Last year was enough society for me to last a lifetime."

"It was awful to be there in town and not be of an age to attend. I, for one, cannot wait to experience it this year," Roselyn returned with a wistful note in her voice. "I'm going to wear the new pink gown I showed you to my first ball." Her fists balled in her lap to keep from clapping in excitement. It was by far her most becoming gown. She'd received it from her modiste weeks ago and had been saving it for the occasion. She would be betrothed to Lord Ayton.

They would dance and everything in her life would fall into place. It would. It had to.

Katie made a sound of disgust. "Months of balls and gatherings. I don't suppose I can wear breeches, can I?"

Perhaps Katie only required some encouragement on the subject. "You should wear your green gown at the first ball we attend. It brings out your eyes. With your pearls. Yes, that will look lovely."

Katie's mother's jet necklace set would look stunning against the pale green, but Roselyn didn't dare refer to her friend's mother's abandoned jewelry. It didn't seem Katie was listening anyway. Instead, she was twisting the wrist of her glove with a faraway look in her eyes.

It was no wonder Katie had no interest in gowns. She'd changed since her mother had abandoned the family. Katie had insisted on moving into that dreadful abandoned gamekeeper's cottage on the property. Ethan had left the country. And now he was home. Why was he back? It shouldn't matter to her...and it didn't. It was only curiosity...

Her mother's voice rang out in the midst of her rampant thoughts. "Roselyn dear, won't you play something on the pianoforte for us?"

"Certainly."

At least this would keep her busy for the remainder of the evening so she could not fret over Lord Ayton's tardiness and wonder over his brother's circumstances. She rose and moved across the room. Picking up the stack of sheet music her mother had insisted she bring to the party, she flipped through the pages.

*Too morbid. No, too cheerful. This one might be nice.*

She spread the music out in front of her and sat down on the wooden stool—tracing her fingers over the lines of the cool keys for a moment.

The piece she'd chosen was one she'd played a few times before, years ago. She stretched her fingers and sank them into the first note in the concerto. Three pages in, she heard the door to the drawing room open.

"Ladies, I hope you don't mind, but we'll be joining you now." Lord Ayton's smooth voice drifted on the air, accenting her piano notes with his deep tones.

"Lord Ayton, we're pleased you're here," her mother said, clearly relieved he had finally arrived. "Roselyn was just entertaining us. Isn't she wonderful? So skilled in the feminine arts."

"Yes, quite talented," he replied, moving further into the room.

Roselyn's gaze darted across the room before swinging back to the sheet music before her. A few gentlemen trailed into the drawing room, including her brother, Devon, who must have just arrived from Thornwood. Lord Ayton's brother, however, was not among them.

Why was she concerned about Mr. Moore? Lord Ayton—he was her focus. She blinked in determination. Her fingers landed on the keys with a little more force than she'd intended, but no one seemed to notice. Lord Ayton was going to be her husband and this was it—that magic moment. The future all hung on this evening. Her heart raced at the possibility of being settled in life so quickly.

A moment later, Roselyn felt his approach. He

stepped up to the side of the instrument and watched her as she concluded the final few bars of the melody.

"Not my favorite piece, but you played it quite well." His voice poured like honey from his lips.

"Thank you. I'm glad you arrived in time to hear it." She was still staring at the music, trying to control her nerves. She could feel the gaze of every nosy matron in the room on her, heating her skin beneath her flowered dress.

"I'm running a bit late with my schedule, so we'll have to hurry things along here. My apologies for that."

"I managed to amuse myself in your absence, but I'm pleased you joined me." She ran her fingers over the instrument in front of her and smiled up at him with her best, most engaging look.

He glanced around, clearly checking to see how many ears were listening to their conversation before turning his attention back to her. "In your idle moments, have you considered your requirements as we discussed?"

"I'll work on it this evening. I've been a bit distracted by the festivities." She was blushing and she knew it. Dratted uncontrollable blushes. Of course she'd been distracted, but the festivities weren't what had held her attention after her archery lesson today. She took a shallow breath and tried to will the color from her cheeks.

"That's regrettable." He frowned and tapped his fingers on the pianoforte in thought as he continued. "I would, however, like to proceed with things this evening, as I'm sure there's nothing objectionable among your requests of me."

"No, not at all." Roselyn sat a fraction straighter on the stool. It was happening.

"Would you care to take a turn around the room with me? I'm sure someone else can take your place at the pianoforte."

"Of course." Roselyn rose from the stool and placed her hand on his arm over his scratchy wool coat.

He waited until they were on the far side of the large room, with another lady now playing a piece of music, before he spoke. It wasn't the secluded garden lit by candles that she'd envisioned for this moment in her life, but it did serve to secure her future while providing them with a small amount of privacy.

"Lady Roselyn," he finally said. "I'm aware I've been preoccupied with estate business since your arrival here at Ormesby Place. This party was ill-timed. However, when one's brother reappears after such a long absence, there seems to be a need to celebrate. We're here now together, however."

"So we are." With her heart racing, she glanced up at him as they rounded the far corner of the room.

"Might I call you Roselyn, my lady? It's much more efficient, don't you agree?"

"Of course...Trevor," she tried his name quietly.

"Roselyn, I would like to join our families together in marriage for the future of our lands, titles, and properties."

Roselyn nodded, unable to form words at the rapid succession of thoughts racing through her mind. Join our families, not join our lives? Lands, titles, properties... It all sounded so formal.

Formal was proper. Formal was what this conversation should be. Fondness and love were notions that couldn't be relied upon. But shouldn't he voice some idea of caring for her? Perhaps it had only been his phrasing.

"Very well, then. I'm pleased to have that bit of business complete," he said a moment later. "After you provide me with your list of requirements for the union, we will make an announcement to the other guests. Tomorrow night, perhaps." He said the words as if filing away an appointment, not making arrangements for marriage.

"After our morning walk?" she asked, dazed by the efficiency of their discussion.

"Indeed. Now if you will excuse me, I have some other matters to see to this evening." With a nod, he left her and moved toward the door.

What had just happened? Was this how her marriage would begin?

The room swam before her until her gaze paused on Devon. Her older brother was leaning against the mantelpiece behind their mother, his narrowed eyes focused on her. They held a question, and she didn't know the answer. She quickly looked away, only to see the shadow of someone in the doorway—someone with dark hair, and eyes that refused to be defined by the laws of color.

She moved back to the pianoforte and began sliding the mess of sheet music into one pile, tapping the edges into place until she had a tidy heap in the crook of her arm. She didn't look up from the pages of music to watch Trevor leave the room, but she knew he was gone. It was done. She was betrothed and tomorrow night everyone would know it. So why did it feel as if she'd just agreed to a dance or a hand of cards and not the sharing of the remainder of her life?

Or, come to think of it, had she agreed at all?

# Three

A FLOWER AND AN ORNATE LEAF—THESE WERE THE only things Roselyn had managed to form with her quill thus far. The sky outside had turned from purple to black while she sat at the writing desk beneath the window, and still her mind wasn't clear on which words to write. Her mother shifted in her sleep across the room. Everyone would be abed at this time of night, but she couldn't sleep. She had a list to write.

It shouldn't be a difficult task. A few short points detailing what she wished of her future husband and it would be done. Only, then it would indeed be done. She would give the list to Trevor tomorrow morning. Announcements would be made tomorrow afternoon. Her future would be set, secure. "Permanent and unchangeable until death do us part," she whispered.

That had been everything she wanted—a predictable life of her own, distanced from her family's past. Was it not what she wanted still?

*I would like to join our families together in marriage for the future of our lands, titles, and properties.*

It was silly, really, this clinging to a few words that

Trevor had said this evening. Their future together was more important than the manner in which he proposed the union, wasn't it?

Her gaze fell on the list he'd given her yesterday afternoon, now spread on the desk beside her own paper. The problem was that Trevor thought of this as their future together, this list of attributes she should possess. His businesslike nature was an honorable characteristic in a future husband. Quite honorable…

She'd decided weeks ago that his organization in all things would lead to the planned life she wanted. There wouldn't be any talk in society of madness or unexpected trips overseas, leaving her alone with her worry. He was everything she'd never known in her own life—stability and predictability. It was only logical to *join their families together in marriage for the future of our lands, titles, and properties.*

Logic. Marriage should be a logical decision, not one based on such volatile things as feelings. Love only led to heartache. She knew that. So why was Trevor's entirely logical list and concise proposal of marriage so bothersome? The problem was that her objections defied logic. She dipped her quill and placed it on the paper.

She must write something on this dratted list. She'd come too far in this plan to abandon it now. She added a flourish to the flower in the corner of her paper as she considered her future with Trevor.

What did she want of him? For him to wait for a response when proposing marriage, for one.

She sighed and shook her head. She wanted them to have some level of friendship, even if it was only recounting the events of the day over dinner. A stable, organized life shouldn't be at the cost of companionship. However, Trevor Moore, Lord Ayton, didn't seem the companionable sort.

Roselyn would get on fine, though. She would have Katie around… Until Katie married, that was. Then she would spend her days with the household staff. She would visit her family since they would be nearby. She would… Ethan Moore's face swam before her eyes before she blinked it away. He had no place in her mind at a time like this.

She needed to think rational thoughts, and something about that man addled her mind. When he was around, all thought, rational or otherwise, fell to pieces. She'd thrown mud at him. She winced, but that quickly turned into a chuckle. She'd laughed with Ethan. Trevor never inspired as much as a giggle.

Would a future with Trevor be a somber one?

It would be an ordinary existence, to be certain, unlike even a few minutes spent in his brother's company. Ethan wasn't ordinary at all. He was unplanned, reckless even.

*Requirements of Lord Ayton:*

Roselyn watched as the ink pooled on the paper where she'd paused. She closed her eyes for a moment, the quill still in her hand. What did she wish to say? What did she truly wish to say? Suddenly, the words came scrawling out from her hand without consideration. In the end, it was more along the lines of a plea for help than a list, but tonight, lists simply were not to be.

*Dear Ethan,*

*There is no way to express to you my thoughts in the light of day, not with so many guests in the house, and not when I don't understand any of this myself. I'm certain I shall regret this missive come morning, yet my future looms before me and I know I must speak with you…*

‾‾‾

Ethan paced the floor again. What was wrong with him? She was engaged to his brother. Of all the ladies in England, she was the one to stay well away from.

When he saw Roselyn strolling around the parlor on Trevor's arm, envy and longing had mixed into a concoction that had soon turned deadly in his gut. One of the few nights in his life that didn't involve a fight, and it was all he could do not to hit someone. Whether he wished to pummel his brother or himself remained to be seen. He spun on his heel and continued pacing his bedchamber.

What bewitching hold did she have on him? There were plenty of chits in this area. He only had to venture into town to find at least four willing women. But he didn't want any woman. He wanted Roselyn. Those gray eyes staring through him into his soul, the way she grinned at him as if her smile was a gift meant only for him, her regal manner when he alone held her muddy secrets… He had to rid his mind of her.

He swore and went to the door. He needed a walk in the cool night air. He needed a strong drink. He needed someone to punch until his thoughts mellowed enough to allow him to sleep this evening. Perhaps a strong drink while walking outside and hitting everyone who crossed his path? Only if they hit him in return and knocked some sense into his head. He threw open the door, but stopped.

"Roselyn." He whispered her name on a sharp intake of breath as he looked down at her. There in the hall, kneeling before his door, was the woman who had him seeking brandy and a fight to cool his thoughts. Her dark hair fell in wild curls around her upturned face. The candle at her side bathed her in golden flickers of light as she twitched a small piece of paper between her fingers with a nervous tremble. "What are you doing here?"

She clambered to her feet. "Oh. I was…" Glancing down at the note in her hand, she blushed and swept it behind her back. "I thought I lost an earring earlier somewhere down this hall. I don't suppose you've seen it?"

"You're searching for a lost earring? Dressed like this?" His eyes raked over her body, taking in every inch of her figure draped in a thin night rail and wrapped in a robe that left nothing to the imagination. His gaze paused on her bare toes, which she wiggled back under the hem of her gown. He pulled his eyes back to her face. "Someone could see you."

"Yes, well…it is the middle of the night. I didn't dress for making social calls. If I had known, I certainly would have dressed for the occasion."

"You didn't think you would find me when you were lurking outside the door to my rooms?" He watched her, but in the dim light of the single candle her thoughts were a mystery.

"You believe I planned to find you roaming the halls at this hour?" She was trying to look innocent and was failing miserably at the task.

What had that paper been about, and what was she doing crawling down the hall? He would have to find out. But he couldn't do that while she lingered outside his door. "It's rather fortuitous that we should find one another, then. Both unable to sleep, you due to the loss of an earring, me due to…"

"I think that would depend on how one chooses to define 'fortuitous,'" she returned, her eyes darting anywhere but at him.

"Perhaps. Come inside before you're seen." He leaned around the door frame to glance down the hall, seeing only darkness.

"I shouldn't. I only came because…"

"You lost an earring?" He lifted one eyebrow in question. "Roselyn, you weren't wearing any earrings today." He would know. Everything about her was etched in his mind and refused to leave—unlike the lady herself. Stepping back, he nodded toward his bedchamber. "Come in."

"Very well." She retrieved her candle and took a cautious step inside. "I shouldn't be here."

He closed the door, never taking his eyes off her. "No, you shouldn't. And yet, you are."

"Yes, I am." She sounded as shocked by her actions as he was. She shifted her weight and looked around the room. She was probably taking in the armchairs before the crackling fire, his jacket slung across a side table, his rumpled bed… He should have straightened things.

Then she froze.

What was she thinking? He needed to know. All Ethan could think of was the silhouette of her body beneath her robe and how her skin would feel as he slipped the robe off her shoulders. He shook his head. He had to keep his wits about him. She was here for a reason, whether she would admit it or not. "Is that a note you have behind your back?"

"No." She turned to face him, her eyes round with guilt.

"Really. Because I thought I saw you with a piece of paper in your hand."

She shook her head, her breasts rising and falling rapidly with every breath. He took a step toward her, his hand settling on her arm where it was still twined behind her back.

"Are you certain? I don't usually see things that don't exist." He wrapped his fingers around her elbow and tugged gently on her arm. She was close, close enough for him to feel the heat of her against his chest. What would happen if he kissed her? His hand slipped down her arm, pulling her closer to his body in the process.

"I...I don't have..." She cleared her throat and closed her eyes to say, "I don't have anything."

"Truly?" he asked with a grin as he grabbed the paper from her fingers and took a step backward with a laugh. He held the note out of her reach—easy enough, given her stature in comparison to his. "Then this would be..." Waving the paper through the air, he watched her stretch to reach it. Then, turning his eyes upward, he assessed the note. "Oh, and look, it has my name written on it. See? *Mr. Ethan Moore.*"

She shoved against his chest with balled fists. "Don't! I shouldn't have. I didn't intend for you to…"

"I wonder what it could say. And with such lovely penmanship." He smiled down into her angry face. "I especially like the little swirl you made when crossing the *T* on Ethan. Nice addition."

"Please give me the note back," Roselyn said in a quiet voice. "I can see now that I was a fool to write it."

His arm dropped to his side at the tearful look in her eyes. *Please don't cry*, he pleaded in silence. He was only having some fun. He'd never meant to hurt her. "You are not, nor will you ever be, a fool. Here, have your note. My apologies."

"Oh." She looked shocked at his change of tack, but took the paper back nevertheless. "Well, thank you. I did write it for you, but it was in a moment of… I don't know what it was in a moment of, to be honest. I sat down to write Trevor's list, but I couldn't. I needed to say this. And then, before I could think better of it, I was already here and then you were here and… I'm running on a bit, aren't I? It's only that I'm not sure what to do, and I'm always sure what to do. Do you understand?"

"No, not at all. Why don't you explain it to me?" He reached out to pull her hand into his grasp, rubbing the pad of his thumb over her palm in an attempt to wipe away the turmoil she was feeling.

She took a breath, looking up into his face as she said, "But that is the issue, isn't it? I shouldn't be explaining anything to you. I should be…" She took a step back, but he didn't release her hand. "I should be in bed."

He moved forward, closing the gap she'd created between them. "I'm happy to oblige on that count," he teased. He couldn't have her, not now, not ever. But he could dream of it without burning for his weakness and being tossed from the family once more.

"My bed! The bed I was provided for my stay here. Not yours!" Her eyes darted to his bed across the room, and a deep blush crept up into her cheeks.

There was a moment of silence in which he caught one dark ringlet in his free hand and spun it around until it encircled his finger, cool and soft. He'd lost a great deal in his life and not just the occasional fight; he'd lost his family, his path, and now he'd lost Roselyn to his brother when he'd only become reacquainted with her yesterday. His timing truly was deplorable, but this was Roselyn. She'd always been his—his friend, his escape.

When they were children, she'd distracted him from the harsh reality he was walking into when he returned to his home at night, and she still distracted him from reality today. Their games had changed, they'd grown up, but her presence still soothed all that hurt and brought much needed laughter into his war-torn life. The only problem was that as soon as she left this room, she wouldn't be his anymore. She would belong to his brother.

Was that what she wanted?

What he wanted was right in front of him. He wanted happiness and laughter with Roselyn's hand in his, to know that he could face tomorrow because she would be there. And he would be lying if he said he didn't want her body wrapped around him the same way her hair was curled around his finger. The idea of her sprawled across his bed—his for the night and his to enjoy, to explore like the fields they had hiked through together years ago—filled his mind with endless possibilities. The wildly adventurous time they would have together brought a smile to his face, even though it was not to be.

Her voice came out in a broken whisper mirroring his own thoughts: "It wouldn't be right."

"So soft. I never realized before," he mused, gazing down at his fingers entwined in her hair.

"I'm sure it is and you have no idea how much it pains me to walk away, but I must."

He chuckled deep in his throat as he ran his fingers across her jaw, watching her eyes drift closed at his touch. "I was speaking of your curls, not my bed. Although, I find it flattering that you would want to warm it."

Her eyes flashed open as she pulled free of his grasp. "On that humiliating note, I will leave you."

Ethan reached for her. "Please, don't be embarrassed. I want…"

"Ah, you say that, and yet I can't help wanting to go crawl under a rock somewhere never to reemerge." She was already moving toward the door.

"Roselyn, wait." He'd played this all wrong. This was what came of not dealing with any ladies for years. He'd forgotten that, unlike barmaids, ladies could only be teased so much before they fled.

"I really do need to get back before my absence is noted." She opened the door and slipped out into the dark hall.

"Roselyn!" he called after her as she scurried back down the hallway, fading into darkness. "I want you too," he whispered into the night on a sigh. He leaned against the door frame for a moment, hoping she would return, even though he knew she wouldn't. He'd straightened and was about to close the door when a movement in the darkness caught his eye.

"Roselyn? If you come back, I promise not to tease you about warming my bed," he tempted, but there were only heavy footsteps moving away down the hall in response. Finally, he gave it up as a loss and closed the door.

He gazed down at the rug in defeat. Only then did he see the forgotten note lying on the floor. Roselyn must have dropped it. He practically dove on it, ripping it open to devour her words the way he wished they both could consume every part of each other.

❧

Roselyn squinted her eyes against the brilliant morning sun as she stepped out onto the gravel path. She should have worn her taupe hat. The brim on her blue hat was much thinner and framed her face to perfection, not to mention accentuating her eyes, but it did nothing to shield her from the glaring light. She could still go back. Of course, then she would look silly for changing accessories at the last moment in front of Trevor. No, she would suffer the light in silence and vow to enjoy the day in spite of it. She offered Trevor a pleasant smile.

"I must return from this errand by early afternoon when the house guests are set to return from their visit into the village. I'll have responsibilities as their host, you know," Trevor stated as he increased their pace down the steps into the garden. His voice sounded a bit more strained than usual, and he'd yet to meet her gaze.

"Of course," she murmured, trying to shake off the uneasiness she felt at spending the morning alone with Trevor.

It appeared Ethan had chosen *not* to join them today. Her stomach turned with foolish regret over going to his room with the note last night, especially now that he was absent. Their short time together was over, it would seem. Wishing for time with Ethan was illogical anyway. She was engaged to his brother. Shame washed over her.

Trevor didn't deserve her irrational thoughts involving his brother. Trevor embodied every ideal she wanted in a husband. He deserved a wife who would be true and steadfast at his side. *I must be that wife for him.* She nodded in determination. The garden path before her feet felt as if it might go on forever, step after step, day after day, with Trevor at her side for all of it.

She stepped forward, aware of the crunch of the gravel under her half boot and the solid arm under her hand. The first step into her future.

"Your gardens are lovely," she offered to fill the gathering silence. It was too quiet this morning, in every way imaginable. This stilted conversation was only the most recent form of silence she'd endured. The halls were empty and the party was devoid of life with everyone in the village for the day. She'd eaten alone this morning, deep in a private shame she would never divulge to anyone. The house itself seemed to be sitting in silent judgment of her trip down the hall last night, even though she knew that wasn't true. She took a breath in an effort to pull herself together.

The red of Trevor's hair glowed in the sunlight. He was rather dashing, she supposed. He was always properly dressed—that was an important attribute. "Ah, yes. I enjoy the view of the garden from my desk. Brightens things up a bit," he said, still sounding distracted.

"I would imagine so. I must admit that I would have a hard time staying inside with such lovely surroundings just outside my window."

"If you were in my garden, I would struggle to stay away from such loveliness as well."

"Trevor, you flatter me."

"A gentleman should flatter his future bride. It will help things run smoothly between us, I believe. That is what you want, isn't it?"

"Certainly."

"Did you have time last night to write your list?" he asked with a bite of something beneath his words that she didn't quite understand.

"No. I began, but I became busy." She looked out across the moors. If she was blushing, he wouldn't see it.

"This afternoon perhaps."

"Should we get a maid to accompany us?" she asked, changing the subject from the list. Her own mother was back in her suite. She'd been overcome with illness upon hearing of Roselyn's plans for the day and had required the use of their maid to recover. She'd looked the other way as Roselyn left for a walk that was entirely inappropriate, and even now she was lying abed, most likely eating sweets. At least her mother was in favor of this union. Roselyn shook her head to clear away her wavering thoughts.

"No one is about this morning to see us, and we're to be married soon anyway. It's not as if *I* would attempt anything less than honorable while on a walk. Would you?"

"No," Roselyn returned, her brows drawing together in concern. What was he getting at?

"Of course not. Your dress would be soiled by the dirt." He spoke in such a matter-of-fact tone that it relieved her worry a bit.

"Yes, a muddy dress would be disastrous," she replied, her voice barely a whisper.

"Come, let us be on our way." He gave her a pleasant smile and increased their pace forward.

They reached the circular fountain, where the path curved away on either side before coming back together and running off to the far side of the garden. That was when she heard footsteps at their backs. Turning, she saw Ethan striding up to greet them. He clapped a hand on his brother's shoulder and broke her contact with Trevor's arm in the process. "Good morning, Brother," he offered before nodding in her direction with a quiet "Lady Roselyn."

Trevor did not look pleased as he seared his brother with a narrow-eyed stare. "Ethan, I thought we determined that you had a prior engagement this morning."

"Yes, I did. However, I received a missive late

last night canceling my meeting." His gaze darted to her for the briefest of seconds before landing back on Trevor. "So here I am, able-bodied tour guide for your exploration of the mines."

"Oh, I am glad you changed your mind," Roselyn muttered around a tight throat. Excitement and worry swirled in her stomach. She was to wed Trevor. No good could come of this, yet she wanted Ethan's presence all the same.

"How could I stay inside on such a beautiful day? Now, we have mines to explore. Let's be on our way, shall we?"

"Well, yes, I suppose so." Roselyn took the offer of Ethan's outstretched arm with a tentative grasp, glancing over her shoulder at Trevor.

Trevor's eyes narrowed at his brother's back for only a fraction of a second, something angry boiling beneath the surface before he fell into step beside them.

"Have you seen the view from the peak of Roseberry Topping before?" Ethan asked from her side as they descended the stone steps to the wilder lower property beyond the house.

"I've seen it from the valley below but I've never been to the top." She shielded her eyes as she gazed up to the tallest hill around, a rocky crest rising from the sea of tall grass that stretched across the moors.

"The view from that point on the property is astounding." He leaned in to add, "And you can see the entrance to the mines from there."

"Perfect!" She stepped around a mud puddle left over from the rains earlier in the week. "Is it a difficult walk to the top?"

"It can be a bit steep in places, but I won't let you lose your footing." He grinned down at her.

Trevor caught up to them within one stride after veering in a wide arc around the puddle. "Brother, I believe that is my responsibility, seeing as this is my outing."

"Yes, but you were going to keep her on level ground gazing at grass in a field or some such. I believe the lady requires a bit more excitement than that. Don't you, Lady Roselyn?"

"A bit of excitement sounds nice, actually." She glanced over her shoulder at Trevor to add, "But I'm sure Trevor's tour would have included many interesting views."

"Certainly," Trevor blustered. "I was going to take you to Drapelsly's Bend."

"Drapelsly's Bend?" Ethan repeated. "That's little more than a shift in the river. It's hardly even a bend. More of a leaning really."

Roselyn could sense an argument beginning and tried to stem it with, "If I recall correctly, it's lovely." However, Trevor wasn't listening.

"There are practically rapids in that area!" he argued.

"Rapids? It's a stream." Ethan chuckled. "I believe the fish are plagued with ennui while swimming in it."

Anger was brewing in Trevor's eyes, but Ethan never turned around to notice. He kept moving forward down the dusty path through the grass, dragging her along with his long strides.

"I will have you know I nearly drowned once at Drapelsly's Bend."

Ethan stopped, then turned to face his brother.

"When we were fishing as children? That water was thigh deep even then. I know. I pulled you to shore."

Roselyn took a step away from the two gentlemen. Perhaps this was why it was advisable to have a chaperone on such occasions. What would she do if this descended into a round of fisticuffs? "I like rivers and streams…and fish," she interjected in a somewhat shrill voice. "Oh, isn't this the perfect day to be out in the sunshine? Days like this one are rare this time of year."

"Indeed." Trevor raised his chin toward his brother. "I will take you to see the dangerous rapids of Drapelsly's Bend some other day. Today, it seems, we will be climbing Roseberry Topping."

After a moment's pause she wrapped her hand around Trevor's extended arm with a smile. "I'm quite excited about both adventures. It's been some years since I've been to Drapelsly's Bend. You'll have to take me to visit the location soon."

"You've been before?" Trevor asked as they wound their way further into the moors.

"Of course," she replied. But she couldn't help adding, "My brother taught me to swim there."

A choke of suppressed laughter came from just ahead. Ethan coughed to cover his amusement, yet never looked back.

Trevor was not quite as amused. "Brother, I do hope this fresh air isn't giving you a cough. You may have to return home."

"Never been better," Ethan called out, striding forward down the path worn through the tall grass.

When they rounded the bend, a small cottage came into view. The walls were made of rock from the surrounding countryside and held up a thatched roof. Smoke puffed from a stone chimney in a merry rhythm before vanishing into a cloudless sky.

"What a charming little cottage," Roselyn mused.

"Hmm… Yes, that is the home of one of our tenants," Trevor offered, his gaze already on the path beyond the cottage.

As they neared, Roselyn noticed a pink-cheeked woman with gray hair escaping from around her bonnet who was beating a rug in the front garden. Her round arms dropped to her sides as she saw them approaching.

"Mr. Moore! I'd heard you were back in these parts. What a sight you are this mornin'."

"A good sight I hope, Mrs. Scatterwald."

"You know you're a right nice sight for the eyes, you rogue," she returned with a hearty laugh.

Ethan smiled broadly in return.

"M'lord, m'lady," she offered in greeting before turning her attention back to Ethan. "Headin' up to the top today, are ye?"

"Yes, ma'am. Don't suppose you still make your famous pies after all these years, do you?"

"For you? You know I do." She smiled at Ethan, turned, and strolled back into her cottage.

When she was inside, Trevor asked, "How do you know Mrs. Scuffield so well? You only just returned home."

"It's Scatterwald, and she lives on our land. How could I help but know her? She keeps everyone at the mines fed. I would have starved for half of my childhood if not for her pies and stews."

"Here you are, some nice pies for your journey."

"They smell delicious as always, Mrs. Scatterwald." Ethan dropped a few coins in her hand and took the bag she offered him. "My thanks. Enjoy this fine weather."

"That I will, Mr. Moore." She nodded in farewell as they continued on past her row of fencing and onto the rocky path leading to the lone hilltop.

"Shall we stop to eat then, Brother?" Trevor asked.

Ethan turned from his path a few paces ahead of them, his cheeks filled with food and a half-eaten pie in his hand. "These are mine. I'm famished from all this walking."

"Ethan!" Trevor reprimanded.

"What?" he asked around a large bite of pie.

"There's a lady present," Trevor hissed in disapproval. "You can't even see fit to share with her?"

"Oh." He paused to pluck an apple from a tree beside the path and tossed it over his shoulder. "Here you go, princess. Enjoy."

By reflex she reached up and caught the apple. It wasn't until she heard Trevor's gasp that she considered the apple in her hand. In hindsight, the ladylike thing to do would have been to cover her head and squeal, but there was no un-catching the fruit that Ethan had hurled at her head. It wasn't something one expected and could therefore prepare for. She should have expected it from Ethan though. He was likely the only man aside from her brother, Devon, who had ever dared throw anything at her. Gentlemen didn't usually throw anything at ladies, but Ethan had known she would catch the apple, having spent an entire autumn sitting cross-legged with her in the shade of a tree and learning to juggle.

Was he attempting to make Trevor doubt his decision to marry her? Her eyes narrowed on Ethan's back. No matter what Ethan's intention, the apple did look delicious, and she'd already caught it in midair. With a sigh, she rubbed the skin of the ripe apple on her dress and bit into the fruit with a loud crunch.

The man at her side gave her a shocked glance before averting his eyes as if she were doing something vulgar. Glancing down at the half-eaten apple in her hand, she grimaced. Was eating an apple so terrible? Certainly if they were indoors, she would have a maid cut it into small bites with a knife, as she had been taught to do by one of her governesses along the way. However, they were in the middle of a field.

But if eating the apple offended Trevor so, she supposed she must refrain from doing it. She sighed as she tossed the apple over her shoulder and licked the last of its sweet juice from the corner of her mouth. This seemed to please Trevor since he gave her a fleeting smile before returning his attention to the path before them.

They walked in stilted silence for a few minutes while Ethan whistled a light tune up ahead between bites of his pie. The path was growing steep. They were winding around large boulders and over smaller rocks pressed into the sparse vegetation when Roselyn stepped over a rocky area, bumped into the side of a boulder, and felt a pebble slip into her boot.

Wincing, she took a step. Perhaps it would shift to a less painful location. Surely if eating an apple wasn't advisable, removing one's shoe was strictly forbidden. She took another step and was forced to add a small hop to avoid the rock stabbing her.

On a large sigh, she asked, "Would it be possible to pause here for a moment? I'm afraid I have a rock in my shoe."

"Of course. Ethan, dust off that stone for her ladyship to sit."

"It's a rock," Ethan said. "Rocks don't require dusting. They aren't like chairs. Actually, I don't believe I've ever dusted anything off before sitting."

"It will be fine," Roselyn interjected. "I only need to perch on the edge to remove the pebble from my boot."

"See? She's fine," Ethan stated.

"She's not yours to declare fine or otherwise, Ethan."

"No, she's not. But she can tell us herself what she thinks, and she says she's fine."

"She's soon to be my wife, and I will make the decisions for her." Trevor shifted his weight in discomfort, though at the situation or the long walk, Roselyn wasn't sure.

"Is she?" Ethan asked in challenge.

"Do you have issue with my decision to marry Lady Roselyn? If so, say your piece." Trevor waved a hand for his brother to proceed.

"I'm quite well. I don't need anyone to speak for me...or dust rocks for me," Roselyn tried to cut in, but she was ignored.

"You've never valued my opinion about anything," Ethan retorted. "Why begin now?"

"I'm...only retrieving the pebble from my boot," Roselyn muttered as she worked to unlace her shoe. The two brothers didn't notice because they were busy glaring daggers at each other. "Are you two even listening to me?"

"Roselyn is mine," Trevor sneered.

Ethan was stepping closer over the rocky terrain. "She isn't your property, Trevor. Or have banns been posted and vows exchanged and I wasn't aware?"

"Well, she certainly doesn't belong to you, Ethan. You don't think I've noticed the two of you together, laughing? When you put your hand on her on the lawn yesterday?" His voice echoed off the hillside as he bellowed, "Why were you touching her?"

"I've done nothing wrong." Ethan shrugged, but she could see the tension in his shoulders.

Roselyn couldn't move as her carefully planned future was picked apart before her eyes. Nothing had happened, yet last night she *had* been with him. If anyone had seen her...if Trevor had somehow found out...

"That's a lie! You're here." Trevor eyed Ethan with hawklike awareness as he stopped before him. "You're trying to seduce Roselyn with talk of danger and adventure. You're my brother! Father was right to rid the family of you years ago. Where is your loyalty?"

"I am loyal!" Ethan exclaimed. "I only came here today because..."

"Why?"

Ethan paused. "I cannot say. You only need know that I changed my plans and was able to attend."

"Your intentions altered in the middle of the night," Trevor said in a dangerous voice. "Last night after you were with Roselyn?"

Roselyn froze, her boot hanging from her hand as she gaped at the two men.

"I wasn't with Roselyn last night, not as you're

intending, anyway. I only…" Ethan stopped. He shot a quick glance to Roselyn.

"I saw her leave your rooms, Ethan."

Roselyn gasped and tried to stand, forgetting she was only wearing one boot, before sitting back down on the rock. "Trevor, I can explain."

"What happened last night?" Trevor asked his brother, as if Roselyn hadn't said a word.

Roselyn's heart pounded in her ears. Her boot became heavy in her hands. Oh no. This could not be happening. No, no, no…

Ethan looked his brother in the eye. "You need to calm yourself, Brother."

"What happened?" Trevor's words thundered through the warm air, knocking the wind from Roselyn's lungs and steeling Ethan's stance against his brother.

Ethan said nothing—only stared his brother down.

"You bastard!" Trevor shoved Ethan in the chest. "You took her into your bed, didn't you? You soiled her!" He shoved Ethan again, this time harder. "You've always wanted everything I have—my title, my inheritance, and now my lady."

"I've never wanted your blasted title. And I don't want—" Ethan began, but his glance at Roselyn undid any lie he was about to tell. He did want her. His eyes held that truth quite clearly.

"Would have been nice if you had been born first, wouldn't it, Ethan? Well, you weren't. I was." Trevor glanced to her with disgust showing in his eyes before turning back to his brother. "This time, you win. This time, you can have my castoffs. I thought I could continue on as if it hadn't happened, as if you didn't exist.

That's been simple enough for the past eight years. But I can't live with the knowledge of *you* and *her*…"

"Trevor, nothing untoward has happened between your brother and me!" Roselyn exclaimed, desperate to cease his assumptions.

Ethan took a step forward. "What she says is true."

"There is nothing between you, then?" Trevor asked.

Roselyn opened her mouth to reply, but her words of denial died on her lips. She may not be guilty of wrongdoing, but she couldn't deny that she'd shared some undefinable something with Ethan. Perhaps she always had. Clearly sharing her same pang of conscience, Ethan only sighed.

"I know what I saw last night in the hall. She's all yours, Ethan. I don't associate with whores."

Roselyn gasped. "What? I am no such thing! I haven't… I didn't…" But she couldn't form any argument that Trevor would hear. It was too late for that.

A whore. Was that what he thought of her? Her chest tightened at the knowledge. Only a few minutes ago they had walked together toward a future marriage, no matter her misgivings on the subject. How had things gone so wrong so fast? Her plans. All of her plans…

Ethan lunged forward, slamming his fist into Trevor's jaw, causing a trail of blood to fly across the stone beside them.

"There's no need to fight. I know the truth and I am innocent," Roselyn tried, but no one was listening. She was forgotten where she sat on the large boulder.

Trevor righted himself and threw an elbow into Ethan's stomach. Ethan barely flinched at the contact. Instead, his fist flew once more to Trevor's face.

"Stop it!" she screamed. Only Ethan turned at the sound of her voice—and was hit a second later for his inattention.

Ethan toppled Trevor to the ground and pummeled him in the stomach two, then three times.

"Stop fighting!" she cried out again.

Ethan pulled back in response to her pleading words. Meanwhile, Trevor gained his footing and took off running up the hill and out of sight. Ethan turned toward his brother and took a step before spinning back to her. The indecision was clear in his eyes, but when his gaze dropped to her stocking-clad foot and the boot still in her hand, he sighed and turned to take off after Trevor, impatience winning in the end.

She tried to stand but only had one boot on. "Blasted boot!" she bellowed to no one since she was alone on a boulder on the side of a mountain. This was not part of her plan!

Trevor had called her a whore. Her stomach recoiled at the thought. Going to Ethan's door with that note had been unwise, but she'd realized that and left. Nothing had happened! Trevor must be made to understand. Her engagement! Her family would be so disappointed. And it had been such a smart and convenient match.

She huffed, stuffing her foot back into her boot. What if her mother found out where she'd been last night? And just now they'd been fighting over her. Ethan had hit his brother in defense of her honor.

Roselyn should be feeling some sense of feminine pride at the moment, but all she felt was hurt. This was her fault. How had she allowed this to happen? It was all because of the note. Of course Ethan had hit Trevor. She'd pushed him into this position. But she'd been confused and... There was no excuse for it. She had to go after them and stop more from happening.

She worked frantically to lace her boot in order to follow them over the crown of the topping. Finally, she stood, hitched up her skirt, and ran up the remainder of the rocks in her path. The grass that survived the rocky terrain grasped at her ankles as she climbed over the hilltop onto a flat surface.

Where had they gone?

The brilliant sunlight reflected off the boulders, making the bright day glaring. Squinting, she noticed movement on the far side of the hilltop. She ran toward the top of the hill—and spotted him.

Ethan was kneeling on the rocks, staring at the ground before him—alone. Where was Trevor?

Her eyes darted around in search of the man. She must make him see reason. Hopefully, Ethan hadn't knocked him too senseless.

She neared Ethan where he knelt, frozen as if he had been turned to stone. His dark hair whipped around his face in the wind. The chatter of distant birds sounded on the air, singing through the silence.

A trickle of blood ran from Ethan's forehead, encircling his reddened eye on its way to drip on the ground. Her eyes followed one red drop as it fell to the rock where he knelt. It was then she saw the glint of a blade on the ground—and the blood smeared across the metal.

Where had Ethan gotten a knife? He hadn't been carrying one earlier, had he? And where was Trevor?

Her gaze snapped to Ethan's face. His eyes didn't waver.

She moved forward and saw what held Ethan's attention.

He wasn't staring at the ground. No. He looked into a jet-black pit in the earth.

"One of the air shafts for the mine," he mumbled. Ethan hovered on the edge of darkness. His breaths were labored. He picked up the knife, the blade shaking in his open palm. The wide mouth of the crevice screamed in silent horror.

She stood dazed for a moment before the truth splintered down her back to wrap its icy fingers around her heart. "Where is Trevor?" she asked, her voice shaking. She already knew the answer. "What happened?" Her eyes began to sting.

Ethan's eyes lifted from the black depths to meet hers with a hollow stare. "Something smashed over my head." He touched the wound at his hairline before looking back toward the cavernous depths again. "He fell. He was here and then…"

"What have you done, Ethan?" she screamed as tears streamed down her cheeks. "What have you done?"

# *Four*

ROSELYN SWAYED TO THE SIDE AS A MAID RUSHED PAST to pack the last of her gowns. He couldn't have killed Trevor. He simply couldn't have. She knew what she'd seen, but Ethan? A killer? Laying a hand on the post at the foot of the bed, she attempted to steady herself while the room spun around her with activity.

"Roselyn, dear. We'll have you home to rest in no time at all." She could hear her mother's voice as if from a great distance away.

"I don't need to rest. I need…" She didn't know what she needed. She only knew that whatever she required, it wouldn't be found today. Perhaps it would never be found and she would forever feel as she did now, tossed about like a tiny ship on the open sea. Gasping for breath as her uncontrollable situation crashed over her and pulled her under, she tightened her grasp on the bedpost. The bustle of activity reached a new level as Devon stepped into the room. Disjointed voices swirled around her in a torrent of words.

"Blasted Himalayan vultures, the lot of them." Her brother shut the door with a loud bang, but Roselyn didn't even look around from her unseeing stare out the window.

"Devon dear, must you use such vulgarity? Your sister is in distress."

"Roselyn has more pressing concerns than my language, Mother."

"Did you meet with the family?" a higher-pitched voice asked. "Such a terrible loss."

"The family is locked away in the library—unavailable to guests."

Katie, she had to tell Katie. Roselyn closed her eyes on the pain she knew she would see on her friend's face when she told her what had happened. Or did she already know? It seemed everyone knew of Trevor's death now, only hours after it happened. But only she'd witnessed it. She swallowed down the truth she'd seen, still feeling as if it was at odds with what she knew of Ethan, and leaned her forehead against the bedpost.

"Roselyn should be allowed to grieve with the family downstairs. She was his fiancée, after all. Even if the betrothal hadn't been announced, the family knew of it," Lily argued.

"Best of luck removing her from this room. The halls are filled with chatter now that everyone has returned from the village. I barely escaped Lady Smeltings with my eyes intact when I told her I knew nothing."

Trevor's fiancée. She hadn't been that any longer by the time they'd reached the hilltop. For a matter of hours, her life had been secure. All she'd ever wanted had been in her grasp for one evening and part of a morning. She'd been on the proper path. She'd had concerns about that path, had even tried to sabotage it with her midnight note to Ethan, but she could have sorted it out with Trevor, couldn't she? She would have been successful if only given a chance to speak with him. Or would their engagement have ended with whispers about her wild nature she'd tried so desperately to stamp out?

In truth, today's events were tinged with the smallest bit of relief on her part.

Shame washed over her at the admission. Trevor's life had been taken from him while only her future had been taken from her, and some small sliver of her was grateful for that. It was sickening. She was awful to think such a thing—truly awful. Speaking to Trevor was not an option she had available, but she would have worked things out with him. He would have understood and proceeded with their engagement. The situation could have been mended, she almost pleaded with herself. But now…

She exhaled a harsh breath. Now Trevor was gone forever, and she must open her eyes and step into uncharted waters.

"Roselyn will grieve Lord Ayton's loss at home, in private. We can be ready in minutes, can't we?" Her mother's commanding voice filled the room.

"Yes, Your Grace."

"Surely we should pay respects to the family before we take our leave," Lily countered.

"It's best if we distance ourselves from this incident, Lily dear. Terrible times. But Roselyn has her future to think of, and soon her debut season…"

"You can't be serious. Did you not hear me

describe those people as birds of prey but a moment ago? You can't take her from this room, much less to London—not this year."

"We must, Devon."

London—her future lay somewhere in London now, even though her thoughts had never been further away than they were right now. She would put the pieces back together again. Wear gowns. Go to balls. Would Katie still attend with her? Her heart ached for her friend.

"Your mother is regrettably correct," Lily said. "The longer we wait, the more stories will form around this day. No one knows what happened, but they do know Roselyn's whereabouts are not accounted for. No one saw her in town today, and now Lord Ayton—with whom her name is quite attached—is gone. There will be talk. If we go to London, perhaps a bit delayed but this season nonetheless, we can insist on our version of the truth—that Roselyn was in her rooms. With any luck, we will reach town before the talk does. Roselyn can't go into mourning for a year over this, or it will follow her forever."

"London, for the season. After this? And they call me mad."

"Roselyn dear, don't listen to your brother. All will be fine."

*Fine.* The word sank like an anchor in her stomach. None of this was fine. She'd seen Ethan with a knife in his hand. She had to come to terms with the fact that he'd killed his brother—over her. And she hadn't told anyone of it. When she'd returned to the house, words had come tumbling from her lips—words like *accident* and *fell*. Why had she lied for him? To protect her secret shame of last night? To protect Ethan? Either way, it was wrong.

Everything about this day was wrong. If she believed what she'd seen with her own eyes, Ethan Moore had murdered his brother, and yet she'd said nothing. That left blame on her as well. He hadn't asked her to tell falsehoods. "Katie," she whispered to herself. But she hadn't done this to protect her friend. How had she made such a muck of her life in less than a day?

"Roselyn, you really should sit, dear. You're looking quite pale."

"We should send for her friend. Surely, they can have a few moments together before we return to Thornwood."

"I asked after Lady Katie already. Apparently she is still out on her daily ride."

That sounded like Katie. She was having a lovely day out in the sun, unaware that her family was in ruin. Let her enjoy her day. Let her live.

Someone sniffed in the corner of the room. "So very close to becoming family, and to have things end like this."

"Now, now, Lily dear. This isn't the end. This is only the beginning. Come along, Roselyn. We must put you to rights so that we can leave this place."

The idea that this was only the beginning made her slightly ill. It seemed like the end of so many things: a gentleman's life, her plans of marriage, a predictable future. All of that was gone. All because of Ethan. She'd seen him holding a bloody knife. She couldn't deny his guilt, yet she was struggling to believe what she'd seen. How had she been so terribly wrong about him? Or perhaps she'd been right about him all along. She should have trusted her initial opinion of the man he'd become and not let his troubling eyes distract her. This was her fault. It was all her fault.

Roselyn pushed off the bedpost to which she'd clung to stay afloat for the past few minutes. A hat was placed on her head and fresh gloves slid over her fingers. She was aware of Lily and her mother leading her to the door. Devon cleared a path for them in the hall. Down the stairs, her feet met each step with an impact she could barely feel. She was numb. Only the guilt that she could have stopped this—all of this—remained.

When they reached the closed door to the library, she paused. Ethan Moore was on the other side of that door. If she saw Ethan again, if she looked in his eyes, would she understand the events of the day? Understand him?

Perhaps he was only a murderer, nothing more.

The man who had killed his brother and her future plans was probably sipping his tea and smiling to himself for a job well done. He'd destroyed her life and gained the title and estates all in one morning. He must be so proud of his achievement. If only she had known the extent of his true nature, the lengths he was willing to go to do what he pleased! Any good in his teasing nature must have been imagined. If she ever looked him in the eye again, she would tell him what she thought of his ways. Whether he was proven guilty or not, she would never fall under his spell again. She would never lose control like that again.

"Roselyn, I know you want to speak with Lord

Ormesby and Lady Katie, but now is not the time. We must go."

She nodded slowly in agreement.

Roselyn floated through the process of walking out the door. Later she wouldn't remember clinging to her mother for support, or the whispers at her back as she left. She wouldn't remember the weather that afternoon or the carriage ride to Thornwood Manor. She would, however, always remember her vow: *I will never fall under his spell again. I will never lose control of my life again.*

❧

Ethan pushed the door to Trevor's private parlor open, half expecting to find him sitting at his desk. The soundless image of his brother falling into the air shaft of the East Mine cycled through his mind again as it had for the past day. With one last glance out into the hall to make sure he was alone, he took a determined step into the room.

Trevor had always been private with his thoughts and actions, unlike Ethan, who was always quick to laugh or throw a punch, depending on the situation. He'd spent nineteen years living under the same roof as his brother and still felt as if he was standing in a stranger's private quarters. Invading. Plundering.

Crossing the floor to the closest window, Ethan pulled back the draperies. He would never find anything in the dark, and as much as he desired to linger and soak up the last of the brother he barely knew, he wanted to be gone from this room just as much. There would be time later to mourn Trevor the way he ought to. Once his killer was captured and brought to justice.

His gaze swept across the well-kept room. Bookshelves flanked the fireplace where volumes were stacked according to size and subject matter, not one out of place. Chairs were grouped together in front of the cold grate, yet nothing of a personal nature was left behind, only a tidy parlor devoid of life. The lack of fire only added to the chilling air of hollowness about the place. Ethan stood for a moment, staring at the chair where his brother must have spent most of his evenings. The dark blue armchair now sat empty, as it would forever.

If Trevor were to walk through the door, would the atmosphere change? It wasn't likely. His brother had never been a warm and inviting individual, and Ethan knew little of his life. Somehow he now had to assemble the remaining pieces and discover what ended Trevor's life. No matter what Roselyn believed to be true, he hadn't killed his brother.

Ethan had shoved him away. He closed his eyes against the memory, but it came back to him just as it had over and over in the past day. Trevor had tried to hit him, but Ethan was too quick. He'd swerved to the side just as the glint of a knife caught the light on the edge of his vision. It happened so fast. Even with his reflexes, he couldn't stop it. He could remember the blinding pain in his head had knocked him to his knees. The hilt of the knife, the knife he'd found in the grass. Trevor staggering backward with a growing circle of red across the white of his shirt.

Their eyes had met for only a moment, too short

to convey any last words. He'd fallen. Ethan reached forward but only grasped air. The shadow of a man had loomed over him, but then he too was gone. He'd seen the knife and lifted it from the grass…

He forced his eyes open as he always did at this point, not wanting to see the accusation in Roselyn's eyes again.

No matter what she believed, there had been another man on Roseberry Topping yesterday morning. The memory of Trevor's visitor that he'd sent away two days ago crossed his mind again.

*Trevor will be out for a walk by the mines, at Roseberry Topping I believe, and will be unavailable. I can speak with the visitor if you'd like…* He shook off the thought. He'd only seen a shadow. That was hardly enough evidence with which to accuse a man of murder, and he'd already questioned Celersworth to no avail. Moreover, there was something about the silhouette he'd seen against the sun that didn't match Trevor's visitor.

However it had happened, someone had been waiting for them—waiting to remove Ethan from the situation and kill Trevor. The thought left him nauseated. How could anyone seek out a man with the sole purpose of killing him? He didn't understand any of it, but he would. Trevor might not have been an ideal brother, but he was the only one Ethan had ever known. He wouldn't allow his murderer to escape unscathed.

Trevor's death couldn't be related to a matter of the heart. Roselyn had been the only lady in his life. Ethan was sure of that much. That left business…the mines. "It must have had something to do with the jet mines," he whispered into the silence.

Turning to the desk on the far wall, he took a second to steady himself. His head still throbbed from where he'd been hit. He'd taken plenty of blows before, but this was the first time he'd been caught off guard with a knife. If he'd been prepared, if he'd seen the danger coming, perhaps he could have braced himself. If the world hadn't gone dark with pain for a moment, if he could have seen beyond the blur of color in that fraction of a second, he could have stopped this from happening. He could have won. Trevor would still be here. The one fight in his life that truly mattered, and he'd lost.

He stepped forward, even more determined than before. Trailing his fingers over the red ribbon that bound the only documents on Trevor's desk, Ethan lifted the neat stack of papers. Something nudged the edge of his memory in regard to the packet of papers, but the throbbing in his forehead overshadowed it. His grip on the documents tightened as his gaze swept across the desk once more. Only an inkwell and a lamp sat on the surface. There were no other personal effects, no hastily written notes, no clues of any sort. Trevor's entire life had been boiled down to a small stack of what appeared to be sales receipts.

Ethan turned to take one last look around the room before leaving. That was when he saw his father standing just inside the door. His arms were wrapped across his chest as he surveyed the room, not meeting Ethan's gaze.

"Most of the guests have left the estate."

"That seems wise on their part," Ethan hedged. He'd gone straight to his father when he returned to the house yesterday. He'd barely spoken to the man since his return to England, but he'd had no choice. His father needed to know of Trevor's death. Ethan had told him everything—or almost everything. The fight over Roselyn didn't need to come into it, now or ever.

Those last few minutes he'd spent with his brother would only hurt Roselyn, not to mention increase the appearance of his own guilt. But he'd told his father the truth about the rest of the morning: the walk to the mines, the shadowed figure who struck him on the head before killing Trevor. His father hadn't said a word. He'd only listened and, when the story was told, had asked him to leave the room.

"I've spoken with the staff," his father said, slicing through Ethan's thoughts. "Preparations are underway for the funeral services." He bit the words out as if by great force.

Ethan nodded, but remained silent.

"Nothing too public. No one needs to know the details of what happened. And, of course, I've already sent for my man of business. There is paperwork to be clarified now that you are...my heir." He seemed to choke on the words before repeating them to himself as if testing them for accuracy. "My heir."

Being the perfect heir was Trevor's job. Ethan had never wanted the burden of the title and estate. He wasn't suited for that sort of life. Where would that leave him? Certainly not where he wanted to be. His gaze dropped to the documents in his arms. He didn't want his life to be calculated in profits and losses on some report, but to live as he always had—by his wits and his fists. Perhaps he couldn't return to Spain now, but he could continue to live his life somewhere. He'd return to St. James and the Spare Heirs Society—but he couldn't live here. "I don't want it—any of it." Although he spoke to himself, his deep voice carried in the quiet room.

"It's a bit too late for notions of that sort," his father replied, squaring his shoulders. His eyes bore a look Ethan had seen many times across the open floor of a boxing salon just before a fight.

His opponents always held the same glare until he knocked it from their faces. But he wouldn't fight his father, even if the man wished it. There were some lines even he wouldn't cross. "The title, the estate, the mines...they were always Trevor's."

"And now they're yours." His father took a step forward, closing the gap between them.

"No." The word was out of Ethan's mouth before he could stop it.

It needed to be said, but the single word of defiance brought his father closer, the menacing gleam growing in his eyes. "You don't have a choice in the matter."

"This isn't why I returned home."

"Why did you return home?"

To hide from his enemies, to escape a terrible mistake. The words flashed in his mind, but he said nothing of his reasons. "Not for this. This." He waved the arm still clutching the documents, indicating the room. "All of this is Trevor's. It always has been and it should remain so."

"Do you believe that?"

"Yes."

"Then why interfere with what you claim is Trevor's property?"

Roselyn. Roselyn had been engaged to Trevor. He never should have... "I don't know what you're referring to," he lied.

"Ever since her arrival you've been after the Grey girl. Did you think I wouldn't notice? That your brother wouldn't notice?"

"I've done nothing." Ethan shifted his weight as he often did to stay limber between punches.

"Why did you go with him to the mines? Was she there as well? Your involvement with her was never going to end well. She belonged to your brother." His voice grew louder as he spoke, until he was yelling.

Ethan watched his father's nostrils flare with every angry breath, but he didn't flinch. The sight had been much more fearsome when he was young, but now he was taller than his father. Today, his father was simply an older man who had just lost his elder son. He needed to rail at someone, and Ethan had nineteen years of practice being on the receiving end of his father's temper. He stood in silence, allowing his father's words to wash over him.

"You should have stayed away as you were instructed. Anyone who sympathizes with that traitorous woman has no room in my home. And yet here you are. My *heir*."

"*That woman* is my mother. It's been eight years, Father. When will you see reason?"

"Trevor said the same. I allowed you room in my home once more for *him*, not for you. His death is on your shoulders, and now you will serve this family. It has become your duty through your own irresponsibility." He took a rasping breath. "Trevor is gone because of you!"

Ethan's eyes narrowed on the older man before him. He couldn't think Ethan guilty of such a crime, could he? But then, his father always thought the worst of him. "Father, I had no part in Trevor's death."

"You followed him to Roseberry Topping and now he's gone. That is all I need know."

"There was someone else there. It's as I told you before. Trevor was involved with something. He must have made enemies."

"That is the last I want to hear of Trevor's enemies. There is too much to be done without chasing an apparition across the moors."

"It wasn't an apparition." Ethan ran his fingers across the gash on his forehead. The man had been quite real, and he had the head wound to prove it.

"The wound on your brother's chest proves nothing, and in order to preserve the future of my title, no one will ever know of it. You should be grateful."

"Grateful? You're allowing his murderer to escape our family's retribution."

"Indeed." His father sneered at him for a moment before continuing. "After the funeral services I'll need you to go to London. There will be talk, and our family needs to see that things don't get out of hand. It could hurt jewelry sales if we allow this to fester. You will go and make the rounds there. Spread the word that Trevor's death was an accident. Accidents happen. Murders don't."

"An accident?" Trevor's death was no accident. Ethan's jaw tightened as he stared his father down.

"Introduce yourself to London society and keep our name strong. We can't allow jet sales to slip during this transition," he continued, ignoring Ethan's protest.

"London? What of grieving? Trevor has been killed, and all you can speak of is profitability?"

"Life doesn't cease because someone is gone, Ethan. You should know that from your mother's abandonment of this family."

"And yet you're asking me to do the same." His grip on the documents tightened as he struggled to control his breathing. "What of Katie?"

"What of her?" His father shrugged off the question and moved away to look out the window.

"We need to remain together to grieve, if only for her sake. She shouldn't have to face this alone."

"Katie can come to me with her concerns."

"That seems likely," Ethan scoffed, knowing that Katie had never been close with their father.

"I've instructed Mrs. Happstings to discover her whereabouts and inform her of this most unfortunate accident."

*Her whereabouts* sounded as if she was lost. Did she not know what had happened? It had been more than a day. "She hasn't been told? Where is she?"

"I haven't any idea. Her horse is missing from the stables. She'll return soon enough."

"No one has gone in search of her?" Ethan was

already moving toward the door. "There's a murderer on the loose!"

"Indeed."

At the single word, Ethan froze. "I'm not guilty of Trevor's murder," he stated, his voice grating out into the still room. He may have accidentally killed a man before, but he hadn't killed his brother. When he punched that man in Spain, he hadn't intended to deliver death with the blow. He'd only meant to win the fight—something he would regret for the remainder of his life. And now his escape from that accident had led him into a worse situation. He tamped down the sorrow over his past to deal with the present.

"You may stay for the services. I will even be generous enough to allow you a small amount of time here after that day, for your sister's sake. Then you will pack your belongings and leave for London. I'll deal with the rest."

Ethan almost stayed to argue. He almost told his father exactly what he thought of his priorities. Almost.

He glanced down at the papers he still held in his hand—sales documents stamped from the London harbor. His father had been right on one score. He did need to go to London, but for a better reason than the damned profitability of the mines. He would find Katie and mourn with her until after the funeral. His sister deserved that much. But his own grief over the loss of his brother would have to wait. He had a mission to complete.

# Five

Dear Ethan,

There is no way to express to you my thoughts in the light of day, not with so many guests in the house, and not when I don't understand any of this myself. I'm certain I shall regret this missive come morning, yet my future looms before me and I know I must speak with you.

Turning to you for help seems mad, I know, and yet when I think about it, it doesn't seem mad at all. You were always there. From my earliest memories of life on the estate, you've been by my side. You know me. And that is why I need you now.

Tonight your brother offered me marriage, and I'm unsure how to face him in the morning with my mind in such doubt. Before your return home, I'd sorted my life. I spent years honing myself into a lady. Society would never look down on me as they did my father. And today I achieved my goal—the promise of marriage to an *honorable gentleman. A lifetime of well-ordered daily pursuits as Lady Ayton should please me, shouldn't it? All reason tells me to go on as planned, yet I didn't plan on you.*

*When I'm near you I forget about everything I was certain I wanted. All I remember is you, and perhaps I'm remembering me as well. I remember the freedom of laughing aloud and the joy that can be found in a shared moment of scandalous mudslinging. I know every word I write here is wrong, yet every word I say to your brother betrays me, the me that I've worked so hard to winnow out. I want to be happy in marriage, but what if happiness isn't to be found there? What if I wake one day to find the life that I've created for myself is like an ill-fitting garment, and I've let go of the life that I tumbled into unaware of its comfortable fit?*

*Please don't leave me alone with your brother when I'm in such distress. I need your strength at my side, your smile, your easy laugh if I'm to face the day. Find a way to come with us. Do anything. I need your help.*

*Roselyn*

The note had been delivered a month ago, and still Roselyn could recall every blasted word. She'd written it in her own hand. *Do anything.* And he had, hadn't he? She would never forget the sight of the knife in his hand. But there had also been the look of shock on his face and the wound on his forehead.

She shook her head. Never mind what she'd thought she knew of the man; the evidence was against him. No matter what she'd imagined she felt for him.

Roselyn forced Ethan from her mind.

She'd asked for this outcome when she wrote that note, and now she must pay the price. That was exactly what she was doing today in the dark parlor. This was how she'd spent most days in the month since Trevor's death. She wasn't quite ready to return to the light—and certainly not the lit ballrooms that awaited her here in London. They'd arrived yesterday and she'd spent her first morning still in secret mourning. It was rather fitting.

Glancing to the pile of Katie's letters she'd brought with her from Thornwood, Roselyn gave the stack a wry smile. If she couldn't be with her friend, she could at least bring a small piece of her to town. Katie remained on Ormesby lands, healing from the riding accident that had happened the same day as Trevor's death. The thought of her friend lying in that field injured while Roselyn had been shoved into a carriage to leave the house party still turned her stomach. She should have been there. Roselyn had attempted to visit, of course, but was forbidden. Therefore they had been sending daily letters to each other.

Katie claimed in her notes that Ethan was caring for her, that they were spending a great deal of time together becoming reacquainted, and he had even come to blows with their father over her care. But that news troubled Roselyn more than it put her worries to rest. The thought of Ethan aiding Katie until she healed from her fall didn't seem to match

the murderous image she had of the man. She'd
asked several times if Katie thought it wise to spend
so much time with her estranged brother, but she'd
been careful not to say too much. Roselyn sighed.
They were siblings, and without revealing all, there
was nothing she could do to prevent their association. And at least with his company Katie wasn't
alone in her awful little cottage as she recovered in
body and spirit.

Roselyn wasn't injured from a fall as her friend was,
but her spirit could certainly use a bit of recovery.
However, she didn't deserve it. She deserved black
gowns and sad surroundings—nothing more. It was
her punishment for her foolishness with Ethan and
her silence about what truly happened that day on
the hilltop, as well as her shameful wavering thoughts
about Trevor before and after his passing. This was the
bleak future she deserved.

"Roselyn dear, what *are* you wearing?" the dowager duchess asked from some distance away.

Roselyn opened one eye as far as necessary before
sinking back into the chair in the upstairs parlor and
closing her eyes once more. "A day dress I brought
with me to town." She'd slipped it into her trunks
when no one was looking, knowing it wouldn't be
allowed in London. Wearing the dress was fitting
payment for her crimes, considering her enjoyment of
gowns and how she'd longed to twirl across a ballroom
floor. Perhaps it would become her new fashion. She
would be known as The Lady in…

"It's black."

"Is it?" she asked without opening her eyes. "Then

it matches my life to perfection—my dismal, woefully disappointing life."

"Come now, Roselyn. We've discussed this." Her mother's voice grew closer. "You mourned and wore black for a month at home, but you are not publicly in mourning, as you were only privately betrothed for one evening. It won't do to be seen about town wearing black for your come-out season."

It would have to do, for today anyway. Tomorrow she might wear color and dance the night away at a ball, but just now she couldn't bring herself to be so cheerful. Even after a month of somber reflection, she felt it was still her fault Trevor was gone, and she'd disgraced his memory by feeling a fleeting sense of relief that the obligation to marry him was taken from her hands. She needed to regain the keen sense of logic and organized reason she'd honed over the past few years, not her sense of fashion.

"You've looked forward to your season in London for so long now. I still remember when you would wear my old dancing slippers and practice the quadrille with your father in the parlor. The two of you would laugh so. He would want you to enjoy your time in town. He would want you to live life again. He would have wanted that for you for some time now."

Roselyn didn't respond. She didn't want to discuss the loss of her father when death was so fresh in her mind. He'd chosen his path and it didn't involve his family. Society had called him mad and driven him to sail away and prove them wrong. He hadn't returned. She'd tried to make logical decisions ever since that day—decisions that wouldn't lead her to his same fate.

Yet here she was, one mad choice one evening leaving her life in ruin, just like her father.

"I know it looks bleak, dear, but all will end well. Your life shall progress onward, like horses or some such."

"Like horses?" Roselyn finally opened her eyes and shifted to better see her mother, who was disgustingly bright-eyed with something that resembled hope as she sauntered across the floor.

"Yes." The dowager duchess danced her hand through the air with a nod of satisfaction.

Roselyn supposed that gesture was to symbolize horses cantering about, which somehow made sense to her mother, judging by the look on her face. It only served to deepen her own sorrow. Not only were her life's plans smashed to bits, but any mention of horses reminded her once more of Katie and how she wished her friend was here with her. Blasted mine shafts. Blasted horses. Just *blast*.

"Mother, I don't want to be a horse," she grumbled, shielding her face from the sun as her mother threw open the draperies. "Not today. Not yet. And while I'm thinking of it, those flowers on the table are far too cheerful. Do you mind ringing for some dead ones to be brought in?"

"Dear. Dear, dear, dear." Her mother sighed, moving to sit in the chair beside Roselyn. "If it would help your situation, I would have you surrounded in flowers past their prime. Of course, once fully gone they would become potpourri, which isn't somber at all."

At the sound of footsteps, her mother turned toward the doorway. "Lily, very good. You can help us. Do you find potpourri to be a somber element of decor?"

"Perhaps. It does smell nice though." Her new sister-in-law shook off the question as she joined them and perched on the edge of a nearby chair. "Roselyn, we have some guests I would like you to meet."

"At a time like this?"

Lily twisted the strand of pearls at her neck around her finger as she considered. "I am sorry for your situation, Roselyn. I know you cared deeply for Lord Ayton."

Roselyn straightened slightly in her seat at the small reminder of her betrayal of the man. She would rather visit with the guests than endure her family's sympathy when she deserved none. "Who are our guests?"

"Some friends I met last year. I think you'll enjoy their company. Will you meet them?"

Roselyn nodded and rose from her chair, moving past her mother's curious gaze over her sudden change of mind.

"I think you'll become fast friends with these ladies, Roselyn. I know it's difficult to be here in London after such a tragic event, but I've found that a well-placed friend can make anything in life bearable."

When Roselyn only nodded in response, Lily continued as they descended the stairs together. "In fact, these ladies are the family of such a friend of mine. Without Sue, I don't know what I would have done last season. Things ended quite well, of course, as I now get to share my life with your brother, but there were quite a few brambles to navigate along that path."

"You're only just back from your wedding trip and already you sound like Devon." With her brother involved, there was always talk of navigating or exploring. It had been the same with her father, until he finally chose his adventures over his family, his duty, and his sanity. For Lily's sake, she hoped Devon proved to be different.

"I'll take my likeness to my new husband as a compliment." Lily laughed and patted Roselyn's arm. "You're going to have a lovely season, Roselyn. Even if it doesn't look optimistic at the moment, all will work out. If Sue hadn't talked my ear off all last season, I don't know that I could have managed it. And yet I did, and so shall you."

Roselyn required more than a friend, in her opinion. "Is your friend here today?" she asked as they reached the bottom of the stairs.

"No. Sue's in France, enjoying married life to Lord Steelings too much to return at the moment, but her younger sister, Evangeline, is in town for her second season. And she's brought along her cousins, Ladies Isabelle and Victoria Fairlyn."

As they entered the small parlor intended for receiving guests, Roselyn was struck by the amount of light in the room. The parlor had never been a particularly dark room, but the present company seemed to illuminate it beyond the normal levels. Perhaps it was her current dark ensemble that made her notice, or perhaps these ladies were simply that bright.

Their dresses ranged from vibrant grass green to a rose pink that rivaled Lily's flowers in the garden outside, and finally was outshone by a yellow that seemed to mimic the sun on a warm afternoon. It was not, however, simply their visitors' dresses that seemed to glow within the room, but their bright smiles, the shine of their hair... She turned a questioning glance at

Lily. Where had she found such a collection of perfection wrapped in silk and wearing fashionable gloves?

"You're wearing black," the lady in the vibrant green dress stated.

"Of course she's wearing black," the pink-clad lady replied. "Lily told us what happened, remember? She was secretly betrothed to Lord Ayton. Don't you listen to Mama when she discusses the latest on-dits with us? He passed." She said the last portion in what was surely intended to be a whisper, but was far too loud to qualify as such.

"You listen when Mother begins all her talk of this lord and that? Who has the time to keep up with such things?" The smirk on the young woman's face disappeared as she turned toward Roselyn. "Good afternoon, I'm Victoria Fairlyn, and this is my evil twin, Isabelle."

"Victoria!" her sister exclaimed, drawing back as if singed by her words. "How could you say such a thing? I'm nothing of the sort. Lady Roselyn, it's a pleasure to make your acquaintance. I'm Isabelle Fairlyn, and I believe you'll find me to be quite good in nature. I heard of your recent misfortune, and I offer my condolences and my silence on the matter. Your secret is safe here. You must be terribly brokenhearted to have had the one you love ripped from your arms..." She broke off to dab her eyes. "It's horrible."

"I'm sure she doesn't wish to relive the ordeal over tea with near strangers, Isabelle. Forgive my cousins. They forget themselves. I'm Evangeline Green." The dark-haired lady in yellow offered a slight curtsy.

"It's no trouble." Roselyn signaled for tea and moved farther into the room, relieved when Lily didn't leave her side as she entered what seemed to her a storm of beautiful females. They were not the sort of storm that rages, but they were fearsome nonetheless.

Lily motioned to the chairs before the fireplace. "Evangeline, have you heard from Sue? Has she eaten all the sweets France has to offer?"

"I wouldn't be surprised if she had, but I haven't yet received a note." Evangeline sat on the edge of the chair nearest the window with her spine straight and her hands folded in her lap as if she were sitting for a portrait.

Roselyn searched for a hair out of place or a wrinkle in her gown, but couldn't find a single flaw to diminish the ideal lady that sat before her. Was this what she was up against in her quest for a husband? *Blasted mine*, she grumbled to herself as she settled back into her seat like a black shadow clinging to the corner.

Evangeline continued speaking as the other ladies found seats and gathered near. "I fear Sue doesn't wish Mother to know her location, but unfortunately that excludes me from knowledge of her whereabouts as well." There was a distant sadness in her eyes as she spoke about her sister that Roselyn found curious, but she didn't pry.

"If I hear word from her, I'll pass it along to you." Lily paused as the tea service was placed on the table between them before continuing, "Are you prepared for the height of the season?"

*Are you prepared?* It was a perfectly appropriate question, and yet it made Roselyn shift in her seat and eye the parlor door. She'd been prepared. Now? She huffed into her teacup. The talk turned to fashion, the latest colors, who would have the gown that was the talk of the town.

Evangeline must have noticed her sour mood, since she asked, "Are you officially in mourning, Roselyn? Lily made it sound as if your mourning was a private one." She possessed such a businesslike manner that Roselyn wondered if some document must be signed to mourn properly. Perhaps there was an official paper in an office somewhere with a solemn list of widows.

"I'm not an official mourner. Since the engagement hadn't been announced yet, the family agreed I wasn't required to go to such lengths. In fact, my mother expressed her disapproval of my ensemble only a few minutes ago."

At Lily's sympathetic tilt of her head, Roselyn continued, "And yet, it doesn't seem appropriate to wear bright colors as if nothing happened. Something did happen." She didn't share the portion of her thoughts that involved her half-truths, her relief, or the guilt that had settled on her as a result. The tea in her hand quivered inside the cup, reminding her of the dark hole in the earth that swallowed up her future—no, Trevor. It swallowed up Trevor. She would do well to remember that distinction. She lowered the saucer to her lap before she spilled it.

Victoria studied her for a moment before saying, "We simply must remove all this black. I'm sorry, but it does nothing for your coloring. If you must mourn the man, mourn him close to your heart. Wear black stays beneath your gowns, but don't arrive at the most talked about ball of the season in bombazine. It's dreadful."

"Victoria!" Evangeline admonished.

"What?" Victoria shrugged. "Don't act as if you weren't thinking it as well. If we are here for the sole purpose of finding a husband—which I find terribly unappealing, by the way—then none of us should go about looking the part of a recent widow."

She was right, of course. Roselyn may have had her life plan shattered by the vile Ethan Moore, but perhaps she should begin again. It wasn't ideal, of course, but the ideal ship had sailed, hadn't it?

No matter what her muddled thoughts were on the matter, there was no sense sitting about the harbor dressed in black, even if it was what she deserved. She needed a new ship, and she wouldn't find one in this dress. Roselyn broke the silence of nervous sips of tea and uncomfortable glances with the clank of her teacup against the saucer. "Indeed. I can't play the widow."

Isabelle smiled over the rim of her cup. "I'm aware no gentleman can take the place of poor Lord Ayton, but there are quite a few gentlemen arriving in town. Perhaps you'll meet someone?"

"Isabelle, not all of us walk about falling in love with every gentleman we meet," Victoria said with a roll of her eyes.

"I don't fall in love with everyone," Isabelle grumbled into her teacup. "And even if I did, it's better to love freely than to refuse it altogether."

Evangeline cleared her throat and shot a warning look at the two blond sisters. They did have the same coloring and features, but they were as different as a garden flower and the blade that chops it down to make an arrangement. Roselyn had little experience with sisters, Lily being the closest she'd come to having one, but it seemed odd that two ladies born on the same day to the same mother could be such opposing forces.

"Have you heard who will be at the Dillsworth ball tomorrow night?" Lily asked in a clear attempt to steer the conversation to safer ground.

"Mr. Brice will be there, I'm sure," Victoria practically sang in her sister's direction while Isabelle glowered.

"As it is held under his family's roof, I would assume he would be in attendance." Lily turned to Roselyn to supply, "Mr. Kelton Brice is the youngest son of Lord Dillsworth."

"And Isabelle's one true love." Victoria pretended to swoon until Isabelle shoved her, forcing her to almost spill her tea.

"He is simply a handsome gentleman and a skilled dancer, nothing more." But Isabelle's blush betrayed her words.

"He's also untitled," Evangeline cut in. "There will be plenty of titled gentlemen who are proper marriage material in town as well, Isabelle." Evangeline tapped her chin in thought. "Of course the talk is all about the new Lord Ayton's arrival in town. There are others though. Let's see. Who else is expected to attend the ball tomorrow?"

"The new Lord Ayton," Roselyn rasped, the words tumbling out of her mouth. Ethan was the new Lord Ayton. It hadn't occurred to her that she would have to see Ethan again so soon. The last she'd seen of him, he'd been kneeling over that mine shaft. If only he could have been left there for good, she could have moved on with her life and pretended none of it had happened. But it had happened. And now he held the title.

"Yes, I'm certain he'll be in attendance. Mother was going on about available lords in town. I'm certain I saw his name on the list I had to memorize yesterday," Evangeline replied, her confusion showing in the form of a single tiny line between her drawn brows.

"He's in London?"

"Mother said that Lady Smeltings saw him walking through the park only yesterday. Did you not know?" Evangeline stopped, panic-stricken. "Oh, Roselyn. I'm terribly sorry. I thought you knew he was about. He was almost your... And now he has the title that was once... I've quite stuck my foot in it, haven't I?"

"Usually I'm the one who makes the poor first impression," Victoria said with an amused quirk of her lips. "I appreciate the assistance in that regard, Evie. It's quite nice to be on this side of things, watching the sport of it all and such."

Isabelle sliced a glance at her sister as she said, "Clearly she's wounded by her profound love for her lost fiancé, Victoria."

"Apologies," Victoria tossed out without a hint of regret. "Even though Evie was the one who destroyed the conversation at tea."

"Thank you, Victoria. That was very helpful," Evangeline said.

"You *are* helpful," Roselyn said through a chuckle.

Their bickering somehow took away the sting of Ethan being in town. If they continued to chatter through the season, perhaps she could face it. She sighed and let her gaze sweep across the colorfully dressed ladies that surrounded her.

They were lovely, but she could already tell they were more than the dazzling smiles and stylish gowns they showed the world. Isabelle was as warmhearted as her sister, Victoria, was barbed, but in a refreshingly honest sort of way. Evangeline seemed to be the voice of reason of the group. With them, her own life might continue.

"All of you are helpful," Roselyn clarified. "I believe Lily was correct earlier. I may survive this season if I have you for company."

"Of course you will," Lily replied with a kind smile.

Roselyn had no plan for her life, but what she did have was a wardrobe filled with ball gowns and a pile of invitations to events this season. Trevor was gone. There was no way to stop the days from passing so that she might wallow in self-pity. Victoria was right—drowning herself in black and slipping into the shadows of life was no plan at all. She ran her hand over her black skirts. This simply would not do. If she was to be in London, she would have to dress the part, at least on the surface where society would take note.

"Tell me what you know of black underthings and available gentlemen," she said with a tentative grin. "I find I'm in need of a plan for the season."

"A plan that involves black underthings and available gentlemen?" Evangeline asked.

"Perhaps." Roselyn smiled her first true smile in a month. The new Lord Ayton would regret his decision to come to London this year. That part of her plan was certain.

❧

He'd been nineteen the last time he'd set foot in this room. Ethan paused in the doorway before stepping inside.

Nothing had changed inside the club's primary gathering space, and yet everything had changed. It still smelled of leather and whiskey. The furniture remained pieced together from what appeared to be ten different drawing rooms, and the far wall still held the crack in the plaster from where his shoulder had collided with it all those years ago. He chuckled at the memory before pulling his gaze from the wall.

Beyond these familiarities, there was an air of newness about the place. Business must be going well in his absence. He moved farther from the door, knowing he didn't belong here anymore, yet refusing to leave. He stepped around a new billiards table that now sat in the center of the room and headed for the front windows that overlooked the street below. New window coverings blocked out most of the afternoon sun—much better than their floral predecessors. Of course, he and Brice had set those on fire at one point, so the change of decor wasn't altogether unexpected.

At one time this had been a widow's home. It was rumored she'd been a friend of the special sort to Fallon St. James. Ethan didn't know the details and St. James had never shared more than was necessary, but he did know that the large home on

Grafton Street was now the headquarters for the
Spare Heirs Society.

The society wasn't a gentlemen's club in the tradi-
tional sense. The doors *were* always open to members
who desired a drink and a hand of cards, as other
clubs in town offered. The Spare Heirs Society, however, offered something more—survival. The band of
second, third, fourth sons that claimed membership
here relied on the Spares for the funds their birth order
denied them. Of course, the various methods with
which those funds were acquired was a topic best not
to be repeated.

Ethan made his way across the room to the table
in the corner, aware of more than one set of eyes
following him as he moved. It was a gamble, coming
here. At one point in his life, he'd belonged under
this roof, even lived in the boarding rooms upstairs
for a time. That time was long ago. Now, thanks to
Trevor's death, he was no longer welcome. His lost
membership was just another tick on the long list of
prices to be paid for his brother's passing. Member
or not, however, he needed to talk to St. James.
This was the one place Ethan knew he could find
the man.

"St. James," Ethan offered in greeting as he joined
him at his table. Some things, he supposed, would
never change. Fallon St. James had aged over the
years, but in that manner ladies always found appealing, with only a few lines at the corners of his dark
eyes and his dark brown hair still holding its color. He
looked as sharp as ever.

His old friend looked up from the paper he was

reading, clearly not surprised to see Ethan after such a long absence. "You should have come to me straight away." Turning the paper around, he slid it across the worn table to Ethan so he could see the headlines.

His gaze fell on a lesser headline, halfway down the page: "Lord Ayton's Demise." News of the event was still being discussed in town—his father's version anyway. Ethan had hoped talk would have diminished among the *ton* by now. He'd spent time with his sister after the funeral services, allowing the weeks to slip past, against his father's will. Arriving after talk had settled hadn't been his reasoning for the delay, but it was still disappointing that the *accident* was in the headlines.

"Damn." That was going to make investigating Trevor's death under the watchful eyes of London society a bit more difficult. He scanned for mention of Roselyn, but saw no hint of Trevor's betrothal. It was as if that part of the story hadn't existed, but the accusation he'd seen in her eyes still burned him a month later. Had she seen this article as well? Had the small likeness of Trevor printed there upset her? The last he'd seen of Roselyn had been her back as she ran away from him, fleeing for her life. He pushed the post and the memory aside, turning his attention back to his friend.

"We have resources available to us that you don't have. Stories like these can be avoided." Fallon took a long drink of the tea that steamed in his cup. "Of course, I would have to be informed of events first-hand and not learn of them in last month's morning post for that to be possible."

"I haven't been back on English soil long," Ethan began.

"Yes, and look at the mire you've managed to sink into in such a short time. According to reports, you witnessed the accident." His friend stood and went to a nearby decanter, pouring a glass for Ethan. He'd never seen St. James drink spirits, but he was always quick to offer hospitality to others.

"There was no way I could have known any of this would happen when I was making travel plans, St. James," Ethan said as he accepted the drink. "Not that I made plans for this trip other than jumping aboard a ship to escape some unfortunate acquaintances on the Continent."

"Unfortunate acquaintances," St. James repeated. As always, he had the ability to narrow in on the part of the story that hinted at danger. Ethan supposed it was a skill honed from years of leading the secretive club in the heart of London without notice.

Ethan sighed, knowing he couldn't avoid at least a small explanation. "His name is Santino."

"His entire name?"

"Alvaro Santino. But Santino is what he's called." Ethan paused, taking his time with a drink from his glass. "When he's dared to be called at all. He has men."

"I have men."

"And what do you do to those who wrong you?"

"Quite." St. James nodded in understanding. "All the more reason you should have renewed your ties with the Spare Heirs Society. We could have prevented much of your current situation, you know. Assisted in your escape from Spain."

"There was no time for that," Ethan cut in.

"But now..." St. James fell silent as he watched Ethan from across the table.

"You won't assist me." Ethan drew his fingers into a fist. He didn't want to argue, but he couldn't find Trevor's killer alone. He wouldn't know where to begin. St. James had to do him this favor. And now, the very thing that was troubling Ethan was also the reason he couldn't have assistance from the society—Trevor's blasted title. "I never asked for this title. You've known me most of my life. You know I've never wanted it!"

"You have my condolences for your loss," St. James said in his usual calm manner as if he wasn't in the middle of a heated discussion. "Take a drink, Moore. Or, I suppose I should call you Lord Ayton now." St. James studied Ethan over the tips of his steepled fingers. He'd always had a flare for the dramatic, and it seemed that hadn't changed. "Tell me the part of this tale of your brother that's not in print for all of London to read."

"He was killed, murdered."

"And this is why you've returned here?"

"I need to learn what dealings my brother had before... I need to find the man responsible, and the only information I have is a pile of sales documents." Ethan remained still, watching, waiting. But as the silence drew out, he knew he had the answer to his question.

He'd wasted enough time here. He drained his glass, pushed his chair back, and stood to leave. If the Spare Heirs wouldn't help him find his brother's killer, he would do it alone.

"Your membership in the club stands. You may have acquired a title, but you were born a second son and we stand by our own."

*We stand by our own.* The words rattled around in his head for a moment as he tried to make himself understand. This band of misfit gentlemen was the only place he'd ever belonged. But it had been years and he now had a title. The lack of a title was the one rule upheld in the group since their establishment. His eyes narrowed on the man across the table. "You'll assist me then."

St. James nodded. "Welcome back to the Spare Heirs Society."

# Six

ROSELYN'S HEART BEAT IN TIME WITH THE QUADRILLE. She tapped her foot beneath the hem of her gown to calm her desire to move to the music. It wouldn't do to be seen swaying to the rhythm as she stood on the side of the large ballroom.

"I'm sure by the next dance you'll be twirling away in the arms of a gentleman," Isabelle said with a sympathetic smile as she hid her offensively full dance card beneath her hand.

Roselyn nodded as Isabelle was led away once more. She looked down at the card tied to her wrist—still blank. Sudden realization struck and she spun on her heel and glared at Devon, catching her brother giving the evil eye to some poor man who dared come near her. "If you stare down every gentleman on this side of the ballroom, I'll never have a dance partner."

"Is that such a terrible fate?"

"Yes!" she and Lily said in unison, drawing a few looks in their direction.

"I've only stopped the ones from approaching who ought to be stopped," he retorted, fairly snarling at a gentleman dressed in a bright coat who made the poor decision of walking past their space of wall.

"You have a reputation, Devon. Your presence is enough to bring the entire ball to a halt. I can't very well attract a gentleman for a dance with you playing your Mad Duke of Thornwood bit over my shoulder."

"Are you suggesting I act mad for the effect of it?"

"Yes!" she and Lily said in unison, once again drawing looks.

"I no longer have a poor reputation. I'm married. Settled. Honorable Duke and all that rot." Devon grinned, clearly knowing what torment he still inflicted upon the *ton* on a daily basis. He was well aware of everything around him, including the effect he was having on Roselyn's dance card.

Roselyn narrowed her eyes. If he could stare down her potential dance partners, she could do the same to him. They had the same steely gray eyes after all. "You were only wed at the end of last season. When most of these people saw you last, you were covered in soot and stealing Lily."

"A day I'm quite thankful for," Lily added, beaming up at her husband. "Roselyn, why don't you take some air by the terrace door while I attempt to remind your brother why he is present this evening."

She didn't need to be told twice. She turned on her heel, ready to conquer this ball without the *assistance* of her family.

"I'm here because you forced me to attend a damn ball," Roselyn heard Devon complain as she walked toward the open terrace doors. Like her, he always had a plan in mind. His just leaned in the direction of exploration while she preferred a life that wouldn't change with the ocean's tide. If she had to bet, she would guess that he was attempting to escape future balls by acting terribly at this one. Although she doubted Lily would let him off the hook that easily.

Now on the other side of the crowd from her family, she scanned the room for gentlemen not on the dance floor. She'd lost too much time already to her brother's antics, and she wasn't about to waste another second. Surely a suitable husband could be found somewhere in this crowd.

Her gaze lingered on the entrance to the ballroom where the crush of people was thickest. And then she saw him. Her eyes widened as she stared across the room, caught between the desire to flee and to attack. He was dressed in black to match his villainous heart. She refused to notice the cut of his coat that stretched across his impossibly broad shoulders, just as she pointedly dismissed how the candlelight glinted off his dark hair.

Her jaw tightened as she took a step backward toward the terrace and away from encountering the one man she didn't wish to speak to this evening. What would she say at any rate? *You're a murderous bastard who stole my future. I'm ashamed I ever thought of you in familiar terms.* Or, the most pressing question on her mind, *why did you come here to torment me further?*

No, it was best to walk away. She was still formulating a plan of action regarding him. It was too soon.

Ethan was laughing at some comment made by the gentleman at his side. Laughing and smiling as he was congratulated on his new title. She watched the swirl of activity around him. He was being honored and seemed to enjoy the attention. Only a guilty man with no remorse for his actions would carry on so.

Her heart pounded with the truth she hadn't fully accepted. The last remaining piece of her that clung to Ethan's innocence—hoping she'd misunderstood what she saw that day, that she hadn't been so terribly wrong about him—was shredded in an instant. She should have reported him as soon as she'd returned from the hilltop. This was what came of remaining silent. Yet the fact that she hadn't told anyone of his guilt was where her remorse ended. She'd spent weeks berating herself for her actions, when the laughing man on the other side of the ballroom was the guilty one.

She ripped her gaze from Ethan and lifted it to the ceiling, fighting to subdue a large amount of anger in the process. There was nothing upsetting about a ceiling. She would simply categorize the architectural features of the ballroom until her breathing returned to normal. The orchestra played from a balcony on the far end of the room. She watched the rise and fall of the violin bows as she attempted to steady her thoughts. The ballroom had a roof of glass, where she imagined the stars would be visible if the candles were allowed to burn out.

"Beeswax candles and roses," she murmured as she exhaled the heavily scented air. This was her debut season, her flower-scented air to breathe. This was her time to find a suitable husband, thanks to Ethan's actions, and she would not allow his presence to destroy this night as he had everything else. She would enjoy the scenery, and she would scarcely think of

Ethan on the other side of the room. Tomorrow she would find a way to prove Ethan's guilt to the world and be rid of him forever, but tonight she would appreciate this fine ballroom and attempt to remain calm. Now, where was she... Oh yes...

Lord Dillsworth had a home built to impress even the most difficult members of the *ton*. She'd heard about the ballroom's glass ceiling before she'd ever set foot inside. And the floor was polished to such a shine that one could almost see the night sky reflected there. It was a magical floor to dance upon—at least that's what Isabelle had told her. Of course even now, Roselyn could barely claim she'd set foot in the room, when thus far she'd only clung to the wall. Would she get to experience the thrill of a dance at all tonight? She'd arrived here with a plan and she had to see it through.

The seed pearls that streamed down her skirt sparkled in the moonlight as she turned and stepped out onto the terrace. Even the pale blue of her gown seemed to glow as she took another step into the night air. With a sigh she turned, watching the movement of couples circling the floor to the music of a waltz. Unfortunately, as she observed the gentlemen in their evening finery with her mind on finding her future husband, her gaze met Ethan's for a fraction of a second. She gasped and backed farther onto the terrace. Perhaps he hadn't seen her. Perhaps he would ignore her out of polite obligation. Perhaps...

The only thing she knew was she couldn't stand about waiting to see whether or not he would approach her. While she had no safe place of retreat on the terrace, she didn't have to stand idle either.

She glanced around for some distraction, but found none. Then inspiration hit. Pulling a pencil from the small beaded reticule she carried, she began scribbling notes on the back of her dance card. It was hardly as effective as her study of the decor of the ballroom, but she could categorize the gentlemen present by rank, apparent wealth, and location of their estate. Her dance card might as well be of some use this evening. She tipped her wrist up to the light streaming out the terrace doors, pressed the card into her palm, and wrote another name.

"Filling out your own dance card," a familiar deep voice sounded in her ear.

Roselyn jumped and dropped the small pencil on the stone floor. Ethan! She would know his voice anywhere. Her heart pounded as she searched again for any escape. This was happening too fast. She couldn't chat about dance cards with him. She couldn't chat about anything with him.

"Writing your own list of names is a bit grasping, isn't it, princess?" he continued, since she'd failed to respond or even turn around. Ethan's fingers wrapped around her wrist, lifting her arm and shifting her balance until she backed into him.

She scooted forward as far as she could while he still held her wrist. "I believe you're the one grasping at the moment, thank you very much," she retorted as he examined the small card.

His grip softened as he traced his fingers around the ribbon attached to her dance card. "My apologies. I only wanted to check on your well-being after..." He broke off as he moved to face her, still holding her forearm beneath his fingers. "Sometimes I forget my own strength."

She might be forced to stand terribly close to him as he looked down into her face, but she wouldn't be intimidated by the situation or the man before her. "I meant that you're traipsing about town, showing off your new title to anyone who will listen. It isn't very becoming to dangle the spoils of an evil deed before the noses of society."

"I've never *dangled spoils* in my life. But I do have my brother's title. There's nothing to be done about that fact now." He paused, his jaw grinding on some unspoken thought. "What's done is done. We must move forward in life."

She couldn't believe this man wasn't accepting any blame for his brother's death, even privately with her. She knew the truth! She hadn't fully accepted it until tonight, but she knew. He owed his family, her, and the country at large his repentance for taking the life of a respectable gentleman. Was he truly going to parade about London without a mention of the man he'd killed to get there? And to think, there was a time when she'd longed for this man above his brother. How wrong she'd been about him. "You have a rather convenient outlook on recent events."

"Do I?" A shadow that almost looked like concern crossed his eyes, visible even in the dim moonlight. Someone this arrogant was never concerned over anything. "It's been rather *inconvenient* from where I'm standing. The question is how do we move forward from here?"

"*We* will not be proceeding anywhere, Lord Ayton." She almost choked on his title.

He didn't respond. His eyes searched hers, pulling at the frayed ends of her memories of him, pleading with her to remember.

Her heart raced as she met his gaze, refusing to look away from him and lose this battle of wills. Somewhere music played. Couples danced. People chatted. And here on the moonlit terrace, time ceased to function. Caught in some sort of spell, she was held there—and not just by his grasp on her wrist. The heat of his hand burned through her glove, making her all the more aware of his touch, yet unable to pull away.

How long had she been standing here with him, close enough to smell his shaving soap, to see his chest rise and fall with every breath? And how long was she to allow his thumb to rub across the inside of her wrist, dragging her into the darkness in which he dwelled? His touch was intoxicating, but like all strong spirits, should be avoided for fear of terrible consequences.

She needed to walk away from him, but her body betrayed her wishes. He was a murderer. He had to be. Yet, she remained, standing alone with him on the terrace. The memory of him covered in mud slipped through her mind. They'd laughed together just as they had as children. This man had always been her friend. He'd accepted her when no one else did. He'd run wild with her. They'd been free then. The freedom she'd felt with him the morning of their mud fight, as if anything was possible… She hadn't felt that way in years. She'd wanted his company then.

It was such a short time ago, and yet everything

had changed between them. There was no freedom to be found with him now. His actions on that hilltop had altered everything. She cast aside the memory and steeled herself to move away from him. She needed to get back to the ballroom, back to the task at hand. No good could come of her prolonged connection to Ethan Moore. The past month had proved that to be true.

His gaze drifted down her neck, heating her skin. And then, with a curious quirk of his lips, he lifted his free hand to the exposed skin at her neck and grasped the shoulder of her gown between his fingers.

"What are you doing?" She should pull away. She should run back to the safety of the well-lit ballroom. His hands were on her! She knew what he was capable of, yet there was a softness in his eyes that kept her still. Any knowledge of what she should do fell away when he was near.

He paused with his fingers resting against her collarbone. "Black underthings? Do most ladies wear black beneath their gowns?"

"No!" She blushed, finally realizing why he'd touched her shoulder. "I don't need to explain myself to you of all people." She leaned away from him, but he finished adjusting her gown anyway, tucking the strap of her new black stays beneath her collar. Was there no escaping this man's torment?

"Your undergarments were visible, just there at your shoulder. Not that I mind the view it provided, but it seemed the gentlemanly thing to do to—"

"To grab a fistful of my gown in the middle of a ball?" She ripped her hand from his grasp and patted the front of her dress to ensure it was where it should be.

"I am attempting to act the gentleman of late." He adjusted the lapels on his coat with a lopsided grin.

"You, a gentleman." She let out a derisive laugh. "What would you know of gentlemanly behavior?"

"Says the lady dressed like a brothel temptress." His gaze trailed down her body as he spoke.

She gasped on principle. No one had ever spoken to her the way he did, without consideration of her rank or the fact that she was a lady. Of course no other man had ever thrown things at her and expected her to catch them either. With Ethan there had never been rules. No matter what had changed between them, that hadn't. She shouldn't like it, just as she shouldn't have allowed him to touch her, but she did.

"I'm privately in mourning, if you must know. And I'm a far sight better at being a lady than you are at acting a lord," she retorted.

His grin faded and he shifted his stance, looking out across the dark garden. "You know my family's background. Father was never interested in society matters, and Mother... You know that tale as well. Then I left home." He fell silent for a moment, lost in some thought or another before continuing, "In truth, tonight is my first ball. But I've learned a bit in the last few days in town, as it happens."

"I suppose you owe it to your newfound title," she bit out.

"It's shocking how educated on societal matters lords are expected to be," he said, turning back to her.

"Of course they are."

"A fact you would know better than I, princess."

"Stop calling me that."

He ignored her and continued, "I was cornered only a few minutes ago to give my thoughts on modern farming techniques."

"Cornered with unwanted conversation? I've never experienced such a thing," she said in mock dismay, her aggravation with him increasing by the second.

He looked back at her, his multicolored eyes catching the light from the ballroom, making him look almost sincere. "I know we've had our differences…"

"Is that what you call what happened between us? Differences? You stole my future away from me. I'm here without your brother at my side because of you."

He ground his jaw for a moment, anger raging beneath his gaze before he replied, "What happened was a terrible tragedy and I grieve his loss as well, but I didn't put you in this position."

"You have a fine way of grieving someone's loss, Lord Ayton. I trust that you will grieve the loss of my company on this terrace to an equal degree." She couldn't be away from him fast enough. She turned and was halfway to the doors before she heard him answer.

"That is undoubtedly true, princess."

Her interaction with him made no sense for two quite prominent reasons. Why was he seeking out her company at a ball after what she had seen? He should want to stay as far away from her as possible. There was no logic in his actions, no order. The more she knew of Lord Ayton, the more she wondered if there was ever logic.

And that brought her to her second quandary of the night. Why hadn't she walked away from him when he first touched her?

She was still stewing on this more concerning question as she crossed the ballroom, intending to find her new friends. Skirting a large group of ladies in deep discussion of the many uses and benefits of a fan, she came face-to-face with Lady Smeltings. Wasn't this evening just grand? She had no definable objection to the lady, only a vague sense of uneasiness when she was near—an uneasiness she could do without tonight.

"Lady Roselyn, how nice it is to see you again." Lady Smeltings's white hair was piled high atop her head as usual, and almost seemed to bounce with every nod or jostle.

"Lady Smeltings," Roselyn offered in greeting.

She tilted her head to the side in sympathy and grabbed Roselyn's hand so she couldn't retreat. "You left Ormesby in such haste that I wasn't able to speak with you. I know you are close with the family. You have my condolences."

"Thank you. My family thought it best to return home." Roselyn tried to smile, but was unsure if she'd achieved it.

"Of course. It's good to see you here in your finery at any rate, continuing on with your plans for the season in spite of tragedy. I was fortunate enough to spy the new Lord Ayton earlier as well. It's such an affirmation of life when you see the loved ones of the deceased continuing on with things, isn't it?"

"I suppose." Roselyn tried to remove her fingers from the older lady's grasp with a gentle tug, but her movement only resulted in a gentle pat on the back of her hand.

"I couldn't imagine not having a Lord Ayton in

town for the season. That's what I told the new Ayton when I saw him. I'm so pleased he was able to forgo the mourning period and attend the events of this year. Aren't you pleased?"

*Pleased* wasn't exactly the word she would use for her feelings on the subject. "Oh, I…"

"Everyone will be so delighted by the sight of such a dashing new lord. I daresay the ladies this season will enjoy his appearance in town."

"I really can't speak on behalf of all ladies…"

"Of course the circumstances are tragic, but having the new Lord Ayton in town is a light in a dark time. I'm quite happy at the result of all of this. I'm sure the late Lord Ayton, God rest his soul, is smiling down on this day, wishing his brother well. Don't you agree?"

Roselyn froze, unable to answer. Well, she had an answer, quite the answer, but not one appropriate to repeat in polite company. She tugged on her hand once more in an effort to free herself, but Lady Smeltings had a grip one simply didn't escape.

"He appears to be fitting in just as he should here in society. It's amusing how things work out and everything falls into place." Lady Smeltings's gaze slid past Roselyn to a point across the ballroom.

Amusing? The word set her nerves on edge. She turned, following the lady's glance across the room. Although Roselyn knew whom she would see when she did so, she looked anyway. There, near the terrace doors, Lord Ayton stood chatting with a lady Roselyn didn't know. Lady Smeltings may find all of this amusing, but she did not. Anger seemed to boil within her bones, making her quake with emotion.

"He fits right in, doesn't he?" Roselyn ground out between teeth clinched into a smile. "Would you excuse me? I must be going now." She ripped free of the conversation and made a line for the front door.

The new Lord Ayton fit in, indeed. He'd made her want him, murdered her betrothed, become far too familiar with her on the terrace, and then walked straight into the arms of another lady. He and the society that had driven her father to madness were fit for each other. She didn't pause until she was in the hall, and then outside the front door of the Dillsworth home.

She took a small gasp of cool night air and stepped down to the wide landing where two lion statues looked over the drive from their wall-top perches. Leaning against the low wall she glanced up at the lion above her. He likely had things well decided—sit here, be stone, look after the carriages. It was a simple lion's life, but it possessed order, something her own life was lacking of late. Lady Smeltings's words still rattled about in her head. Was the entirety of the *ton* truly pleased that Ethan was in London?

One thing she knew with certainty—Trevor was *not* smiling down upon his brother. She shook her head and pushed off from the wall where she rested.

The evening was quiet on this side of the large oak door. Footmen loitered about, waiting to become busy once again when the crowd inside began to disperse. But for now they were gathered around a tall, blond gentleman who seemed to be telling a story.

"M'lady, do you need your carriage brought around?" one of the footmen inquired.

"Perhaps in a moment. For now, I would like to catch my breath." She should return to the ball, but she couldn't bring herself to continue the torture this evening had become. Perhaps she should hop in the carriage and not look back. Tonight seemed to be a lost effort. But her Mother and Lily would worry, and Devon certainly wouldn't approve since he was trapped within a crush of a party he hadn't wanted to attend.

"Certainly, m'lady. May I inform you of the terrace off the ballroom if you require air during the ball."

Roselyn almost laughed. "Oh, I found the terrace just fine on my own, thank you."

"I sense there's a story there," the blond gentleman mused.

"Indeed. I don't, however, wish to discuss it."

"Clearly. Perhaps your issue is the lack of a chaperone, if I may be so bold," he said with a twinkle in his eye as he crossed the landing toward her.

"My *chaperone* was chasing away every available gentleman at the ball."

"Chaperones can be difficult that way," he sympathized. "Mr. Brice at your service, my lady, youngest of this fine home and a quite unavailable gentleman."

Isabelle's Mr. Brice? He was Dillsworth's fourth son, was he not? "Roselyn Grey. I have an acquaintance who will be most distressed at your lack of availability."

"I suppose I'm available in the technical sense, although I have no wish to make that official with a leg shackle. Confirmed bachelor," he added to be exceedingly clear on the subject.

"Ah, I see. Between us, I'm in mourning in the

technical sense although I have no wish to make that official either."

"Then you have come to the proper place for unofficial entertainment."

"Finally, fortune has turned in my favor this evening. What is our unofficial entertainment?"

"Same as every gentleman's entertainment—bawdy tales and wagers." A few of the footmen chuckled on the other side of the landing, and Roselyn instantly relaxed. The prim facade she had to show the world didn't matter on this side of the large oak door, and she felt free for the first time in a month.

"That sounds delightful." There was an overall goodness to Mr. Brice, and Roselyn now understood Isabelle's attraction to him. He was handsome and charming, and though he was of a similar large build to Ethan, he had a gentle quality that the new Lord Ayton could never possess. Even so, there was something about this gentleman that reminded her of Ethan—or perhaps it was the easy nature of the situation that reminded her of what they'd once shared. Before she could examine it further or learn more about Mr. Brice or his bawdy tales though, Devon stepped outside.

"Roselyn, what are you doing outside, alone, with the likes of Brice?"

"Your Grace." Mr. Brice nodded. His pleasant demeanor changed in an instant, as if a candle had been blown out. Devon seemed to have that effect on many people.

Roselyn turned her attention back to her brother. "The company is better here than on the terrace, of that I am certain."

"What happened on the terrace?" he growled, his gray eyes narrowing on her.

"I encountered the new Lord Ayton."

Brice let out a bark-like laugh which he attempted to cover with a cough.

"Rest assured, Mr. Brice here is a marked improvement," Roselyn continued, unsure what the gentleman found so amusing.

"That doesn't seem likely. Brice, have you put on a show of respectability for my sister?"

"Of course." He grinned. "But I thought it better than the alternative when your sister came outside alone."

"Indeed."

"I was in need of air," Roselyn complained. "And now I find I am ready for that carriage you offered a few minutes ago."

"Yes, m'lady."

"We're leaving? Thank God." Devon was already descending the steps toward the carriages as he called out orders to the footmen who lingered on the landing. "Send for my wife and mother."

"I'll try not to be offended by your desertion of my family's ball, Your Grace," Brice called after him.

"Ah, but you have hundreds of others for company, not to mention more damn flowers than should be allowed in one room. It's dreadful. Enjoy."

Roselyn heard Mr. Brice's loud, hearty laugh as she climbed into the carriage. Her first ball had been a disaster, much like the rest of her life of late. And the common thread that bound every bit of misfortune in her life together was Ethan Moore, the new Lord Ayton.

# *Seven*

ON THE JOURNEY TO LONDON, ETHAN HAD CONSOLED himself with the glimmer of hope that he would see Roselyn again. How wrong he'd been. When the mission ahead of him was so daunting, with no cause for happiness, she was the light that pulled him forward. And then he'd seen her, a vision in blue. But everything after that moment had gone quite wrong. He still carried the note she'd written with him every day, and tonight it seemed to burn him through his pocket, much like the fiery lady in question. They'd only spent brief moments together at his home, and now even those small slivers of time were smashed to dust.

He'd spent the past month remembering the adventures and laughter they'd shared as children, how he now treasured that long-ago friendship with her. His dreams had been filled with the lady Roselyn had become, the one who'd thrown mud at him and stolen to his bedchamber with a note. Meanwhile she'd clearly been fixating on the knife Ethan had picked up after his assailant had dropped it. Unsure of how to proceed with her tonight on the terrace, he'd watched her walk away—for now.

Ethan scanned the ballroom for the true reason he'd come to this ball. Aside from mucking things up with Roselyn, he'd come here to find Kelton Brice. This was his family's home, so he must be about somewhere. His height and, if memory served, his propensity for wearing bright colors should make him terribly obvious. Ethan had often told Brice that his work for the Spare Heirs Society would be easier if he didn't draw so much attention to himself with his looks and his manner. But Brice had never agreed and he never would. He was most likely the only paid henchman, for lack of a better term, who *henched* while wearing a large smile and bright clothing.

Ethan pushed off of the terrace door frame and moved farther into the room. Before he could take more than two steps, someone clasped a hand on his shoulder. Ethan tensed, prepared to throw the first punch. Turning, he saw his father's business partner at his side. He sighed and released his fingers from the fist that he'd formed. "Cladhart, I almost took your head off."

"You could try," Cladhart returned with a grin.

"It'd be a pity to break the Dillsworth ballroom."

"The entire ballroom?" Cladhart raised one brow.

Ethan shrugged and glanced around at the room that was practically made of glass and filled with vases. It seemed likely that a fight could bring down the roof of this place.

"I didn't expect to see you here. When did you arrive in town?" Cladhart asked as they stepped to the side to allow a group of ladies to pass.

"Only a few days ago. I thought you were still sorting things at the mines."

"Business, it changes every day," Cladhart explained. "Did you open Ormesby House now that you're in London?"

"No." Ethan pulled at the tight knot of his cravat. "It didn't seem right. I have his title, his inheritance—I don't need his town house as well."

"Trevor's title, inheritance, London home, his lady…"

Ethan exhaled a harsh breath. Roselyn didn't seem to have any interest in him, not anymore. "I don't think the lady in question can be acquired like a home or a title."

"Are you losing your touch?" Cladhart asked with a jab of his elbow in Ethan's arm. "And just when you have a title to bandy about town. Such a pity."

"Keep your pity, old man."

"This old man has a lady on his arm this evening. Do you?"

"I don't believe you." Ethan glanced around for evidence of a lady. "Who would attend a ball with the likes of you, Cladhart? I fear for the soundness of her mind."

"It's not her mind that I'm interested in tonight," Cladhart said under his breath before turning to beckon a woman at the base of the nearest column to come closer. She was fine-looking, even if she did carry a certain desperation about her.

"Lord Ayton, I'd like to introduce my new friend, Lady Mantooth. Ayton here is the son of my business partner."

"My lady," Ethan offered with a nod of his head.

"Lord Ayton, Cladhart tells me he has access to an unlimited wealth of jewels, only I have yet to receive a single bauble. Tell me, are there truly mines in the north, or is your business associate having a go at me?" She smiled a practiced grin he was sure she'd used to empty the pockets of many a gentleman.

"Not a single bauble?" Ethan asked, shock dripping from his words. "Cladhart, this lady requires jewels for enduring your company. Have a care and give her a piece from your *unlimited wealth*."

"Ayton," the older man said with an uncomfortable laugh. "You know there are rules about such things. Your father made it clear years ago..."

"Rules are made to be broken, I always say. Don't you agree, Lady Mantooth?"

She laughed, swatting his arm with a playful tap of her fan. "Lord Ayton, I believe we will get along quite well."

"That might well be true," Ethan lied. He'd toyed with many a barmaid, but he could never dally with a lady. The price was too high for such a brief entertainment. The thought of Roselyn slipped through his mind, but he dismissed the contradiction. Roselyn was different—she always had been. He'd never met a lady who could sling mud at his face one moment and then curtsy with ingrained grace in the next.

Roselyn was still the same girl he'd known when they were children. Her wild love for life could now be seen in her quick glances when she thought no one was watching, and when she truly looked at him, it was with genuine emotion, even if tonight that emotion had been anger. He had to find a way through that anger. He needed to see her smile at him once more. He wanted his friend back in his life.

"Ayton, might I speak with you a moment?" Cladhart asked, drawing him out of his thoughts. His nostrils were flared like one of those angry bulls they kept in Spain. "Alone?"

Lady Mantooth pouted but took a step backward in the direction of the parlor that held the refreshments. "I suppose I've overstayed my welcome, gentlemen. Please, excuse me."

As soon as she was beyond earshot, Cladhart began, "Ethan, must you put ideas into her head in such a fashion? I can't empty the mines for the likes of a grasping widow."

"I'm aware." Ethan smiled, amused by the tightness of the older gentleman's jaw and panicked look about his eyes.

"You miserable sod of a bastard," Cladhart muttered under his breath.

"You're welcome."

"Why are you in town anyway, other than to make my life more difficult?"

The smile slid from Ethan's face. He was here for one reason; it wasn't for his father's benefit, and as he'd reminded himself on many occasions, it was not to see Roselyn again. "Looking for the truth."

"The truth... You don't mean about Trevor?" Cladhart drew back in surprise. "Your father told me of your suspicions, but I thought you'd seen reason. Ethan, you can't—"

"I need to know who killed my brother," he stated without preamble. "And I won't rest until I find him."

Cladhart glanced around them before pulling Ethan deeper into the shadows under the balcony. "Trevor passed away in an accident. That is the story your own family is spreading. You have responsibilities now."

"Yes, I do. I have an important responsibility to see that Trevor's killer is brought to justice."

"Shhh," Cladhart said, looking around to see if anyone was within earshot of their conversation. "Ethan, no good can come of your digging about in your brother's life."

"Justice for my brother isn't good? Avenging his death?" Ethan sighed, forcing himself to breathe to defuse his anger. "I have to know who is responsible for killing him. I have no choice."

"Is this to prove your father wrong? I know there's bad blood between you, but this is taking it a bit far. I can speak to Ormesby. I'll—"

"Father has nothing to do with this," Ethan cut in. "He sent me to town to smooth things over in society."

"Then that is what you must do. Forget searching for a killer."

"No." Ethan's jaw tightened around the single word as he stared at Cladhart. Trevor deserved peace, and to achieve that peace, Ethan had to find the one responsible for his death, to see that justice was served. And perhaps, once he'd completed his task, Roselyn would know he was innocent. It might not change a thing in her mind, but at least he would have tried to set things to rights.

"I see your mind is firm on the matter."

"It is."

"Damn." Cladhart grew silent for a moment before adding, "What information do you have that led you to London?"

"Sales documents." It was an admittedly small trail to follow to the truth, but he would pound his answers from the papers if it was the last thing he did. "I think Trevor discovered something with the mines, something it was worth ending his life to conceal."

"With the mines? I would know of it too if that were the case." Cladhart shook his head in confusion before sighing in resignation. "I'll ask a few questions if it will keep that crooked nose of yours clean."

Ethan pulled back, not expecting help from someone so closely tied to his father, even if he had always been close with the man. These were the mines they were discussing, and business had always outweighed anything else, in his experience. "You wish to assist with my investigation?"

"Better to assist you than to find you dead as well." With a clap on Ethan's back, Cladhart walked away. Ethan watched him leave. He may have a rotten excuse for a father, but at least he had Cladhart on his side.

Shaking off the morbid conversation, he moved toward the entrance of the ballroom, no longer caring for banter this evening. His new title and position were like an ill-fitting suit that tugged at his shoulders, constricting his breathing. He longed to throw them off and move about as he used to do, but there was no choice now but to stretch the fabric of his life until it fit. And that process began with finding Kelton Brice and spending the remainder of the evening studying those blasted papers.

Twenty minutes later, he had to admit defeat. Although St. James had instructed him that Brice would be in attendance, the man was nowhere to be found. Ethan left the house, taking a minute for his eyes to adjust to the dim light…and saw the very man he'd been searching for all evening. Ethan descended the steps to the wide landing. "I should have begun my search for you by looking in the garden beneath a lady's skirts," Ethan said, waiting for Brice to turn around.

A second later Brice's smile was visible even in the near-darkness. "Moore! I heard you were in town, and sporting a new title."

"I see you don't deny the bit about being beneath a lady's skirts."

"Thornwood's sister was here a minute ago. Could have been a lovely evening beneath the stars if her brother hadn't arrived."

"Careful…" Ethan's voice grated. The very idea of Roselyn with Brice had him ready to throw a punch in his friend's direction.

"Nothing happened with her." Brice put his hands up in a show of innocence. "She left untouched by me, and with her family. Your reaction is interesting though. She said she saw you on the terrace earlier." Brice laughed, slapping Ethan on the arm.

"Stay away from that one."

"I'll try, but only with that one. The ladies find me charming." Brice shrugged.

"Charming as an opponent in a fight, appearing harmless yet ready to pounce," Ethan teased.

"Ah, but unlike your usual opponents, I have all my teeth."

"Indeed. Even though I've tried on many occasions to remove them." Ethan couldn't remain angry with

Brice. There was too much history, too many adventures between them to ignore.

"It's good to have you back. St. James told me you moved back into your old rooms at headquarters."

Ethan nodded. He'd needed a place to stay. He wouldn't be sleeping in Trevor's bed and dining at his place at the table—ever. "Did he mention anything else?"

"Only something about you chasing down a murderer. Not much to tell, really."

"Yes, only that." Ethan smirked.

"Chasing down a murderer is a damn sight more interesting than the ball this evening."

"You would think so. Glad to see some things never change." The terrace had been plenty to hold Ethan's interest. Of course, that was before Roselyn had fled his company. He should regret the way he'd touched her, yet that had been his favorite part of this evening. He regretted nothing. He stifled a grin with a cough and leaned a hip on the low wall at his side.

Brice nodded to one of the departing guests before turning back to Ethan. "Did you like the additions to the club? I told St. James that if he didn't replace the flowered draperies we attempted to burn that time, I was going to start wearing gowns and practicing my curtsy."

"And yet you had him keep the hole in the wall from our *discussion* that time. Your sentimentality impresses me." Ethan crossed his arms over his chest.

"That was St. James's doing. It's a warning to the new members."

"A warning not to fight in the drawing room?" Ethan frowned in thought. "Seems reasonable."

"No, to finish what you begin. Or maybe it was to make a lasting change on society, not a damn hole in the wall?" Brice shook his head. "I forget."

Ethan chuckled. He couldn't even remember now what he and Brice had argued over, but he remembered the resulting fight well enough. "It was a nice hit. St. James must admit that much."

"St. James never admits anything." Brice laughed. "It's good to have you back, even with the business about your brother. Condolences."

Ethan waved away his friend's nicety. He had no time for condolences; he was on a mission. He'd spent the past month caring for his sister and considering his loss. At the end of it he'd realized he'd lost more than a brother—he'd lost the past eight years with his family. His brother, a man he lived a separate life from, a man that he never really knew, was dead. They'd lost years to their disagreements. In truth, what Ethan mourned was the loss of the hope that they could have found some bond in future years. Trevor seemed to hold everyone in his life at arm's length, something he'd learned from their father. Had he been of the same mind about Roselyn? Perhaps not. She was wearing black next to her heart.

Ethan heaved a great sigh to fend off the sudden pang of jealousy. Everyone dealt with loss differently. Roselyn could wear her black underthings. He would hunt. "I don't have much of a trail to follow," he mused.

"I could break in somewhere, get what you need. Discuss the situation with a few people and encourage them to talk."

"Brice, you have my word. When there are skulls to be beaten, you will be the first person I alert."

"Just what I like to hear."

"Pardon me, gentlemen. Just passing through," a dark-haired gentleman commented as he pushed past them.

As Ethan and Brice paused to watch him make a hasty retreat down the steps, two footmen threw the door open and came speeding out in pursuit, the first one calling out, "Lord Crosby!"

"Lord Dillsworth wishes to speak with you, sir! Come back at once," the other footman called after the man.

In one quick shared glance, Ethan knew his conversation with Brice was over. Kelton Brice was many things, but willing to overlook excitement on his doorstep wasn't one of them.

"I'll retrieve him," Brice stated, already running after the man.

"Do you require assistance?" Ethan called after him, but Brice waved him off just before he disappeared into the night.

Ethan paused for a moment, listening for Brice to yell back to join the chase, but heard nothing. Brice could handle himself even if it came to blows with the young gentleman. After all, he did far worse in an average evening while following orders from St. James. With a shrug, Ethan followed them down the steps but then turned in the opposite direction. The Spare Heirs Society wasn't a far walk from here, and he had quite a few things to consider before he would be buried beneath sales documents for the remainder of the evening.

First, what business brought Cladhart to London when his father required him at the mines to assist in Trevor's absence? Was it something to do with Trevor's death? Perhaps his father knew more than he let on. And second, when would he catch sight of Roselyn again? It was this second question that hung in his mind like low fog in the morning. He rubbed his fingers together. The heat of her skin was etched into his memory, and her heartbeat still pounded in his ears, the rhythm matching the sound of his boots against the ground.

With the prospect of reviewing sales ledgers for clues for the remainder of the evening, he would cling to thoughts of Roselyn as long as possible.

∽

"You must tell me every word he said, Roselyn." Isabelle practically fell into the chair at her side, her eyes wide as she waited for Roselyn to speak.

"It's just as I said. Mr. Brice was entertaining the footmen when I arrived on the steps. He introduced himself, and we spoke for a moment before my brother arrived."

Isabelle closed her eyes and sighed, sinking farther into the chair. "What was he wearing?"

"Attire appropriate for a ball…a dark coat and waistcoat. Blue, I believe."

"Blue. I'm sure it matched his eyes."

"Isabelle, I may become ill if you continue this conversation," Victoria cut in. She removed a flask from her reticule and poured something that Roselyn suspected was whiskey into her teacup. "Everything about that man is false. He acts the charming gentleman in his horrid flashy clothing, yet he associates with blackguards. And *I* heard he killed a man last season."

"Vicious rumors. He once served in the army, Victoria," Isabelle stated as if that settled everything. "And there's nothing wrong with his acquaintances either. He's perfect."

Roselyn cleared her throat as she dropped a cube of sugar into her tea. "I saw the new Lord Ayton last evening."

"Did he speak to you?" Victoria asked as she took a sip of her whiskey-infused tea.

"He did," Roselyn stated. "Is London society pleased he's here this season?"

Victoria shrugged. "Most likely. You know how people enjoy talk, and he's a new subject to discuss."

Roselyn considered Victoria for a second before blurting out, "But he has no right to be here."

Isabelle's large eyes turned down in shared sorrow. "I know it grieves you to discuss it, but he does in fact have the title now, Roselyn."

"That's precisely the problem."

"Evie, what do you think? You're always proper," Victoria said with a grin. "Should he be in town this season?"

There was no answer.

"Evie?"

"Yes?" she asked, dragging her gaze from the window at her side.

"Is something wrong?" Isabelle asked.

"No. Of course not." But even Roselyn could see she wasn't being truthful.

"Did something happen at last night's ball?" Roselyn asked.

"It's true you never returned from repairing your gown," Isabelle mused. "Is it your gown? Is that what has you at odds?"

"My gown is in fine order, but thank you for your concern, Isabelle."

"Evie has met someone!" Victoria exclaimed.

"No, don't be absurd. If I'd met someone, you would have seen me dancing with the gentleman in question. His name would be on my dance card, and everything would be aboveboard as it should be."

"Indeed," Victoria said with a knowing smile. "If you don't wish to discuss the gentleman you met in the darkened alcove when you left to repair your gown, so be it."

"I wasn't in a darkened alcove," Evangeline was a bit too quick to retort. Her cheeks were rosy, and she took a sip of tea to hide her eyes.

"Victoria, I don't think any corner of the Dillsworth home is ever dark," Isabelle said, scrunching up her nose in thought. "Did you see how many candles they possessed?"

"I don't think she meant a true darkened alcove, Isabelle, only the idea of one," Roselyn added.

"Oh!" Victoria exclaimed, her gaze still on Evangeline. "It wasn't a darkened alcove. It was a darkened hall, wasn't it? A garden bench? The stairs like your sister last year? A carriage, a gazebo, an empty library…"

"Victoria," Evangeline warned.

"So it was the library." Victoria leaned back in her

chair, pleased with herself. "How naughty of you. I've never been so proud."

"I don't consort with gentlemen in darkened or empty anywhere," Evangeline blustered. "I don't know what would give you such an idea."

"Very well. Keep your secrets. Roselyn will simply entertain us with her sighting of Lord Ayton. Won't you, Roselyn?"

"I didn't find it entertaining in the least. The man is vile, and *I* don't believe it would *ever* be proper for him to be allowed in society," Roselyn proclaimed as she set her teacup on the table beside her. "He is personally responsible for the destruction of my life, and he sought me out last night! He should avoid me, with what I alone know of his character, or lack thereof.

"But, no. Lord Ayton forces a conversation with me, and I'm in turn required to speak to him. If he would simply stay far from me and continue charming ladies on the other side of the ballroom, I might be all right. I might survive his presence..." Her voice trailed off as she thought of the lady he was speaking with last night. Glancing down, she realized she was rubbing the hand he'd held within his as if she could wipe away the memory.

"This is entertaining," Victoria said, her eyes bright with glee.

"Roselyn, if I may be so bold, how is this gentleman responsible for the destruction of your life?" Evangeline asked, concern filling her voice.

"He... We...and by 'we' I mean..." Roselyn looked from one lady to another, damning the curiosity reflected three times over. "Can we forget I said that part of the story?"

"That's not likely," Victoria stated with a shake of her head.

Roselyn swallowed. She shouldn't repeat any of the events of that day; any blame she placed publicly on Ethan would only hurt her as a result. Could these ladies be trusted with the truth? She'd only known them a few days. And yet her heart was about to burst open with the knowledge she held. "He should be hanged."

"Roselyn, if he is such a terrible fellow, then prove he is so. You know how fickle society can be. Turn them against him. Drive him from town with the very society he is currently charming," Victoria stated.

"Could that be done?"

"Ask your sister-in-law. She drove quite a few gentlemen from town last season as I've heard it," Evangeline added, then blushed at the mention of wrongdoing, looking down at her clasped hands.

"No. If I do this, it is without my family's knowledge. Devon would never approve."

"How exciting!" Isabelle practically bounced in her seat. "If your brother wouldn't approve, it must be scandalous!"

"It began as scandalous," Roselyn replied. "Once you've surpassed scandal, what does one call events?"

"Dangerous," Evangeline said.

"Dramatic." Isabelle leaned forward, clearly not wanting to miss a word of the discussion.

"I'd call it fun." Victoria lifted her teacup to Roselyn in celebration of her decision.

But Roselyn was confused. "I'm not sure how to begin proving Lord Ayton is the villain I know him to be. Where do I start?"

"When I'm planning to wager on a horse, I begin by learning all I can about the mount in question," Victoria replied, her lips pursed as she thought.

"You mean you spy on horses before you bet on them?" Roselyn asked.

"If you want to use such a clandestine word, then yes. I spy."

"Victoria, you've been gambling again?" Isabelle cut in with dismay written across her face. "Mother will have fits."

"Not if you keep your mouth closed."

"But remember what Father threatened? I couldn't bear it, Victoria. You have to stay with me in London."

"Of course I'm staying with you in London, Isabelle. I rarely place a wager. I won't be sent away."

With as much as the two sisters bickered, it was surprising they would miss one another at all. Roselyn smiled at the glimpse of love.

"What do you believe a spy would wear on a day out in London?" she mused.

"Black, I would think," Evangeline replied as she took a sip of her tea. "Not that I condone such activity."

"I did bring the one black day dress with me to town," Roselyn said with a smile. Finally, she had a plan. "And I have the perfect necklace to match."

"Roselyn, I'm fairly confident the point of spy work is *not* to be seen," Victoria admonished.

"Very well. But I do have lovely new black dancing

slippers with tiny roses stitched onto the toes." Roselyn held up her fingers to indicate the embroidery on an invisible shoe in the air before her. "I've been waiting for the perfect ensemble to match."

"Dancing slippers? Are you spying at a ball?" Victoria asked.

"That would be safer than spy work in a dark London alley, would it not?" Evangeline asked.

Roselyn ignored them because she was busy envisioning herself slipping from windows and fleeing into the distance. "It's the ideal shoe choice for quiet getaways."

"You should weave roses into your hair to match," Isabelle cut in. "That would set off the shoes."

Victoria shook her head in defeat. "Flowers in her hair? The lot of you would make rotten spies."

"Are being fashionable and completing spy work mutually exclusive?" Roselyn asked with mock outrage, choking back her laughter.

"To my knowledge, yes." Victoria grumbled her answer.

"Then I shall start a trend," Roselyn returned with a grin. It was all too easy to become caught up in her friends' suggestions for her spy wardrobe. For the first time since she arrived in London, she laughed, allowing their conversation to chase away the morose feelings that had haunted her for weeks.

"I can see it now." Victoria waved a hand before her. "Soon all of the country's spies will be wearing flowered dancing slippers."

"Won't it be grand?" Isabelle added with a dreamy sigh.

Indeed. Roselyn's plans would be grand. She would learn the true story of what happened while she was stuck pulling a pebble from her boot that day on the hillside. Whether he realized it or not, Ethan would provide all the evidence she required to have the truth known. Roselyn would be free of her guilt over what happened that day, and free of him. Then she would dance across London—in her fabulous spy shoes.

# Eight

CLADHART DRUMMED HIS FINGERS ON THE DESK, listening to the tap, tap, tap of his nails on the wooden surface rather than the ongoing report of profits and losses being recited for his entertainment. He'd asked Sharpe to keep him informed of any whispers of instability due to the *unfortunate accident*, as they were calling it. And yet he hadn't heard a word the man had said since he arrived.

His mind was still circling the events of last night— and *not* the time he'd spent with Lady Mantooth. She only wanted the gifts he could provide and was keeping her legs closed until she had something around her neck that caught the light. He released a sigh and stared across the room. Lady Mantooth didn't matter. No woman had mattered to him for some years. There had only been one, and she was gone, just like Trevor. And now Ethan was headed in the same direction. He must find a way to stop the man.

It looked to be a clear day beyond the walls of his library—a pleasant day to visit the Bond Street location of their business, then perhaps the harbor.

Ethan had mentioned sales documents he'd obtained from Trevor, but Trevor wouldn't have had the only copies. He needed to retrieve the documents from the harbor warehouse to truly understand the situation. His fingers rapped across the desk again.

"Sharpe," Cladhart interrupted.

"Yes, my lord?" the man asked as he looked up from the papers in his hands and pushed his glasses higher on his nose.

"I find I'm in need of Catting once again, and perhaps that friend of his, if he can be trusted."

"Catting's associate is a trustworthy fellow, I believe. As much as a man in his position can be. Use of such ruffians in business always makes me uneasy, but if we must…" He tapped the papers into a straight stack against his legs and turned his attention back to the small print. "I can send for them when we've completed the mining reports."

"Consider the mining reports complete," Cladhart said.

"I hadn't yet reached the sales projections for London." The man stared down at the stack of documents in his hands for a moment before sitting them aside and meeting Cladhart's stern gaze. "Very well, my lord."

"I plan to look in on the Bond Street shop this afternoon. We can discuss it then." Cladhart stood and moved to pour himself a drink, returning a moment later with two glasses of whiskey.

Sharpe gave a small nod of appreciation as he accepted his drink. "What shall I tell Catting you need from him?"

"Information."

"That's certainly a simpler task than I'd imagined. As your man of business, of sorts, I could gather the information you require. My work at the shop doesn't take all of my time."

Always such an eager bootlicker. It was both an admirable and a sickening quality. Sharpe was irritating, but the man had worked for him since they were young. He knew all there was to know about the business and fit his position like a pair of old, worn gloves that couldn't be given away.

"It's not the sort of information contained in a library." Cladhart took a swallow of his drink.

"I see. I'm sure Catting can assist you, then. Would you be seeking documents of a private nature?" Sharpe asked with a wary look in his eyes. "Items best recovered at night?"

"Perhaps." He took another drink.

"Will they need to gain access to any homes?" He raised his brows in alarm.

"You ask too many questions."

"Which is precisely why you keep me about," Sharpe said, glaring at him through the thick lenses of his glasses.

Not precisely, but Cladhart was in no mood to argue with the man. He rubbed a hand over his weary eyes. "Lord Ayton is looking into the death of his brother."

There was a pause in the conversation, punctuated only by Sharpe setting his drained glass of whiskey on the desktop. "His father can't have approved that. The implications on business… When did you discover this?"

"He attended the ball last night."

"You have to stop him, my lord. He listens to you. You could—"

"Do you think I didn't try that?" Cladhart asked. "He won't listen to me on the subject."

"He must see reason. He'll drag the mining company and his own family through the mud if anyone hears of this. Not to mention…"

"Things that ought not to be mentioned should not be mentioned," Cladhart warned before tossing back the last of his drink. The last thing he needed was for Sharpe's excitement to draw undue attention to Ethan's investigation. All that he'd worked for, all that he'd built through the mining company could topple with such a scandal.

"Indeed." Sharpe glanced around to ensure the library door was closed. "I don't know where my head was."

Cladhart rose and walked to the window, resting his forearm on the frame. He couldn't sit any longer. He needed action. He needed to settle this situation before it got out of hand. And he would do that by any means necessary. "So, now you see the need for Catting and his friend? We need information, to know every detail the late Lord Ayton might have discovered."

"Quite. We can't allow this to become the talk about town."

"If we can find the documentation the new Lord Ayton is seeking, then we can protect him from what may come."

"Quite. Is he in possession of anything of import?" It would have been a nonchalant question if not for the tremor in the man's voice. They both knew the dangers of the waters they were wading into.

"He mentioned sales documents of some sort," Cladhart replied.

"I see. That would indicate that a search of the harbor office is necessary."

"I'm glad we see eye to eye on this matter," Cladhart said as he turned back to the room.

"I'll see to it that it's done." Sharpe stood to leave, pausing to study his hand as he gripped the edge of Cladhart's desk. "I don't want to see the new Lord Ayton fall into any trouble. There has been far too much of that of late."

Cladhart didn't reply; there was no need to. Sharpe was correct. If everyone would leave well enough alone and go about their business, no one would come to harm. But he'd known Ethan all his life. An adventurous child had turned into a rebellious boy and grown into a reckless man.

A man like Ethan would never leave well enough alone. And that was the problem.

# Nine

ROSELYN'S PLAN HAD SEEMED BRILLIANT THIS MORNING when she'd learned from her brother where Ethan was expected to be today. She smiled at the memory of her own cleverness, even if it had led her to this quite unsavory location. Spies must suffer for their work at times, and today was a day of suffering on her part. It all began this morning when she'd cornered Devon while he ate breakfast.

"Are all gentlemen in town as obsessed with maps and foreign plants as you are, Devon?" she'd asked him as she took a sip of tea.

"No, unfortunately. Dreadfully dull, lot on the whole," he'd grumbled as he took a bite of the food on his plate. "Sorry to disappoint you, Roselyn."

"Then where do they go on an average afternoon if they don't skulk about in their libraries?"

Devon had shrugged. "To clubs. Tattersalls, Gentleman Jackson's Boxing Salon, and the like. They wager and drink the day away—as I said, quite dull."

"Do you think that's how Trevor would have spent his days?" she'd asked, trying to appear the very image of forlorn so he wouldn't become suspicious over her questions.

"I'm sure not," her brother had rushed to say.

"And the new Lord Ayton?"

"That's precisely how he's spending his afternoon. He's to be at Jackson's for a fight midday."

"Oh, how dreadful," she'd replied just before excusing herself from the small family dining room.

After that she'd only required a slight change in her proposed spy wardrobe before slipping from the rear of the house unnoticed. And now she was here. She tugged on the front of the waistcoat she wore in an effort to further hide her breasts. There was no wearing her black dress and matching dancing slippers in this location, but her current disguise was working quite well thus far. She'd slipped through the door without notice, wearing clothes nicked from one of the footmen at her home. Of course, that had been the easy—and pleasant-smelling—part of her plan.

Years of sweaty masculinity seemed to be baked into the floorboards at Gentleman Jackson's, like cinnamon in the bread Roselyn had eaten this morning, only much less appetizing. She crinkled her nose as she moved farther into the establishment. How could such a foul-smelling place be so popular with gentlemen? If any respectable dress shop or milliner on Bond Street kept their facilities in a similar fashion, ladies would cross the street to be away from it.

Roselyn rose to her toes to see through the gathered crowd. The male half of town all seemed to be packed inside on this unseasonably warm afternoon. *Go to the park*, she longed to tell them. *Take your family for a picnic and enjoy the fine weather.* But they wouldn't listen to a young boy who'd wandered in from the streets anyway. She straightened her hat, making sure her hair was still bound inside the costume.

At least the crowd served to hide her existence— that should be worth something. No one looked at her twice. Did her brilliant spy work know no bounds? Perhaps if marriage didn't go in her favor, she would pursue espionage for her country. It wasn't difficult. Don a costume. Sneak about. Waltz away with valuable information. She shimmied between gentlemen in an effort to get a better view, but only managed to see the backs of shoulders and heads.

"My money is on Ayton today," she heard someone to her right say.

Money on Ayton? If there was a wager involved with this crowd, then all eyes would be on him. She knew he was present, but was he truly at the center of this crowd? Her shoulders sank beneath the lawn shirt. How was she to pick his pockets and find evidence to prove his guilt if everyone was here to observe and gamble on him?

She grumbled at the complication and pushed her way through the gathered gentlemen. But with the excitement of the crowd, pushing ever forward toward the center of the room, there was no hope of someone of her stature getting any kind of view. Elbows jabbed at her as she was shoved out of the way again and again.

*I'll leave here with nothing but bruises to show for my afternoon.* She shifted sideways through the crowd, searching for an empty space of floor, only to be pushed back again. Finally, with a huff of exasperation that threatened to reveal her true identity as a high-born lady, she stiffened her own elbows. To the devil with these gentlemen, she would stand where she pleased. She stomped her foot down hard on the floor—only her heel didn't meet floor. It met the toe of the gentleman behind her.

She gasped and twisted around, ready to offer an apology when the man's meaty hand wrapped around her arm. "I didn't mean to…"

"Jackson, I believe I have Ayton's next opponent right here," the man snarled, cutting off any explanation she might have made.

Roselyn blinked, shocked by his announcement. He couldn't mean her. "No, I don't want to fight anyone," she tried, but her voice didn't carry across the din the way the man's had.

"Don't you?" he sneered at her, his anger burning through each word. "You're the one who scuffed my boots. Dirty scamp."

She wiggled to free herself from his grasp, but clearly she'd stepped on the wrong toes. Increasingly desperate, she kicked her foot back at the man's shin, but her heel only glanced off the side of his leg as he shoved her forward through the crowd.

"Who has volunteered?" another man asked as he moved closer to investigate.

"This fellow." The man's grip on her arm finally slackened. But before she could flee from this awful situation, she was shoved forward into a clear area of floor.

The surrounding men turned to look at her. She was fairly certain this was poor form for a spy—and certainly for a lady. She worked to control her breathing as she tugged her hat lower over her forehead, silently willing everyone to look the other way.

"He's but a boy," the official-looking man before her argued. Although that statement was rather flawed, she was in agreement with him.

"That's true. I'm only a small boy of meager background and disappointing strength," she offered in a voice deeper than her own, while looking around for the nearest door to the street. This had been a terrible idea. She needed to leave straightaway.

The man continued speaking as if she would be quite disappointed by his refusal to allow her to compete. "Apologies, lad, but you aren't capable of holding your own with a great gentleman like Ayton."

"A great gentleman," she scoffed, her head snapping up to meet the man's gaze.

"Aye, he's new to town. Perhaps you haven't heard of him."

"Oh, I've heard of him," she mumbled.

"Then you know that he is much more powerful than you are. Many strong men have tried to best him, and he destroys them all. You're no match for him." The man didn't move away but was already searching the crowd for another opponent.

She should leave while she had the opportunity, but she found herself staring at the owner of the boxing salon instead. Had he meant what he said? No man in London was strong enough to take Ethan down a peg? Perhaps that was true when it came to hitting one another over the head, but it struck her that it was true on a larger scale as well. She'd seen the way he was treated at the ball the other night. He had the title and that was all that mattered to society. She alone saw the truth behind his rise to *greatness*. Only she could make that truth known.

"I have to try." The muttered words were out of her mouth before she could control her tongue. What was wrong with her? These men would think she meant with her fists. That wasn't what she'd meant at all. The heat of a blush rushed through her face.

"Sounds like he's a willing victim, Jackson," stated the man behind her who'd set up this entire situation.

Yes, it had sounded that way, hadn't it? *Idiot*, she said to herself, even as she called out, "No."

"It isn't my practice to put young boys forward to fight," the official-looking man said as he turned his attention back to her.

"Honorable of you." Roselyn nodded as she spoke in the deep, false voice again. Her heart was pounding as she glanced around for a possible escape from the room. This was hardly the afternoon she'd planned. The door stood at too great a distance from her, as did the windows on the far wall.

"Is there no man here who wishes to best Ayton?" the man called across the ocean of gentlemen.

How could she make someone find the courage to step forward and get her out of this mess? "Yes," Roselyn added in her overly deep voice. "Ayton could be bested by a sickly goat. He has weakness in his veins and longs to be facedown on the floor." Surely that would do it.

When even the rumble of chatter in the room grew quiet, she continued, "His fists are made of pudding, and his punches feel like licks of a puppy's tongue." There. Any moment now a willing opponent would make his move.

"Bring the boy forward," Ethan said from the other side of the wall of gentlemen.

What? *No! No, no, no.* Someone was supposed to be compelled to fight Ayton based on her words. She dug in her heels, but hands on her back pushed her across the worn planks. She flailed her arms like windmills, trying to hold herself steady.

"No backing down now, son. You've gone and angered the man."

"I didn't mean to… I only thought…" But she was shoved into the center of the crowd, and the words died on her lips.

Ethan was standing before her half-naked. Her mouth dropped open as she reminded herself to stay upright. She'd had no idea men entertained themselves in such a manner. This place was called a salon. One did not disrobe in the center of a gathering at a salon! She'd never imagined… She blinked.

She should look away. It wasn't seemly to stare.

Ethan was looking down at the bindings that covered his hands, adjusting something at his wrist. His dark hair hid his face from view, but his chest was on full display for most of the gentlemen in London to admire. Although it was doubtful anyone here was looking at every bulge of muscle as she was. Some things in life should be committed to memory for safekeeping, and this was one of those things. Her eyes went wide as she savored every detail of his body.

"You wish to fight me, do you?" He barely glanced up, his gaze not reaching her face.

"No." She watched as a bead of sweat snaked down his arm, rounding over his muscles before threatening to crash onto his forearm.

"That was a great deal of talk for someone who doesn't wish his nose to be broken." Ethan turned his back on her and wiped his face on a towel. "Gentlemen, place your bets wisely. This boy may well be the end of me," he added to another round of laughter.

"Meant no offense," she mumbled, staring at the muscles rippling in his back as he moved. The cocked tilt of his hips made her mouth go dry. She licked her lips and tried to look away from him. She didn't look away, but at least she could claim that she'd attempted it if questioned.

"No offense?" he asked as he lifted his face from the towel. His arms tensed with the motion, and she stared at their size. "We'll see if my blows feel like… What did you liken them to? Licks from a dog?" Laughter from the crowd seemed to punctuate his words.

"A puppy," she corrected, regretting her thoughtless taunts. She shuffled her feet on the floor. Ethan was larger than she'd imagined. Muscles seemed to stack on top of other muscles and then tapered down to hips that were, thankfully, still clad in black breeches or she might well need smelling salts to revive her from this experience. How had she not noticed his size beneath his clothing? She'd known he wasn't a small man, but… Her gaze trailed down his spine, memorizing the tanned color of his skin, the way his hair almost curled at the back of his thick neck.

"A puppy." He chuckled as he handed the towel back to the man in the crowd. "Even better. You'll soon find out, won't you?"

He turned and took a step toward her, a menacing scowl written across his face—at least until his eyes met hers. He blinked before narrowing his gaze to study her. He didn't move for a long moment. Was he deciding how best to kill her? She wished she could read the thoughts that had his lips mouthing a soundless oath. He glanced to the men who encircled them for but a second before his gaze returned to hers. It was only then that his shoulders relaxed a fraction and his lips quirked up in a crooked, all-knowing grin. Blast it all. She knew what that look meant for her disguise.

"Do you have a name?" he finally asked.

"Thomas." She blurted out the first name that came to mind, that of the footman whose clothes she'd stolen.

"Yes, you look like a Thomas." He smirked and ran his hand over the stubble of his beard to hide any further hint of amusement.

"And you look…" She'd set out to insult him, but found she couldn't when he was looming over her like a dark cloud on the horizon. Her cheeks burned, betraying her thoughts.

"It seems Thomas here will insult me from across the room, but not to my face." His gaze flitted from her to the crowd and back to her as if assessing the situation. He knew who she was. Would he tear her disguise away and reveal her identity to the room?

She held her breath, waiting for him to move, to say something, but he remained still. Was he unsure how to proceed, knowing who she was, or was he waiting for her to make a move?

"Hit him!" someone yelled.

"Throw a punch, Ayton!"

Roselyn glanced at the gentlemen surrounding them. How had she gotten herself into such a mess? There was no escaping this. He was clearly ready for a battle and she…was not. She forced herself to breathe.

Ethan was not backing down. Did that mean they were to fight in earnest?

There was nothing for it. If this crowd wanted to see a fight, they would see one. Ethan was watching her. Was there some signal to begin that one waited for in these situations? Perhaps there was a horn blast or a shot fired to signal the beginning of pugilist matches. It was one clearly valuable subject not covered by any governess.

She refused to stand about waiting for her fate to be announced. No gentleman would tell her when she was to do anything. She was Lady Roselyn Grey! She tilted her chin higher and squared her shoulders to her enemy.

Pulling her arm back as she'd once seen a village shopkeeper do to remove someone from his establishment, she thrust it forward though the air with the force of her entire body. Her fist collided with the warm flesh of Ethan's skin with a small thwack.

He didn't flinch, only stood with his arms hanging at his sides.

She frowned at the lack of impact her blow had on the man and pulled back to swing at him again. But when she looked up, she saw the laughter in his eyes. He was amused!

She'd come here at great risk to learn the facts behind a terrible crime, and he was laughing at her. It was true that he towered over her and could send her sailing across the room with a single move of his arms, but must he be so obvious about it? She wanted that smug look to land on the floor along with the rest of him. She was swinging at him before she could stop herself. This time she aimed for his face.

A shot of pain seared up her arm as her fist collided with his eye. His head turned as she staggered forward from the impact of the blow. She'd done it! She hadn't expected it would hurt her as much as it did. But she'd hit him. She rubbed the pain from her knuckles.

She'd pounded the smug look from those eyes that refused to adhere to one color. Those eyes that had been warm on her skin just two nights ago at the ball. She turned, looking up at him to see what damage she'd done.

He stared at her, no longer amused. She'd wanted to hurt him, but the mental blow appeared to have sunk much deeper than her fist was able to penetrate. Emotion crossed his face in an instant before it hardened before her eyes.

"This foe is too great for me," he stated in a deep, carrying voice. "I forfeit."

"Come now, Ayton," one of the men pleaded.

"It's a hustle!" someone bellowed from the back of the crowd.

But Ethan shook his head and raised his hands in surrender.

That was when she realized that he'd never made a fist. He'd been taunting her with words, but he'd never planned on hitting her, even when he thought her a boy. How odd that a man she knew to be a murderer would have such ethics in sport. She ripped her gaze from him and focused on her aching red knuckles.

As the crowd began to shift around them, yelling taunts and grumbling in anger, she slipped across the room. Perhaps there was a rear door out of this den of sweat and wagers. She moved to the back wall in search of an alternate escape—other than climbing through a window—though she would do what she must to be gone from this place before her situation became worse.

She dodged a group of gentlemen exchanging money and skirted another. Finally, she reached the rear wall of the building. Any door here would lead to the alley behind the building where she could easily escape on foot. The crowd shifted, and she saw a hall that led farther to the back of the establishment. There!

She was about to step around a bench near the corner and run for freedom, but then she saw it. There on the bench was a pile of black clothing.

She spun around to scan the room behind her. Everyone else present was wearing a shirt and coat— every gentleman but one. Ethan was still across the room talking to a man she didn't recognize. She turned back to the clothes and lifted the jacket. It had to be Ethan's, not only because of the size, but also because it was black. With Ethan, everything was black, even his heart. It was rather fitting.

She slipped her hand inside the pocket. There simply had to be evidence of some wrongdoing. She only took a second to inhale the lingering scent of his shaving soap before focusing on her task. Her fingers found a piece of paper. She'd done it! Whatever the document, it was sure to prove Ethan's guilt.

"Princess." The word was whispered in her ear, making her jump.

She turned but kept her hands behind her back. "I don't know what you're talking about," she said in an overly husky voice. He knew her identity, but she was unwilling to give up her disguise even now. Especially now.

"What are you doing with your hands in my pockets?"

"I didn't…" She broke off when she realized one hand was still in his jacket pocket.

"I have a grand idea." He reached around her, so close he brushed against her shoulder, and picked up his shirt. "I'll put my clothes on, and then you can resume digging around in my pockets. That will be much more to my liking."

She turned away as he slipped the black shirt over his head so as not to witness the fabric falling over his sleek body. She needed to keep her wits if she was to escape him. "Do you speak to all the young boys this way?"

"Young boys don't have shapely thighs visible beneath their breeches—something I've tried repeatedly to explain to my sister."

The heat of his gaze warmed her skin through the breeches she was wearing. Was her costume so obvious? She'd fooled everyone else today. It was a shame it hadn't worked on Ethan as well. She would simply have to increase her efforts tomorrow. He grabbed the coat from the bench, and when she turned back to him, he was shrugging it onto his wide shoulders.

"You cost me my winnings, I'll have you know," he mused as he attempted to tie his cravat.

"Pardon me if I have no remorse for decreasing the size of your pile of ill-gotten funds."

"Have you no care how I dine this evening?" He was still attempting to tie a knot beneath his chin and failing at it.

"You will dine quite well, I presume—at Ormesby House where your servants now cater to your every need. *Lord Ayton, how can we serve the new lord of the house?*" she mocked. "*Might I get you additional sweets, Lord Ayton? Allow me to lift that fork to your mouth so that you don't have to trouble yourself, Lord Ayton.*" She finally grew weary of watching him tie his cravat and pushed his hands away to attempt to repair the damage he'd done, a skill she'd learned from watching her father and his valet as a child.

"If that is the lordly life, perhaps I should visit Ormesby House."

"Visit?" She paused in her work and looked up at him. A moment later she dropped her hands to her sides. She was sure his cravat was suitable for an afternoon out, although she wasn't looking at it to make that assessment.

"What are you doing here?" he asked as he stared down at her.

She cleared her throat. "You aren't staying at Ormesby House while you're in town?"

He quirked a brow at her. "You haven't answered my question."

She couldn't answer his question. She couldn't tell Ethan she was investigating him for his brother's murder. A guilty man would destroy any evidence she might otherwise find. "I should leave."

"Something a wise lady would have done some time ago. The smell alone…" He broke off with a smile.

"A wise lady wouldn't have come in the first place," she said with a shrug. She had her reasons though. If only she could have retrieved that paper from his pocket before he'd spied her.

"Winnings or no, this has been my favorite match. You throw quite the punch, *Thomas*."

Dragging her gaze back to his face from his coat where the paper resided, she said, "I'm only as good as my target."

He drew back in shock. "Was that a compliment?"

"No, only a statement of how irritating I find you."

"Happy to be of assistance." He gave her a small bow.

She needed to leave if this was to only be idle chat with no relevance to her quest for information. Shifting to the side to move past him, she was annoyed when he moved as well to block her path. "Even now, I long to hit you again."

"I wasn't aware of your violent tendencies, princess."

"*My* violent tendencies? You are the one who…" She broke off. She was sure he would soon be found guilty of murder, but it would do no good to yell it to the rafters of a boxing salon. "If you will excuse me, I'll be going now." She sidestepped him and walked away, focusing only on the front door and her path beyond that. She would see him rot for his crimes, and his thickly muscled arms and attempts at charm could rot with him. She was almost to the door of the now-empty room when she heard his footsteps behind her.

"By what means will you return home?" he asked as he caught up with her. He reached for her arm to slow her pace, but she slipped from his grasp. "Are you planning to walk back to Mayfair alone?"

"No, I have the carriage waiting for my return."

He placed his hand on the door, stopping her from leaving. "You're planning to walk out of Gentleman Jackson's dressed as a boy, having just drawn far too much attention to yourself, and hop into the carriage with your brother's seal on the door? Most gentlemen who bet on this match were none too pleased with the result."

Did he think her so careless? Of course she'd considered her escape, even if she hadn't considered her mission well enough. This was only her first attempt. She would try again and next time she would walk away successful, with a smile on her face. And those gentlemen deserved what they got for their gambling ways. "The carriage is waiting a block away."

"Very well." He opened the door and stepped outside behind her.

Moving forward, she walked straight into a wall of gentlemen. How had she not noticed the crowd from one of the windows? There were raised voices and angry glares as she attempted to push past them and reach the street beyond. What was happening?

"There he is!" someone yelled.

She turned to see if Ethan was standing just behind her but found no one. Were they looking at her? Surely not. They should be glad she'd hit such an awful excuse for a gentleman, no matter their losses over the match. And yet, they seemed quite out of sorts. She took a step away from them, almost stumbling into Ethan.

"Gentlemen, the boy did nothing that isn't allowed, and neither did I when I ended the match," he called out to the gathered group. His words had no effect, however; anger rippled through the crowd as the men looked at her.

"Cost me all the money in my pocket 's what the both of you did," one man proclaimed.

"Aye. It's a ruse and it needs to be dealt with."

"Jackson wouldn't approve of such talk," Ethan warned in a deep voice.

"We're outside, are we not?" the man in the front of the crowd, the apparent leader of the group, asked as he moved toward her.

"Indeed. But no one is getting hurt today," Ethan stated. A second's pause later, his hand wrapped around her waist, slinging her over his shoulder.

She gasped as her ribs were crushed into his shoulder and they left the gathering behind. Most of the men watched them go with looks of disgust on their faces, but a small group, a younger group, followed. "What are you doing?" she struggled to ask.

He adjusted her higher on his shoulder with one arm wrapped around her waist to increase his speed, easing the pain in her side as he did so. "Saving your arse."

"My rear end is just fine, thank you."

He slid his other hand over the back of her thigh to hold her to his chest as he moved down the street. "So it is." He chuckled as he increased the gap between them and those who pursued them.

How dare he? The heat of his hand warmed her skin through the breeches she wore, just below the curve of her rear. It was indecent. But if she was to be toted about town like a sack of flour, she'd rather not hit the ground in the process. Her breaths were ragged in spite of the fact that it was Ethan who ran down the street. He'd never been overly concerned with what was proper, but the way he was holding her was scandalous and she knew it. "If anyone sees this…"

"It's no different from the many times I've helped you to the lowest branch of a tree."

"This feels entirely different from tree climbing," she grumbled.

"You weren't so shapely back then," he returned between breaths as he ran.

Her face heated at his admission. He was the one who should be suffering. She huffed and attempted to steady herself since there didn't seem to be an escape from her torment at the moment. "It isn't lordly behavior to notice or comment on a lady's rear, I'll have you know."

His grip on her waist tightened a fraction. "I'm no lord."

"You are now! You saw to that!"

He grumbled something she couldn't quite understand as they rounded a corner. It was most likely his great pleasure over having received such a title. He was enjoying all the benefits that came from his actions on the hilltop that day. It was just as he'd planned it, she supposed. Though it hadn't seemed planned at the time. She'd asked him to come with them on their walk after all. *Roselyn, are you defending this murderous man?* She cringed at the thought.

What was it about Ethan that made her forget all reason? She would have to be more careful of her reconnaissance in the future. She would stay well away from him. But for now, he was—as much as she hated to admit it—saving her arse. And as much as she wished to wiggle free, there was no place for her to go.

She sighed and braced an elbow on his back to see the group of men chasing them around the corner. They certainly weren't what she would expect of angry pursuers. She rested her chin on her wrist and watched them follow half a block behind. "I've only read of angry mobs before today. I thought they carried pitchforks and torches with them."

"You're complaining about the lack of organization of the men chasing us down the street?" he asked between breaths as he ran.

"Well, they do seem rather ill-prepared." She braced herself as he turned again, doubling back toward Gentleman Jackson's in an effort to lose the men. His hand shifted on her rear, though she tried not to notice.

"To be honest, princess, I would rather them be angry over empty pockets than us angry over singed arses."

"I suppose," she mused.

"Spoken like someone who has never had to run for her life."

"I ran from you."

His footsteps faltered before he found his pace again. "I would never hurt you, Roselyn."

He hadn't hurt her, yet. But he'd attacked Trevor. She'd seen him with that blade in his hand. How could she ever trust a man who had done such a thing? But he hadn't attempted to fight her today. He'd only stood there and taken her punches. She should fear him. And yet, somehow, she didn't.

She was truly losing her mind. She had been there to spy on the man, but she was allowing him to carry her away from an angry mob of gentlemen...after having punched him in a pugilist club. There must be a better way to go about this investigation. A less violent way, at any rate.

He spun around to check the men's progress before continuing down the deserted street. The men were still losing ground. One more turn, and Roselyn and Ethan would disappear into the twisted streets of London.

"Does it hurt?" she asked to pass the time, setting aside her anger with the man for a moment. Ladies should, after all, strive to make conversation even in the most strained of circumstances. Running from an angry mob on the back of a murderer most likely qualified as such.

"What? The eye you punched? It will heal to a charming yellow by tomorrow."

"Pugilism is barbaric," she stated with disgust.

"Ha!" He let out a bark of laughter. "That's why ladies shouldn't attend matches at Gentleman Jackson's, let alone step forward and hit a man."

"It claims to be a salon," she complained, ignoring his comment. "Tea wasn't even served."

"Sometimes we read poetry and embroider."

She elbowed him in the back, which only made him laugh. It was a hearty laugh that shook through her body, making her more annoyed with him than before. The men chasing them were quite a distance away now. They'd escaped. So why was she still allowing him to haul her through London? She could find her carriage from here, she was certain. But the more she knew of this man, the more she could piece the truth together. She had to understand. And for that, she needed to stay put.

Turning a corner into an alley, he slowed his pace, shifting her in his arms so her legs were draped over one of his arms and her elbows could no longer do him damage. Of course now she was face-to-face with the man. She crossed her arms, refusing to hold on to him for support. He could put her down if he so desired. Apparently he didn't.

"I've been punched plenty—just not by ladies," he said, strolling down the empty alley. "Usually, I do more damage than is done to me. That's the secret to the sport."

"Sport. You call that a sport?"

"My sport, my livelihood, my life…up until recently, anyway." He swallowed and looked down the street, the hard, square lines of his jaw tightening with the motion.

If he was looking for her sympathy over Trevor's loss, he would wait forever. But at least he was speaking on the subject. "You inflicted more pain than you received on that occasion as well, as I recall."

"That wasn't what I was referring to."

"Oh." Of course not, because that would make her

mission simple. But he was talking, and that would lead to answers of some sort. It had to. She looked up at him as she attempted to understand. "What *were* you referring to?"

"I had a life before I returned to England, princess. I didn't begin life the day we met again in the drive at Ormesby."

"I'm aware." She wasn't that naive. Men did not sprout fully formed from the ground like flowers in the spring.

"Pugilism was my life in Spain. It's how I ate…had a roof above my head."

"Sounds like a lavish lifestyle," she muttered.

"Not by your standards, but it was the life I chose."

Why would he choose such an existence? Why not act like the wild second son in England? He seemed well suited to it. "You chose to have men hit you every day?"

"I try to have it work in the reverse of that. Of course, mistakes happen. It isn't an exact science."

That still didn't explain why he'd chosen such a life for himself, nor did it answer any of the other questions she had about him. She studied his crooked nose for a moment until he caught her looking at him.

"That happened several years ago. Large Russian fellow with fists like hammers—not licks of a puppy's tongue as you suggested."

"Can you still smell properly?"

He pressed his crooked nose to a spot just behind her ear where a bit of her hair had escaped the hat she wore. "Some sort of flower. I think it works."

"It's lavender," she said as she struggled to keep

her breathing steady. No other gentleman would dare to touch her as he did, let alone smell her neck. She shouldn't allow him to be near her at all. He was dangerous! She'd seen him with that knife. She would do well to remember that when in his company. Perhaps there was more truth to the talk about her family being mad than she'd realized. This had gone on long enough.

"I want you to put me down," she said. "I don't want you..." *Touching me. Confusing me. Reminding me how easy things are with you.* "Just...put me down."

"Princess," he began, immediately setting her on her feet.

"I believe I can find my carriage from here, thank you," she cut in before he could weaken her more.

She turned, setting off down the alley that led to the corner where her carriage waited for her. But when she turned back, he was already walking away. No words of farewell. Roselyn watched him go with some question she couldn't quite place lingering in her mind.

One day she would lay out proof of who Ethan Moore truly was. All her questions would be answered. Society would know the truth about him...and perhaps by then so would she.

⤬

Gentleman Jackson's was certainly the last place Ethan had expected to see Lady Roselyn Grey. He was still unclear on her reason for sneaking around in there. He'd seen her go through his pockets, but the only item in them was still there—the note from her.

Carrying it was foolish at best; he knew that. But he carried the bit of paper in his pocket anyway. When he was weary of looking at sales documents or chatting with society, he would read it again.

It was his escape. Like looking through the bars of a prison window, he could see a world where grass grew and life was lived. Then he would fold it back into a square and put it away for another time.

It was what could have been, but now never would be. Perhaps she would have made amends with Trevor and they would have married. Or perhaps, in some other reality where his brother hadn't died, she could have been... *They* could have been.

He swore and turned to walk down a less-traveled street.

He should throw the note into the fire. He'd tried that once, but it was still in his pocket. Those words were committed to memory now, and he would remember each of them until his last day of life.

It did not matter, though. What had been between them would never be again. Today, instead of a relief from the day's torment, the letter only served to remind him of how everything had gone wrong that day on their walk. If he found Trevor's killer, would Roselyn look at him like she had before? Perhaps the past was lost forever, but he had to try, not only for his brother, but for Roselyn as well. She deserved happiness, to move forward with no lingering thoughts of death on a hilltop.

There must be some element he'd missed in Trevor's papers, some involvement with criminals willing to stoop to murder to keep Trevor quiet forever. If only he could lure the culprit into the light. If only…

He stopped in the center of the street. He was going about this business in the wrong manner. *I wasn't the only one there on the hilltop. I wasn't the only witness.*

Roselyn hadn't seen anything, true. By the time she arrived over the crest of the hill, the man had fled. But who knew that small detail besides him? Trevor's murderer wouldn't have taken the time to learn her location. Was he even aware that she had been at Roseberry that day?

When an opponent expects a blow from the right, a left hook will send him to his back. If the murderer somehow learned that Roselyn had witnessed Trevor's death? Boom. Left hook.

He heard footsteps behind him, and he turned. One of the men from the crowd earlier must have tracked him down. He flexed his fingers.

"I have no wish to beat you senseless, but I shall." He'd made a vow to himself long ago that he would only fight for the means to live, not to bash heads in dark alleys. But the mob had threatened Roselyn. That changed the rules.

The man stopped, still too far away for Ethan to see his face.

"If you wanted a fight with me, you should have stepped forward in the salon." Ethan squinted, trying to get a closer look at his opponent through the shadows of the alley. It was odd. The man appeared to be wearing the clothing of a laborer, not someone who would have attended the match. In fact, Ethan would wager he'd never set foot in this section of town before, based on the worn look of his boots and the age of his garments.

Who was he? The two remained on opposite ends of the small stretch of street for a moment, each waiting for the other to move. A carriage rolled through the intersection of the street visible behind the man. Ethan surged forward down the alley as the man dove for the back of the conveyance, grabbing the ledge intended for trunks and holding on. The carriage turned the corner and in an instant was gone.

Ethan stood for a second, waiting for some new surprise. The man had vanished as soon as he'd appeared; what had he wanted? Ethan shook his head and turned back toward headquarters. There were no footsteps at his back the rest of the walk home. He knew the sort of gentleman who haunted Jackson's, and the man in the alley hadn't fit into that category. Perhaps he was closer to piecing together his brother's final days than he realized.

Had Trevor listened for footsteps at his back in the days leading up to his death?

If that man thought to push Ethan into a mine shaft, he needed to reconsider. Ethan wasn't so easily pushed. He grinned but there was no humor behind his thoughts. He would lure the villain out from the shadows, and he would do so at once. He and Roselyn were in this mess together, and it was time Trevor's murderer learned of the second witness to his crime.

# *Ten*

"St. James," Ethan said in an attempt to gain his friend's attention. "St. James. Fallon." He tried the man's given name as he tapped him on the shoulder with the billiard cue in his hand.

St. James looked up, a distant stare on his face. "My turn already?"

"It was your turn five minutes ago before I left to get a drink." Ethan lifted the glass in his hand in salute before taking a sip of the amber liquid.

"Right." St. James took the shot, clanking the balls around on the felt surface.

Whatever was occupying his friend's thoughts today, it wasn't their game of billiards. Ethan winced at the terrible shot that gained not a single point. "Damn."

St. James narrowed his eyes on him across the table.

Ethan continued. "Do you require lessons in billiards? I can send for my little sister, because even she could have made that shot. Or if it's easier, I could go to the park and round up some children and allow them to tutor you in the game."

"I'm quite skilled at billiards, I'll have you know."

"Clearly." Ethan grinned.

"You're an arse."

Ethan took a small gentlemanly bow. If it were any other friend, he would ask what was troubling him, but Ethan knew better when it came to St. James. The man only spoke when he had a purpose for doing so, and his own concerns never ranked high enough to require words. Ethan set his drink aside and leaned forward to line up the balls on the table. "I need the sales ledgers and shipping records from the Bond Street location."

"I thought you might. Your documents from the mining office are only half of the equation," St. James said so casually that he might only be half listening.

"Should I send for Brice?" Ethan asked, motioning for St. James to take his turn. He would go to Bond Street himself if not for word of his inquiries reaching his father if he did so.

"He should be here later this afternoon once he wakes for the day. I'll speak with him about retrieving what you need."

"I can accompany him," Ethan offered, although he hoped he wouldn't be needed.

"He works better alone. You know how he can be when anyone is about."

Ethan grinned at that. Since their school days together, his friend had always been one to chat whenever there was an ear to listen. He couldn't help himself.

Between his need to fill the world with the sound of his rather loud voice and his tendency to wear outlandish colors, Brice made for an interesting choice of heavy. He moved about under the cover of night, a loud flash of color doing the society's dirtiest work. Yet it was a job he seemed to embrace.

Amicable silence fell between Ethan and St. James as they lined up shots and moved around the table. The bump and clank of the balls echoed in the silence of the room. Headquarters were quiet today. Even the newest resident, Ash Claughbane, the so-called *Lord Crosby*, wasn't about. He'd arrived in town after Ethan with some great plan that St. James wanted to keep quiet, something to do with steam. Was that what had his friend distracted today? It didn't seem likely. St. James could always be counted upon to hold not only his own business in his mind, but that of everyone around him. It made him the perfect leader, but for the past few days, something had been troubling him. Ethan had heard mention that a member was back in town after being tossed from the Spare Heirs years ago, but he had no involvement in the matter as of yet. He was certain his friend would handle that issue as he did all others—with cleverness and efficiency.

Ethan had planned to speak to St. James at some length about the next steps in his plan, but perhaps it would be better to handle the first steps without him. Spreading gossip through London didn't seem like a difficult task and the head of the society had much to deal with at the moment.

"If you're trying to stare me down to ruin my play, you needn't bother as you've already noted I'm off my game," St. James said.

"Staring could only improve this travesty of a match. I would accuse you of being deep in your cups by the look of that last shot, if I didn't know better. It might help if you take up drinking. From the looks of this game, it couldn't hurt."

St. James tossed his cue onto the felt surface with a muttered curse and turned away from the table.

"I suppose that's a forfeit," Ethan mused as he leaned on his cue. "That makes pugilism, rowing, and billiards all sports at which I can best you."

"Ah, but I will strip your pockets clean every time when we sit at the card table," St. James called over his shoulder as he walked across the room to his standard table in the corner.

"If that makes you feel better about losing today…" Ethan broke off with a shrug, tossing his cue onto the billiards table.

St. James turned, warning flashing in his dark eyes. "Do you want to try your hand? Right now?"

Ethan threw his hands up in surrender. He was doing that a great deal of late, first with Roselyn at Jackson's and now with St. James.

"Ladies complicate everything," Ethan stated as he fell into the chair opposite Fallon's. "Life is difficult enough without their involvement. They come along and soon our thoughts are on end. Much like the rest of us."

"Is it that obvious?" St. James asked as he ran a hand over his eyes. "I hardly know her. I don't know why her opinions matter. They don't. I manage my affairs in quite the orderly fashion."

"I was referring to a lady with whom I'm having troubles, but perhaps you're sailing the same boat. Do tell."

St. James shot Ethan a lethal glare before settling

back in his seat. "There is nothing wrong with the manner in which I handle my life. Fanciful thoughts and heartfelt smiles are for gentlemen of leisure. I have the Spares to think of."

"You're saying if you didn't have us misfits mucking things up, you would be leisurely and fanciful." Ethan couldn't help the chuckle that escaped his lips.

"That was once the goal of this group. Don't you remember?"

"A leisurely gentleman's life? That was the dream of a few young boys who knew nothing of the world's unfortunate realities." Ethan took a sip of his drink, lost in old memories for a moment.

"I suppose."

"What's this about, St. James?"

He shook his head. "Never mind. It's nothing to be concerned over."

Ethan saw the brief door into his friend's life slam shut as he closed the subject. He smirked as he asked, "Is she another Lady Lydia?"

"I haven't heard that name in ten years."

"She had opinions about your future pursuits as well, if I recall."

"Her idea of future pursuits involved the local parish and something about schoolchildren." St. James shook his head. "My ideas were somewhat different."

"Her ideas involved a wedding as well."

"My ideas on that were *quite* different."

"And this lady isn't interested in the same?" Ethan asked.

"Caring for schoolchildren? I can't imagine many want such a life."

"You know I'm speaking of marriage."

"This lady…" St. James pursed his lips and tapped his fingers on the arm of the chair in thought. The tapping of his fingers slowed and he gave Ethan a shake of his head. Clearly, he was done divulging information.

"This is a different situation," Ethan returned.

"You mentioned difficulties with a lady?"

"Yes. I need to spread news around town about one."

St. James raised a dark brow in question. "They don't like that sort of thing as a general rule."

"It can't be helped. Word needs to return to my brother's killer that there was a witness to his crime. Lady Roselyn Grey."

"And you will keep the lady in question from meeting the same fate your brother found?"

Ethan blinked at the reminder of the danger involved. All would be fine—he would make sure of it. He was only doing what was necessary to find a killer. With such a person on the loose, all of London was in danger. "Keeping an eye on her isn't an issue, if that's what you're asking."

"Are you certain?"

"Of course. I would protect her with my life. Satisfied?" Something flared inside him at the idea that he would allow Roselyn to be injured. "Now, how do I spread talk about her to the furthest reaches of London?"

"I'll have it done by nightfall."

Ethan nodded his thanks and rose from his chair, prepared to leave his friend alone with his muddled thoughts. Moving past the window, he saw a cloaked figure slip into the shadows of the alleyway across the street. He froze. The shape seemed familiar. The same man from the alley yesterday? Or had he imagined it? The price of too many blows to the head over the years?

"What is it?" St. James asked at his back.

"Nothing," Ethan muttered. He'd discussed enough problems today. This one, he could handle alone.

⁓

Roselyn blinked into the concerned faces of her family. "Thank you for informing me." Something that lived in the space between sorrow and rage ticked within her heart, pounding audibly in her ears. She turned away, unable to bear their looks of disappointment on top of her own. Looking out the window offered a moment's escape, but even the leaves on the trees in the front garden seemed to whisper her plight with every gust of wind. *Roselyn is ruined. Ruined.* She tightened her fists until her nails bit half-moon crescents into her palms. This couldn't be happening. All of her plans were destroyed, blown away on that blasted wind.

She crossed the parlor to the fireplace, since the burning heat and curling flames suited her current mood more than a garden view. Trying not to choke on her emotions, she asked, "Is that the tale being told in its entirety?"

"Should there be more?" Devon asked. "Not only are everyone's suspicions confirmed that you were engaged to Ayton, but they also know you were there with him when he died." He ran a hand through his already disheveled hair with a mumbled curse.

Roselyn turned back to the fire. Fire could always

be counted upon to burn. It had a purpose that it cheerfully fulfilled. Why couldn't she simply be a gentleman's wife? She wished to do her duty and marry, and yet she was doused with water at every turn. The *ton* knew she'd been with Trevor that day. *Splash.* She'd been engaged to the man and had witnessed his death. *Splash, splash.*

"The current talk is quite enough to be getting on with, dear," her mother said, cutting through her thoughts.

"They say Trevor and I walked alone that day?"

"They do," Devon practically growled.

"Oh my, I should have come with you that morning. Alone with a gentleman…" Her mother broke off with a shake of her head. "What will Lady Smeltings say? And I cannot even think about Lady Rightworth. We need to contain this scandal before word spreads."

"Mother," Devon warned. "The need for smelling salts would only complicate matters this afternoon. Calm yourself."

The dowager duchess whimpered another "alone" before throwing a hand over her forehead as if ill from all the talk.

"Roselyn, if I could change this news…" Devon broke off at the sight of her upraised hand.

"There is no changing news. It is fact and as such can only be understood." Roselyn tried to offer a polite smile. She wasn't angry with her brother. He'd done her a service, really. Now she knew the obstacles in her path.

There had been no mention of Ethan and no mention of the fight over her honor. Thank God for small mercies. She sighed as she watched the flames lap hungrily at the coals in the grate. Even if everyone thought she'd been a bit too friendly with Trevor, he'd been her intended, and now he was gone. This was, mind you, the better option than the truth of what had taken place on the hillside that day. It would cost her the hope of marriage this season, but it was a scandal she had hope of one day recovering from. It was of small consolation on this dark day, but consolation nonetheless.

"We were so careful," Lily said, joining the conversation. "How did this news spread?"

"Someone from the party must have seen Roselyn leave with Ayton," Devon replied, moving to the decanter and pouring himself a glass. "Although I can't discern how anyone would have known the details of the betrothal. It had yet to be announced."

"Who at the club told you this?" her mother asked as if she might personally take the man to task for his impertinence. "Who spoke of your sister before you?"

"Mother, it was on the lips of every gentleman last night."

"Every…" She pursed her lips in disapproval as her head fell back against the chair once more. "Oh dear."

"Indeed," her brother agreed.

"Devon, tell us exactly what they said. We must know every detail of what we're dealing with."

"I've already done so," he said, bracing a shoulder against the mantel.

Her mother lifted her head, leveling him with a glare. "Tell me once more."

Roselyn could almost hear his eyes roll before he

began. "There was talk of a secret betrothal between Ayton and Roselyn."

"Yes, a secret betrothal," her mother repeated.

"There was speculation over the nature of their relationship," he said, wincing over his words.

"Speculation? That's madness, Devon! Roselyn has always been chaste in these situations, haven't you, dear?"

Roselyn opened her mouth to speak, but said nothing. She and Trevor had never been anything but appropriate. However, her visit to Ethan's room the night before their walk was on the shady border of awful behavior and had caused the quarrel that ended in Trevor's death. But that was far too cumbersome to wrap in a bow and present to her mother.

"This isn't *my* madness," Devon stated, drawing their mother's attention away from Roselyn. "I was simply stating…"

"Go on, go on." Her mother waved a dismissive hand in the air.

Roselyn exhaled a harsh breath. No one need know about Trevor and Ethan's fight that day. She would prove Ethan's guilt. He would rot. And she would carry her other memories to the grave.

"There is speculation, because it is said that they walked alone that day and Roselyn witnessed his passing." Devon looked at her with narrowed eyes as if he believed none of his own words.

Perhaps she'd relaxed a bit too soon. But how could her brother possibly know the thoughts speeding though her mind? He'd always been perceptive, but in this instance, he could keep his sharp eyes and clever thoughts to himself. Roselyn sank into the nearest chair in the parlor. One lapse in judgment in the form of a note to a black-hearted gentleman, and she was going to pay with her future. "I've made such an effort to do everything right," she mumbled mostly to herself.

"You have."

"Why is this happening?" She looked up, meeting her brother's gaze. "I was the one who found a gentleman to marry before the season even began. I courted him through the autumn. Do you know how rainy it was on the moors last September?" She shook her head in despair. "My hair was a sight all autumn from making calls on Katie. It was awful. But I did what needed to be done. I had my entire future planned. And when it fell apart, I moved on. I left Ormesby Place as I was asked to do. I came to London as I was asked to do. I've worn the proper gowns, smiled at the proper gentlemen..." She paused on a small gasping breath. "What more could I do?"

"Roselyn, you aren't to blame for any of this," Lily cut in. "The timing of it all was no help. If there'd been a year for talk to chatter itself quiet..."

"This is why society is a great load of rhinoceros dung," Devon declared as he set his glass on the mantel.

"Devon," her mother complained.

"It is." He shrugged. "We could go back to Thornwood Manor. You'll come with me on my next expedition, Roselyn. Perhaps we can find a nice Yank for you overseas."

Her mother gasped. "She'll do no such thing. We are in London, and in London we shall stay. I did not rise to the station of Dowager Duchess of Thornwood to be chased away by some silly talk in a club."

"It was a topic of discussion in every club in town, or so I'm told, Mother."

Silence filled every corner of the room. What was there to say? She was in the middle of a scandal and there was nothing to be done to change it.

She'd spent years refining herself into a lady. Now every practiced smile, every learned appropriate response was null and void. She'd done everything she could think of to secure her future, only to land in the exact place her former wild ways would have put her—alone and shunned in London. No one would come near her now. She had no hope of marriage this year, but she wouldn't run away either.

"Mama has the right of it, Devon," she finally said. "I can't flee. We already tried that once, remember? And now we are here."

Lily rose to her feet to pace the room. "I can scarcely understand why this news is being spread about now. If the events of Ormesby Place were going to come to light, they would have done so a month ago. I was even prepared for it the night of the first ball, but now…" She paused her pacing in the center of the room. Her head tilted to the side in sorrow. "Oh, Roselyn."

"Why now indeed," Roselyn said. She had a good idea. Ethan had been pleased to prance about London with his new title, pleased at her failed attempt at marriage, so why not be pleased at her failed season? One thing was certain. He would have a second blackened eye when she next saw him.

"Roselyn, did you tell us the full story of what happened that day?" Devon asked, making her snap her head up and causing a sharp pain in her neck.

"Of course," she said a bit too quickly as she rubbed the side of her neck. "Trevor was injured, fell into an air shaft, and was killed while on our walk. There's nothing more to tell."

Devon's eyes narrowed on her until she looked away. "Clearly," he replied.

She turned to her mother. "What am I to do now? I scarcely know where I stand. Do I ready myself to attend tonight's ball?"

"You must, dear. Put on a strong face and your loveliest gown."

"There will be whispers. What if no one desires a dance? I'll have to return home unmarried at the end of the season. All of my hard work, and my first season is a failure."

"You haven't failed yet, dear. And if this season is not to be, it isn't the end of your life. You'll return to London next year."

"Next year. Another year of my life wasted? After coming this far?" Roselyn shook her head.

"Then I suppose we need to look our best for the ball this evening."

❧

"Would you care to dance?" Ethan extended his arm and waited.

Roselyn didn't move. She looked like a portrait this evening—poised, still, untouchable—and he couldn't pull his gaze away from the sight of her. She was the image of beauty every gentleman longed to have at his side. Yet she stood alone. To the casual observer she appeared to possess a hint of a smile and a pleasant look in her eye, but he knew the sorrow that lay behind her elegant exterior. Her eyes didn't sparkle now as they did when she was happy. He wanted to make the portrait move, to make her smile. He needed to see her eyes shine once more…very well, twice more, if not every damn day for the rest of time.

"A dance." Her gaze stayed warily fixed on his extended arm as if it might harm her if she so much as flinched. "With you?"

"As opposed to the long queue of gentlemen to my right?" He stepped to the side to make way for the nonexistent gentlemen, gesturing for an invisible man to pass with a small wave of his arm.

Clearly this wasn't going to be as simple as leading her onto the floor and turning about a bit. Who knew? Other gentlemen made the process appear so effortless.

"My lack of a dance partner is entirely your fault."

"Is it? Because I'm fairly certain I just asked you to dance."

"You are one gentleman."

"I am." What the devil was she going on about? He narrowed his eyes on her. He'd expected her to be upset over her name being tossed about, but what did that have to do with dancing? "Are you feeling well this evening?"

"Of course I'm well," she said loud enough to turn heads in their direction. She passed a smile about as if doling out sweets to children before turning back to him and lowering her voice. "No thanks to you. I would have a queue of gentlemen, you know, quite the queue."

"I can see why. You look lovely this evening."

"Flattery will get you nowhere, my lord. You were responsible for telling everyone I was with Trevor when he passed, were you not?"

There didn't seem to be a correct answer in his mind. He paused for a moment before deciding on the safest reply he could think of. "I'm sorry you're distressed this evening. Perhaps I can make amends."

"There's no way to redeem my reputation now."

"Your reputation. That's what has you at odds?" Thoughts of her reputation being harmed with his words hadn't crossed his mind. The only outcome he'd considered was the one that led to Trevor's killer's capture. He'd only seen the need to keep her safe from a murder, not to protect her reputation. He *had* been away from society too long.

"I was alone with a man. I dare not think what would happen if the truth came to light, what's being said is damaging enough," she whispered. Her eyes were wide as she pleaded for him to understand.

Unfortunately, she spoke in the foreign language of societal rules. That was a language he hadn't spoken since he was a boy, and even then it hadn't been a priority in his upbringing. His family was unusual with their thoughts on such things—a fact he was cursing tonight. "You were betrothed to him. I suppose that's not allowed…"

She shook her head, whether as a way of saying no or a way of expressing her disbelief, he didn't know.

"A dance seems to be the least I can do under the circumstances, princess."

"Stop calling me that. Dances don't unmake the past." Her words were strong, but something seemed to soften in her eyes that gave him hope.

"They don't. But it's more pleasurable than blackening my eye."

"That's debatable." The corner of her mouth tipped up, almost approaching a smile yet not quite reaching its goal before she contained it.

"You outshine the other ladies this evening. It would be a crime not to dance on such a night." He only wanted to please her, but had he gone too far with his compliment? He waited.

"Thank you," she finally said, looking down to run her fingers over the fabric. "It's my favorite gown."

"I prefer the breeches on you, but if you like frills and such…" He broke off with a shrug.

She looked up, cocking her head to the side as she considered him. "Sometimes I forget you're Katie's brother. And then you say things like that."

"Have you heard from her?" he asked, offering her his arm again in an attempt to lead her to the floor.

"From Katie? Of course I have. We write quite often." She laid a hand on his arm in resignation over their dance. "But she's your sister. You haven't heard from her?"

"No. I haven't had correspondence from home since my arrival in London."

"Your family is grieving," she stated, stopping their progress to the dance floor, her brows drawing together in accusation. "How nice it must be for you not to be encumbered by such a sad state as that."

"I'm grieving as well." He gave up on taking her to a nice area of open floor and turned toward her where they stood.

Her eyes raked over him in disapproval as she took his hand for the waltz. "Wearing black to a ball isn't grieving."

"But wearing black underthings to a ball is?"

"I'm dealing with this situation in my own way."

"As am I," he said, stepping in the same manner the other couples appeared to be moving.

"By destroying my reputation?"

"What exactly have you heard?" he hedged. He was no doubt responsible, but the less he had to confess, the better.

"Enough to know you told someone I was there with your brother when he died—and that we were alone." Her eyes flared in accusation.

This was not how he'd envisioned his first attempt at a waltz. It involved a great deal more arguing than he'd planned upon, not to mention the steps he was feigning knowledge of—both of which left him feeling a bit off.

He held no regrets though, only the soft form of Roselyn in his arms until the music ended. She could rail at him all she liked as long as he could inhale her faint scent of flowers and hold her close. Even arguing with her was time spent in her company. Life as a pugilist did make one learn to enjoy the day in spite of a few blows, and he would savor the next few minutes in the same way.

"He was correct," Ethan mused as they narrowly avoided colliding with another couple. "Word does spread quickly in town."

"I don't give a care who was correct. I only care that now everyone in town believes I was alone with Trevor. That he and I were…close."

"You were close. You were engaged." Ethan shook his head as he looked down at her, not understanding her meaning. Was she saying what he thought she was saying, or was that simply where his mind traveled after too many years spent in Spanish taverns?

"We weren't *close* when he passed. And now every-one believes we were. Ouch!" She stifled a cry as he stepped on her toe.

"Apologies, I was distracted."

She glowered at him. "Any future I might have found is now gone because of you. People think that I…that he and I…"

Indeed, they were speaking on the same subject, and he couldn't have been more interested in what she had to say on the matter. "You and Trevor may not have been caught in a passionate moment when he died, but—"

"How could you mention such a thing?" she asked, looking around to see if anyone had heard him.

"You're the one discussing it in the middle of a dance floor." He took a step in the wrong direction and trod on her toe again. "Apologies again," he mut-tered, anxious to return to the subject at hand. "I was only going to ask…"

"You're as good a dancer as you are a gentleman." She scowled.

"I am trying," he said, leading her to the side of the room where he could no longer injure her toes.

"Try harder, my lord. My life was planned before

I met you. I had everything sorted out. Now no one will come near me. My reputation is tattered and bruised, much like one of your opponents in fisticuffs. And you are to blame. You're to blame for all of it. And here you are, parading around like the world is made of sunshine."

Made of sunshine? "The world is made of battles yet to be fought and villains yet to be unearthed," he corrected.

"Am I your opponent in battle then? Because I certainly have the scars."

He had to explain, to make her understand that he'd never meant to hurt her. She already thought the worst of him; he couldn't bear her being angry about more on top of that. He always rushed into situations without thought. That's what his father had claimed through most of his life anyway. His reckless nature had led to the severed ties with his family years ago, and now it had led him here. He fought to find the right words. "I didn't think about how your being alone with a dead man would hurt your reputation."

"Being alone with any man, dead or alive, is a crime for a lady."

"You've been alone with me," he countered, thinking of the night she'd come to his bedchamber.

"Something I regret every day."

"Really." It wasn't a question, but a dawning realization that sank like a knife to his heart. "You'll excuse me if I don't feel the same."

"No, I won't excuse you." She tilted her chin up as if leading the charge into battle. "Everything about you is wrong, from your cold heart to your crooked nose."

"I suppose I'm wrong to enjoy the fact that due to my blunder, I'm the only one to dance with you tonight." His words were perhaps a bit too honest, but damn if they weren't true. He guided her further toward the wall so a couple could pass, his hand lingering on her elbow.

"It's beyond a silly dance. Your careless words have cost me my ability to gain a husband."

He took a small step toward her, his hand still on her elbow as if anchoring her to him in the storm that raged around them. And that was when he realized the truth. She was upset over the demise of her plans. She'd raged at him through the entirety of their dance, her only dance, because he'd destroyed her life's schedule. It was the sort of thing Trevor would have been angry about. There was no saving Trevor now, no helping him to enjoy life and find happiness. However, Roselyn could be helped. And she was, above all else, his lifelong friend.

He studied her a moment before beginning. "When I was a child, my father tried to teach me about the jet mining business. There were documents with numbers and words, but I never saw any of them, not truly at any rate. I only saw the stack of papers that kept him from living his life. He buried himself behind a wall of reports, taking no notice at all of his family. I always found my way outside the walls of my home, to you, but he never once tried to set aside his work to live."

"What does that have to do with your careless words?"

"You bury yourself behind plans and expectations. It's only when you dress as another and sneak about town that I even see a glimmer of the wild girl I knew as a child. Forget what society thinks of you. When was the last time you stepped out of your door as Lady Roselyn Grey and lived? You chose not to enjoy that dance, Roselyn. But I enjoyed it for both of us. When was the last time you reveled in the uncertain promise of today?" He shook his head, allowing his hand to drift down her arm to her wrist. "What happened to the girl who used to run free across the moors, the lady in the drive at Ormesby Place with mud covering her hands? I wish she would come back to me."

She flinched at his words but said nothing. A second later she spun on her heel and marched away.

Apparently, *that* was what it took to overstep one's bounds. He frowned and shook his head, taking a moment to watch her leave before he entered the fray once more. He caught up with her halfway across the room, forcing her to walk the remainder of the way at his side. She was silent even through his attempts to gain her attention. Out of a large room filled with ladies willing to dance, why did he only want to dance with the one who hated him?

He delivered her to the fringes of her group, notably smaller this evening than at the last event. A hum of conversation seemed to be moving around the room. Stepping closer, he tried to pick up the topic of the chatter this evening, hoping it wasn't more talk of Roselyn's reputation. If it was, he'd never get back into her good graces. He'd wanted to catch a killer, not drive Roselyn away from him.

"Emerged from the flames in the arms of a gentleman," he heard one lady say.

Flames? This certainly wasn't about Roselyn, but he listened anyway.

"I heard her dress melted from her limbs."

"Dresses don't melt."

"Might I ask what you're speaking of?" Ethan cut in.

"Haven't you heard of the fire? Terrible business."

"What fire?" he asked.

"On Bond Street. Apparently, the Fairlyn girl was injured."

"Which one?" Roselyn asked as she stepped forward, her eyes growing wide with concern.

"Is there more than one?"

"Of course there is," Roselyn retorted.

"Twins," Ethan added for clarity. He'd seen Roselyn with them at the last ball.

"Perverse bit of nature, twins, if you'd like my opinion."

"I don't want your opinion," Roselyn snapped.

"Well, I never," the lady said.

One of Roselyn's other friends stepped between them before they could come to blows. "I'll take it from here, if you please, Mother. Roselyn, it's Victoria. She barely escaped death while on an errand to the milliner. Thank heavens for Mr. Brice. She owes him her life."

"Mr. Brice?" Ethan asked, already wincing at what was to come.

"Yes, he saved her life. Carried her from the building. He's being touted as quite a hero."

"Where on Bond Street was this fire?" he asked, somehow already knowing the answer.

"At that new milliner's shop everyone is so fond of, the one next to the jewelers with all the jet pieces in the window," Lady Evangeline replied.

"Will you excuse me? There's something I must see to." Ethan didn't wait for a response. He was already moving toward the door. All he'd asked of the Spares was assistance with retrieving a file from the store. He could have even done the job himself during business hours, if not for the risk of his father learning of his investigation. It was his family's shop, and Brice had thought it wise to burn the place to the ground?

With a backward glance, he saw the curious look in Roselyn's eyes but she didn't follow him. As long as she remained with her friends and family, she would be safe from harm. He didn't like leaving her, but what choice had Brice left him? His friend might not have died in the fire today, but his life would certainly be in danger once Ethan found him.

# Eleven

THE SHELL OF THE FORMER MILLINER'S STOOD BEFORE them, still smoldering from yesterday's flames. Bits of singed feathers and charred ribbon littered Bond Street. Roselyn caught a piece of yellow ribbon floating on the breeze and inspected it in the palm of her hand. It was hard to fathom this had once graced the top of a hat, perfect, complete, ready to be sold. Now it was reduced to the shred she held in her hand. How had such a rapid blaze occurred to cause this amount of destruction?

She glanced up, her eyes sweeping across the row of shops. Habersham's Antiquities didn't seem to have sustained any damage, but the jeweler on the other side of the milliner's couldn't claim such good fortune. The front window was broken and men milled about inside, surveying the damage and overseeing repairs.

Roselyn narrowed her eyes on the men. Ethan.

Imagine that. Lord Destruction-and-Death was standing amid the wreckage, seemingly unaffected by the damage done. Perhaps it was unreasonable to assume his guilt in the blaze, but reason didn't matter when it came to Ethan. In any matter of misfortune in the past months, he'd been to blame—and he was to blame now. *She* had no doubt of his involvement. Victoria had been caught in that blaze, and word had not yet been spread of the milliner's health.

First her fiancé and now her friend, both only guilty of standing in the way of an arrogant gentleman getting what he desired. Was there no end to his malicious behavior? Anger wrapped around her as she looked through the haze of ash and debris at the man surely responsible for this travesty.

However, a thought tickled the edge of her mind, demanding explanation. What was he after? He could barely be counted on to wear a cravat, let alone jewelry. What need would he have of jewels?

"Have you spoken with Victoria?" Lily asked at her side, pulling her thoughts from the scene inside the burned shop.

"She isn't receiving guests." It wasn't surprising at all; Isabelle had mentioned that her twin had been forced to cut her singed hair quite short. It was a wonder that was the only damage done, but losing one's hair was devastating in and of itself.

"It's hard to believe she wasn't burned worse." Lily breathed out, leaning around a group of gentlemen for a better view of the wreckage.

"I don't believe fire would dare harm a lady like Victoria. She no doubt found a means of out-burning it."

Lily chuckled. "Indeed. And, I'm sure the flames learned a few new words yesterday—along with anyone else within earshot."

"It was good that Mr. Brice was about," Roselyn said, pulling Lily to the side so that a carriage could pass through the crowded street. Since the fire had occurred late in the day yesterday, many people were only now coming to see the terrible sight. And what a terrible sight it was. Roselyn shook her head. "Even Victoria would burn if left within that building a moment longer."

"He played quite the hero in yesterday's events. It's odd that he isn't about today," Lily mused. "One would think he'd be enjoying his fame. Invitations must be pouring into the Dillsworth residence today."

"I'm not sure that he enjoys being in the center of things. When we met, I found him avoiding his own father's ball by chatting up the footmen. There's something about that man that doesn't equal his parts."

"I suppose I miscalculated him." Lily paused. "Roselyn, is that Lord Ayton amid the ashes?"

Roselyn only grumbled in response. A moment ticked past before she asked, "Do you know anything of the shops affected by the blaze?"

"I have some experience with Mr. Habersham and his antiquities, as it happens."

"And the jewelry shop?" Roselyn pressed.

Lily turned to her, confusion drawing her thin blond brows together. "Lord Ayton's family produces jet, does it not? I believe that store is known for having a nice selection of jet pieces."

"Jet…the mines! That's it! It was about the mines. I only happened to be about. All this time I thought…"

"What are you talking about?"

"The connection between the fire and Lord Ayton."

He'd killed Trevor at the mouth of the mine. There must be some evidence inside that shop, evidence he wanted destroyed. She saw Ethan slip a black, rectangular velvet box into his pocket and move toward the rear of the shop. "We must follow him. Apologies, Lily, but you need to either come with me or look the other way and later tell Mother you lost me in a shop."

"I believe I would rather follow you into yesterday's inferno than tell your mother I lost you."

"Come on then. He's getting away."

"Wait. I have another idea," Lily said, tugging on Roselyn's arm to make her stay.

"Wait? Lily, I must follow him! I need information."

"Yes, and we'll find all we need to know by questioning the shopkeeper."

"The shopkeeper," Roselyn repeated. What was Lily talking about? The jeweler wouldn't know anything of import. She needed to follow Ethan, discover what he'd stashed away in his pocket.

"I happen to have some experience in this. You would be amazed at the wealth of knowledge shopkeepers hold." There was confidence in Lily's movements as they crossed the street like officers marching into battle.

"Lily, sometimes I believe *I've* miscalculated *you*," Roselyn said, linking arms with her sister-in-law.

"It's actually an amusing story. I'll have to share it with you one day. Today, however, we have a jewelry clerk to question." She touched her hand to her hair to ensure it was still in place. "A shame there's nothing left here to steal. That worked quite well for me in similar circumstances."

"I appreciate your enthusiasm for this mission, but I'm fairly certain Lord Ayton is the one doing the stealing today."

"We shall find out. If there's one thing shopkeepers can be counted upon to do, it is to chat up the highborn who visit their shop. If he took something, we'll soon know the story."

Roselyn was more confident of her spy capabilities than ever. Perhaps it was the familiar Bond Street setting or the thrill of placing two clues together to discover the link to the mines, but she knew today would be successful. She stepped into the jewelry shop, Lily at her side. Today she would prove Ethan's guilt, and that would begin with this shopkeeper.

"Excuse me, sir," Roselyn called out. "Could you tell me when your shop will open again? Such a terrible event. This is your shop, isn't it?"

"I oversee things for the owner," the man hedged, eyeing them as they strolled through the ruins of display tables.

"The poor owner. Not to diminish your losses, but to have your business burn…" Roselyn sidestepped a swept-up pile of broken glass as she neared the man. "Who does own this shop? I'd like to offer my sympathies. I'm Roselyn Grey, by the way, and this is my sister-in-law, the Duchess of Thornwood. So rude of me not to offer introductions sooner. And you are?"

"Sharpe, Your Grace, my lady," he offered with a bow, looking quite pleased to have them in his shop. "I can see if there are clean chairs in the storeroom, though I'm doubtful."

"And the owner of the shop?" Roselyn prodded,

ignoring the man's frantic glances around in search of better offerings for two ladies of their station.

"The owner of the shop is remaining quiet in this fire business. Nobility in trade and all," he explained in a low voice.

"I see. Well, it is too bad," Roselyn said with a large sigh. "We came here today unaware of the fire. We wanted to purchase a few pieces of jet jewelry."

"More than a few," Lily corrected at her side. "There's no need for modesty about such things."

"It is the latest fashion," Roselyn added, hoping they sounded genuine enough for the man to take the bait and give them more information.

"Oh." Then a bright gleam came into his eyes and he stepped forward, glancing around to see if anyone was about to hear him. "I shouldn't mention it, but there is a place you can go for such wares down by the harbor. There was a shipment of jet that left here only yesterday. You didn't hear this from me, of course, but there's a warehouse by the docks that might be of use to you. If you were to go there in about an hour…"

"A warehouse at the harbor?" Lily drew back in dismay that would have seemed quite real if Roselyn hadn't known their ruse. "I'm quite particular about the jewelry I'm seen wearing. No paste will do, you know."

"The stones are of the highest quality," Sharpe assured her. "You'll see when you visit the warehouse. They're from mines in the north," he whispered as he pulled a small calling card from his pocket and held it out to them.

"Are they? From Ormesby lands?" Roselyn asked

with a smile, taking the card from Sharpe before Lily could move. Then the Moore family did own this shop. It made sense that they wouldn't mention such a thing in public since being connected to trade would certainly be frowned upon, as Mr. Sharpe himself had mentioned. "That would explain why we saw Lord Ayton here only a moment ago. Do you know where he was off to in such a hurry?" She looked down at the card, seeing only an address printed there with no name. How odd. Then again, this entire interview had been odd.

"I apologize, but Lord Ayton didn't inform me of his plans."

"It's just as well. Thank you for your assistance, Mr. Sharpe." Roselyn shot a glance at Lily, indicating it was time for them to leave.

Sharpe nodded and returned to his work with a smile as they made their way out of the shop. She'd walked inside hoping for information about Ethan, but she left with only more questions. The only thing she knew was that Ethan was somehow involved with the fire—he simply had to be. And something with the business of the jewelry shop was a bit off.

She seemed further from discovering the truth behind Trevor's death than ever. Yet, she didn't think it had been an accident that his death occurred at the mines. She glanced around her at the broken display cases and pieces of jet jewelry scattered around amid debris from the fire and glass from the front window. Everything seemed to be linked together in one confusing chain of events—Trevor's death, Ethan's appearance in London, the fire. And at the center of it were the jet mines.

"Lily?" Roselyn mused as they stepped out onto the street. "Do you find it odd that a shop would send merchandise to a warehouse at the harbor instead of selling it?"

"I do."

"Have you ever wanted to visit a warehouse near the London harbor?" Roselyn asked, her eyes on the small card the shop owner had given her.

"I can't think of any other place I'd rather go on this fine afternoon than a dirty warehouse," Lily replied with a smile, linking her arm through Roselyn's.

"You really have spent too much time in my brother's company if you can say that without laughing," Roselyn replied, already pulling her sister-in-law down the street toward the harbor.

∽

"Was burning the place to the ground really necessary?" Ethan asked.

Brice shrugged. "Things got a bit out of hand when the Fairlyn girl arrived."

"Do you think so? Thanks to you, there's ash covering half of Bond Street!"

"I was only trying to defend myself. She was throwing hats."

"She threw a hat," Ethan repeated. "Have you ever known a bonnet to kill someone? Look at yourself. You're claiming that fire was due to a woman tossing a hat at you?"

"It was more than one hat," Brice mumbled.

Ethan glared at him for a moment before turning away. "Did you even manage to retrieve the papers you went to find?"

Brice shoved a journal filled with numbers at Ethan. "Of course I did. I succeeded in my mission. There was just a bit of…"

"Fire?"

"I was going to say 'trouble with my escape.'"

Ethan took the journal, folded it, and shoved it into his pocket. "Mind telling me why we're meeting in the foulest-smelling alley in London instead of at headquarters?"

"There was a man sifting through the rubble at daybreak this morning. I followed him here." Brice nodded toward the old stone building across the street.

"Working early this morning?"

"What's morning to some is early evening to others."

Ethan shook his head, knowing the odd hours his friend kept. Brice always had preferred night to day, which fit both his social life and his work with the Spares. "You think the man you followed is involved?"

Brice raised a golden brow and nodded toward the building across the street.

Following his gaze, Ethan looked at the stone warehouse tucked beside a large wooden structure that bordered the water. It was small compared to others used for freight storage. He squinted his eyes to read the small sign beside the door. *W. B. Exports—Fine Jewelry.* He turned to Brice with a questioning glance. "What of it?"

"A shipment of jet left here only a few hours ago.

Saw it stamped on the side of a crate. Does your family own the only mine about?"

"Ours is the only one that I know of."

"Then I suppose this is more than just competition. Rough business, mining."

"Some might say cutthroat," Ethan stated with a hollow voice. Was this why Trevor had been killed? Did some knowledge of W. B. Exports end his brother's life?

His hands curled into fists with the longing to hit someone. He was close to the truth. He could sense it on the pungent air. He turned to stare at the building, looking for any sign of movement. The window appeared to look into an office; on the left he could see a large opening in the wall made for loading and unloading crates. He needed a closer look. He would never find answers while hiding in shadows across the street. He took a step into the street, only to have Brice pull him back by the neck of his coat.

"What was that for?"

Brice held a finger to his lips and shook his head.

Ethan glanced around but saw nothing of note. However, the man's instincts proved to be correct.

Chatter echoed off the brick wall beside him. Feminine chatter? Ethan peered around the corner, wondering what girl in her right mind would come to a place filled with warehouses and the stench of rubbish. Its only point of pride was proximity to the harbor, and given the type of men who lingered around the London harbor, those bragging rights weren't much to speak of.

Then he heard something that made his pulse quicken even as his breathing stopped—Roselyn's laughter.

"What the devil?"

"Were you followed?" Brice asked, as he pulled Ethan back toward the brick wall.

"No. I checked, just as you taught me to do."

"Then what is your lady doing here?"

"She isn't my lady."

"What brought her here if she didn't follow you?"

"You think I know?" Ethan asked, still staring at Roselyn and trying to understand her intentions. If she was taking his advice from last night to throw off her plans and live, this was certainly an odd place to begin. But he knew her presence here wasn't arbitrary. It had to do with him. He just didn't know how. "This is the second time I've found her someplace unexpected," he mused.

"Ladies don't go out of their way to unexpected places like this one unless they have a reason to do so."

"It isn't what you think. She hates me. Blames me for ruining her life."

Brice gave a low whistle that almost pulled Roselyn's attention their way. "I suppose ladies can simply be difficult, whether following us without us realizing or throwing hats."

Ethan turned and glared at his friend. "If you're angling for an apology for berating you, you'll have to do better than that. You burned Bond Street."

Brice grumbled at his side before murmuring, "It's a great loss for you, I know. Your fondness of shopping is legendary."

"What?" Ethan glanced at Brice to see he was

grinning. Looking down, he ran a hand over his current ensemble. It was serviceable and black. What more was necessary? He shoved Brice in the shoulder, whispering. "At least I don't sneak about London on secret missions dressed in clothes that could turn the head of a blind man."

"I like to look nice. It's for the ladies," Brice returned.

"The ones with or without hats?"

Just then the chattering became louder as the ladies neared the corner where Brice and Ethan hid. "Roselyn," he breathed.

"Perhaps I'm not the only one with lady troubles," Brice teased. "Beware her hat. They look soft but the ones with the flowers can open your flesh."

Ethan watched Roselyn walk past with the Duchess of Thornwood as if out for a stroll in the countryside. She motioned to the sign on the side of the building and her sister-in-law smiled in return, but they didn't stop. Roselyn's eyes cut to the side, searching the area, while she kept up a steady conversation about shoes. If she was looking for him, she'd missed her mark already. Ethan let her go. It would do no good to step out of the shadows to confront her now.

He was so focused on watching her movements as she walked down the street that he'd missed the two men slipping around the side of the warehouse. He tensed, preparing for a fight, but the men weren't walking in his direction. They were trailing after Roselyn.

"Remain here and watch for activity," Ethan said, his hand grazing the brick as he plowed forward from the shadowed side street.

He was rounding the corner and out of earshot before Brice had a chance to reply. Knots seemed to tie his stomach together as he watched the men gain ground on the ladies' more leisurely pace. He wanted to shout a warning to run, but there was no need. He would catch them. Roselyn was safe as long as he was here. Maybe this would be good. He would pound answers from the men in pursuit of Roselyn, and they would lead him closer to Trevor's killer. He only needed to gain a bit more ground without raising the alarm.

The gap between them closed. The ladies rounded a bend toward the outskirts of the bustle of harbor business. More people. More witnesses. Ethan wasn't sure whether that was of benefit or not, but he followed anyway.

Close enough now to see the men more clearly, he took note of their clothes, their gaits. They bore the look of common laborers, and if not for their menacing pursuit of the ladies, he would believe their cover. "Ruffians, most likely," he mumbled to himself as he neared them. He didn't recognize either of them from the hilltop that fateful day. Still, there was something familiar about the shorter one. Where had he seen the man before?

The ladies rounded a corner and caught sight of their pursuers for the first time. He heard Roselyn's gasp even from this distance. The taller of the two men increased his pace, preparing to attack.

Ethan moved forward with the speed he was known for, lunging for the man at Roselyn's back. He brought the tall man to the ground, but the other—a wide man with meaty, lumbering movements—sped up.

Ethan struck the man beneath him in the jaw, knocking his head to the side. He needed to down this man for the foreseeable future to get to Roselyn in time. He hit the man again, desperate for him to stay down.

He glanced up to see that the ladies had stopped and turned to confront the shorter man. "Don't stop. Run!" Ethan yelled as the tall man's fist met Ethan's cheekbone with a shock of blinding pain.

He pounded the man again. Blinking away the stars in his vision, he looked up from his current opponent to find the ladies. Would wonders never cease? Roselyn and the duchess were now beating the shorter man about the ears with their reticules.

Roselyn took great hacks at the man's head as if using an ax on a tree, while the duchess was busy rapping every piece of exposed skin with the fan she carried. Together they made a formidable opponent.

He almost grinned, but in between blows the now-injured shorter man made grasping motions toward them. No one was allowed to touch Roselyn in that manner. Anger flared inside him, his fist connecting with the tall man's jaw once more. Why wouldn't he stay down? Of all the days to have a worthy opponent in a fight, this was not the ideal time.

Ethan lifted him from the ground by his shirt to pummel him again, determination making his hits more powerful than before. When the man made no further move to retaliate, Ethan slung the limp body into the gutter and moved forward. He had to reach

Roselyn before the other man could gain the upper hand in their fight. But, just then, someone stepped out into the street between him and his quarry.

"Unhand her," the man said in a dangerous tone.

Ethan pushed the newcomer aside and swung at the shorter man. With force backed by anger, he drove his fist into the man's face. He staggered back a step before Ethan reached for him. Ethan pulled him within range of his hits, knocking him to the ground with a mighty blow. The sound echoed off the surrounding buildings as he watched the man to ensure he posed no more threat. Even though the scoundrel had a bloodied face, Ethan knew he'd seen this man before, but where? He shook off the thought.

He turned to see Roselyn and the duchess's shocked faces and curious glances from onlookers, and finally looked around to see who had interrupted his fight.

He drew back, not expecting to see the Duke of Thornwood in such a place. Of course, his wife and sister were in the same situation, but they were here because of him. Weren't they? Or was this some sort of bizarre family gathering?

"What are you doing here?" Ethan asked Roselyn.

"Your presence is rather suspect as well, my lord," Roselyn retorted. "So I will ask the same of you."

Thornwood stepped forward, staring at his wife and sister. "What the devil are you doing here? Don't you know the part of town you're in?"

"I do." The duchess eyed the tavern from which Thornwood had walked only minutes ago. "What are *you* doing here?"

"I asked you first."

"Actually, I believe I asked first, Your Grace." Ethan glared at Roselyn.

"I owe you no explanations, Lord Ayton," Roselyn replied with as much dignity as one could muster after beating a ruffian with a reticule.

"But you do owe *me* one," Thornwood cut in.

The duchess only eyed her husband, revealing nothing.

Thornwood sighed. "Interviewing a man for the position of captain of the latest ship added to my fleet."

"At a tavern?" his wife asked.

"Jealous? I know how you enjoy the occasional rum punch."

"I... Perhaps." The duchess smiled.

"This is a lovely chat for afternoon tea, but if you'll excuse me, I must be leaving." Ethan bowed and turned back to where he'd left the nearest man on the ground.

Somehow, in the brief moments he'd looked away, the man had disappeared. Ethan whirled, searching the street. He'd been sure the man was unconscious when he turned his back. It wasn't a blunder Ethan made often, if ever. Mistakes like that never ended well. He looked up the street to see the two men running in the opposite direction. "Damn." Even with his speed, he couldn't catch them. That was when he remembered the man's identity—Trevor's visitor the day before his death. And now he was out of reach. Ethan sighed.

At least he'd protected Roselyn from harm. That was the important part.

"Lord Ayton, what business do you have in the area to bring you so far afield of your home?" Roselyn asked at his back.

"Boxing practice, it would seem." That wouldn't satisfy her; she wanted to know more. He wanted the same. Unfortunately, information was the one thing around here that seemed in short supply.

"You're bleeding," Roselyn exclaimed, taking a step forward.

"Am I?" He reached up to his head and dabbed at the moisture gathered there at his hairline.

"Yes, quite profusely."

"At least you're safe."

"You came from nowhere to assist us, and now you're wounded." She began digging in her reticule in search of something to stem the bleeding, but he produced a handkerchief first. "It's black," she said as he pressed the square of fabric to his forehead.

"Black doesn't stain with blood."

"Is that the true reason for your fondness of the color?" she asked.

"No." He chuckled. "It's rather convenient at the moment though, wouldn't you agree?"

She looked up at him with warmth instead of disdain, clearly overcome with relief for her safety after being attacked. "Agree with you on a subject? The skies might fall."

"We wouldn't want that, not with all of us standing in the middle of the street." He grinned at her, wishing things could remain this way between them if only for a few minutes. Her looking at him with concern in her eyes instead of anger. Him speaking without saying all the wrong things. It was a much-appreciated break from their usual encounters—in spite of his bleeding head. He should save her from ruffians more often.

"Does it hurt terribly?"

"When the sky falls? I wouldn't know."

"Why are you going on so? Your head wound must be worse than I thought. This is my fault. You wouldn't be injured if not for me." There was a tenderness in her gaze that he hadn't seen there in a month.

"It isn't your fault. You were attacked. I couldn't allow those men to hurt you."

"No, I suppose not. It's only... Thank you." She looked at him for a long moment with confusion drawing her brows together before turning away from him to gain her brother's attention. "Devon, he requires a doctor. Where is your carriage?"

"Where is yours?" Thornwood asked.

"Bond Street," the duchess replied.

"How did you get here? Never mind, I don't want to know the answer."

"I don't need a doctor," Ethan stated, cutting into their family squabble.

"Yes, you do," Roselyn insisted. "You're bleeding, your mind is addled, and you aren't acting yourself at all."

"I'm the same as I've always been, and my mind is as clear as ever."

"No, you're acting quite different—heroic even. It's the head wound," she explained and turned back to her brother. "Devon, make him listen to reason."

"Roselyn, I believe he'll live. Leave the poor gentleman be."

"Poor gentleman," she repeated, clearly doubting the description. Roselyn looked back at Ethan, concern warring with wariness in her eyes. The moment hung between them, while he silently hoped the concern would win. He would take her worry over him rather than anger any day.

"I've been wounded much worse than this on occasion, princess," he finally said in an effort to reassure her.

Roselyn only nodded as a blush crept over her face. Was she ashamed she'd admitted her fear for him in front of her brother and his wife, or ashamed she'd been concerned for his well-being for even a moment? Either way, he'd never enjoyed a head wound so much in his life.

"I appreciate your assistance, Ayton," Thornwood said, pulling Ethan's thoughts away from Roselyn for a moment.

He shrugged. "I was in the area."

"Yes, it's curious that you, my wife, and my sister were in the same area today, given the area in question."

"Curious circumstances keep life interesting at times," the duchess replied, wrapping a fortifying arm around Roselyn.

"Ayton, let us be clear. Where my sister is concerned, curiosity killed the cat and then I killed curiosity many times over…with great pleasure."

"Devon Grey," his wife hissed at him, before turning a polite smile on Ethan. "I think we should return home for tea now. Will you excuse us?"

Ethan didn't answer, only looked at Roselyn. Some of her hair had slipped from the confines of her elaborate braids and trailed down her neck in tantalizing curls. She was safe. Now he only needed to keep her that way. Next time, he would simply have to be closer to her, ready to strike. With any luck, he would bleed again and Roselyn would look at him as if she cared about him once more.

# Twelve

ROSELYN HELPED HERSELF TO A SMALL TEA CAKE FROM the platter on the table in the middle of their gathering in the parlor. She sat back next to Victoria, who fidgeted with the ends of her short hair. Clearly she wasn't used to the new style even after a few days of wear. Some called it a shame that her hair had been singed in the fire, but Roselyn thought her new fashion rather becoming. It managed to convey Victoria at a glance: no level of fussiness and an air of rebellion.

Roselyn smiled and took a bite of her cake. At least one good thing had come from the fire.

"I see Isabelle isn't with you today," her mother said from the other end of the settee, causing Roselyn to suck in a quick breath. Leave it to her mother to point out the elephant in the parlor.

"No. She was otherwise engaged," Victoria stated, dropping her hand to her lap.

"Oh? It is a busy time with the season in full force."

"It is. However, Isabelle was too busy not speaking to me to attend. I'm sure it's nothing against the company you provide." The twins were never apart, never until the fire and its aftermath. Now, as Roselyn had heard it, the two were barely speaking. She couldn't blame Isabelle; she was heartbroken, after all. She'd held a great love for Mr. Brice, and now, quite suddenly, he was gifted with a title for his heroism and a betrothal to her own sister. The situation was painful on all sides, Roselyn believed, because Victoria had no desire to marry at all, let alone be paired with a gentleman her sister pined after.

"She's still upset over your upcoming nuptials?" Lily asked.

Victoria's eyes glazed over with clear anger even as she appeared to offer a polite smile. "I believe that, aside from my father, everyone involved finds my upcoming nuptials bitter medicine to take. I, for one, would rather stay ill."

"Is it as terrible as that?" Roselyn's mother asked, leaning forward to take another biscuit from the tray. "Surely Mr. Brice is pleased. Or should I call him Lord Hardaway now? His new title does have a nice ring to it," she mused as she popped the small biscuit into her mouth in one bite.

"It was given to him as a reward, which, in my opinion, is an entirely false means of possessing a title," Victoria said dismissively.

"Victoria! He's to be your husband," Roselyn's mother scolded in the haughty manner only a dowager duchess could achieve, yet mixed with the concern Roselyn knew the woman had for those around her.

Victoria shrugged and took a sip of the tea Roselyn had seen her spike with liquor earlier. "He knows my thoughts on the matter."

"Other gentlemen acquire titles upon a relative's death," Lily cut in. "Your own father received his rank from a distant cousin not long ago, did he not?"

"That's different. Those gentlemen are not Kelton Brice." Victoria spat the name as if it contained poison.

"I see," the dowager duchess replied, her pursed lips hiding a hint of a smile. "It is difficult when you despise a gentleman who can't seem to let you be. Don't you agree, Lily?"

Lily smiled into her teacup. "Quite so. Gentlemen can be rather cumbersome at times. But then, they have other lovely qualities they keep hidden beneath the surface."

She was speaking of Devon. Roselyn knew the story. She'd seen bits of it last season. Everything had fallen into place in the end, even if Lily had been put through her paces during the season. Perhaps Victoria would find the same happiness with Lord Hardaway. Roselyn wished her the best. Although she had to admit, it was difficult to watch a friend find a husband when she was so far from her own target. It was even a bit more difficult to hear her complain of it when that was a fate Roselyn wished for daily.

Roselyn had been so close to being settled in marriage, like Victoria soon would be. If only she hadn't destroyed her chances with that letter. Or if the delivery of that letter had ended differently, in some other life would she be engaged to Ethan? Would he have read her words and come to her rescue like he did yesterday, only with Trevor's blessing?

Apparently, it was not to be for her with any gentleman now. Ethan had seen to that quite well. He seemed to be everywhere she looked. He'd invaded her life, and now he was invading her thoughts as well. *Blast you, Ethan.*

"How is the situation with Lord Ayton, Roselyn?" Victoria asked.

Had she said his name aloud, or had the conversation moved on without her? She wasn't sure how to reply. The heat of a blush crept up her neck, and she took a sip of tea to hide her discomfort. "In regard to what exactly?" she finally asked, knowing everyone was watching her.

"He was most valiant in coming to our aid a few days ago on the street," Lily offered.

Roselyn huffed into her tea before looking up. "The situation he was assisting with was most likely his own doing."

"You don't know that, Roselyn," Lily countered.

"You don't know otherwise," she argued. They didn't understand. He was a blackguard, a murderer with a stolen title. It was her fault no one knew the truth, but that was a situation she was working every day to remedy, despite the wicked way he had of turning her head. She would work on steeling herself against the effects he had on her when she next saw him. For now, she could only attempt to cast doubt on his character. Soon. His time would come soon. She sighed and met Lily's concerned gaze. "Wherever there is trouble in this life, that's where Lord Ayton can be found. He's awful."

"What sort of trouble, dear?" her mother asked. "Is this about his brother's death?"

"Nothing to fuss over," Roselyn rushed to say,

because lies were easier told quickly. "We simply do not find one another suitable for conversation. And yet he finds me at every ball and then the other day on the street. I can't seem to escape him or his torment."

"Roselyn, are you certain he feels the same? That he doesn't find you suitable for conversation?"

"*I'm* enjoyable to be near; *he's* the one who finds new ways to make *my* life miserable on a daily basis."

"You don't enjoy speaking to one another and yet he seeks you out on a daily basis?" her mother asked.

The dowager duchess was known for her love of playing the matchmaker, but she could work her charms on Victoria, not her. *Roselyn* would never allow a weed to grow between her and Ethan, let alone feelings. Any kind of connection she'd toyed with in the past had died with Trevor on that hilltop, by Ethan's own hand. That bit with the head wound had only been common decency and concern for the welfare of those around her. Regardless of how he'd stepped in to save her, he would never be her hero.

Roselyn took a steadying breath, forcing any fond thoughts of Ethan from her mind. "Don't insinuate ideas like that, Mama. Ayton is vile. There is no happy ending in this mess for me. Not with him."

"We shall see, dear."

"Mother!" Roselyn turned to exclaim, ignoring the two other ladies in the room. "He's a black-hearted man who fights for coin. He's already destroyed one pair of my dancing slippers with his poor footwork. He brawled with a man just this week on the street in front of us. He's no gentleman."

"The law of this land declares otherwise."

"Very well, but I can barely tolerate his company. And he wears black," she finished meekly as she sank back into her corner of the settee, unable to think of another insult that didn't involve accusations of foul play.

"He cuts a rather fine figure in evening wear, if you ask me," her mother mused.

"I didn't ask," Roselyn grumbled, but no one heard her over Victoria's carrying voice.

"I don't care for so many muscles on a man," Victoria announced as she bit into a tea cake. "He and Hardaway are too large. It's not surprising they're friends."

"Gentlemen should be strong, shouldn't they?" Lily asked.

"Some men wear their strength simply for people to notice," Victoria said before finishing the cake with an unladylike bite.

"I don't think either of them display themselves in such a manner," Lily said.

"Really, Victoria, dear," the dowager duchess added. "You act as if these gentlemen are walking about London without clothing. No gentleman would ever…"

"Clearly, you haven't seen Ayton at the boxing salon," Roselyn muttered to herself over the rim of her teacup.

"What was that, dear?"

"What?" She blinked her mind back into focus. "The point to this entire discussion is that I find everything about Lord Ayton to be irritating. He's a pugilist, violent to his core."

"Lily tells me he was quite kind when he intervened on your behalf on the street, even acquiring a head wound in the process." Her mother's eyebrows rose to her hairline as she gave Roselyn a knowing smile.

"Well, yes, he did arrive at an opportune time, I suppose. Throwing punches though," she added to drive her point home.

"Has he ever been violent toward you? Other than stepping on your toes while dancing?" her mother asked.

"No, he would never hurt *me*." Whatever else she thought of him, Roselyn knew that much to be true—and she refused to let that awareness soften her toward him. "But that isn't the point."

"Interesting."

"No, it isn't interesting in the least," Roselyn retorted. "He—"

"Roselyn, when I met your father, he was fresh from a ship where he'd spent the past year with sailors. He was to inherit a dukedom." She paused and smiled at the fond memory. "He spoke as if he had been raised in a brothel. He had tanned skin, which in that day simply wasn't done. I realize today it's only marginally overlooked, but it was a fashion faux pas back then, to be sure."

"Mama, we don't need to know of the fashions in the dark ages."

"No. However, you do need to know this, dear." She pinned Roselyn with her sharp gray-eyed stare. "Gentlemen are not always what you imagined gentlemen to be when you were dreaming of them in the schoolroom. Real gentlemen may have unfashionably tanned skin, curse like sailors, and have an abundance of muscles. They are inherently irritating and torment us at every turn."

"But, Mama, you don't understand. He's awful, violent."

"You said he would never hurt you, and whether you care to admit it or not, you said it with great ease. Perhaps instead of testing that theory, you need to discover why that fact is true."

"I haven't tested anything."

"Truly? Then why, dear, did I spy you crawling in the window not two weeks ago, dressed in the footman's clothes after asking your brother of the man's plans for the afternoon? I turned a blind eye, but I still find it quite interesting. Am I to understand that had nothing to do with Ayton?"

"*You?* In servants' clothes?" Victoria laughed.

"None of this is as it seems, and I'm told the breeches looked quite nice," Roselyn mumbled.

"I'm sure he appreciated your ensemble," her mother stated.

How did the woman possess the ability to know every move her daughter made, even when she was spying? It was infuriating, to say the least. Roselyn opened her mouth to retort, but knew that in this match her mother was the victor. "I… Very well." Roselyn heaved a great sigh. "I'll see if I can tolerate a conversation with the man."

"Then I believe this is a successful tea. Now, Victoria, about your Lord Hardaway."

Roselyn stopped listening. Perhaps her mother was right. Conversations could be quite enlightening. And if she could make it through an amiable conversation with Ethan, she might be able to get the answers she sought, right from his mouth.

No more sneaking about dressed as a boy, no more peering around corners of dark alleys... Well, perhaps she wouldn't eliminate her spy work entirely, but she *would* use Ethan's own words against him.

Roselyn smiled. Her mother really should be more careful what she wished for in the future.

❧

"I know why Trevor was killed," Ethan stated as he tossed the sales journal onto Cladhart's desk.

"Do you?" Cladhart asked as he laid his book aside. "You also know you should wait to be announced by the butler, knock for entry, all that societal hubbub?"

Ethan shrugged off his comment. This was more important than proper entry into a library. "Someone has been stealing from the mines."

"Ethan, we've had to deal with small theft at the mines for years." Cladhart leaned his arm on the polished desktop and looked up. "I know you want to find answers for what happened, but theft is nothing that would have been worth killing your brother for."

Ethan pressed a finger to the top of the journal, pushing it toward his father's business partner. "This is no small theft."

"What have you found?" Cladhart asked, eyeing the book of numbers as if it might contain some kind of plague.

"Not enough, but I'm getting closer." Ethan needed to make Cladhart understand the importance of this plot against them. His father had trusted him, and now Ethan needed this man—practically an uncle and a far better man than his father—to set things right.

"This could be dangerous, Ethan." Cladhart tapped the top page of the journal with his finger as he spoke. "I told you I would look into things. I don't want you involved if this is indeed what Trevor was—"

"Trevor found out about this," Ethan insisted. "That's why he was killed. I'm sure of it."

"And it will kill you," Cladhart pleaded. "Let it go. Don't look into it any further. I beg you."

"Aren't you even interested?" Ethan flipped open the ledger he'd pored over for the last two days. "Whoever is responsible has stolen enough for an entire shipping facility. I saw it! W. B. Exports and Fine Jewelry."

"Do you know who at the mine might be involved? Who would be willing to kill to cover their tracks?" Cladhart asked.

"Not yet."

"Then close this journal and walk away, Ethan." Cladhart sighed and leaned back in his chair. "I've always been fond of you. If any harm comes from this…" He swore and looked away. "Promise you'll allow me to see to this investigation."

"You'll look at the documents?" Ethan pressed.

"Of course I will. This is valuable information indeed, but it can't name your brother's killer. How do you know Trevor wasn't involved with some lady? He could have had gambling debts. It could have happened for a number of reasons. Desperation can lead a man to bad ends."

"That's not what happened."

Cladhart raised a brow. "How do you know?"

"Because I saw a man that day. A man with a knife."

"You now know who you saw? If you have the man identified…"

"Not in any detail, but I know it wasn't about unrequited love on Trevor's part, or debts. It had something to do with the mine. I'm certain."

"What of the Grey girl? They say she witnessed Trevor's accident. Perhaps she's involved."

"Lady Roselyn? No, she has nothing to do with this," Ethan insisted. Why didn't Cladhart understand? The answers were so close at hand.

"Could you identify the man you saw to the magistrates?" Cladhart asked.

"No, but I will find him."

"Sit down, Ethan."

"I'd rather stand."

Cladhart ignored his stubbornness and stood, moving to the decanter on the table under the front window. "You're no closer to catching your brother's killer than when you arrived in London."

"If you only look at the ledgers, you would see—"

"I don't need to look at the ledgers," Cladhart insisted. He lowered a hand to the table, his spine stiff. His shoulders rose and fell with a slow breath, and when he turned back to Ethan, a drink clutched in his hand, any trace of emotion was wiped from his face. "I look at ledgers every day for this business. I know the inner workings of this company. If a theft of the magnitude you suggest exists, I would know of it."

"Cladhart, I didn't mean to suggest—"

"To suggest what? That I am not skilled at my work?" He leaned a hip against his desk as he continued, "Because you surely aren't suggesting that I'm somehow associated with a theft at the mines." He took a sip of his drink. "Are you?"

"No. God, no. Listen, Cladhart. You're family to me. Even my own father..." Ethan sighed. Where had this meeting gone awry? "What I'm trying to say is that I never considered that you could be involved with this. It took a great deal of digging to even find this much information. That's why I came to you, so you could see to things."

"Then allow me to do so. You don't have to pound out every problem with those great fists of yours."

"You'll look at the ledger?"

"Yes. Leave it with me. I'll see to it that all is taken care of."

"And if you come closer to finding Trevor's killer?"

"I don't want you involved, Ethan."

"I only want justice for my brother and for it to be known who the true killer is. I won't stop until I see a proper end to this matter."

"That's what I'm afraid of."

Ethan crossed his arms and stared at Cladhart. He wished he could offer the man some encouragement that would clear the concern from his eyes, but there was nothing left to say. Cladhart had the journal, filled with correlations to the documents Ethan had found in Trevor's rooms. There was nothing more to be done about the theft. Trevor's murderer, on the other hand, had never been closer. If Ethan could stay near Roselyn while luring the man into the open, he could end this.

He pushed off from the desk and gave Cladhart a nod of farewell. Roselyn would be seeing a great deal of him, whether she thought him addled in the head or not.

# *Thirteen*

"I'D LIKE TO STOP FOR A MOMENT," ROSELYN CALLED to the driver, barely waiting for his answering nod before gathering her skirts. If she sat here any longer, she would lose Ethan altogether. She'd spotted him on foot when they rounded the last bend in the road and had spent every moment between then and now in silent debate over following after him.

It was a bright day, but the ground was still soft from yesterday's rain and nothing could destroy the hem of a dress faster than the muck of the park grounds. She enjoyed Hyde Park. It was lovely, but she, like most of society, would rather take the air from an open-topped carriage when wearing a new day dress. Some things, however, could not be helped. She'd promised her mother she would at least try to be civilized with the man, and here there wouldn't be any witnesses if she couldn't manage it and felt the need to hit him again. She leaned outside and cringed at the mud below the carriage wheel.

"My lady, you shouldn't pitch yourself over the

carriage side. It isn't safe," the young maid said from the opposite seat.

Pulling herself upright, Roselyn said, "Stay here. I'll return in a bit." She was already hopping down from the conveyance and carefully sidestepping a mud puddle before Alice could reply.

"My lady," she heard the maid call after her in a halfhearted attempt at propriety.

Roselyn smiled, not bothering to look back. Alice would stay put in the carriage. This was why Roselyn had chosen her to be a chaperone today. The woman counted as a chaperone, although she was far too fond of resting from the bustle of the house to actually accomplish the task. Roselyn moved away from the carriage, crossing Rotten Row where she dodged another carriage that was traveling far too fast for the park. She'd spotted Ethan only a few minutes ago, on foot and moving toward the area where she'd enjoyed having picnics as a child. She picked up her pace.

Cresting a hill behind a grouping of trees, she shaded her eyes. Where had the man gone? She hitched up the hem of her dress and edged down toward the grassy banks of the Serpentine below.

"Are you following me again?" a deep voice rumbled in her ear, setting her nerves on edge and sending shivers down her spine. How did he always manage to sneak up on her?

Spinning on her heel, she came nose to chest with Ethan. "Oh!" she exclaimed. Her gasping breath filled her lungs with the warm, male scent that clung to his clothing.

Taking a step away from him to a more civilized

distance, she caught her heel on the hem of her dress that she'd let fall to the wet ground behind her. Time slowed in that annoying manner it had when one simply had to appreciate the agony of the moment. She waved her hands about to steady her backward topple down the embankment. Fingertips grazed hard muscle as she grasped at anything solid within reach. His hand wrapped around her wrist. Her eyes widened with horror as she instinctively grabbed at the waist of his breeches and he was tugged a step toward her.

Then, all at once, time sped forward and a shooting pain drove up through her ankle.

She attempted a polite smile up at him as she regained her balance. Perhaps she could pretend it never happened. That would really be the best option. "How am I to know you aren't following me?" she asked, her voice breathless and high-pitched even to her ears.

"Are you all right? I didn't mean to startle you." Concern clouded his eyes as he looked down at her.

"Fine, fine, fine. That was nothing. I'm fine," she blustered.

"Are you certain?"

"Of course I'm certain. Certain as can be. Just as I'm certain you were the one in pursuit this afternoon. I would never stoop so low as to trail after a gentleman."

He was grinning. The blasted man was amused by all of this and standing too close to her for civil conversation. "I was here when I saw you flitting over the hill from your carriage."

"You saw me… Well, that is rather incriminating."

"Are you certain you aren't hurt? Because you're maintaining a rather tight grasp on my breeches."

"That's rather incriminating as well," she admitted, releasing her grip on the fabric.

She tugged to remove her gloved hand from the most indecent of places for it to be, but it didn't move. Giving up on tugging, she gave her hand an unladylike yank, yet her hand remained pressed low on his hip, caught on his clothing. She could feel the heat of a blush rush up her neck.

Why had she thought it a good idea to seek him out for conversation today? And why was her hand attached to his breeches as if by glue? She blamed her mother's insistence on polite conversation with the man. She would have to remember to tell Mama how wrong she'd been about that later this evening—while leaving out a few details, of course.

"You're awfully quiet," she accused while jerking her wrist about.

"When a lady has her hand in your drawers, it tends to divert the conversation." His deep voice rumbled around her, setting her nerves further on edge.

"Why can't I get away from you?"

"It doesn't seem as if you truly want to," he teased.

"Why does everyone say that?" she asked, pulling on the edge of her glove with her other hand.

"Stop," he warned. Removing his gloves, he wrapped his fingers around her wrist until he found the offending clasp on her bracelet. She'd forgotten she was wearing the piece of jewelry that was currently bound up in the threads of his clothing. "You're caught."

"Really? I hadn't noticed."

"Who is everyone?" he asked as he fumbled with her bracelet.

"Have we gone from quiet to philosophical? Or are we passing the time by speaking of fellow park attendees?" She was talking too much, but if she kept chatting, she wouldn't have to think about the fact that her fingers were currently stuck down his breeches. She could also ignore the slight brush of his hand against her wrist as he worked—mostly.

"The 'everyone' who says you don't truly want to be away from me," he clarified. "We're the only ones in this area of the park."

"Thankfully," she retorted as she glanced around for signs of life. "I'd hate to think how this would look to passersby."

"I'm fairly confident I know exactly how this would look to passersby."

The arrogance in his tone made her look back at him. "Rather cocky about the situation, aren't you?"

"At the moment? Pretty damn." He smirked and leaned closer to see what he was doing. "You didn't answer my question. Who claimed that you don't want to be rid of my company?"

Why had she admitted that? She squirmed in her desire to get away from him. "And if I don't wish to discuss it?"

"You brought it up, princess. And the fact that you don't want to talk about it tells me all I need to know." With a twist of his wrist, he unwrapped the threads from about her bracelet clasp, allowing her to pull her hand to freedom.

"Finally," she exclaimed, wiggling her fingers in the air. She moved to turn away from him, but the pain in her ankle wouldn't allow it.

"I was on my way to that bench over there." He nodded toward a spot barely visible through the tree branches that separated them. "You should sit."

She looked at his offered arm, glanced toward the other side of the hill where her carriage waited, and looked back at his arm.

"You've spent the past few minutes with your hand in my breeches, and yet you find issue with taking my arm?"

"You make it sound so tawdry. I did nothing wrong... I wouldn't even... Might we simply go sit on the bench and not touch one another for a few minutes?" She threw her hand onto his arm and raised her chin toward the bench beyond the trees.

"If that's what you would like, I'm happy to oblige."

Pain shot through her foot with every step, but she refused to lower herself to lean on Ethan for support. "I enjoy this location as well. It provides the perfect view of..."

"The swans," they said in unison as they shot each other curious glances.

"Don't look so shocked. Did you expect me to come here for the view of the dirt and grass?"

"Along with other dirty things rich with dark color. Swans are a bit too white for your tastes, aren't they?"

"Everything is better in black." His gaze lingered on her hair.

She tried to ignore his attention. Heat filled her cheeks as she turned the conversation back to the park around them. "You don't seem the sort to appreciate the grace and beauty of swans in the afternoon."

"You may like them for their grace and beauty, as

you say, but I like them because they're angry little blighters. They look unassuming and pristine, but that's only to lure their enemies into a false sense of security. Next thing you know…" His hand snapped through the air to down an imaginary opponent. "*Whap!* A great many things can be learned from watching swans in action."

"We're in Hyde Park. The swans here have no enemies."

"Tell that to the boy who poked one with a stick last week. He got the swan version of a left hook."

"Oh my! Was he injured?"

"Swan bites aren't lethal, last I checked," Ethan teased as he assisted her to the bench and sat beside her.

"Have you always been interested in the barbaric arts? I don't recall it ever being mentioned when we were young."

"No." He chuckled. "My interest in *barbaric* pursuits grew out of necessity. I was nineteen years of age with nowhere to turn, no skill with which to survive. I used what I had."

"Didn't you have friends, a distant relation to turn to in such a time?" Of course, she remembered and had heard plenty of rumors. Ethan's father had renounced him when he was nineteen. It was just after his mother disappeared. Roselyn wasn't sure what had occurred behind the closed doors of the Moores' home, but she and everyone else who lived in the area knew the outcome. Ethan had been banished from the estate; Katie had fled to her cottage in the woods; and Trevor had remained to pick up the pieces like a good heir to the title and estate.

"I turned to a particular group of gentlemen for a time. They trained me as a pugilist, fed me, gave me rooms."

"That was kind of them."

He nodded. "It's a debt I continue to repay."

"But then you left the country, lived in Spain," she supplied, filling in the gaps of his life.

"Eventually." He stared at the swans for a moment, his eyes trained on their constant glide across the waters of the Serpentine. "I began in France. It was the logical place to begin since my mother's lover was reportedly French."

"Your mother…" Her mouth dropped open as she turned to look at him. "Did you leave the country to find your mother?"

"And pound to dust the man who had taken her from her family," he clarified.

Small pieces that made Ethan who he was fell into place in her mind. She shook her head in disbelief. How had she not suspected as much before now? "That's why you trained as a pugilist—to confront your mother's lover?"

"Yes. Although it proved a convenient skill to have once I was on the Continent and away from any assistance I had while in London."

"If it was revenge you sought, why not use a pistol? Why take a year, if not more, learning your craft?"

"My mother taught me to be honorable. She wouldn't want me to take a man's life, even if it was to honor her good name. Every happy memory of my childhood came from her. She gave our home balance. No one truly understood that until she was gone and my father tilted the scales in his favor." He bit the words out. It was clearly a poorly healed wound that still bled if prodded overmuch. "He managed to rid himself of Katie and me all at once. Trevor was the only one who ever held value to him, and that was simply because he required an heir."

"An honor now passed to you."

"An honor." He scoffed and shook his head. "Any honor I have is a result of the woman he drove away."

"A woman who wouldn't want you to take a life with a pistol," she said, her gaze on him.

"Or with a knife." His eyes held her there.

It was as if a thick fog that hung between them was burning off in the heat of the sun. She could see him for the first time, at first faint but becoming clearer the longer they sat there together. "You didn't kill Trevor."

"No, princess. I didn't."

She'd been so certain of his guilt. All this time, she'd wrapped herself in her anger toward him, shielding herself from what she should have seen from the start. Of course Ethan wouldn't kill his brother, even for her. She'd known him her entire life, yet she'd ignored it all to focus on how the situation appeared. How had she gotten this so terribly wrong? She was breathless as she opened her mouth to speak, desperate to put the pieces together and understand. "You were fighting, and when I came over the hill…"

"I picked up the knife from the grass. I'm aware of how it must have looked to you. I've revisited the scene more times than I can count, always ending with the accusation in your eyes when you found me."

"You were holding a knife and Trevor was gone.

When I saw you…" When she'd seen him, she'd laid all blame on him without consideration. Shame washed over her. She'd abandoned Ethan when he needed her most. He lost his brother that day. What had she lost? She looked down at her hands, unable to meet his gaze.

But a second later he reached for her, lifting her chin until their eyes met. "I'm sorry, Roselyn."

"For what? I'm the one who has been set on proving your guilt and seeing you in chains."

"In chains?" he asked with a wry smile, his hand slipping down her arm with a tender touch. "I should have suspected as much."

"When I saw you in London, I thought…" She broke off, blaming her silence on an unwillingness to say more words that would hurt him. She'd hurt him enough. But she knew that was a lie. She was protecting herself now, not him. The truth was, every time she'd caught a glimpse of the man she knew him to truly be, she'd dismissed it, insisting instead on the worst about his character.

Why had she done such a thing? She'd known Ethan since she was a child. She knew him now. And he was no murderer.

"I should have known it wasn't as it seemed." Perhaps she had known and was simply unwilling to admit it. She'd needed him to be guilty. She'd needed her own anger toward him in order to keep going. She had to say it. She had to confess the worst to him and beg his forgiveness, or it would haunt her forever. She'd blamed him so she wouldn't have to blame herself.

"You believed what seemed to be truth. It's not your fault." He wrapped her hand within his, stroking her palm with his fingers.

"That isn't true," she said quietly. "I placed the blame for this on you because it was easy to do so. If not, I would have to accept that I destroyed my own plans. The words I expressed in that letter... I didn't want the future I'd planned for myself. I needed to blame you for Trevor's death, to be angry with you, when really I was to blame."

"You didn't kill Trevor, Roselyn."

"No, but I blamed his death on you so I didn't have to dwell on my mistakes."

He tensed and his hand tightened around hers. "You still believe it was a mistake to give me the letter?"

"Wasn't it? It proves I'm just as mad as my family. No matter how hard I've tried to prove myself otherwise."

His gaze softened as he looked at her. "It proves you are who I always knew you to be, and that lady is not mad."

"Yet I ignored the truth of you. When I saw you laughing at that first ball..."

"I came to London because my father instructed me to do so. I wasn't going to follow his edict, but clues to finding my brother's killer led me in this direction as well." He shifted on the bench beside her. He seemed to be searching for the correct words to fill the space between them. Heaving a great breath, he added, "And truth be told, I wished to see you again."

"Lady Roselyn," Alice called from the hilltop, but neither of them turned in her direction.

"You're not here to enjoy the season with your

new title?" she asked, confirming her new belief in him.

Ethan didn't answer, but the truth was written on his face. He wasn't in town for society's pleasures—he was here for her, for his brother, for every reason she'd ignored.

"I've made a grave mistake," she whispered.

"By thinking me a killer or by sitting with me too long on a park bench while your maid screams for you?"

"Lady Roselyn?" Alice cried.

"It would seem both."

"Allow me to alert her and have your carriage brought closer. You shouldn't walk on that ankle."

"Ethan?" she said. She watched as his body went rigid at the sound of his given name on her lips.

He turned back toward their bench, his gaze intent on her. His eyes seemed to burn, and even through his coat she could see the rise and fall of his chest on quickened breaths.

"Forgive me," she said.

He crouched low before her and lifted one hand from her lap, his eyes never leaving her face. Placing a kiss on her knuckles, he gave her hand a small squeeze before releasing it. "There was never a need to ask."

He rose and walked away to inform her panicking maid of her whereabouts, leaving Roselyn to watch his retreat. Her hand was still warm from his touch. It was as if the last month hadn't occurred and they were back at Ormesby Place. She'd been wrong about him in the worst possible manner, and yet he'd forgiven her in an instant.

Their past had fallen away, along with her anger toward him, and now they were here. "Here," she muttered to herself. *Here* seemed to be a more complicated place than ever before.

# Fourteen

ROSELYN LEANED AGAINST THE COLUMN NEAR THE edge of the Sutton ballroom. It was hardly proper to slouch in such a manner, but her ankle ached beneath the wrapping hidden under her gown. The shift in position allowed her to ease the pain, if only for a moment. It wasn't as if anyone was going to look in her direction anyway. A few weeks ago, she would have taken offense at such a slight, but now she was too busy enjoying the reprieve from proper conduct.

Across the ballroom, a dark-haired gentleman seemed to hold everyone's attention as he spoke. She'd never seen such command of a crowd, except perhaps for that time at the harvest festival when the man in the large cloak had made objects disappear before everyone's eyes.

From this distance Roselyn couldn't hear his words, but whatever they might be, they certainly held Evangeline's attention. Evangeline's usually guarded exterior seemed to be a few locks short of secure this evening. Was that curiosity or something stronger that shone in her eyes? Roselyn couldn't be certain, but she did know one thing—she'd never seen the emotion in her friend's eyes before.

"I didn't expect to see you tonight," Ethan said as he approached, making her jump.

She'd been so preoccupied with watching Evangeline and the gentleman at the center of the crowd gathered along the opposite wall that she hadn't noticed Ethan's arrival. He was in his all-black finery as usual, and his eyes seemed to dance more than they had in a month. "I didn't think you were attending either. The ball is half over."

"I was delayed with a bit of business." His gaze drifted across the room to the crowd when they all laughed at something the gentleman at their center said.

"You had to hit someone for sport this late at night?"

"I have other business dealings on occasion," he teased. "Things that don't involve broken noses."

"Truly?"

"On occasion." He glanced back to the dark-haired man across the ballroom and gave him a small nod.

"Who is that? He seems quite popular this evening." Her gaze drifted over Evangeline before turning back to Ethan.

"Lord Crosby. He's most likely discussing his new investment opportunity."

"Investments? Why would Evangeline care about such a thing?"

"I don't think it's the investments your friend is interested in," Ethan said in a low voice only she could hear.

"She has been acting a bit off of late. Perhaps this Lord Crosby is to blame."

"I'm sure he would like to think so." He chuckled.

"He would like to think of her being at odds? Why must you gentlemen be so aggravating?"

"We gentlemen? Don't sort me into the same bin as Crosby. I've done nothing to you...this evening," he added with an unapologetic grin.

"Yet."

The smile slipped from his face, and his eyes grew dark for a moment before he seemed to collect his thoughts. "Shouldn't you be resting your foot?"

"I won't be dancing, but I doubt that's an issue anyway." She looked around with open arms as if inviting a large number of gentlemen to join her.

"It's an issue for me," he countered in a soft voice, regaining her attention. "I rather like dancing with you."

"The slippers you destroyed disagree."

He frowned in thought. "I suppose moving about in a fight and moving on the dance floor don't have that much in common after all."

"I don't know... My feet took a good pummeling," she teased.

"To avoid further injury, would you like to join me on the terrace during the next dance?"

"That sounds safe enough," she offered with a smile.

"Does it?"

Something in his gaze made her heart race faster the longer she looked at him. "I'm sure a few ladies would disagree with the safety of a terrace in your company, but we'll ignore those ladies."

"Good. They sound rather dull anyway. Complete lack of adventure and all."

Smiling up at him, she took his arm. Life had

certainly been an adventure since he'd returned to the country. It was difficult to believe that not too long ago she'd been content to wed his brother. Although everything had changed in a moment, she was glad to be here now.

It was a shocking thought. Her loyalty should still lie with Trevor, and yet she now wondered if it ever had. She'd been pleased to check "marriage" off her list of life's plans. But an afternoon at Trevor's side had never made her limbs buzz as if alive with bees while her mind worked to sort rampant thoughts. He'd never left her wanting more, curious to discover the answer to some riddle, to live a life greater than she'd anticipated. Not like Ethan.

And yet, they were brothers. Should she have her hand wrapped around the arm of the brother of her deceased almost-husband when the man had passed only recently? She was quite certain she shouldn't enjoy their conversations or the strength of the arm beneath her palm.

She allowed him to lead her toward the terrace. It was only a stroll during a dance. It was nothing. They were nothing of importance to each other after all. Only old friends.

"You purse your lips when you're deep in thought."

She bit her lip to stop the telling gesture. "My governess used to reprimand me for doing just that when reciting poetry. She thought I was attempting to look alluring."

"She wasn't wrong."

He thought her alluring. The heat of a blush washed over her cheeks, but she pushed the thought from her mind. "My governess never truly understood. I was thinking about the words and how they pieced together into verse."

She made an effort to ensure she was no longer pursing her lips. She shouldn't be alluring to him, should she? He was Trevor's brother, after all. People would talk. If she was to be honest, however… Beneath it all, she wanted to be alluring to him. She enjoyed his attention. Was that so wrong?

"And now? Are you thinking of poetry? Because, I must admit, I know none."

"Do you think happiness is earned or deserved?" she blurted out.

"Perhaps I do prefer poetry." He laughed. "I know *you* deserve happiness."

"But you do not?" she asked, looking up at him.

He shrugged. "What brings such a weighty subject as happiness to mind?"

"Do you never woolgather over weighty subjects?"

"I do, indeed. Just this afternoon, I sat wondering how hard I would have to hit a man to lift him from the floor."

"That's a weighty subject?" she asked.

"You didn't see the man in question." He pulled a face as he added, "He was quite large."

She stepped through the door to the stone terrace and breathed in the scent of leaves on the cool evening air.

"It's a shame there isn't seating outside. It's such a lovely night, but I confess my ankle is beginning to ache even with that small amount of walking."

Ethan turned to survey the empty terrace. "Allow

me to assist." With a quick movement she hadn't time to brace for, he lifted her from the ground and sat her on the top rail of the stone wall that ran the length of the space.

She gasped and gripped his upper arms for support in her precarious position. "I'll fall into the garden below."

"You've room to sit," he said with all the confidence she lacked. "It's the best I can offer at the moment."

"I'd feel better standing." But the pain in her ankle was already fading as she sat, swinging her legs below her. She glanced over her shoulder at the bushes in the garden at her back. It wasn't far enough to break bones if she slipped, but that didn't mean she wished to experience it.

"I won't let you fall," he said, reading her thoughts. The heat of his gaze burned a trail down her neck, drawing her attention back to him. He'd settled his hands on her waist where he left them, the warmth of his grasp seeping through her gown and through her veins until her feet stopped swinging below her.

*This is no different than a waltz*, she told herself. There was closeness when dancing and that was an acceptable activity. This was simply the still version of a waltz. But it was more than a dance and she knew the truth of that. Theirs was a near-embrace, alone on a moonlit terrace.

"This seems rather scandalous if anyone were to see us," she said in a breathless voice.

"You're injured and needed to rest your foot." He shrugged. "And I made sure you were in the shadows of Sutton House. I wouldn't want to damage your reputation again."

"Your reasoning seems quite sound." She released her grip on his arms to slip her hands to his shoulders.

Although she wanted more than anything to wrap her arms around him and hold on to this moment and secure her place within it, she settled for a polite touch. Even through layers of clothing, gloves, coat, and shirt, she could feel the warmth of his body close to hers. The steady rhythm of his breaths pulsed beneath her palms. Time could only be measured in heartbeats and the increasing longing she had to kiss him.

The wall had brought her to eye level with him. His lips were so close to her own. What would he taste like? Was he wondering the same? And then a terrible thought occurred to her—what if he wasn't wondering the same? What if he was only being a gentleman and assisting an injured lady in need?

"Roselyn?"

"Mmmm?"

"I want to smash your reputation to a point beyond repair right now."

Her gaze lifted from his lips to his eyes—dark eyes that reflected the dangers of being alone with him. "You do?" she asked in a small voice as hope soared through her body. She bit her lip to try to hold back the words but lost the battle after a second. "How would something of that nature begin?"

"Don't ask me that," he warned as his fingers bit into her sides.

Did he not want to kiss her as she did him? She didn't want to be the only one thinking such tantalizing thoughts. But she would never know either way if she didn't ask. She took a small breath. "Why not?"

"Because I'll show you." His gaze dropped to her mouth.

One part of her silently pleaded for his touch, to taste his lips, just as the other remained mortified at the brazen thoughts hanging in her mind. She pursed her lips as she looked at him. Did she dare? Her heart pounded in her ears as she drew the courage to speak. "Show me."

He slipped his hands to her lower back, drawing her in to his body. He was so close. If she stretched forward only a breath, he would be hers. Her gaze was focused there on the beckoning temptation of his mouth. *Please, kiss me; please, kiss me*, her heart chanted until finally his lips met hers in a soft caress. Her eyes drifted closed into darkness as the warm touch of his lips invited her farther into his embrace.

The heat of his skin beneath her hands. The press of his lips to hers. She didn't know what she was doing, but she knew she wanted more. Like a decadent serving of sweets of which one couldn't take only one bite, he filled her senses and left her begging for more. What began as something tender quickly turned needful. Her grasp on his shoulders tightened as he traced the seam of her lips with a teasing lick of his tongue. They melted into one another in a frenzy of desire and seeking kisses.

She bit at his lower lip, sucking into her mouth the only soft part of this world-hardened man. One hand came up to cup her cheek as he slipped past the barrier of her lips to taste her. Matching his movements, she tangled her tongue with his. She dug her fingers into his shoulders with greedy grasps, wrinkling his coat beneath her hands. She didn't care. The bulky garment was only another barrier between them. He shifted forward a fraction and pulled her into his embrace as their kiss deepened.

A moment later she realized she was no longer sitting on the wall but poised on its edge as Ethan held her close and kept her from falling. She ripped her glove off and slid her hand into his hair, soft warm strands weaving in and out of her fingers as she clung to him.

He wouldn't let her fall. She wasn't sure where the thought came from but she knew it was true. As long as he was with her, she didn't have to strain for stability. She didn't have to hold on to anything but him. It was odd that hanging a second from falling and losing oneself in passionate kisses with a man she once feared left her free. Unplanned, reckless freedom—he tasted of it, and she licked it from his lips.

She could remain here forever. Freedom and intoxicating kisses *should* last forever. But Ethan had made her no promises of forever. He gave her lip a playful bite before soothing it with his tongue and making her forget for a moment why forever mattered. Only tonight was important. Only tonight held the magic of this moment. Only tonight would she allow him to... She deepened their kiss, again demanding more. If this was only to be tonight, she would experience all this night had to offer.

A noise escaped his throat, almost a growl and entirely male. He took all that she offered and demanded more until she broke away on a gasping breath. He pressed his forehead to hers for a moment.

"Ethan, what are we doing?"

"Kissing, last I checked," he said with a crooked grin. His voice was husky and his eyes dark.

"Beyond this. With each other…if anyone saw us together." She broke off with a shake of her head.

"Because you were engaged to my brother." He supplied the words for her racing thoughts, his heated gaze turning cold.

"His passing was rather recent." He must understand that there would be talk of this, were word to spread.

"Trevor always caught the bigger fish, shot the closest arrow to the target. Even now, he's finding a way to best me." He loosened his hold on her. Had he stepped back, or did she only imagine the distance now between them?

She licked her lips, wishing she hadn't spoken to break their connection, not yet anyway. "There is no besting in this situation, Ethan."

"Isn't there?"

She reached forward and grabbed the lapels of his coat, pulling him closer. What could she say to make him understand when she could hardly fathom the implications herself? She'd never been with a man like this, never desired a man like she did now.

Lifting her lips to his, she kissed him with all the desperation that coursed through her limbs. His body seemed to sigh into hers as he trailed his lips down her jaw to her neck. She turned her head to the side. She'd never experienced such a sensation. How could something so tender cause her such anxious exhilaration? She blinked her eyes open, needing to remain in reality or slide off this ledge with him into darkness.

That was when she saw movement in the shadows of the garden below. Her grasp on Ethan tightened. Perhaps she imagined it, but then something caught her eye again. "Ethan," she whispered.

An inarticulate sound vibrated across her skin in response.

"Ethan, I think someone is watching us."

&

Ethan's gaze lifted briefly in search of their audience, but he saw no one. His mouth was not so obedient. Even as he searched, he continued to breathe in the scent of Roselyn's hair where a piece fell artfully over her shoulder, to feel the smooth skin of her neck with his lips. "We're alone," he murmured. After all, he'd made sure they were alone when they arrived.

He'd waited and wished for so long now. She wasn't his, but she was in his arms. *If you let go, you'll lose her*, some voice in his head told him, and he wasn't about to test that thought. His heart picked up speed, ready for a battle with some unknown stranger even as his hands refused to leave her. He wasn't thinking entirely clear thoughts at the moment, but he knew he could shield her from society's talk somehow and protect her from harm if it came to that—which it wouldn't. He would simply wait for that harm to get a bit closer before he was forced to release her. More time, more of her.

"Ethan," she said in a breathless voice. "I saw something. The shadow of a man in the garden, or perhaps…"

"Does he look the type to tell tales in a ballroom?" he asked as he kissed the exposed skin along the top edge of her gown. Palming her breast and producing a moan from her throat that made him smile, he added, "There's a breeze. It was most likely a tree, and I have to tell you, I'm not inclined to care how many trees see us at the moment."

"Perhaps," she whispered as she dug her fingers into his hair.

He pressed his hand to her breast again, running his fingers under the trim on her gown as he lifted his mouth to the base of her neck where her pulse beat a wild rhythm. He trapped her heartbeat there beneath his lips, enjoying her small gasp and the arch of her back pushing her farther into his grasp.

"Eth...Ethan," she whispered. "I saw it again, and it's not a tree branch..."

"I don't want this to end," he murmured as he lifted his head, kissing her again. He pulled back just far enough to see into her eyes, but not far enough to break their contact. He didn't want to let her go, not now, not yet. "Where did you see this shadow of a man?"

"At the base of the terrace steps. Be careful."

He brushed his lips against hers. Damn whoever was interrupting them. This was the moment he'd dreamed of for far too many nights. The man who was apparently lurking in the shadows was about to get the full force of Ethan's rage for his poor timing. He ran the pad of his thumb over Roselyn's kiss-swollen lips. The last thing he wanted to do was to walk away from her. But if it would keep her safe and put her mind at ease, so be it. "Wait here," he said, forcing himself to release her.

"Ethan," he heard at his back as he turned, but he was already moving toward the terrace steps.

Whatever she'd been about to say was lost to the rush of his footsteps on the stone floor.

He would discover who was watching them and why, force the man to cease, then return to Roselyn to continue what they had begun. It was blasted painful to leave her, considering he'd longed to kiss her for weeks, but if someone was lurking nearby, he needed to ensure her safety before he could continue. If anything happened to her, he would never forgive himself.

A scream pierced the night.

"Roselyn?" He turned and looked to the terrace wall where he'd left her but saw only empty railing. He turned back to the terrace steps, gripping the stone rail for a second. There was no other way off the terrace except through a crowded ballroom. He turned, squinting into the darkness.

Where had she gone? All at once, the pieces clicked into place. The man in the garden. The trap he'd set for Trevor's killer. Roselyn perched so precariously on the terrace ledge, within easy reach of anyone lurking in the darkness. *Oh, God, no.* What had he done? "Roselyn!" he called as he ran out into the dark garden.

He'd brought her out into the cover of night and then had become distracted. Someone was attempting to take her from him, and he was the one who had lured her captor to her. This was his fault. When would he learn?

"Roselyn!" he cried again, his boots eating up ground as he moved to the far side of the walled area. Pushing past bushes and jumping low hedges, he scanned for movement. Finally spotting a man attempting to scale the back wall of the garden, Ethan ran for him. No one would harm Roselyn. Not tonight. Not on his watch.

He reached for the man, wrapping his hand around the leg that still hung over the wall. Pulling him back to the ground, Ethan grabbed a fistful of the man's shirt. It was the tall man from the harbor. Hadn't he beaten this man enough already to keep him away? He tightened his grip on the man's clothing. "Where is she? What have you done with her?"

"I didn't touch your lady. Only to follow for now," the man gasped as he pulled at Ethan's hands in an attempt to free his shirt.

"Why are you watching me?" Ethan ground out. "Did you kill Trevor? *Where is Roselyn?*" He raised his fist, ready to beat the truth out of the man if he had to. Terror raced through his blood. God, if anything happened to her... If she was hurt, taken, *killed*... "Tell me!"

"I didn't..." the man began, visibly frightened. He squirmed to get away. "I... Your brother—"

But before he could say more, a small voice called out from the other end of the garden. "Ethan?"

*Roselyn?*

He needed to hear whatever the man had been about to confess, but he had to help her more. She could be hurt.

Releasing the man to fall to his knees at the base of the wall, Ethan turned and ran to her. Branches scratched his face and shoulders, tearing at his breeches but not slowing his pace. He had to find her. He stopped in the gravel walk that ran beside the bushes that lined the terrace.

Turning, he squinted into the dark. "Roselyn? Where are you? Are you injured?"

"Of course I'm injured," she said from the ground just ahead. Dropping to his knees, he spotted her on the ground between two bushes, lying on her back.

"How did he hurt you? Are you bleeding? Can you move?" he asked as he pulled her onto the gravel path, holding her in his arms.

"I'm fine. Did you catch that man?"

He ran his hands up and down her spine in search of wounds. "Never mind him. He hurt you."

"No, he didn't."

"He didn't hurt you." He breathed the words in relief as he pulled her tighter against his chest. "We should have stayed inside the ball. I'll never take such chances with you again. It was wrong. This was my fault."

"I agree." Roselyn's voice was muffled by his coat, but he didn't need to hear her accusations. She was right.

He'd been reckless with her life, and she'd almost paid the price. No outcome was worth that risk. What a blind fool he'd been to think he could use her as bait! The sheer terror he'd felt belied that idea.

He released his hold on her, realizing he was in danger of choking the life from her in his relief. Cradling her head in the crook of his arm, he brushed a stray twig from her hair and ran his hand over her shoulder to check for injury. It was hard to believe she'd survived the attack when his brother hadn't. "Are you sure he didn't harm you? I thought you were gone."

"He didn't lay a finger on me."

His relief that she was well subsided enough for him to understand her words. He glanced around, from the broken branches on the bush to the empty garden around them, and finally up to the ledge of the terrace wall above them—the wall where he'd left Roselyn to wait for his return. He winced at his mistake.

"I told you I'd be more comfortable on solid ground."

"It looks like you got your wish."

"Falling into a bush wasn't what I had in mind."

He glanced back to the shadowed corner of the garden in time to see the silhouette of a man drop over the wall and disappear. "None of this was what I had in mind."

"None of it?" she asked, pulling his attention back to her.

"Well, I admit I had hoped for the parts on the terrace."

Her eyes grew wide. "You had?"

He'd admitted too much. If she knew how much he'd thought about touching her, holding her in his arms and kissing her, she would run from him. Or worse, she could rethink her change of heart about his guilt. After all, he'd longed for her even before Trevor's death. His heart pounded in his chest. If she knew he'd been dreaming of her since that day in the drive at Ormesby Place, she would think the worst of him again. The moment stretched out between them as he searched for the right words. Finally, after a few failed attempts, he glanced away. "It was an enjoyable diversion from the ball this evening, don't you agree?"

He held his breath, waiting for her to answer,

willing her to accept his callous reasoning over the truth.

"An evening's amusement." She nodded as she sat forward and tried to gain her feet with her back to him. "That's what I thought as well."

It was odd. Those were the words he wanted to hear, for they meant his lie had been believed, his secret was safe. But something tightened in his chest at the sound of them. Was it only entertainment for her, a break during a dull event? Perhaps so. But he could have sworn when she was in his arms that there had been something more. It could have been wishful thinking on his part, but he couldn't have dreamed the look in her passion-hazed eyes or the feel of her hands in his hair, pulling him closer.

"Who was that man?" she asked in a tight voice, pulling his thoughts back to their present predicament.

"I don't know, but I plan to find out. It wasn't the first time we've met. He was one of the men who followed you by the harbor."

"I thought he looked familiar. He was from the harbor, then." She shivered and turned to look at him. "Ethan, was that man Trevor's killer?"

"I don't know, but I do know where I can find answers."

"Where?" she asked with wide eyes.

"I'm not sure who is behind it, but that warehouse at the harbor is involved—W. B. Exports and Fine Jewelry. I don't know what I'm looking for, or what I'll find for that matter, but I have to go there."

"I'll come with you."

His heart jerked as he attempted to understand her

words. He watched as the moonlight danced off her pale face, the glow of her skin only interrupted by an escaped curl that blew across her cheek in the night breeze. What was she talking about? She couldn't possibly intend to sneak around London with him. "What? You want to come with me to the harbor? Absolutely not."

"I can fend for myself. I stopped one of the men with only a reticule just the other day, didn't I?" she said as she dusted off her gown.

"You aren't coming with me."

"Yes, I am. That man came here tonight for a reason, and I don't plan to sit by and wait for him to come again."

"You can't go there. It will most definitely be dangerous. I'll have to go at night when I can sneak in without being seen."

"Then I know exactly what I'll wear for the occasion."

"It's not an occasion." He reached for her arm. She must understand. He couldn't risk her life, not again. "There will be no ball gowns or borrowed men's breeches. There will be nothing at all since you aren't coming with me."

"I wasn't going to wear a ball gown," she said. "Clothing should always match the destination."

"The slums of London. This is how you wish to dress?" He slid his hand down to her wrist, stilling her movements and forcing her to look at him.

"I have just the ensemble in mind," she said again with her chin raised in challenge.

"You are not going, princess."

"We should go back to the ball." She looked down

at her hand now wrapped in his and shook free of his grasp. "I think our *evening's amusement* has lasted long enough." Her eyes held some emotion he couldn't place as she looked at him. Her mouth quirked up in a wry smile for a second and then she was gone.

"Roselyn," he called after her, but she was already limping up the terrace steps in spite of her injuries and didn't seem inclined to stop for further conversation.

Ethan watched her leave. She was moving back toward the safety of the ballroom. The thought should please him. He'd endangered her life. She was safe within the light of nearly a hundred candles—with her family, her friends, the rest of society—yet he itched to be at her side. He wanted to be the one to keep her safe from harm, not the one placing her in danger. "It won't happen again, princess," he muttered into the night. "I've lost too many. I can't lose you as well."

If only his mistakes could be unmade as easily as words could be spoken.

# Fifteen

ROSELYN SLIPPED FROM THE CARRIAGE LIKE A WISP OF black smoke against the night sky. She crept to the door of the warehouse without being seen. Pleased she was on good terms with her driver, especially when engaging in spy work, she watched her coach roll around the corner as instructed.

Pausing to admire her dark silhouette in the small pane of glass in the door, she gave herself a wicked grin. "You should have become a spy months ago."

Really, why didn't young ladies become spies? She looked delightful in black and had the ability to walk across floorboards without making them squeak. And she rather enjoyed being out in the night air, although the air at this location was rather pungent. She wrinkled her nose and reached for the doorknob, but the door pushed open beneath her fingers.

Splintered pieces of wood littered the floor at her feet. Someone without her skills was already here. "Smashed to bits," she whispered to herself. The lack of tact with the lock screamed of Ethan. She stepped inside and closed the door behind her.

She appeared to be in an office of some sort. Moonlight streamed in the one small window in the door, lighting the surfaces of several desks. Perhaps there was some documentation written here, a note left behind, or… What was she looking for? Trevor had been murdered almost two months ago; it hardly seemed likely that any plans for it would be lying about. Her gaze landed on a stack of papers on the corner of a desk on the far wall. She wasn't sure what she was searching for, but that was as good a place to begin as any.

She thumbed through the first stack of rag papers, which appeared to be old shipping receipts. There were plenty of mentions of W. B. Exports, which was the name on the outside of the building, but none of it had any meaning to her. She shook her head and continued. Still, it was odd that shipments were being made from Bond Street to this dank place. Who would venture here to buy a bauble for anyone? It made no sense, nor did it provide any clues about Trevor.

*Clunk.*

She spun on her heel. Although it was most assuredly the sound of Ethan snooping about the adjoining warehouse, she should be wary. And come to think of it, she should be wary of him—more so than some stranger. He hadn't wanted her to come tonight. "Humph." She would show him who the better spy was.

Stalking to the door at the back of the office, she opened it ever so slightly and slipped through into the larger room. Clinging to the walls and crouching low behind crates stamped with the W. B. Exports emblem, a *W* and a *B* wound together with vines, she put her skills to the test.

That was when she saw them—two men ripping into a crate not ten paces away. Only the thin light of a single candle lit them. She recognized Ethan's broad shoulders and wild hair in an instant, but who was with him? He seemed familiar, but she couldn't quite place him.

"Don't know why you felt the need to accompany me tonight," the unknown man said in a booming voice.

Ethan picked through straw, his attention on the contents of the crate as he spoke. "Needed something to keep me busy."

"From what I've heard, you have a lady that would oblige you in that regard."

"What did you hear?" Ethan asked, muffling Roselyn's gasp with his words.

"My *fiancée* mentioned it," the man said. She could practically hear his eyes rolling. "It was nothing. Seriously, Ethan, you can stop scowling at me now."

Ethan. So they were close. Roselyn squinted, trying to make out the man's features. A large man with blond hair. Could that be Lord Hardaway?

Victoria had mentioned that the men were friends. Roselyn just hadn't imagined they were the *break into a building together in the dead of night* sort of friends. She looked around, catching sight of the heavy beams above in the flickering candlelight. This sort of place would either bring friends together or tear them apart. Or perhaps this was the type of activity that gentlemen enjoyed in their leisure time. She'd heard Lily reference Devon's love of dirty taverns on occasion. And after the smell inside that boxing salon, she didn't give men much credit for taste. She settled back on her heels and listened. Perhaps she would learn something this evening after all.

"How are things with the fiancée?" Ethan asked as he replaced the lid to the crate and began prying another one open.

"How well can they be? I'm to wed Lady Victoria Fairlyn."

"Yes, a title and a beautiful bride. I can see how difficult life has become for you."

"You have the title bit now. In my experience, that's halfway to being saddled with a wife," Hardaway replied.

"It's not working out to be as simple as that in my case."

Roselyn held her breath and listened more closely.

"You almost sound as if you want to be wed. I'd happily trade circumstances," Hardaway said with a loud laugh.

"It's complicated," Ethan muttered. "She was engaged to my brother. I'm told it isn't done and people would talk."

He didn't only want an evening's amusement? If that was true, why had he said otherwise?

"Aren't you turning into the right fancy gentleman, considering society talk? Next you know, you'll be taking up needlework. Stitch me a nice pillow for the drawing room, won't you, Ayton?" Hardaway said the last bit in what was clearly meant to be a lady's voice.

Ethan shoved Hardaway in the shoulder, and the crate toppled to the floor with a bang. Then Hardaway jabbed Ethan in the ribs and laughter rang through the nearly empty warehouse. A dog barked outside and Hardaway extinguished the candle, throwing them into complete darkness.

Roselyn stood. There was no need to hide when it was so dark no one could see their hand before their face.

"Damn it all, Ayton," Hardaway said in something that was intended to be a whisper. "This is why I don't bring you with me on Spares business. Tossing crates around with no thought to where they land. You're a great bull of a man and you make a racket. This is to be a secret investigation. I have a mission. I know this is personal for you, but it's my work. Only last week, I was saying…"

"You'd talk to the empty room if I left you be," Ethan countered.

"I'm someone who has much to say."

"I've noticed."

"People find me quite entertaining."

"And humble," Ethan said.

There was a shuffling of boots on the wood plank floor, and another round of laughter cut short by what she guessed was a friendly punch to the gut.

Roselyn shifted closer. What was *Spares Business*? Were Ethan and Hardaway involved in some enterprise together? Perhaps Ethan had more than one reason for keeping her away from this place tonight. And Victoria had been correct about Hardaway from the beginning. She wasn't sure what was happening, but she knew she would have to get closer to find out more.

She felt her way forward, making sure she didn't walk into anything or anyone. If she could circle the crates they were investigating, then when they relit the lantern, she would be able to see inside. Walking on the tips of her toes and gritting her teeth against the slight pain that still plagued her ankle, she was almost through the open area where the men stood. Barely daring to breathe, she stepped past them. The hem of her dress brushed something. She froze.

"What was that?"

"What?"

"Something brushed against my leg."

"I would think this a rather nice home by rat standards—close to the water, within walking distance of several taverns," Ethan mused.

"Shut it, Ayton. You know I can't abide rodents."

"All those years living in the Dillsworth home have made you weak. You should have seen the accommodations I had in Spain."

"Remind me not to return to Spain any time soon. Once was plenty for me."

A gnawing sound echoed in the room. It was much too loud to be a rat, and yet she jumped anyway. And so did Hardaway, it would seem from the commotion at her side.

"Was that you?" Hardaway asked.

"No, it was a rat the size of an alley cat." Ethan cried out, "It has my arm!"

"Not your pathetic attempts at rat noises, you arse. I heard footsteps."

Before Roselyn could move, the lantern blazed to light. She wasn't two paces from Ethan.

"I believe I found our rat," Ethan offered as he stared her down like he would one of his opponents in a fight.

"I didn't know rats dressed up so," Hardaway answered with a grin.

"Could you give us a minute? I think Lady Roselyn and I have a few things to discuss."

"Don't mind me," Hardaway tossed out as he replaced the lid on the crate they'd been searching and lifted the lantern high in the air. "I'll just be rooting through crates of jewels in search of... What are we looking for again, Ayton?"

"Hell if I know. But keep looking."

Hardaway nodded and walked away to the far side of the warehouse, taking the light with him.

Ethan didn't know what he was searching for either. That was interesting. Disappointing, but interesting. What of the business Hardaway had referenced? Tonight certainly had created more questions than answers. She met Ethan's hard stare in the dim light.

"A black mourning dress?" he asked with an arched brow as he prowled closer to her.

She glanced down at her spy ensemble and smoothed the folds of the fabric. "It's perfect, isn't it?" But when she looked back up at Ethan, he was only glaring at her. Clearly, he didn't mean his question as a compliment. She shrugged.

Unlike in the cool moonlight of last night, this evening he looked dangerous. It must be the atmosphere in this place. A terrace on an unseasonably warm night it was not.

"I thought I told you not to come here," he said, taking another step in her direction.

"You shouldn't have told me where you were going, then."

"A mistake I won't repeat."

Why couldn't he understand that she needed to be here searching for answers every bit as much as he did? She was not going to sit by while he sniffed out a killer without her involvement.

"You need my assistance," she said in a soft voice.

"No, I don't." Even in the gray haze of light between them, she could see his jaw tighten as his gaze pierced through her.

"Of course you do. Have you found Trevor's killer yet?" She smiled, knowing her blow had hit its mark.

Ethan turned away with a muttered curse on his lips. He took two steps, ran a hand through his hair, and turned back to her, covering the ground he'd lost and then some. He didn't stop until he was looming over her. "If you think turning up here in a fancy dress is helpful…"

"This is a day dress," she corrected. Her heels knocked against wood as she hit a stack of crates, stopping her retreat.

He leaned toward her, resting his hands on the crate on either side of her shoulders. "You can't be here, Roselyn. Do you truly think dressing in dark colors will hide you from danger?" His brows drew together as he looked at her, concern hanging heavy in his eyes. "You can't hide from this."

"I'm here to catch a murderer just as you are. Now, if you will excuse me, I need to search for

evidence. I don't have time to poke fun at *your* clothing when there is work to be done." She tried to
duck under his arm but he stopped her with a touch
to her shoulder.

"Roselyn, I have to keep you safe." His hand
drifted down her side in a possessive motion.

"My safety isn't your responsibility," she said,
trying not to think about the warmth of his hand
where it rested on her hip. She'd stood with him
too long, and the temptation to stay longer warred
within her. She swallowed the treacherous thoughts.
"You're of no relation to me. I'm not sure what you
are to me. You're not even my future brother-in-law
anymore."

"A fact I'm most thankful for," he growled as he
lifted her from her feet and tossed her over his shoulder. *Again*.

He was too fast for her, and now she was winded
and had a jostled view of the world from his back. She
tried to push free of him, but he only tightened his
grasp on her hip.

"What are you doing?" she snapped as soon as she
could breathe.

"Seeing that you return home." He was already
striding toward the door to the office.

"Is this your solution to every problem? Hauling
me away to my carriage?"

"If my problems continue to be you showing up
where you shouldn't be, then yes." He was already
throwing open the door that led to the street. "I will
toss you onto my shoulder every day if I must." He
ran his other hand over the back of her thigh in a bold

gesture as the night air whipped around her exposed ankles. Was he enjoying this?

"I'm not your problem," she choked out as she jabbed him in the shoulder with her elbow, but he barely flinched. If anything, he increased his pace away from the warehouse door. Shifting about, she tried to free herself of his grasp. Even if her efforts landed her face down on the street as a result, they would be worth it. But the more she wiggled, the more indecent his grasp on her rear became.

She gasped, torn between aggravation and her own shameful enjoyment of his touch, but aggravation won a second later when he grumbled, "Solve this problem for good."

"Put me down!" She pounded her fists against his back.

To her surprise, he stopped. They were close to the corner where she'd left the carriage, yet still too far for the driver to see the commotion on such a dark street.

"My pleasure," he murmured in a low—somewhat dangerous—voice.

She stilled, waiting for him to lower her to the ground. But instead of setting her down as if being handed down from a carriage, he moved his hands farther around her back, roaming them over her body and pulling her close. "What are you..." she began, but her words faded as he lowered her from his shoulder.

He slid her down his body in one seemingly endless motion until they were face-to-face. He had a reckless gleam in his eyes and a hint of a smile on his lips that she'd only seen once before—last night just before he'd kissed her. Was that his solution to the problem she represented? If he thought to distract her from their disagreement by seducing her, then he...could try his best. She was a worthy adversary after all. Her heart pounded as she met his wild gaze.

In a minute she would escape him. She would slip away, away from the muscular arms that held her, and away from the hungry stare from the man she desired. But perhaps not just yet. Right now she wanted nothing more than to discover where this clandestine meeting would go. What would happen next? Caught up in this increasingly heated exchange, she wound her arms around his neck and held on tight instead of letting go.

His hands moved to her hips as she slipped down the hard planes of his stomach by tiny fractions, the friction stirring a greater need within her. He followed her descent with his head, his lips only a breath away from hers. She arched into his grasp. Her hands trailed down his chest, sensing every beat of his heart, every breath he took—an action that stole her own breath away.

"Roselyn," he whispered against her lips. She didn't know if it was a warning or a plea, but she understood it nonetheless.

She couldn't be warned away, not tonight. She wanted the adventure, the excitement of being with him like this, and the freedom she knew could only be found when she was in his arms. It was a desire matched in the untamed look in his eyes. Her lashes batted shut as his lips met hers. She kissed him back, meeting his seeking kisses and demanding more. Their connection turned from needy to raving mad, and for the first time in her life she didn't care if anyone who might see her thought her mad. She was mad—mad for this man.

Time stretched out on the dark London street in a frenzy of tangled tongues and playful bites, but she wanted more. She began pulling at the knot of his cravat with hasty tugs. She needed to touch him, more of him. Clearly he felt the same since a second later he shifted his grip on her and she found her hips pulled tight against his as he held her rear.

"Ethan," she breathed in desperation. But he caught her bottom lip between his teeth and pulled her back into another scorching kiss. She didn't know where this was leading, but as long as she was with Ethan, she didn't care. The feel of his hard body against hers—while he plundered her mouth and she plundered his right back—left her wanting more. More wild kisses, more excitement, just *more*.

He pulled back a second later and pressed his forehead to hers as he caught his breath. "I want this, but you're not safe here." His voice was rough, and the deep vibration of it sent shivers down her spine in spite of the words he spoke.

But a second later he was kissing her again, his actions contradicting the thoughts that must be pounding in his head. He finally released her enough for her toes to touch the ground. But he didn't let go, instead moving forward to trap her against the stone wall of the warehouse. He bent to trail his lips down the side of her neck as he framed her breasts with his hands.

"I'm safe with you," she murmured as she delved her fingers into his dark hair, holding him to her.

"That's debatable at the moment," he said between the kisses he was placing on the exposed skin above the neckline of her dress.

"I want to be here with you," she said, not caring how wanton it may sound. It was true.

He sighed and straightened. Lifting her once more from the ground, he began to move down the street with her in his arms.

"Where are you taking…" But then he was kissing her again, though this time he seemed to be savoring every moment like she was the last bite of cake in the country. She would memorize this kiss to keep with her forever. Slow and sweet, leading her to… Where was he leading her?

Just then she heard a clunking noise at her back and Ethan set her down on a cushioned seat. A cushioned seat? She blinked up at the velvet interior of her carriage, and every fond thought she'd had for this man shattered. "You tricked me."

"I know," he said sheepishly.

Well, he could look sheepish all he liked, that didn't change what he'd done. "You know?" she asked, her voice growing louder by the second.

"Roselyn, you should be at home where you're safe, in your bedchamber."

"Do you think I will sit by, brush my hair, and lounge about on my bed while you prowl through the worst parts of London without me?"

"Yes. You must." He was shifting his weight as if expecting her to throw a punch in his direction…and he wasn't wrong.

He couldn't throw her into a carriage and walk

away. She wouldn't allow it. Lunging forward, she braced her hand against the door, coming face-to-face with Ethan in the process. "How could you do this? You are the one who suggested I step out of my doorway and live life."

He reached up to brush a fallen curl from her forehead, trailing his fingers down her cheek. "I will be the one at risk in the damp London streets tonight." The set of his shoulders, the stern look in his eye, everything about his stance said he was willing to fight her on this point. Why did it matter to him?

She'd been near Trevor's killer before, had even warned Ethan of danger at last night's ball. So why did he send her away now?

Had he only kissed her to manipulate her without any true desire on his part? It was a horribly embarrassing thought that had her shrinking into the corner of the carriage even as anger raged within her.

But as he closed the door she could have sworn she heard a faint, "Lounging about on her bed…in your dreams, Ethan."

It was odd for a man who only used kisses as a distraction to dream of her at all. Then with a swift bang on the side of the carriage, he was gone.

～

Ethan had accepted a dinner invitation from the dowager duchess and had spent every second after that regretting it. The door to the Thornwood residence now stood a finger's width from his raised hand. He had been standing there for longer than he'd care to admit. Once he knocked for entry, there would be no turning back from an evening spent with the family of a lady who hated him—again. "This should be large, steaming piles of enjoyment. Just as well to have it begin now," he mumbled to himself as he rapped his knuckles on the door.

A moment later he was shown into a parlor where the Grey family was gathered. The duke and duchess were sitting together on a settee under the front window, while the dowager duchess occupied a chair before the fire.

The duchess offered him a warm smile and waved toward a nearby chair. "Welcome, Lord Ayton. Do have a seat so that we might visit before we dine together."

"Of course," Ethan returned as he sat down. His gaze combed the room but Roselyn wasn't present. Was she so angry over last night that she was refusing to see him? There was a sound at the door and he spun in his chair, hoping Roselyn was entering the room, but it was only a footman taking his post in the corner.

"I'm so pleased you received our invitation," the duchess said, cutting into his thoughts. "Our man had a time of it finding your accommodations. I was afraid it would be tomorrow before you were invited to dinner this evening."

"That would have been problematic," Ethan offered, attempting good-natured humor.

"I was simply pleased he made it inside the house," Thornwood said under his breath just before getting elbowed in the ribs by his smiling wife.

Ethan sighed, wishing he'd realized the parlor offered a perfect view of the front steps. Nothing for it but to carry on, he supposed. If they'd already witnessed his indecision over attending, there was really nothing to be lost by asking the one question on his mind. "Will Lady Roselyn be joining us this evening?"

"Eventually," Thornwood responded. "She's spent most of the afternoon preparing for dinner."

The dowager duchess leaned on the arm of her chair to better see everyone in the room. Giving Thornwood a piercing glare she said, "There's nothing wrong with caring for one's looks, dear. You would do well to care a bit more, if you ask me."

"I'm presentable," Thornwood countered as he straightened his coat on his shoulders and pulled at the knot of his hastily tied cravat. "Though I do find it interesting that Roselyn was content to wear any old gown until she discovered we were entertaining a guest."

Ethan tensed as three sets of eyes turned on him. Had she given a care for her wardrobe because he was their guest? Perhaps she wasn't made aware of who their guest would be and her attention to her wardrobe was out of polite respect.

Either way he shifted in his seat in anticipation of seeing her. He shouldn't be so drawn to her. She'd made it clear she didn't care for him, and it was most likely bad form to spend time with one's dead brother's former fiancée. But two nights ago on the terrace, she'd kissed him back. And again last night... best not to think of last night since it was such a blunder, but the terrace—that had been something to cling to.

"Roselyn will be down shortly, I'm sure. She only needed to repair her hair when I checked in on her a bit ago," the duchess said.

"No small task, taming her hair," the dowager duchess mused.

Who would seek to tame anything about Roselyn? He liked the way her hair was always escaping its confines—it matched the woman herself. The true woman, not the polished shell she tried to present to the world. Ethan opened his mouth before he could think better of it. "Lady Roselyn always looks…"

Roselyn stepped into the parlor. Her hair was tucked and twisted onto her head. Not a single ringlet escaped, and he longed to ruffle it like a bird's feathers until it fell in wild curls around her shoulders. "You were saying," she prodded, her light gray eyes slicing him to the core.

"Lovely," Ethan finished. "You always look lovely." He watched as she walked past him to sit in the farthest corner from his present location, even though the chair beside his remained empty.

"I find it interesting that you say so, Lord Ayton, when so recently you found fault with the color of my dress."

"It wasn't the color. It was the fact that you…" Ethan broke off. "Perhaps this isn't a subject for predinner conversation."

"On the contrary, I find I'm quite enjoying this," Thornwood cut in.

"Do you often toss people into carriages and send them away like lost dogs? Perhaps it's sport for you?" Roselyn asked. Clearly she didn't share his reticence.

"When I'm attempting to protect someone from danger, then yes, I do," he replied, too irritated not to respond in kind.

"Dogs aren't usually sent away via carriage, Ros," Thornwood offered as he studied Ethan and ran a hand over his chin in thought.

The dowager duchess leaned forward, joining the conversation. "When did this happen, dear? Did someone lose a dog? How awful."

"There was no danger other than rats of your own invention," Roselyn retorted, ignoring her mother's questions.

"That was only to annoy Hardaway," Ethan said.

"He doesn't seem to be the sort to fear such things," the duchess mused.

"I'm told you came to my sister's aid in the garden at the Sutton ball," Thornwood cut in. "Rats aren't usually seen in the garden. When did this occur, Ayton?" His tone was as menacing as the glare he leveled at Ethan.

"There's no need to begin an interrogation, Devon," Roselyn said.

Thornwood only shot her a quick glance in return before turning back to Ethan. "You seem to have been about when my sister was in danger a number of times."

"A situation I'm attempting to remedy, I assure you," Ethan replied. This was not going well at all. He should have stayed on the front steps.

"Ha!" Roselyn said.

"Would you rather he allow you to get hurt, dear?" her mother asked.

"Remedies can be a bitter drink in Lord Ayton's case," Roselyn said, her gaze falling to the rug in front of her feet.

The conversation fell silent for a moment as Ethan

watched Roselyn. He'd only come to this blasted dinner to see her. Now he not only had her ire to contend with but her brother's as well.

"Drink?" Thornwood asked as he shoved a glass into Ethan's hand.

Ethan hadn't even realized the man had moved.

"I think I could use one, thank you." He watched Roselyn over the rim of his glass as he took a sip, allowing the fire of the liquid to burn a path down his throat and melt his trepidation. She might be angry with him for forcing her to return home, but the important thing was that she was unharmed.

"I would like a drink as well, if you don't mind," she said with her chin raised.

"Roselyn," her mother warned. "Dear, I believe you've been too long in the company of your friend Lady Victoria. Ladies don't swill liquor."

"I'm sure a drink wouldn't scandalize our guest too terribly—not from what I've seen of his lordship, at any rate."

Ethan choked on his whiskey.

"It's lovely to have someone from home visit for dinner," the duchess said with a nervous laugh as she attempted to steer the conversation back to neutral ground. "I enjoy London but I do miss the peace of the estate. My lord, you have much to become reacquainted with upon your return."

"My stay at Ormesby Place *was* rather brief. I look forward to seeing the changes to the area. I was amazed at the difference eight years made to the parts of the area I was able to explore."

"Eight years. I still remember you running about

with the local children." The dowager duchess smiled. "Roselyn, do you remember your younger days together? Such a happy time that was."

"How could I forget?" Roselyn asked, taking a sip from the small glass of sherry she'd been allowed. "He was the gangly boy who put a snake on my chair."

Ethan almost laughed, both at the memory of once being considered gangly and the joke he'd apparently accomplished all those years ago. "Did I?"

"You did."

"Apologies," he offered with a sympathetic nod of his head.

"Oh! See, everyone, he does know how to apologize. It only takes him twelve years to do so."

"Perhaps you've had enough to drink, dear," her mother replied.

"We should adjourn to the dining room." The duchess stood, inviting everyone else to do the same.

"Oh God. We have another hour of this torture, don't we?" Thornwood asked.

"At least that much. Come along, darling," his wife answered.

"You said they were on friendly terms," Thornwood stated. "This is dreadful."

Ethan moved to the parlor door, surprised when Roselyn took his arm for escort. "I thought you were angry with me."

"I am."

"Good to know."

They entered the dining room and sat down. It was a smaller room than he'd anticipated. When one thought of a ducal residence, even in town, opulence was the expectation. He should have known better—the Grey family was a unique sort. A long line of explorers had led to the current duke of Thornwood. Some called him "mad," but from what Ethan had seen, that was a load of fustian nonsense.

Ethan hadn't been old enough to keep up with Thornwood and the older boys when they were young, but Thornwood had always seemed nice enough—plain-speaking and rather to the point with his thoughts, but pleasant on the whole.

His gaze must have lingered too long on their surroundings because the duchess leaned forward to explain. "This is the small dining room, reserved for family meals."

"You were expecting a more formal evening?" the dowager duchess asked.

"I wasn't sure what to expect when I arrived here tonight." He answered the question, but he spoke only to Roselyn. "I admit I've become accustomed to a bachelor's life. Living alone, life is rather casual."

"You poor dear. No gentleman should be forced into a bachelor's life."

"Mother," Thornwood said. "I know you will never grasp this concept, but some rare gentlemen prefer a bachelor's life to a leg shackle."

"Those gentlemen don't know any better."

"It did seem to sort itself to rights for us," the duchess added over the rim of her wineglass, her blue eyes batting in her husband's direction.

"And so it shall for Lord Ayton. Fear not, we shall have you wed in no time." The Dowager Duchess of

Thornwood raised her glass and drank to the mission she'd set for herself.

"Mother, he'll flee our table at such talk," Thornwood argued as the first course was served.

Meanwhile, Roselyn remained silent. She didn't even lift her face from the task of pretending to eat soup until the topic moved to gentry living on the moors. Ethan couldn't fathom what she was thinking and gave up the attempt.

Their family was far different than he'd imagined. Perhaps this was how all families interacted—with good-natured ribbing, concern, and a general sense of interest in one another's goings-on. The conversation was the sort he imagined he would have had with Katie had he been present the past few years. His family, such as it was, couldn't have been more opposite to the Greys if they tried. The longer he sat in their company, the more he didn't wish to leave. Even if Roselyn was angry with him, he was still here with her—exactly where he wanted to be.

"Don't you agree, Lord Ayton?" the duchess asked.

"I…" He turned toward the Duchess of Thornwood, realizing too late that he'd been staring at Roselyn across the table and not listening to the ongoing discussion about their homes in the north. Roselyn had been glaring at him in return, only offering biting retorts to any comment he made and huffs of indignation when he remained silent.

"The answer is clear then, isn't it, dears?" the dowager duchess chimed in.

"The answer?" Ethan asked.

"My mother and wife are far too sympathetic to

your plight, Ayton," Thornwood said with a shake of his head.

"I take offense at this entire course of conversation," Roselyn cut in as she pushed her chair back from the table.

"I clearly missed something," Ethan interjected. "I have no plight this evening."

"He's so out of sorts, he can't think clearly, the dear. Ayton, remain here and discuss your differences with my daughter. We will be in the drawing room." The older woman turned to Roselyn with a stern look in her eye. "Roselyn, when you can gather yourself to speak with civility to our guest, the two of you may join us."

What was happening? He rose from his chair as everyone filed from the room. Thornwood shook his head as he was pulled from the room first. The dowager duchess gave Ethan an encouraging smile before she followed in the duke's wake. Turning to Roselyn, Ethan saw that she was rounding the table as well. He wasn't accustomed to family dinners, but this one was most unusual.

"Roselyn," he said, reaching for her arm to stop her retreat.

"I suppose you're pleased with yourself. Clearly, you've won over my family."

"I wasn't aware there was a battle for them."

"Everything is a battle with you," she said, shaking free of his grasp.

"Is it?" He didn't wish it to be.

"You think you know best, just like every other male in the country."

"Do I?" How odd, because at the moment he had no ideas on how to handle her. What the devil had her this upset? He knew he'd angered her last night, but this seemed to go beyond the indignity of being hauled from a portside warehouse at midnight. "Roselyn, why don't you sit? It can be useful to size up an opponent before a fight. Learn all you can." He motioned to the empty dining chairs.

"If it would help me win over you, then by all means…" She broke off with a shrug and glared at him, but she made no move to sit down.

"It doesn't seem as if there is a winner here, princess."

"Isn't there? You want me to sit at home and wait for you to find Trevor's killer."

"Yes, that's precisely what I want." Was her safety such a far thing to reach for?

"I suppose that makes me the lady in all of this."

"You are a lady, princess, very much so if I'm not mistaken."

"I'll have a hand in my own life, thank you." She spun on her heel and stomped a few paces away before turning around and pacing back. "I have no interest in sitting idle and filling my days with sketches and pianoforte while a killer is on the loose."

"I sent you home because you were in danger."

"As were you!"

"Roselyn, I can handle myself in a brawl. You know that."

"I can take care of myself as well. I've spent my entire life sitting at home, waiting, hoping for the best while someone else fights the battles. My actions, my life should be under my control."

"I'm a poor excuse for a gentleman, but even I know that isn't the way of things."

"Damn the way of things. It's never worked out well for me or any other lady of my acquaintance."

"The way of things keeps you safe, keeps you alive."

"Yes, and it can also leave me to pick up the pieces when you don't return."

He blinked in surprise. "Are you...*concerned* for me? Is that what this is truly about?"

"Of course I am. Once you've lost..." She paused her pacing, turning back to look at him. "Do you know the story of my father?"

"I've heard pieces of the tale," he hedged. Everyone had heard parts of her father's struggle, but it seemed she needed to tell the story. If it explained her anger, he was ready to listen.

"Pieces. That was all that was left when it was over."

"Sit," he offered, but when she shook her head he shrugged, pivoting his chair toward her before sitting.

"Have you ever known something to be true even though it sounded like a wild tale to those around you?"

"Rather recently, as a matter of fact. Remember when you thought me a killer?"

"That was precisely what happened to my father. He knew a foreign civilization to exist. Society called him mad. He boarded a ship to prove them wrong and left Mother and me to deal with the Mad Duke of Thornwood nonsense." She pursed her lips in thought. "It isn't easy having a father whom everyone thinks is mad, even if he was only committed to science. I suppose that was the problem. He was committed to the pursuit of science and not our family's welfare. He walked away from us and never returned."

Ethan reached out and grabbed her hand as she paced in front of him, stopping her path. "Roselyn, I'm not going to board a ship in pursuit of a murderer."

"You don't know that. And if you do, I would rather be in danger than left behind to mend the pieces that return, if that much!"

He glanced at the dining room door, noting it was barely cracked and no one stood guard before tugging on her hand to pull her closer. "I've had to mend pieces as well. Everyone has."

"Then you should understand my upset."

"I do." He glanced back to the sliver of open door leading to the hall before he pulled her down onto his lap.

She gasped and whipped her head around to the cracked door. "Someone could see."

"No one is watching. I made sure of it." He lifted a hand to her cheek to gain her attention. "I'll protect you now as I did last night. I know that isn't what you want, but I've lost people just as you have."

"I don't plan on being lost to you."

"I don't plan on being lost to you either."

The moment stretched out between them as their argument dissolved, leaving behind a simmering stew of raw emotions. Roselyn was here with him, and she was no longer angry. Where was this leading? No courtship began as theirs had. But were they courting? He wasn't even sure of that fact. He did spend a great deal of time in her company. He was at her home for a family dinner. Roselyn couldn't want him to court her, however. She'd traveled that path with his brother rather recently and still wore the black stays to prove it. He needed to tread carefully. He knew this, but his mind was clouded with the desire to touch her.

She shifted closer on his lap even though her hands were still folded together. "I don't think this is what my mother had in mind when she asked us to settle our differences."

"I still see quite a few differences between us."

"Oh?" she asked in a breathless voice. "Then I suppose we should discuss them."

"We should, shouldn't we? Very well, I'll begin." He traced the arch of her cheekbone with his fingers, barely believing the direction their argument had turned. "Your skin is soft and smooth against my callused hands. Quite different."

"Mmmm, I have to agree." She bit back a smile, tugging on her lip with her teeth the way he longed to. "Your hair is short whereas mine is long?" she asked, clearly gaining confidence in their play.

She unlaced her fingers and lifted her arm, watching her own hand as she sank her fingers into his hair. Her nails scratched gently against his scalp and he tilted his head into her hand.

When he'd regained his wits, he offered, "I won't prove the truth of that difference, or we would leave this room looking rather guilty of indiscretion."

She smiled down at him and his chest tightened. It was her true smile, the one she saved just for him.

He followed the line of her jaw down the side of her neck to her shoulder. "You have the delicate shoulders of a lady," he said, tracing the silhouette of her collarbone with his fingers. "Quite unlike mine."

"Quite," she replied as she slipped one hand under the lapel of his coat. "Your broad chest..." she began but stopped just as quickly with a shake of her head. She blushed, obviously realizing she would have to finish the sentence.

He took pity on her and added, "Is most definitely different from yours." He rounded his hand over the curve of her breast and felt her resulting twitch against his own chest where her palm was still pressed against him. The tenderness of the moment wrapped around them, growing warmer by the second. Her slight weight bore down on his legs, and he tightened the hold of the arm that encircled her waist. She didn't seem to mind being held so close to him—a fact he tested as he teased the nipple under his hand into awareness with his thumb.

Her breaths became shallow and she sat with complete stillness, as if afraid he would stop if she flinched. "It's your turn," she whispered.

"My turn?" he asked, his voice rough with desire, before remembering their increasingly heated discussion. "Right." He looked up at her and named the first thing that came to mind. "Your lips are the color of roses in the early spring, full, lush, inviting." He released a small sigh. "I'm certain mine don't look as kissable as yours do."

"That's not true."

"Have we struck upon something we have in common? Perhaps we should test our theory."

He couldn't wait any longer. He needed to quench

his thirst for her. Reaching up, he wrapped a hand around the back of her neck and pulled her closer until his mouth was on hers. Seconds slid into uncounted minutes.

She matched his movements, learning from him and giving it all back with every flick of her tongue and caress of her sweet lips. He struggled for more even as he knew he must remain in control. As much as he wanted to drown in the feel of her body against his, if he let go of reason, he would take her here on the family dining table. But that didn't mean he couldn't enjoy every second of this encounter with her.

He pulled her closer into his embrace until her back was arched into him as he dipped his head to taste her skin, trailing kisses down her neck. He slid his hands down her back, allowing himself to explore her body, the curve of her bottom over her hip to her thigh.

She let out a small whimper of need as he kissed the base of her neck, and wrapped her hand in the hair at the back of his neck, holding him to her. "This isn't about one evening's diversion, is it?" she whispered.

"God, no. I could never have enough of you," he said without thought before realizing his admission. He stilled, not sure how to proceed.

She pulled back from him a fraction and met his troubled gaze. "Good," she said, and then she kissed him once more.

Footsteps sounded in the hall outside the door. Apparently, this moment he was allowed with her was coming to an end. She must have heard the sound too because she leaped from his arms before he could resign himself to ending their time together. He steadied her with his hands on her waist and nudged a chair closer to his with a kick of his foot, pushing her into it.

A second later when Thornwood pushed the door open, Roselyn was sitting at a respectable distance from Ethan as he lifted his wineglass to his lips for something to occupy his hands.

Thornwood surveyed the scene as he spoke. "I've been sent to inquire if you are able to set your differences aside in favor of civil conversation over cards."

"I believe we have found common ground between us," Roselyn said. Her cheeks were still pink and her breathing unsteady, but hopefully her brother didn't notice.

"Indeed. Unfortunately, I'm unable to stay for cards this evening. I have business to see to elsewhere," Ethan said.

"Very well. We enjoyed your company this evening." Thornwood turned to leave the room, but stopped. Looking back, he added, "Ayton, when trying to give the appearance of innocence, it's generally good practice not to drink from an empty wineglass. Good evening."

Ethan heard Roselyn's sharp intake of breath before he could turn back to her. Perhaps he'd been a bit too cavalier with her this evening. He should work harder to shield her from possible downfall, but he couldn't find a shred of regret within his heart for his actions tonight. She'd wanted his nearness, his touch.

Roselyn had been concerned for him last night. He couldn't keep his mind from circling back to her earlier admission. No one had ever worried over him before.

His family certainly hadn't wasted the effort. The Spares were allies, a brotherhood, but he'd always been expected to fend for himself within their ranks. He'd never had difficulty defending himself in less-than-ideal situations, and yet the refined lady he'd held in his arms was worried about his safety. She was a precious gift, a respite from the troubles of the world, and he would treasure every moment he was allowed with her.

Perhaps tomorrow he would know how to proceed. Tonight, he was too busy celebrating his victory in this round to care if he drank from empty glasses forever.

# *Sixteen*

"DOES MY HAT MATCH THIS DRESS?" ROSELYN ASKED, twirling the tail of ribbon between her fingers. When she'd selected this shade of green, it had clearly been before the sun decided to appear. Now, standing in the bright garden, she wasn't so sure of her choice.

"Your hat always matches your dress. As does mine." Evangeline stared off toward a distant row of roses. "Roselyn, do you ever want to *not* wear a matching hat? Perhaps arrive at a garden party with no hat at all, lift our faces to the sun, and encourage freckles?"

She turned to consider Evangeline. "One of my dear friends has freckles, and I find them charming on her. I don't know that I could pull off the look myself." Roselyn missed Katie more every time she thought of her. They wrote to each other, but there were some things that couldn't be explained in a letter. She supposed she could tell Katie about Ethan…but perhaps it was best not to divulge too much where Ethan was concerned. Roselyn smiled. She hadn't caught sight of him yet today. Taking a breath, she focused on what Evangeline was saying.

"I find I no longer care how it will look. I want to feel the sun on my skin and the breeze in my hair."

Roselyn drew back in shock from her always-pristine friend. "Who are you and what have you done with Evangeline?"

"I know. It's shameful, isn't it? Mother would scrub me down and cover me in perfumed powders at the mention of such a thing."

"I won't tell," Roselyn said with a grin and a nudge to Evangeline's elbow.

"I may not be as trustworthy," a male voice said over their shoulders, making both ladies jump.

Turning, Roselyn saw the man who had gathered a crowd around him a few nights ago at the ball. He was tall and lean, with chiseled features. His light-blue eyes glinted with some hidden jest as he looked at Evangeline. Roselyn looked at her friend as well. Could he be the reason for the difference she'd seen in Evangeline recently? Roselyn wasn't sure what she thought of this gentleman, but her friend's smile spoke volumes in his favor.

"Lady Roselyn Grey," Evangeline said, seeming to realize no introductions had been made. "This is Lord Crosby. Crosby, Lady Roselyn is…"

"Far too busy to talk to the likes of you," Ethan finished with a grin as he joined them.

"Never," Roselyn said as she looked from Crosby to Ethan and then back again. "I hope you will pardon my friend Lord Ayton, who has *no* control over *my* schedule."

"I approve of this friendship, Ayton," Crosby offered as he clasped Ethan on the shoulder in greeting. "Anyone who can put you in your place deserves a medal of some sort."

"I fear she would be so weighted down with awards that she would be unable to move." Ethan spoke to Crosby, but his gaze never left her.

"Then she won't mind when I steal her friend away for a turn in the garden?" Crosby asked.

Roselyn cleared her throat and pulled her attention from Ethan and how handsome he looked this afternoon. "Of course not."

"Roselyn, if my mother comes looking for me, tell her I've gone inside to avoid the sun. *That* activity, I'm sure she would condone."

Roselyn nodded and watched them leave. Turning back to Ethan, she was surprised to see him watching her and not the retreating couple. "You're friends with Lord Crosby."

"We share an affiliation," he hedged.

"And Lord Hardaway."

"Do you have a point?"

"No, I'm simply sizing up my opponent. Someone taught me to do that recently."

"Sounds like a fascinating fellow," he said.

"Not particularly." She shrugged and managed a straight face for a moment before laughter escaped her lips.

Ethan glanced around at the smattering of good society members chatting in the shade of a great tree, sipping lemonade and eating food from one of the refreshment tables. "What does one *do* at a garden party?"

"I believe we are already doing it," she said with a lowered voice so as not to offend their hosts.

"Somewhat anticlimactic, don't you think?"

"I suppose if you were expecting garish party decor, flowing drink, and cheap women…"

"That does sound enticing. I find, however, I'm rather enjoying this sort of party at the moment." He leaned close under the guise of placing her hand on his arm. "It must be the company. Though I can think of one improvement we could make." His fingers lingered over hers for a second longer than was appropriate.

"Ethan," she whispered. "Not here. I know our friends just wandered away together, but that was only for a stroll among the flowers. We can't very well slip between the bushes to continue what we began last night."

"I wasn't going to suggest that. But I appreciate that your mind turned in that direction. Do you always think such salacious thoughts, princess?"

"No! I only assumed…" Was he not going to escort her away and kiss her again? Her embarrassment at her miscalculation warred with regret. She stared at the ground as they strolled toward one of the refreshment tables. She had to explain. "You're the one who…"

"Shhh. I'm sure I'm to blame for any less-than-angelic thoughts in your mind."

"I'm thinking some rather choice ones at the moment." She lifted her face to see him properly. "Care to hear them?"

"That doesn't seem wise," he mused with a wry smile.

"Your loss."

"Roselyn, it occurs to me that I need to make amends."

"I'm not truly out of sorts, just a bit embarrassed that I jumped to conclusions. To be accused of *salacious thoughts* when I always try so to be prudent. Desire has never entered into my thoughts...until recently anyway."

"You desire something now?" He stopped walking and looked down at her, seemingly hanging on her answer.

"I desire this afternoon."

Ethan raised a brow in question. "Warm lemonade and idle chatter?"

"Among other things." She tightened her grip on his arm for a moment, pulling him to continue walking.

"Please tell me you aren't speaking of your dress or breaking in new shoes."

She rose to her toes to whisper, "I've had these shoes for ages."

"I've never been so honored to be compared to old shoes," he replied with a grin.

Roselyn couldn't help the bubble of laughter that escaped her throat. "You're welcome. Now, I believe you wished to make amends for some wrong."

"I did." He allowed her hand to drop from his arm and turned to face her. His gaze was intent on her, unswerving. He pulled a rectangular velvet box from his pocket. It was the one she'd seen him drop into his pocket that day on Bond Street. But what was he doing with it here in the middle of a garden party? They weren't exactly in the middle of a crowd, but where they stood offered a partial view of their interactions.

She glanced around, noticing for the first time how quiet the party had grown. She'd been so focused on

Ethan that she hadn't noticed that all conversation around them had lowered to a rumble. Her heart pounded as her eyes raced from face to face, taking in their looks of keen interest, curiosity, and dismay.

Ethan stood poised with a box most assuredly containing jewelry. He couldn't give her jewelry. Everyone present would think the worst of her. She'd be branded a demimondaine. She could perhaps live down being alone with her fiancé at the time of his death, but a public gift from a gentleman? This couldn't happen. The whispers had already begun, and Ethan was staring so intently at her that he didn't seem to notice.

"...rather friendly with the brother," Roselyn heard one lady say, but it was all she needed.

She laid her hand over Ethan's before he could open the box. She had to stop him, to somehow reverse the progression of time. "Not now, my lord." She barely breathed the words through gritted teeth.

"I don't want these hard feelings to continue between us."

"I don't either, which is why you need to stop."

He wasn't listening, as his mind was clearly on the words he wanted to say. "I made your life difficult with my talk about town, and as a result I put you in a dangerous situation."

"You don't say." Her voice came out in a high-pitched ring of panic. She had to repair the damage he was causing. *Think, Roselyn, think.* She offered the nearest group of ladies, who were now straining to be within earshot, a gracious smile before turning back to Ethan. "You really shouldn't do this," she said in an urgent whisper. "Ethan!" she hissed between clenched teeth, but he was staring down at the box between them, plowing forward heedless of her words.

"I've spent so much of my life removed from society. I know it's no excuse for my actions, but perhaps this will compensate for my faults."

She would need compensation for the faults he was revealing at this moment. How could he be of the peerage and not know this wasn't done? But then, he also wasn't expecting the title and was raised in the same unconventional home that had produced breeches-wearing, horse-obsessed Katie. Blast the originality of the Moore family and their brazen lack of knowledge of society! "Lord Ayton, you really need to listen to me."

But in the next moment, he opened the box in spite of her hand resting on top. A sparkling jet necklace set in silver was displayed inside. She gasped at the beauty of the extravagant gift for a split second before slamming the box shut with a *whap*.

"It's from my family's mines. I got it from the shop on Bond Street. The black reminded me of…" Ethan broke off, his brows drawn together in concern. "Do you not like it?"

"No, I…" She stopped, resisting at the hurt visible in his eyes. There must be a means of changing the situation without causing that look to cross his face. She didn't want to cause him pain. He was trying to give her a gift—a lovely gift. Her fingers itched to touch the piece. She wanted to see it draped about her neck, to feel the weight of it and know that Ethan had chosen it with her in mind. If only the situation was different.

He reopened the box and pulled out a necklace that rivaled the finest any true princess would ever wear. Teardrops of jet cascaded down from a central circle of black and silver. A hush came over the crowd as he laid it across the palm of her hand.

She glanced around at the shocked looks on the faces of those present and leaped at the first misguided idea that came to mind.

"As you can see," she said in a carrying voice as she turned from Ethan and held the necklace high in the air, "the stores of Bond Street are very much in business after the recent fire. Your patronage is always appreciated during difficult times such as these. I have long been a proponent of…shopping. As such, Lord Ayton has asked me to say a few words. Haven't you, my lord?"

"I have?" he murmured, brow furrowed, before turning to the gathered group. "I have indeed."

Roselyn nodded in agreement as she took a small step forward. "If we could have a moment of silence for the losses those shopkeepers suffered?" A hush fell over the crowd and heads lowered. Roselyn shot a quick glance at Ethan, who looked both taken aback and amused.

"Sorry?" he mouthed, as if finally realizing what he had done.

She shrugged and plowed ahead, hoping the ruse would work. "Now, we will pass a bowl around for donations to go to…" She shot a pleading look at Ethan, not knowing what donations would go toward.

"Damages to the stores affected," he supplied.

"Yes, and children," she added with a smile.

"Children?"

"Mmmm-hmmm…children in need of…"

"Food?" Ethan cut in over the top of her pronouncement of "Shoes."

"Yes, food and shoes for children," she clarified. If anyone believed this, it would be shocking. She reached behind her and pulled a bowl of fruit from the table, littering the ground behind her skirts with strawberries, grapes, and slices of apple. She shoved the bowl at the nearest lady and kept walking toward the entrance to the garden.

"Is this a charity event?"

"How lovely to give back after such a tragedy."

The necklace hung from Roselyn's gloved hand, adding weight to the maneuver she'd accomplished. If anyone suspected the truth, they said nothing. She stopped her retreat to glance back at Ethan who was now surrounded in conversation, smiles, and friendly nods. She would have to discuss the gift with him at a later time. Especially since she hadn't any idea what to say on the subject. Her fingers tightened on the necklace as she turned back to the garden gate, only to find her path blocked.

"What an unexpected turn," the hostess stated, catching Roselyn by the arm.

"My apologies for not warning you prior to my speech, Lady Pepridge."

"My garden party is the talk of London. No apologies necessary."

Just then, Lily caught up with her, an amused smile barely contained on her usually serene face. "Lady Roselyn has such a mind for philanthropy.

It's wonderful, is it not?" Lily covered the necklace in Roselyn's hand with the end of her shawl as she spoke. "Roselyn, we really must go. Lovely party, Lady Pepridge."

Roselyn let Lily lead her through the garden gate. They only dared to speak in glances until they were well away from the gathering. As they neared the carriage, Lily slowed her pace, giving Roselyn a sympathetic look and a pat on the arm as she adjusted her shawl back on her shoulders.

"Do you think anyone suspected the truth?" Roselyn finally asked.

"Your mother almost required smelling salts."

"Is she terribly upset with me?"

"On the contrary," Lily said with a smile. "You overturned the fruit bowl and not the platter with the cakes she's been pilfering all afternoon. If you had tossed her sweets to the ground, you might have started a war."

"But the necklace…"

"Is lovely and a subject for discussion later, at home."

Roselyn glanced down at the stones clutched between her fingers where they caught the sunlight. Lily was right; she didn't need to decide how to approach Ethan just yet. For now, she would enjoy the glow her time with him had left in her heart, which was closely matched by the jewelry she held in her hand.

৵

"It is lovely," Isabelle said, sighing. She held the jet necklace to her own throat and admired it in the mirror.

"And I'm sure it's quite valuable," Roselyn added from her perch on the end of her bed.

"No one thought it unattractive or made of paste." Evangeline spun on her seat at the dressing table to look up at Isabelle. "That's the issue. If a gentleman were to give you an imitation trinket of no concern and unfortunate appeal, society would hardly notice. That, however, is not an easily forgettable necklace. You did well to disguise the entire event as charity, but you can't wear it out anywhere now."

"Won't you at least try it on?" Isabelle asked. How would she look if she knew the truth? That Roselyn had slept in the piece last night and stayed abed for an extra half hour, admiring it in a hand mirror.

"I don't see why not." Roselyn was off the bed and across the room with Isabelle in a heartbeat.

"Am *I* the only one who sees why not? Once you've experienced something grand, there's no returning to ordinary. Sometimes rebellions like these are a curse, because you must go on and pretend nothing happened." There was a sadness in Evangeline's eyes. How much of a gentleman had Lord Crosby been yesterday in the garden?

But then Isabelle placed the necklace around her throat and Roselyn forgot her train of thought.

"She isn't going to wear it to a ball, which is a shame since it's so beautiful." Isabelle turned back to Evangeline. "She's simply going to show it to us properly within the confines of her bedchamber."

"After which you will return it to Lord Ayton?" Evangeline asked.

"I suppose I must."

"It is a shame," Evangeline admitted. "If only he'd had the good sense to give you this gift in private, you might be able to keep it. No one would be the wiser."

"Since when has Lord Ayton had good sense?" Roselyn asked.

"Since when has Evangeline changed her views on perfect behavior even behind closed doors?" Isabelle added, clearly noting the change in Evangeline as well.

"I'm not perfect behind closed doors. Unfortunately, I never have been. And you're changing the subject."

"To a very intriguing one," Roselyn replied as Isabelle latched the clasp at the back of her neck.

Isabelle rested her arm around Roselyn's shoulders and looked into the mirror with her. "It is lovely, isn't it?"

The black stones glistened at her throat, reminding her of a certain black-clad gentleman. It was fitting that his family mines produced jet. Somehow the brilliant tones of rubies or sapphires wouldn't fit Ethan as this did. It was as though she wore a small piece of him about her neck, dark and heavy yet catching the light with a twinkle—just how Ethan looked at her.

"You would shine on every ballroom floor," Isabelle said at her side.

Roselyn trailed her fingers over the stones, warm against her skin. "And yet it will never be seen on a ballroom floor."

Isabelle got a dangerous look in her eye and grinned. "Perhaps if you…"

"Isabelle," Evangeline warned as she stood from her seat at the dressing table. "Don't make this more difficult than it must be. It's hard enough for Roselyn to continue on, knowing she possessed something so lovely for a time, something she can't possibly keep."

Roselyn turned toward her friend, watching as she blinked away tears she knew had nothing to do with any necklace and everything to do with Lord Crosby. "Are you all right, Evangeline?"

She sniffed and raised her chin. "Of course I am. Why do you ask?"

Roselyn and Isabelle exchanged disbelieving glances but said nothing.

She took one last admiring look in the mirror before reaching up to unhook the necklace. As it slid from her neck to land in her palm, she sighed.

That was when she noticed it—a tiny marking on the back of the piece, etched into the silver of the clasp. Lifting it to the light, she squinted to make out what it said: the letters *W* and *B*, entwined with vines.

"W. B... W. B. Exports. The warehouse at the harbor?" *But he took this necklace from the shop on Bond, didn't he?*

Evangeline peered over her shoulder to see what held Roselyn's attention. "Looks to be a maker's mark. I have a necklace with that marking on the back as well."

"But this necklace was from—" She stopped herself before sharing that Ethan's family owned the jewelry store on Bond that had burned. "It's from a shop on Bond, and they receive inventory from the mines on Lord Ayton's family lands."

"That must be the mark of their wares."

"That's the problem." Roselyn looked up at the confused looks on her friends' faces. "It *isn't* their marking." The significance of this discovery was lost on them, but Ethan would understand. This might just be the clue he'd been searching for. He may not want her involved in this investigation, but it was too late for that. He'd placed the key to the puzzle right in her hand.

She stared at the marking on the necklace. Why would the Moore family mine for jet, have jewelry crafted from it, and ship that jewelry to their shop in London, only to have it remarked with the W. B. emblem and sent to the harbor? "They wouldn't," she whispered to herself. Someone who wished to steal from the family would, though. And a theft of this size would leave a trail—a trail that led to a killer.

Trevor must have discovered the plot against his family. He'd always been careful and considerate about everything involving his family's estate and mines. She ran a finger over the engraved letters. This wouldn't have slipped his notice for long. And once he'd learned who was behind the massive theft, he'd been killed to ensure his silence. *Ethan and I were simply bystanders to a greater plot than I could have imagined*. But Trevor had known the truth. Why hadn't she thought of it before?

She blinked up at her friends who were watching her with a mix of curiosity and concern. "I think my black dress is going to get another use. I need to break into Ormesby House."

⁂

Roselyn stowed the hairpin back in the thick braids on her head and leaned against the inside of the front door of Ormesby House. She was only a short walk away from her family's Mayfair residence, but the walk here alone at night had kept her on her toes. Once she'd even had to dive behind a large shrub while a few gentlemen passed on horseback.

She sighed, her eyes combing the interior of the home. She'd visited Katie here last season, but it didn't seem the same now without her friend, without even a single candle to light her way. White covers blanketed the furniture. The grates were empty, and the chill of the night pushed its way in through the windowpanes.

This had to be done though, and after her last two failed attempts at spy work, she needed to accomplish this task herself. Ethan's company might well be appreciated while inside this tomb of a home, but she'd wanted to come here alone to prove she could succeed without his assistance. And she was about to prowl through her former fiancé's belongings. Some privacy might be necessary.

She shivered and moved forward. "No turning back now," she muttered.

Glancing into the rooms as she passed, she thought back to last season. Katie had always been either in the mews in the rear of the house or—when forced to be ladylike for the afternoon—she could be found in the parlor. Trevor hadn't haunted the same locations when he was about. Roselyn shook off the thought of Trevor haunting anything at all. What a lovely image that was when faced with prowling through a dead man's possessions for answers. Glancing up the dark staircase that led to an even darker second floor, she took a fortifying breath and moved into the shadows.

On the second try, she found what must be Trevor's rooms because there was a portrait of him over the fireplace. She stood in the doorway for a moment, watching the painting. It was eerie to see his likeness again, yet it seemed a lifetime ago that she'd known the man the portrait depicted. So much had happened. Was it wrong to root through his belongings? Well, it wasn't as if he was around to complain. "Apologies," she said to the portrait. "I'm only trying to find your killer." She fell silent on the part about how that involved assisting his brother and subsequently kissing him. "You're a portrait. That's all you need to know." With a nod she went to the nearest piece of furniture and began removing the white sheets.

A moment later she'd pulled the draperies back to allow moonlight within the room and she was standing at Trevor's desk—Trevor's empty desk. She wasn't sure what she'd been expecting. It wasn't likely that a pile of evidence would be waiting for her with the name of his killer clearly printed in black ink. Although she had been hopeful about just such a thing.

Sinking into the chair, she rapped her fingers on the wooden surface. Where would Trevor keep information about a theft at the mines?

Her gaze fell to the drawer of his desk. Pulling it open, she saw carefully labeled files marching in rows. With a smile over Trevor's organization in all things, she began thumbing through the sorted and grouped papers. Accounts receivable, accounts payable, mining this, mining that—it would take hours to sort through all of the information here. Hours she didn't have since she would certainly be missed at home by then. That was when she spied a parcel labeled *Personal*.

She laid the packet on the desk and glanced back to the portrait of Trevor before tearing into it. "Apologies again. But I believe murder to be a quite personal matter."

The parcel, however, was filled with notes of some sort... Were these love notes? Perhaps Trevor hadn't been as innocent as she once believed him. "You were capable of composing a love note?" she asked the portrait.

She opened the top missive in the pile and began to read.

*Dearest Katherine,*

"Katherine?" Roselyn muttered. He had quite the pattern with ladies named Katherine. That was Katie's true name, though she was violently opposed to being called by such. She'd been named for their mother. Curiosity pulled her further into the note. Her eyes skimmed across the words on the paper.

*I was pleased to see you this morning while you were out for your ride. Every moment I'm able to spend in your company is a precious gift.*

"A precious gift, was it? All you ever offered me were two nights a year on a list," Roselyn grumbled, but returned to the note once more. She wasn't truly upset over the slight, only surprised at how little she had known Trevor.

*I was disappointed that you had to return so soon to see to the children. I watched you ride away across the moors as beautiful as the day I met you so long ago. Remember our first season together in London? I think of it more often than you know. One day when you find the courage to leave that man, we can spend every day together. You will no longer be pulled away from me for the sake of his offspring. And I will hold you in my arms forever.*

Roselyn looked up from the note, something in the words not ringing true to even the vaguest knowledge of Trevor. He'd met Katherine during the season long ago and now she had a husband and children. Trevor would never lure a married lady away from her family. It wasn't in his character. In fact, the only person she knew who would abandon a family at home in favor of a lover was…Lady Ormesby.

Her eyes grew wide at the realization. This note wasn't from Trevor to a lover, it was from a lover to his mother! Trevor had found the identity of the Frenchman who'd stolen his mother away. Roselyn gasped, her gaze flying to the bottom of the note.

*Yours always,*
*Herold*

Herold didn't sound like the name of the Frenchman she was reported to have left her family for. Herold sounded entirely British, but if so, then why the tale of the French lover?

She pressed the note out flat on the desk and

moved her hand over the words. Ethan had only spoken of his mother once. The pain she'd seen in his eyes had been clear that day in the park when he talked of her abandonment of the family. If he knew of this, would it only bring him further hurt? Ethan had been hurt enough, hadn't he? She would have to be careful how she broke this news to him. In the meantime, she would read the words written to his mother in search of clues to Trevor's death. It wasn't a perfect plan, but even perfect plans had flaws, in her experience.

Roselyn stood from the chair and scooped up the love notes in her arms. After replacing the covers over the furniture, she turned to look at the portrait above the fireplace one last time.

"The theft at W. B. Exports and the details about your mother's lover who wasn't French at all... You certainly had a few secrets, Trevor. And perhaps you had more." She moved closer. "The question is, which secret got you killed?"

❦

"Who established the brilliant rule that one can't give a gift to a lady?" Ethan grumbled as he settled deeper into his chair at headquarters, still sulking a day after the damned garden party.

"Gentlemen who don't wish to part with their money?" Hardaway suggested, taking a hearty gulp of the whiskey in his hand.

Ethan rubbed his aching forehead, trying to understand at what point in his life he'd gotten everything wrong. "When a lady is angry, you give her flowers or jewelry. It was the only lesson I ever learned from my father, and now it seems even that is rubbish."

"It does put us at the disadvantage of not being able to purchase our way out of trouble, I agree," St. James added as he took his standard seat across the table from Ethan.

Ethan leaned his head back against the soft leather of the chair. Although he would dash out the door in a heartbeat if Roselyn were near, he was enjoying the commiseration of like-minded men at the moment. "I see why you remain unattached, St. James," he muttered. "Much simpler."

St. James didn't answer, only studied the cup of black tea he was pouring.

"Lady Roselyn pulled you out of the muck—from what I heard anyway," Crosby mused from behind the daily post he held in his hands before lowering it to his lap. "She'd play a fine part in a scheme, you know. Quick to act when problems arise amid society."

"She'll have no part in your steam pursuits, Crosby...or should I say Claughbane," Ethan countered with a wry grin, knowing the use of the man's true name would cut deeper than a knife wound.

Lord Crosby, as he was known in town, was in reality Ash Claughbane—a smooth-talking swindler, youngest brother of a duke from the Isle of Man and the most recent member of the Spare Heirs Society. But no one beyond this table knew his secret. For a time, only St. James had known the truth, but Hardaway had finally convinced him to talk. As much as Ethan didn't care for secrets, he had to admit that the young confidence man was a friendly sort and a welcome addition to the Spares.

"That hurts, mate. Really it does," Crosby mocked. "My *steam pursuits*, as you put it, are quickly becoming the talk of the town."

"Precisely why I don't want Lady Roselyn involved, no matter the quality of her fine lying skills. You do plenty of that without her."

Crosby sat back in his seat with a proud grin. "I prefer to think of my words as possessing the promise of truth. I sell hope, Ayton." His bright blue eyes twinkled as he spoke. "People need hope."

Ethan took a swallow of his drink. Hope was in short supply at the moment. He still hadn't heard back from Cladhart about the theft. Clearly it was a complicated matter since he'd looked at the warehouse himself. He'd found plenty of jet, but that didn't prove who was behind such a crime. Cladhart must be having the same struggles. Perhaps there was another mine now and he had the entire situation wrong— Ethan had been away for some time. Things changed in time. The truth was his search for Trevor's killer had hit a wall, and until he heard from Cladhart, that didn't have much hope of improvement. All he had in his life were a few stolen moments with Roselyn, and he'd managed to muck them up as well. "I could use some hope—hope of setting things right with Lady Roselyn," he muttered.

"Apologies. That kind of hope isn't for sale."

Hardaway let out a loud laugh. "Crosby may, however, have some of the raspberry cordial he sold as a love potion in his trunk upstairs. Quality liqueur, I hear."

"If it helps your situation, the last vial is yours for five pounds," Crosby cut in.

"Five pounds?" Ethan exclaimed.

"That's the price of love, mate," Crosby said with a grin.

"It won't make her forgive you for the stunt with the necklace this afternoon, but it'll take the edge off your bitterness over it," Hardaway mused, lifting his glass in salute.

No love potion or raspberry cordial would fix the mess he'd made with Roselyn. "I'll survive," Ethan mumbled.

"Hmmm," St. James said as he looked out the window beside them.

"Do you disagree? You could be right. I may not survive this."

"A social misstep you will survive." St. James took a sip of his tea, a thoughtful frown clouding his face. "Those men across the street who are stalking your every move, however, may prove otherwise."

Hardaway stood and peered around the draperies to the street in front of the house. "Those aren't the same men. Damn, Ayton. How many enemies do you have trailing after you?" He said the words in the tone one would use when offering a compliment; for Hardaway, more enemies meant a job well done.

Ethan turned just enough in his chair to spot the two men on the opposite corner, watching them through the window. He was expecting to see the same men from the docks but Hardaway was right—this time was different. This time he drew back in shock.

"Santino's men," he whispered as his eyes met St. James's. They couldn't have found him, not here. He'd been careful to protect the location of headquarters.

He curled his hands into fists without realizing he was doing so. If they wanted him, they would have a fight to deal with first.

"Are you certain?" St. James asked.

Ethan only nodded as St. James looked down to the street again.

"I've escaped an angry mob on occasion, but there were never any among them that looked like that." Crosby winced as he spoke. "It might be a good turn that your lady isn't pleased with you at the moment. You wouldn't want that arriving on her doorstep."

As much as Crosby dealt in falsehoods, Ethan knew the unfortunate truth when he heard it. Between hunting a killer and being hunted by a killer, he was in no place to court a lady. But he was in no place to walk away from her either.

# Seventeen

ETHAN CUT ACROSS THE BALLROOM, SPYING ROSELYN near the opposite corner. She wasn't difficult to find, because she was wearing a near-blinding dress the color of an orange's peel. The gown would have been garish on anyone else, but against Roselyn's pale skin it only made her glow. Her dark hair slipped over one shoulder in stark contrast.

There was danger lurking somewhere outside the walls of this ballroom, but it wasn't here. There would be time to think of all that had come between them and all that watched from the shadows, he told himself. He'd planned on a rather heavy discussion, but now that he was here, he only wanted to be near the lady in orange. He grinned at her, narrowly missing a lady who was twirling in his direction. Sidestepping one couple who almost careened into him and ducking beneath another's outstretched arms, he reached the other side of the floor. "I came to speak with you."

"Obviously," Roselyn replied. "As it happens, I need the same."

He turned far enough to gesture to the dance floor as he asked, "Care to dance?"

"Not particularly. I believe you just made quite a few enemies while crossing the floor. And I like these shoes."

"Really?" he asked, eyeing the bright-orange concoctions peeking out from the bottom of her gown.

"Yes, really. They're quite stylish." She hit him on the arm with her fan, making him smile.

"If you say so," he teased. She was beautiful no matter what she wore.

"Not everything can be black, you know."

He ran a hand down the lapels of his coat and shot her a grin, his eyes lingering on the ringlet of coal-black hair that he longed to lift from her shoulder. "Everything looks better in black."

"Fishing for compliments this evening?"

"No, simply stating fact."

"You are the most arrogant, poorest excuse for a gentleman in my acquaintance."

She was teasing, but something about her words struck a chord. What was he doing, eyeing her like she was an orange cake about to be served at tea? This hadn't been his plan. He'd had a plan. He needed to warn her off any involvement with him. He *was* a terrible excuse for a gentleman. He was awful, and his actions had put her in danger and nearly destroyed her reputation. Men lurked in the streets, watching him, and they were only drawing nearer. If she stayed well away from him, she wouldn't become tangled in the mess of his past. If she stayed well away from him, she'd be safe.

They needed a quiet place to speak. Subtly tipping his head toward one of the back exits—if he remembered correctly, there was very little toward that corner of the house to signify—Ethan led the way out of the crowded ballroom. The hall was very nearly empty, the ball seeming to fade away more and more with each step. The occasional guest still slipped past on the way to a nearly empty card room, however. They needed yet more privacy. He glanced around, noticing an extra set of closed draperies that matched the ones at the windows. That was just the place.

He pulled her inside, expecting a small alcove, and instead walked straight into a large tree. This must be a small morning room converted into a storage area to make space for the ball. Potted plants filled almost every available space of the floor, branches arching to the ceiling of the earthy-smelling room, transforming it into a conservatory. Turning, he ensured that the draperies were closed behind them, the door having been removed.

"Roselyn," he started, but she disappeared behind the containers of greenery and the words died on his lips. Stepping farther into the small, wood-paneled room, he followed her into the shadows.

"Isn't this lovely," she announced, sitting on the bench seat below the far window. "You could barely tell the place existed behind those curtains. I wonder why they have it hidden away like this."

He considered the ballroom, where light glinted from every surface and watchful eyes surveyed the room. "I could venture a guess."

"Never mind that. I have quite a few things to

tell you." She took a small breath, appearing nervous as she pulled the necklace he'd given her out of her reticule, the silver and polished stones catching the moonlight that spilled over her shoulder.

He sat. This was it. She was giving back his gift and walking away. And he was going to let her. It was for the best, but that didn't stop his chest from constricting with the news. "There's no need for explanation. I should have known all along."

"How could you have known? I saw the evidence as plainly as you did, and it took my admiring the necklace to truly see."

*Evidence* was an odd way to phrase it, but he allowed her to continue. He didn't deserve her. He knew it. She must know it now as well, but was there evidence? If there was documentation of such a thing, he wouldn't put it past his Roselyn to find it.

She turned his hand over on his leg and thrust the necklace into his grasp. It shouldn't be surprising, and yet he drew back from the piece that lay like lead in his open palm.

"Go on," she encouraged. "Look for yourself."

"Look at what? The gift you're refusing? I've seen it. I selected it from my family's store only last week."

"Ethan," her voice was soft, drawing his gaze to hers. "I'm not returning it because I don't want it. That's far from the case. But it isn't proper. I can't accept a gift of this sort from a gentleman, and I certainly can't wear it."

"Society rules. That's why you're giving it back to me?" He was having trouble keeping his breathing even.

"That and I needed to show you what I

found—at least some of what I found." Her fingers grazed his palm as she lifted the necklace and held it up to the moonlight.

And right there, under his nose, hanging in the silver light of the moon was the same marking that he'd seen over and over these past few weeks. W. B. with tiny vines growing around the letters. W. B. Exports—he'd gotten this piece from his family's shop, not from the harbor warehouse.

This proved that the crates he'd seen that night did not come from some new mine but from his family's lands. It was theft, and a large one at that. They'd had time to set up a warehouse, to establish customers to sell the pieces to. None of this had occurred overnight—it would take months, years even. He pulled it from her grasp and lifted it higher into the light to examine the markings once more.

"W. B. could be someone's initials," he mused.

"The vines around the letters remind me of an estate name. Yet I can't think of an estate in the area that would be symbolized by W. B."

"An estate," he repeated. Was this the work of a neighboring lord? And if so, how was it kept quiet for so long? "W. B…W. B…" Then the truth hit him. "It is a place, but not an estate."

"Where?" she asked, leaning closer as if the answer was stamped there in the silver in his hand.

"Whitby." He turned to look at her. "W. B. is Whitby. It has to be. The town is close enough to the mines for the culprit to maintain a steady theft, yet far enough away not to be discovered."

"I was right to show it to you then," she said as

she watched the necklace sway in his fingers. "Do you know what this means? We can follow this clue. We're one step closer."

Closer to what, he wasn't certain. All he knew was she hadn't presented him with evidence that he should stay far away from her and for that he was thankful. Though there were still Santino's men from Spain, a killer on the loose, and countless reasons why she was too good for the likes of him. *You had a plan.* "Plans are meant to be changed," he whispered to himself as he looked at the necklace.

"What?"

He tucked the necklace into his coat pocket and looked back at her, bracing one arm on the window ledge behind them. "This wasn't planned, Roselyn. None of this was supposed to happen."

"Plans are tricky things that way, aren't they?" There was an uneasiness beneath her words.

He was feeling a bit uneasy as well. What he knew he must do was now at war with what he wanted right in front of him. "When life throws an unexpected punch, what are we to do?"

"I would say cover our faces to avoid a broken nose, but something tells me you disagree." The tension he'd seen in her eyes lessened as she leaned into him and ran a finger down the ridge of his nose.

He caught her fingers within his as he dropped his hand to rest on his knee. "You are always the wise one."

"Not always," she said, glancing around at their current surroundings.

"I suppose you do spend time in my company," he teased. "That doesn't speak too highly of your wisdom."

"Sometimes ignoring all wisdom is the wisest course of action, isn't it?" She pursed her lips in thought as her eyes searched his, clearly needing his agreement. "Furthermore, simply because we possess knowledge doesn't mean it's wise to share that knowledge, since part of wisdom is knowing when not to be wise. If that wisdom could hurt someone, for example."

He didn't know what the devil she was talking about, but he nodded anyway. "Ignore all the wisdom you care to ignore. There's most assuredly something wrong with your logic, but I don't care to argue with it just now."

"That's terribly wise of you, Ethan Moore." A smile lingered on her lips, enticing him closer.

"I thought so too," he mumbled as he closed the gap slightly between them. He needed her, needed to know that amid the danger surrounding them, she was truly there. That her desire for him was real. A breath away from her lips, he paused, allowing her to choose. She'd returned his gift, but with good reason. The necklace hung heavy in his pocket nonetheless. The heat from her body warmed his skin. If he were to shift forward a hair, he could claim her sweet lips— and yet he held still, waiting.

She tightened her grasp on his hand as she moved closer, her lips meeting his in the moonlight. At the light pressure of her lips against his own, his heart soared. She wanted him. And in that instant, he lost the control he'd fought to hold on to. He'd been dreaming of touching her again for days now, not to mention the torturous nights alone in his bed. He reached for her waist, releasing her hand and dragging her with him across the cushioned seat until he was leaning back against the wall, Roselyn draped across his chest.

Her breasts pressed tightly against him, but he wanted more. Damn her binding undergarments and orange gown. He splayed his hands across her lower back, enjoying the slight arch of her body into his. Capturing her mouth with his lips, he beckoned to her with tender kisses until she opened to him. She grasped at his shoulders as he tasted her sweet mouth. The minutes passed in a tangle of desire, both reaching for more.

She let out a small squeak of alarm against his lips as he splayed his hands over her round curves and pulled her farther across his body. But she melted into his embrace with a playful nip at his lip, her body molding to his. He grasped greedy handfuls of her lush body as she moved her lips across the rough line of his jaw. She was gentle, barely brushing her mouth against his jaw until she reached the soft bit of skin just below his ear. He couldn't control himself, not when she was licking his neck and biting at his ear like this. Lifting his hips, he pressed his arousal against her, needing the contact with her body.

He heard her quick intake of breath, and a second later her wide eyes were on him.

"Sorry, princess." His voice was rough with passion as he spoke.

"Is this what I do to you?" she asked, moving one hand to his breeches and tracing the length of him with her fingers.

"Dear God," he murmured as he pulled her

back down onto his chest to kiss her again. He was half hoping she would stop touching him when he shifted her body back over his, and half of him was desperately thankful when her curious caress continued. He would regret this for the remainder of the evening, but damn, the feeling of her small fingers on him was magical.

Their kiss deepened until she broke away on a ragged breath.

Her hand was still on the bulge in his breeches when she said, "This is wrong, isn't it? I should go. I... This... We're at a ball. Anyone could pull back that bit of fabric and find us here."

"They could. But that's no reason to rush off." He lifted her hands to encircle his neck, pulling her back into his embrace. Damn his aching body! If she left here tonight, would he ever have her like this again? It was a chilling thought and he plundered her mouth to rid himself of it. Everything about her was small, smooth, and frail beneath his rough hands. Like a healing tonic to his heavily beaten and bruised life, she washed over him, giving him reason to heal, reason to hope. He held her against his body, reveling in the scent of lavender that surrounded them, the pliable warmth of her in his arms. In this moment, she was his.

"This is all so reckless," she murmured.

"Agreed. But you are reckless, princess. You always have been." But she was already pulling away from him. Damn responsibility and consequences, he wanted her too much. But his grip loosened nonetheless. If she wanted to leave, he had to let her go.

"Someone might come looking for me and we would be found."

"How would they find us?" he asked. "Would they see me touching you like this?" He ran a possessive hand over her arse, pulling her close.

"Or would they find my lips on your body? I could be kissing you here." He paused to kiss along her jaw. "Or here," he added, kissing her lips. "Or when they find us, I could be kissing some other part of you, something you haven't even experienced yet." He punctuated the imagery with a teasing grin. "Don't you want to find out what could happen if you stay?"

He knew what he was doing to her, and he knew Roselyn couldn't resist a challenge. She was always ready for an adventure, and this was the most tempting adventure he could offer her.

"I do have to return to the ball eventually. But perhaps…"

There was a loud round of laughter on the other side of the draperies that shielded them from view and someone bumped the velvet as they passed, making it flutter for a second on the other side of the potted trees.

She gasped and pushed to her feet. There was a sadness in her gray eyes as she said, "It's too dangerous, Ethan. There would be consequences."

He should let her go. It was for the best. He watched as she turned away from him, her shoulders heaving a great sigh. His fingers twitched. He blinked. It wasn't wise at all, but wisdom was overrated—she'd said as much herself. He stood from the bench behind her, pulling her against his chest as he did so.

"In a moment, but not yet," he murmured in her ear. The words seemed to beat through his heart in an uneven rhythm. *Not yet. Not yet.* He knew he had to allow her to leave, not just this alcove but to leave him for good. Only everything inside him screamed at the thought. Just one more minute, only one more day, he bargained with himself.

Her head fell back against his chest as she breathed his name, the force of it hitting him like a fierce wind pushing him forward into a storm. His lips skimmed down the column of her neck as he followed the silhouette of her moonlit body with his hands, finding the outsides of her breasts, dipping in to her waist before rounding over her hips. He slid his hand down her leg, gathering the fabric as he moved.

"Ethan, what are you doing?" she whispered, her voice a siren's call in the dark.

"Hopefully driving you as mad as you drive me," he said against her skin as he licked at the pulse that beat wildly at the base of her throat.

"Yes, but…" She tried to speak, but lost the battle and reached up to sink her fingers into his hair instead.

"I'll protect you from harm, from prying eyes. You're safe here with me. Just stay." He trailed his fingers up and down the front of her thigh, enjoying the resulting shiver that moved her farther into his embrace.

"I'm beginning to see why this alcove was filled with plants and hidden by curtains. It's a dangerous sort of place."

"If you still wish to leave…" He swallowed his fear as he waited for her response. "You could return to the ball as if this never happened, as if we never met." He kept the constant movement over her skin, moving one hand to cup her breast, teasing her nipple into a hardened peak beneath his fingers.

"No. I don't want to leave."

"Thank God." He smiled as he moved his hand up the inside of her thigh.

"I... What..." She breathed words that attempted to be strung together into thought but failed.

"Shhh," he whispered against the rim of her ear. "Do you trust me?"

At the small nod of her head against his chest, he skated his hand over her soft skin to the apex of her thighs. He pressed her silken curls beneath his palm in a gentle caress as he kissed her neck. As much as he wanted her now, to have her collapsing in his arms, sated from the pleasure he'd given her, the moment was one to be savored. He moved his hand lower, stroking her with seeking touches that pulled a whimper from her throat.

He knew the feeling; he still ached with need for her. Slipping his fingers into the damp heat of her body, he explored her soft flesh. He toyed with the small bud beneath his fingers, feeling the tension build in her body as he held her. He closed his eyes, groaning at the slick heat of her body against his hand. He held her close as he thrust into her, never ceasing his contact with the most sensitive part of her. Moving his lips up her neck, he tugged at her earlobe with his teeth as he kept up a constant rhythm.

She tensed, shuddering against him even as she wrapped her fingers around his wrist, holding him to her. He grinned against her skin and increased his play, reveling in the feel of her passion all around him.

"Ethan!" she said a bit too loudly as she twisted to look up at him in desperation. A second later, the planter her foot rested against tumbled over, forcing him to shift his stance to keep her from falling, but he didn't stop touching her even through the chaos of the fallen planter. Her cry a moment later was muffled by the shaking leaves of a large bush and the thud of the planter as it came to rest, spilling dirt across the floor. Off balance and reaching for something to steady her, she grabbed the trunk of the nearest tree.

The next second passed in a blur of falling leaves as the tree toppled over, knocking them back onto the bench seat. He was still holding her when they fell, landing her between his legs. Neither one moved as they waited to see if anyone would be drawn to investigate the noise. They lay like that for a few minutes, as the fear of being discovered slipped away and was replaced by sighs of relief and more than one chuckle over the mess they'd made. They truly were in their own little world, it seemed. She was settled against his chest, and he continued to trace the folds of her skin. He should stop, but he didn't seem to possess the ability to be sensible with her. Finally, just when he forced himself to begin tugging her gown back over her, hiding her body from view, she turned in his arms.

She said nothing but the wild look in her eyes was the same one that had always come just before she jumped from a high tree branch or rolled down a steep hill. Reaching for the fall of his breeches left no doubt in his mind which high branch she wished to leap from tonight. He only had a second's surprise at her intentions before he assisted her, freeing himself and looking up into her face.

"Are you certain you want…" But his words of concern didn't seem necessary as she pulled the edge of her gown up one thigh and gave him an inviting smile. This was an invitation he couldn't turn down.

Guiding her to her back on the soft bench, he slid his hand up her thigh, pushing her gown from his path. She'd made it clear that she wanted this, but he'd be damned if he was going to rush things with her. This was Roselyn, his Roselyn, unguarded and open to him. He'd waited so long for this, had thought it would never be, and now he was here. He knelt between her thighs and leaned forward, capturing her lips beneath his as he moved his hands over her hips. She was pliable beneath him, making room for him between her legs.

She slid her fingers down his back and grasped him tighter in a plea for more. He wanted to give her more—she had no idea how much that was true. But he had to hold on to some fragment of control for her sake. He deepened their kiss as he trailed his fingers over her moist heat. When she arched her hips into his touch, he knew he couldn't wait any longer and neither could she.

Angling her hips, he pulled back from their kiss to look into her eyes. He wanted to remember this moment. She was flushed and beautiful in the moonlight. He would never forget the wonder and anticipation in her eyes as she looked at him. She parted her lips and mouthed his name soundlessly as he thrust into her. She squeezed her eyes shut for only a moment before she relaxed beneath him.

Then she smiled and moved her hands down to his sides. That small smile of anticipation for the adventure ahead was his undoing. Losing all control, he tossed off the idea of acting the gentleman even in this situation and drove into her with the untamed desire that he felt for her. She surrounded him, drawing him in deeper and deeper with each thrust. She arched beneath him and he palmed her breast through her gown, but it wasn't enough.

He shifted forward even as he kept the rhythm with her body, grasping her nipple with his teeth through her gown. If he was a savage beast, she was the one driving him to it. Roselyn gasped and rose to meet his movements with a new desperation. Her body was tense with need for him—it encircled him and pushed him forward, matching his own desire for her. She hung on the edge of surrendering to her own desire, and it was an inspiring sight. Her fingers dug into his sides as she looked up at him, overwhelmed yet silently begging for more.

She was wild and beautiful, and in this moment she was his.

"Come for me, Roselyn," he whispered. "Let go."

He increased his pace with his words, watching as she jumped from that high branch. As reckless and beautiful as ever. She drew in tight around his body, driving him mad. He couldn't wait much longer. She arched beneath him, reaching for her release. And he kissed her to muffle the scream he knew was coming as she clung to him, her body pulsing around him with ecstasy.

That was the last he could endure as he drove into her one last time, jumping—as he always had—with Roselyn. His body was slick with sweat as he came careening out of control back to her. He was spent and yet he already wanted her again. Would he ever tire of her? Not a chance.

A moment later, he shifted back to his position against the wall, pulling her with him. "Roselyn," he whispered with reverence as he brushed an escaped ringlet of her hair from her forehead.

She pressed her cheek against him and made a content humming sound in response that reverberated through his chest with a satisfying vibration. Winding his arms around her, he held her tight, thankful for this night.

When he was with her, he was home. He hadn't had a true home since he was a child, and even then that home had been at her side. They'd grown. Everything between them had changed, yet she was still his center, his shelter from life's storms, his family, and his love.

He loved her.

The realization didn't sneak up on him like a blow to the head; rather, the shocking part was that he *hadn't* seen it earlier. His love for her had always been there. Perhaps he'd always loved her. He couldn't recall a time when he hadn't at least felt fondness for his friend from the neighboring estate. She was his Roselyn and she always had been. Of course he loved her.

"I know I called it dangerous, but I rather like this place," Roselyn mused, pulling him from his thoughts of her.

"The redecoration helped on that count." He chuckled, eying the fallen tree. "And an overloud orchestra outside, come to think of it."

"Being here with you helped more. When I'm with you, I'm free. I can be that reckless girl you once knew because of you."

He kissed the top of her head. "We should consider a trip to the tropics after all is settled here. I find I have a sudden fondness for greenery."

"I…" Her eyes grew wide as she looked up at him, filled with a misty awe he'd never seen there before. What was that about? She swallowed before opening her mouth to attempt to speak again. "I hope things are settled here soon then."

"I hope so too." His greatest wish was that he and Roselyn could lie beneath trees one day, no threat lingering in the world.

"Ethan? Thank you. For tonight…"

"I know I overstepped my bounds. I didn't set out to—"

"You were the perfect gentleman," she said, cutting him off. "You would never allow me to get hurt, even if I did think you a murderer for a time."

"Roselyn, I will do everything in my power to keep you safe." And that was exactly the problem.

❧

The second her maid dozed off against the tree trunk where their blanket was spread, Roselyn was on her feet. "One glass of wine does it every time." She smiled down at Alice. She should feel some sense of remorse for leaving the woman propped against a tree in Hyde Park, but she'd only be gone a few minutes. It was nearly one in the afternoon. If she hurried she wouldn't be late to meet Ethan.

She'd been reluctant to leave their alcove last night after what she'd experienced with him. The memory of their time together added a skip to her step as she moved away from her dozing maid.

She'd seen him pass by on foot only a few minutes ago. Her anticipation over discovering his progress with the theft and the conclusion of their investigation quickened her footsteps. After all, there wouldn't be another evening like last night until Trevor's death was just an unfortunate memory. The necklace was the key to the mystery. She knew it. There was no need to tell Ethan about the love notes from Herold when they had no bearing on Trevor's death. Finding Trevor's murderer was what mattered at the moment. One day she would tell Ethan what she'd found at Ormesby House, but today was not that day.

Leaving the sanctuary of the trees, she wound her way down one of the well-traveled paths of the park, jumping over mud puddles and sidestepping large areas where the rain from this morning had turned the path to muck. Her shoes would be destroyed, but they were a worthy sacrifice if she was able to catch him.

The park was remarkably empty for such a sunny afternoon. The rain earlier must have sent everyone into their homes before the shock of sun emerged in the sky. Not everyone, she supposed, had been sitting at the window all morning, waiting for one o'clock no matter the weather outside.

As she rounded a bend in the road she finally caught sight of him, striding down the path ahead of her with no regard to the squelch of mud beneath his boots. She grinned at the splatter of rich, dark mud flying in every direction. It seemed a lifetime ago when she'd slung mud at him in the misting rain. He'd been an aggravating near-stranger then. Now he filled her hours with his company, her thoughts when he was away, even her dreams. She blushed and picked up her pace to close the gap between them.

He paused at the sound of her hurried footsteps, looking over his shoulder to find the source of the noise. "Roselyn, what are you doing here alone? You should have a chaperone, family, someone who could protect you. Better yet, I should have canceled this meeting." His brows furrowed in concern as he turned toward her.

"I'm not alone." She stopped in front of him with the same playful grin she'd been wearing all morning. "Or are you not truly here?" She tapped her finger on his arm to prove his existence.

"You're not alone *now*," he countered, glancing around for enemies among the trees.

"Then you have nothing to worry about."

"Nothing at all," he said with a wry laugh, and rubbed at his eyes.

"I trust you had a pleasant morning," she said, attempting a change of subject.

"Nothing could match my evening," he said with a warm smile. "The clerk at the jewelry store was away making a delivery when I stopped in."

"Oh," she replied, a bit crestfallen. She'd hoped

everything would have been made clear to Ethan and the mystery surrounding Trevor's death would have been solved. Then they could put this bit of ugliness behind them and... She wasn't sure what came after that, but she knew something must.

"It's been less than a day, princess. I'm quick on my feet, but not that quick." His eyes were tinged with red, as if he hadn't slept well last night. To be honest, neither had she, yet something else was troubling him today. He seemed glad to see her, but ill at ease all the same. Perhaps this was to be a quick meeting due to some prior engagement this afternoon and she was keeping him from his plans.

"I suppose having the investigation complete was wishful thinking on my part. I should go," she said without moving to do so. She didn't want to go back to her sleeping maid just yet. She shifted her weight and glanced around for some topic of conversation.

"Is that all you wanted of me?" he asked, taking a step toward her. "To ask about the maker's mark on the necklace? Nothing more? When we made plans for you to meet me today..."

She pursed her lips and looked down at her hands, searching for the correct answer to his question. "If you have some other place to be..."

"No, there's nowhere else but here with you." His words rushed out as if he was begging her to believe them. He whispered a curse and moved closer to her. "It's only that when I entered the park I thought I saw someone I knew."

"Am I keeping you from a reunion of sorts?" she

asked, looking around as if some distant relation was about to bound out of the bushes.

"No. A reunion of sorts is exactly what I would like to avoid."

She whipped her head around to meet his gaze. "It wasn't the man from the Sutton ball, was it? The one who scaled the garden wall."

"No. Recently I find that I've been catching glimpses of people I once knew in Spain and would very much like to not see again." His mouth quirked up in a crooked smile, easing her rising alarm. "It's nothing to concern yourself over."

"Are you certain?"

"Of course." But he didn't meet her gaze when he spoke, instead glancing over his shoulder to search the woods. After all, there wouldn't be another evening like last night until Trevor's death was just an unfortunate memory. "When I left, I made sure I wasn't followed, trading ships, doubling back over my own path. It was known that I was English of course, but nothing more. This country is a large place to search for one Ethan Moore." He fell silent and looked around, proving that he didn't believe his own words of comfort.

"Does trouble follow you everywhere you go?"

"It would seem so, but then so do you…"

"Are you calling me trouble? I believe I prefer 'princess' if those are to be my only options."

"I happen to be fond of troublesome princesses. One in particular, as a matter of fact." His eyes twinkled as he looked at her, making her heart race.

"Then you won't mind escorting this troublesome

princess back across the park to her abandoned picnic blanket and dozing maid. I can't stay long this afternoon." He was fond of her! Fond! The simple claim shouldn't excite her after all they'd shared last night, but it did.

"You left your maid sleeping alone in the park?" he asked as he extended his arm to her. "See? Trouble."

"There are certain benefits to having a maid prone to naps in the afternoon," she said, taking his arm.

"Like walks with gentlemen who attract trouble," he leaned close to her ear to say.

"I happen to be fond of troublesome gentlemen. One in particular, as a matter of fact." She smiled as she repeated his words back to him.

They walked for a minute in companionable silence, marked only by quick glances at each other and smiles. Were they courting in some roundabout manner? She'd always assumed that courting involved dancing, chatting over tea, and strolling about a garden under the watchful eye of a chaperone.

They were strolling, but this muddy version of life was hardly what she'd envisioned for herself. She almost laughed. *Think of all the dirt-covered adventures you would have missed if you'd been at Trevor's side.* Of course, that relationship had been leading to marriage. Where was this one headed?

"Do you remember when we were caught throwing rocks at passing carriages?" Ethan asked, dragging her thoughts away from more serious questions that held no answers.

"You mean as children?"

"Taking into account that I haven't thrown a rock

at a vehicle since the age of fourteen, yes, when we were children." He nudged her gently with his arm and shook his head.

"I remember sulking because I wasn't allowed sweets for a week."

"I suppose I've always been a bad influence on you. I should have known then."

The smile slipped from her face as she looked up at him. "Known what?"

"That I'd met my match." He squeezed the fingers that lay on his arm. It was a quick touch, but accompanied by his words, she felt it through to her toes. "Anyone who could outthrow my sister was bound to have a mean punch one day," he teased.

"I'm sorry I hit you."

"If you knew what I was thinking of you in those breeches, you would know how much I deserved it. Even the memory distracts me." He stepped unseeing into ankle-deep mud and laughed as he released her hand so she could go around the wet section of the path.

"Between my punch and the mud covering your boots, I'd think we're even," she said, turning back to him from a few paces down the path.

"Perhaps."

"What will you do next?" she asked as she wrapped her hand around his arm once more.

"Return home and clean my muddy boots, I suppose," he mused, pulling her into the tall grass that bordered the path so they could avoid the mud altogether.

"After that," she corrected. "After Trevor's murder is settled, after the season in London?"

"I don't know." He kicked a fallen tree branch from in front of her. "To be honest, I've never thought beyond tomorrow before."

"Ha!" She let out an amused burst of laughter. "I remain so mindful of my plans for tomorrow that today often goes unnoticed."

"Tomorrow is a luxury. In my profession, only today matters."

"Ethan…"

"Hmm?"

"Please don't take offense at this…"

"I don't offend easily, princess."

"Very well." She took a few steps, considering her words before she spoke. "You are Lord Ayton now, and one day you will become Lord Ormesby," she began. "I believe your days of fighting for your dinner are over. You have a responsibility to your title, your family. What will happen to the mines and your land once your father passes?"

"That's many tomorrows away," he replied with a shake of his head.

"One never knows." She stepped through the grass, the height of it dragging against the hem of her dress and slowing her progress. "We've seen the evidence of life being cut quite short, have we not? I find recently my thoughts have changed regarding tomorrow. Life can't be lived on a day that's yet to occur. We must seize the day, as they say. I don't believe I've seized anything until recently."

"Today is all I've ever known. The trouble is once the day is seized, what then? I've led quite the reckless life, but there's always a price to be paid for my actions come the following morning." He tossed her an easy smile, adding, "You taught me that."

"Did I?"

"Yes, when I nearly destroyed your reputation... twice."

"Four times, but who's keeping tally?"

"Not me." He chuckled as they continued through the grass. "Perhaps I do need to consider what to do with myself."

"I have vast experience in preparing for tomorrow," she offered.

He covered her hand with his, intertwining his fingers with hers. "If I assist you in your enjoyment of today, would you come to my aid in my preparations?"

"Of course." She leaned into his side for a heartbeat before pulling herself upright. "Together, perhaps we could navigate a week."

"Perhaps longer."

She turned to look at him. What did he mean by that? Her heart clung to the promise of his words. "How much longer?"

"What do you plan to do after the London season is over? After things are resolved with the investigation and we're no longer in danger from the murderer at large?"

"Return to Thornwood Manor until next season," she replied, dismissing his question. "What did you mean by longer?"

"I'm not sure what I meant. Don't you ever say words without thinking through their implications?"

"Only with you."

He shook his head with a smirk on his lips and looked away from her.

She hadn't come to the park today expecting a marriage proposal, but now that he seemed to be taking away even a hint of one, she bristled. *Why are you upset, Roselyn? It's not as if you love him. You don't believe in such logic-lacking notions.*

But this wasn't any gentleman. This was Ethan. And she *did* love him.

The thought practically pounded her over the head. She could try to deny it, but it was the truth. Beyond logic or reason, she loved Ethan. And now it was all she could think of. She had to know if he felt the same, but that wasn't a question one simply asked.

If he wanted to include her in future plans, then he at least considered her a companion of sorts, didn't he? A friend? They'd always been friends. One didn't form bonds with those one didn't care for, and he'd already admitted he was fond of her. Fondness wasn't the same as love, but it was something, a start, a place to build. But she had to understand more. She opened her mouth and attempted to ask the question central in her mind. "Do you mean you had no intention of… that you have no intention…"

"Do you wish me to have intentions because of last night?"

*Yes, more than anything*, a small voice rang out in her head, but not because of last night. Because she loved him. She wasn't thinking logically. None of this made sense. Only two weeks ago she'd thought him a killer, and the chaos from Trevor's death was anything but resolved. Wouldn't it be wise to sleep on such a decision as marriage? To wait for the investigation to be over? And he'd yet to even make that offer. He'd only mentioned planning his life beyond a week and she'd pounced like a madwoman. Perhaps madness did run in her family. She blinked away her rampant thoughts.

"I'm as unsure of my intentions as you are, Roselyn. But I know I enjoy our time together. And after last night, I owe you certain things. However, I'm not in a place..." He turned away on a string of curses. "This is why I got no sleep last night."

She grabbed his arm. "Ethan, it wasn't my plan to press you for information you didn't have or to cause you a sleepless night." This afternoon was certainly taking an unusual turn from her plan to discuss the theft with him. "I only..." She stopped, squeezing her eyes shut for a second. "I don't know what is happening between us."

"Then we have reached the same conclusion."

"What is that?" she asked. If he'd reached some conclusion, she wished he would share it, because her thoughts were rather muddled on the subject.

"We should be confounded over the future together."

"Together," she repeated. It wasn't a marriage proposal or a declaration of love, but it was a shining beacon of hope and she clung to it like a ship lost at sea. She loved this man and today, on this day she was seizing, *together* was exactly what she wanted. Love and marriage could be considered tomorrow.

He glanced around to see if they were alone, then

reached up to cup her cheek in his hand and brushed his lips over hers in a brief whisper of a kiss.

There in that kiss, within the lingering touch of his fingers and warmed by the heat of his eyes, was the only promise of tomorrow she needed.

# *Eighteen*

ETHAN HAD CIRCLED BACK THROUGH THE PARK AFTER seeing Roselyn safely returned to her maid. He'd taken his time, stopping to watch the swans. No one from Spain would expect that of him. They would search nearby taverns, not peaceful corners of a park. It was a blasted waste of his day when he only wanted to put an end to the search for a killer and think of a future where he could be with Roselyn, but he didn't care to face down Santino's men alone. They wanted him dead after all.

When he'd arrived in England, he'd thought he could disappear forever. Then Trevor had died and Ethan's name had been splashed across the post, leading his enemies to his doorstep. Coming back here had been yet another mistake in a long list of wrongs. But how was he to make any of it right?

He was working to find Trevor's murderer. In fact, he was on his way to call on Cladhart—if he could escape danger long enough to do so. Once the theft and the murder were settled, he would set up a meeting with Santino on his terms, not in a back alley surrounded by his men. They could come to some understanding that included Ethan keeping his limbs and his life—he hoped. As for the last item on his list of wrongs that needed sorting… He sighed. His situation with Roselyn wasn't as easily solved as murder and agreements with Spanish crime lords.

He moved down the walk toward the townhouse Cladhart kept in the city.

"Our favorite fighter." The accented voice that sounded over his shoulder in broken English froze Ethan's movements as if he'd just sunk into icy waters.

"Where are you going, fighter?" Alvaro Santino called out.

Ethan turned, raking his eyes over his surroundings in search of an escape route. He'd given Santino's men the slip twice before and was certain he would be able to do it again, but the crime lord himself? Santino had followed him from Spain and wasn't likely to give up now. If Ethan disappeared down the nearest alley, Santino would simply find him again. He seemed to do a damn good job of it—a bit too good.

If Ethan stood his ground and heard the man out, he might put an end to this particular battle. As Roselyn had said, trouble did follow him wherever he went, but he didn't want that trend to continue. He was alone on the street and this man would likely kill him, but he had to try.

"Santino, I didn't think I would see you here." He began taking a step toward the man. "You do realize you're in England? Not deep in your cups and lost, are you?" Ethan tried to laugh, but the sound was hollow even to his ears.

"You left me no choice," Santino replied, his broad-shouldered build filling the walk that led back into the park. "In Spain, we have honor. We stay, we fight."

"That's amusing. In England, we prefer a nice cup of tea while we talk." Ethan offered a polite nod to two nursemaids out for a walk with their charges as they passed, their eyes wide as if expecting the men to come to blows any second. From the look in Santino's eye, they weren't wrong.

"Amuse? You think this funny, fighter?" Santino asked, stepping toward Ethan.

Could he count this bit of conversation as having tried to talk things out? It was clear Santino wanted a fight. That wasn't something Ethan was ready to do just outside the entrance to Hyde Park in the middle of the afternoon when small children were about. It seemed some shred of him was a gentleman after all. Roselyn would be pleased.

"In Spain, you pay for your crimes," Santino said, moving closer. "I've come to make you pay, fighter."

"It's unfortunate you feel that way," Ethan said with a sigh. There was nothing for it. Apparently this little meeting was happening here, whether he wished it otherwise or not. Ethan lunged forward with the weight of his body behind his fist. It collided with the man's jaw and he staggered back several steps.

With a glance, Ethan saw several men now moving in his direction. He was outnumbered. Ethan didn't wait. There was only one advantage against this many men, and that was height. He moved toward the low wall that bordered the park, prepared to attack the men from above.

"Running to your woman friend?" Santino yelled.

Ethan stopped. Turning, he watched as the man spat blood onto the cobblestone street and held a hand up to stay his men. Ethan pushed forward with a lengthy stride. "Don't even speak of her!"

"She's a beautiful girl. Too beautiful for you."

"Something we agree upon," he said as he studied the Spanish man. There was something Santino wasn't telling him. Ethan's heart sped as he forced his breathing to remain steady.

Santino knew of Roselyn. She wasn't safe from him. She'd left the park with nothing but a sleepy maid for protection. Ethan had to get to her, to make sure she was safe.

"What do you want, Santino?" he asked, shifting his weight.

"What I lost," the Spaniard ground out in anger.

"That may prove difficult. I can try to find a potion to wake the dead, but short of that…"

"No more tricks. No more chasing."

"Santino…" Ethan began, unsure how he was to make amends for accidentally killing the man's brother. Returning the prize money from the fight in question would be difficult enough; he'd spent it on the journey back to England. He couldn't, however, bring anyone back from the dead or he would have done so for his own family.

"You have until tomorrow."

"Until tomorrow to do what?" Ethan asked.

"Return what you stole from me, or I will do as the English lord asks and kill you and your lady."

"The English lord… What English lord?"

"The English lord who sent for us to finish the job when your countrymen failed."

"Who hired you? What is his name?" Ethan demanded.

"You have until tomorrow," Santino said again as his men joined him on the street.

There was no hope of beating the truth out of Santino with so much opposition. "I can't bring your brother back to life, and the money…"

"The money will do, for now."

Ethan didn't answer. He'd managed to earn enough from his daily fights at Gentleman Jackson's to cover his board and dine well enough, but the funds Santino had lost were gone. He could fight all afternoon, and he would still fall short by tomorrow. Even if he was willing to go to his father for assistance, it wouldn't be settled by tomorrow.

"Bring the money to the park tomorrow."

"And if I have another engagement and miss our meeting?"

Santino smiled, showing a row of small, yellowing teeth. "I will find you and your lady. The English lord will pay if you do not."

A carriage pulled up beside them and the men climbed inside. Ethan watched as it rolled away, heart pounding. Roselyn. She was in danger and it was his fault. He took off down the street toward Mayfair. With any luck, she and her maid would have returned home straightaway.

He had to reach her in time and explain the situation. And if he had any good fortune in this life at all, one day she would forgive him.

◦◦◦

"Lord Ayton," Roselyn said in a voice the entire house could hear. "What a surprise. I haven't seen you since we spoke briefly at yesterday's ball." Walking toward him in the receiving parlor, she glanced around to see if they were alone before adding in a whisper, "I'm in a bit of hot water over allowing my maid to rest in the park. Apparently, a squirrel woke her."

"I need to speak with you," Ethan said as he moved around the room. He walked to each window, looked outside in every direction, checked the latch, and drew the draperies closed.

"I gathered that much since you are here, and we parted company not two hours ago." She watched him in confusion until he reached the third window. "What are you doing?" she finally asked.

"Has anyone been here? Have you had any callers?"

"I've only just arrived home. Ethan, you look pale. Are you ill?"

"I'm fine," he said, brushing her comment away as he secured the last window and closed the draperies, throwing them into shade. "I'm more concerned about you. Are *you* all right?"

"I'm quite well. I changed my dress to one with no mud at the hem and repaired my hair only a few minutes ago. Do I look poorly? Because I believe if you saw your own coloring, I would look quite healthy by comparison."

"And you need to stay healthy. Roselyn, we should sit. Can we sit? I'd like to sit."

"I can't blame you, in your state." She sat beside him on the settee and arranged her skirts around her legs to fall in perfect folds to the floor. What was this about? He looked as if he'd seen an apparition since they parted company in the park. And even then he'd seemed troubled, not like last night.

"Is your family about?" he asked.

"I left the door cracked for propriety, if that's your concern." Mind you, if that was his concern, he wouldn't have eliminated most of the light in the room. The usually sunny parlor was lit only by slivers of sun shining through the gaps in the hastily closed windows.

"Then they are home. Your brother?" he added, his brows drawn together in alarm. "He seems the sort to keep weapons about in case of emergency."

Weapons? Why would they need weapons? "Are you in trouble?" Her eyes were wide as she reached for his hand in an attempt to offer him support. "Is it the necklace? Trevor's killer…"

"It's all connected. Roselyn, I must explain."

"Yes, you must because I don't understand any of this." She wrapped her fingers tighter with his and began stroking soothing patterns up and down his arm. "Let me help you."

"There are things in my past, things you don't know. No one knows. One of them caught up with me a few minutes ago on the street outside the park." He squeezed her hand within hers. "The man who killed Trevor is a lord and somehow he discovered my past. But how?" He rubbed his eyes, clearly trying to make sense of something, but meanwhile he was making no sense to her.

"Perhaps if you start in a logical location, the beginning for instance."

He nodded and turned further toward her on the settee, bracing an elbow on the back of the furniture between them. Taking a breath, he began, "I survived in Spain by various means—winnings from fights, games of chance, and on one occasion…I was paid to lose to an opponent." His eyes were dark with a pain deeper than she'd ever seen there. Countless hits, and this was when he showed anguish.

She traced his fingers with hers as she listened, willing him to tell her everything. From the sound of it, it was clear she was about to learn.

"There was a man named Santino, a crime lord with a brother who wished to show his strength. It was a new endeavor and Santino never refused his family—just like no one ever refused him. He set up a match, paid me to be defeated, and gambled heavily on the outcome. His brother would become a feared man about town and bolster his credibility as a pugilist, and Santino would heavily line his pockets."

"That doesn't seem very honest."

"It wasn't. And that's why I couldn't go through with it. When the time came to take the fall…I threw a punch instead."

"Sounds rather noble to me," she offered with a small smile as she scooted closer to him on the settee.

"It's not generally considered noble to kill a man with a blow after taking money to allow him to win. Taking the winnings from the match doesn't help matters either." He stopped, looking at Roselyn. "I didn't mean to kill him, but I did. It turns out he was ill. He appeared well enough to fight, but in the end…I didn't know of the illness or I would have never thrown that punch. When he couldn't be revived, I panicked. I gathered the winnings, slipped out the alley door, and bought passage on the first ship I could find. I returned to England, unsure of where to go, what to do. A few days later, I met you in the drive of my father's home."

She didn't reply. What were the appropriate words for this situation? This had not been covered by any of her lessons. He'd killed a man with his fists? She didn't even know that was possible.

"You see, I might not have killed my brother, but I am a murderer, Roselyn. I threw a punch that..." He broke off, squeezing his eyes closed as he looked away from her.

"It was an accident, Ethan," she said, placing a hand on his cheek. "You're a good man. Look at the way you've served your family since your return, the way you've protected me from harm."

"Yes, look at that. My brother is dead, and you've had to save yourself from me more than I've saved you."

"Ethan, everyone makes mistakes. But I know you would never hurt me. You're no murderer."

"I've put you in danger, Roselyn. Santino is here in London. He's demanding retribution for my crimes."

Her hand fell away from him. "How did he find you?"

Ethan shook his head. "He was hired by the same lord who had Trevor killed."

"How do you know that?"

"Santino said as much." Fear was written on his face as clearly as if in black ink. "Roselyn, you aren't safe. These men..." He broke off with a curse and leaned forward, bracing his forearms on his knees.

A second passed while her mind whirled with ideas. There must be a way out of this mess. "I'm only in danger because they saw me with you in the park today, correct? So, if we were known not to associate with each other, then I wouldn't be involved. We could cause a scene at the next ball or have an argument in the park. I wouldn't mean it, of course, but it could work." She reached forward and touched his hunched shoulder. "Once free of danger, I could work to help you without risking anything. We can find a way through this, Ethan, together."

"A public display would only serve to hurt your reputation," he said in a downcast voice.

"That hardly matters now. You need me. I'm not going to allow you to fight this alone."

"Roselyn…"

"What issue could you possibly have with my plan?" she asked, beginning to become exasperated with him. "Believe me when I say that you are more important than my reputation. I know it isn't done to admit such a thing, but just today in the park we decided to face the future together. Last night we…"

"You're not making this easy," he mumbled as he sat up to face her once more. "Roselyn…your plan to distance yourself from me won't work. It's too late for that."

"Really?" She could hardly bear the thought of quarreling with him, even if it wasn't a real fight, but she would do it if they must. It was reassuring, however, to know he felt the same hesitation.

"It's too late because it is known that you were there when Trevor died."

"I don't understand. Everyone knows that now."

"Yes, thanks to me." He sighed, seeming to come to some conclusion she didn't quite grasp. His eyes were hollow as he looked at her, just as they had been when Trevor was killed and he stared into darkness. "When I spread word that you witnessed my brother's death, it wasn't idle conversation that got out of hand."

She narrowed her gaze on him. "What do you mean?"

His entire body tensed, bracing for some impact. "I was determined to find the killer at any cost...so I set a trap."

"A trap."

"Whoever killed Trevor knew that I'd been there. I have the scar on my forehead to prove it." He touched the small red line as he spoke. "But you... your presence was unknown."

A moment passed in silence while his words sank into her mind. He hadn't told someone she'd been present that day by accident—he'd spread word to a killer. The murderer hadn't known about her, and she'd been safe. Until Ethan used her. She'd danced with him the same night word had been spread about her. He'd acted as if he hadn't known he'd destroyed her reputation, but he'd done far worse on purpose.

She searched his eyes, looking for something she could understand. "You used me as bait?"

"Not bait. I only needed to lure the murderer from the shadows. I never considered this outcome. I..."

"That's why you took me out onto that terrace. It wasn't about me. You only wanted to hang me out over a wall like a worm on a hook." She was having trouble breathing, the laces of her stays all at once too tight. How could she have fallen for such a scheme? Humiliation washed over her in great waves.

"No, that night wasn't part of my plan."

The truth slapped her again and again as she considered their encounters. "The men who followed me that day at the harbor. You allowed it." She squared her shoulders toward him. "What would you have done if Devon hadn't arrived? Anything?"

"I was attacking before I even knew of Thornwood's presence," he countered.

"Was the alcove last night some plot to have me attacked gone awry as well? Was a henchman supposed to be waiting in there with the trees?" She'd kissed him. She'd allowed him to touch her. She'd given herself to him. And, worse, she'd enjoyed it. She'd convinced herself it was love. He surely had some laugh at her expense after she left the ball.

"No. I would never..."

"Don't speak to me of what you would never do." Her breaths were coming out in forced puffs of air. "You said you would never hurt me."

"Roselyn," he murmured, reaching for her, but she recoiled from his touch. His hand hung in the air between them for a moment before it fell back to his knee.

"You kept me safe in the same way a fox is kept before a hunt. No wonder you were intent on forcing me out of the investigation. I might have uncovered the truth." She stood, unable to sit beside him any longer, and began pacing.

"I didn't want you to fall into a killer's hands."

She turned, looking him in the eye. "And yet I seem to have done just that."

He nodded, accepting her accounting of him. "I'll find a way to repair this, Roselyn." There was desperation in his voice that she didn't understand. He'd gotten what he wanted, hadn't he? He was a step closer to finding Trevor's killer now. And her part in his plans was over.

"This isn't a scratch from one of your fights," she said, wrapping her arms around her waist to keep from shaking. "There is no bandage great enough for this wound. You put me in danger, all the while proclaiming you would protect me from harm. You're a liar. You used me and I fell for your games."

"I've never lied to you." His voice was low and solid. It almost sounded trustworthy, if she didn't know differently.

"When you said you were fond of me?" she asked with a cracking voice, not wanting to hear the answer, but knowing she must. "How horribly I've twisted our situation in my mind. I thought we might have a future together. I thought…"

"I'm more than fond of you, Roselyn," he said, standing from the settee to face her. "You have to believe me."

"I don't have to do a thing where you're concerned!"

"What I did was wrong, careless." He took a step toward her, but no closer. "I made a mistake, and for the first time in my life I'm going to stay and fix it. I'll make it right."

"You can't make this right. I trusted you, Ethan." She blinked as a tear threatened to fall down her cheek. She was not going to give him the satisfaction of knowing how deeply he'd hurt her. "You need to leave," she struggled to spit out. "Go!"

"I'll leave your home, Roselyn. But I'll never leave you."

And some traitorous part of her that she would keep locked away forever would never leave him. She pointed to the door with the last of her strength, her finger trembling. "Leave now." A tear threatened to crash down her cheek, and she did nothing to push it away. "Please, just leave," she whispered.

❧

Somehow Ethan managed to walk as far as the front hall. *Let her be.* That had been his plan yesterday before the ball. She was better off without him. But that had been yesterday. Today, he couldn't make himself move past her front door. He met the butler's gaze and, with a single raised and shaking finger, silently asked for one more minute. The older man nodded, but gave him a warning glare. Eventually he would have to walk from this room, descend the steps, and move on with his life.

One more minute, his heart demanded. It couldn't be over—not yet.

"Roselyn, I'm truly sorry," he said, gripping his hand on the bottom of the stair rail for stability. He turned back to where she stood in the door to the parlor, his fingers curling into the wooden rail. "Even if you never forgive me, I'm going to mend what I've broken. I'll find a way to remove your name from this situation. It shouldn't be your burden to carry."

"Forgiveness," she repeated. "Is that what you want? You used me. Your words have been nothing but deceit, and you seek to earn my forgiveness?" She shook her head in disbelief.

"There were no tricks on my part, Roselyn. Everything between us has been real."

"More lies," she breathed. "Go, Ethan."

"Do you know what I carry with me every day?" he asked, desperation to hold on to what he had with her whirling through him.

When she didn't answer, he continued, "The note you wrote to me that night." Pulling the tattered piece of paper from his pocket, he held it out for her to see. "I've carried it with me since that night just to have a piece of you to hold on to. Roselyn, I wasn't trying to deceive you in any way. Things became complicated between us, and I made mistakes."

"The blasted note I wrote that began this mess? You think reminding me of such a foolish night will make me forgive you?"

"No, but I was hoping it would make you understand."

"This is what I understand." She pulled the note from his fingers. "You needed me to fill a void in your schemes." A tear fell from her cheek, but she didn't stop even though her voice shook with emotion. "You toyed with my affections to keep me within reach. And now you're trying to use words I wrote in haste against me. I won't be used by you anymore."

"No!" he exclaimed, reaching for the paper, but she was already ripping it in half.

He watched as she repeated the process until tiny

shreds of paper floated to the floor between them. He couldn't breathe. He'd held that note for so long it had become a part of him. All hope that Roselyn might want him again as she had that night was torn to pieces. All hope that she might love him, gone. Looking back up at her all he could see was the cold steel in her eyes behind the tears.

"Go!" she screamed, pointing to the door with a shaking hand.

The butler was approaching. Ethan could take the man, but to what end? He'd lost her.

Just like that, it was over. There were no words left to be said between them; there was no argument that could be made in his favor. He gave her a slight nod of his head, refusing to look at the pieces of paper that he so desperately wanted to scoop up and take away with him. It would do no good. He'd lost enough people in his life to know a note could never bring one back.

With that, he turned and walked away. The pieces of paper caught the breeze when the butler opened the door. Ethan could hear the rustle of them swirling in the air behind him until the door shut at his back. He turned, looking at the solid door for a moment before descending the steps into the still afternoon.

When his mother left, he'd pursued her. When Trevor was killed, he'd sought out his killer. When he'd accidentally killed Santino's brother, he'd fled back home. But with the slam of Roselyn's door, he couldn't move at all. He made it to the street before stumbling to a stop. He'd lost her, and it was his own blasted fault.

# Nineteen

"My mother thought you could use nourishment," Thornwood said as he sat down beside Ethan on the stone walk.

"Thank you," Ethan mumbled, pulling his coat closer around him. He wasn't sure how long he'd been here, but if his numb legs were any indication, it had been a while. He knew he should leave, but as long as he was here guarding her door, Roselyn was safe. He would have to go eventually. Right now, however, he sat.

"Don't thank me. I said you could rot for making my sister cry, but I'm told it's wrong to leave a lord sitting outside alone."

"Is it?"

"Damn if I know," Thornwood replied. "The only thing that is certain is that my wife and mother wished for me to bring you tea." He shoved a flask into Ethan's hand.

"This is tea?" Ethan asked, eyeing the metal flask.

"No."

Ethan tipped the flask to his mouth in an attempt

to drown his thoughts of Roselyn. It didn't work. "Roselyn doesn't know I'm here?" he asked.

"We thought it best not to inform her." Thornwood shrugged. "*I* thought it best. I don't care for hysterics." He settled back against the lamppost, bracing his arms on his knees.

"I never meant to hurt her, you know."

"Ah, I thought an explanation of the tears inside my home might be forthcoming."

Ethan nodded. He needed to confess as much. Thornwood had the right to know what was happening in his home. "I…" he began, unsure how to explain his quickly unraveling situation. In his mind, everything began at Ormesby Place. Perhaps that's where his story began as well. He took a breath and dove in. "I was with Roselyn the day Trevor died." He paused to see if Thornwood was going to react, but he said nothing.

"From the moment I saw Roselyn in the drive at Ormesby…" Ethan looked away on a curse as he rubbed his hand over his eyes. "Go ahead and pummel me, Your Grace. I know I deserve it."

"Keep talking."

"I couldn't stay away from her. Damn it all, I still can't stay away from her." Ethan leaned back against the lamppost. "I went along on her walk with Trevor. Only we fought—Trevor and I, that is. Then before I knew what was happening, a man was there. I took the hilt of a knife to the head, and Trevor… You know that part. But Roselyn wasn't to the top of the hill yet. Trevor's killer never saw her."

"Trevor's killer," Thornwood repeated. "There's

been a murderer not only near my sister but on a property adjacent to my own—and you never thought to tell me? I may kill you now, Ayton."

Ethan held up a hand. If he was to be killed, it should be for the proper reasons. "That isn't the worst bit."

"By all means, continue."

"I spread it about that Roselyn was there that day, in an attempt to catch the killer. Once he came after her, I would have him. I was an idiot. I acted without thought, but then I always do. And now…" He broke off.

"You used her to bait a killer?"

"Her words as well. How could she think our time together meant nothing to me? I admittedly erred. But I swear I didn't further my acquaintance with Roselyn for any foul purpose."

"We'll come back to the *furthering your acquaintance with my sister* bit in a moment," Thornwood ground out. "Where is this man now? I assume he's close since you're guarding the door to my home."

"The man he hired is close. I haven't yet discovered the identity of the man behind it all."

"Then I suggest we begin searching for him. I'll need any evidence you have on this man, a team to help with the hunt, and my flask back. Any day that requires use of the term *furthering acquaintances* also requires a stiff drink."

"You'll help me," Ethan stated as he cocked his head to the side to look at the man.

"You brought this battle to my doorstep."

"I suppose I did." Ethan nodded and pushed to his feet. He never intended for Thornwood to become involved in his troubles. No matter what he did, he couldn't seem to cease dragging those around him into the mire of his poor decisions. He looked up at the facade of the house. Roselyn deserved far better in life than anything he could provide. She was safe now, hidden behind a fence and the walls of her home. She was safe from him. He took a ragged breath and released it.

"Tell me, Ayton, how long have you been in love with my sister?" Thornwood asked as he rose to his feet, watching Ethan.

"That obvious, is it?"

"To all but the lady in question." Thornwood chuckled, though Ethan found no humor in the situation.

"She'll have a better life without me," Ethan stated as if memorizing a mantra he would recite for the remainder of his life.

"Perhaps," Thornwood said as he frowned up at his home.

Perhaps? Roselyn deserved a peaceful life with an honorable man at her side, even if the thought made his hands twitch with the need to punch someone. She would be happy and that's what mattered. Only, he was having trouble picturing a smile on her face as she walked away on the arm of another gentleman. She would be pleased with her life without him in it, wouldn't she? It's what she wanted. He shook off his wavering thoughts on the subject. "It's no matter. She won't consider forgiving me…"

"Let's manage the simple parts of this mess and remove the price from her head, shall we?" Thornwood asked, clapping a hand on Ethan's shoulder. "Then you can deal with her feelings."

"Catching a killer is easier than finding forgiveness?"

"When compared with ladies, murderous plots are always easier to solve. Now, about the evidence in your possession and a team to assist with the hunt…"

༺∾༻

Roselyn stacked the last of the items from her dressing table into her valise. Glass bottles clanked together in her trembling fingers and perfumed powders puffed up, making her cough and feel vaguely nauseated. She'd been shaking for the last hour. Snapping the bag shut, she set it aside and ran her hands over the cool, empty surface of the table.

She'd been offered tea and even something stronger, but she had no desire to drink, eat, or continue on with any kind of life in London. She only wanted to sit and stare until the house could be packed and the carriage prepared.

Her mother stirred behind her. "Are you certain you want to cut your season short, dear? It's all so rushed. We could wait until tomorrow when you're well rested from the day. I haven't even spoken with your brother."

"I shouldn't have come at all."

"Come-out seasons are always a bit sticky, truth be told. There's so much anticipation for such a short span of time. Most don't live up to a young girl's dreams."

"Mama, this has nothing to do with my dreams." Roselyn stood and walked to the foot of her bed, watching her mother sort through the stack of gloves in her wardrobe. "I simply cannot set foot in another ballroom this year knowing what a fool I've been." She turned away, brushing a tear from her cheek.

"Roselyn," her mother began, abandoning the pile of gloves for a maid to deal with and crossing the room to her daughter. "I've known a few ladies over my years in society, and you are the least foolish I've ever encountered. When your father left us, I watched as you placed stone after stone around your fragile heart. No matter how I tried to stop you, you walled yourself behind lists, agendas, and goals. This season has been the first time I've had a glimpse of my daughter behind those walls in a very long time." She tucked a stray curl behind Roselyn's ear with a thin smile. "Some may call it foolish. But I know who you truly are, Roselyn Grey."

"Mama, how can I go on here after…"

"After your heart has been broken? You are not the first lady to ask that question, my dear, and I daresay you won't be the last. We'll return home if that's what you wish, and you'll have time to mend before next season. For now, rest. I need to see about something in the kitchen. Who knew arranging tea to be sent outside would be such an ordeal? Should have been served an hour ago, if you ask me," she grumbled as she left the room.

Roselyn couldn't stand still, but neither did she have the energy to move. She shuffled to the window and stared, unseeing, into the back garden. *Time to mend.* She repeated her mother's words in her mind. Was mending possible? It seemed having a whole heart would only place her farther from this day and her memories of Ethan. It was a mad thought—needing to hold on to the hurt so she wouldn't have to let go of the man. But then, what was love but madness?

Another wave of tears fell, and she fell with them onto her bed, collapsing as sobs shook her body. She loved him. Whatever his intentions had been, for her part, she loved him and she always would.

The quilted counterpane of her bed pressed lines into her cheek as she traced the threads with her fingers. She'd done the right thing, just as she should have done. He'd used her and she'd forced him to leave. "The correct decision," she mumbled into her bedding.

Good decisions shouldn't crush one's body under their tremendous weight. And then there was the note she'd written him... Even though it seemed everything between them had been said, she still had questions. She supposed she always would. Another tear slid down her cheek as the sun sank lower outside her window.

At the tap on her door, she glanced up.

"My lady, you have a caller," one of the maids reported.

"I'm in no fit state to entertain," she replied, her voice thick with emotion. She wiped her hand across her eyes to remove the tears.

"He's most insistent."

"He?" Roselyn sat up, not waiting for an answer, but moving toward the door instead. "Ethan," she said breathlessly. He must have come back. But why? She flew down the stairs, her feet barely hitting the edge of each step in her haste. The front door stood open. That was odd. The door was never left open. And their butler was nowhere in sight.

She spun around in the hall, looking for Ethan. When she turned back to the open door, a hand covered her mouth. A sickly sweet smell flooded her nose as a man's arm wrapped around her from behind. She tried to scream, but everything spun instead. A moment later, her legs collapsed beneath her and her eyes drifted shut.

"Ethan!" She tried to call out, but she was already falling into darkness.

❧

The pile of documents Ethan had collected were strewn across a table in the corner of Spares headquarters along with the necklace Roselyn had returned to him. Ethan gritted his teeth, desperate to find answers among the papers. He had to solve this before Roselyn was put in danger. He'd even pulled her brother into the mix of things, bringing him into headquarters and, in doing so, breaking a vow he'd taken long ago to keep the Spare Heirs Society a secret.

St. James had been shooting him stern looks for the past half hour, but Ethan ignored him. He'd had enough ire for one day. He rubbed his weary eyes and leaned over the documents he'd damn near memorized weeks ago.

"This Alvaro Santino was the fellow we saw across the street?" Crosby asked from across the table.

"Those were his men," Ethan replied. "It appears he was behind the surveillance of headquarters. He said he was contacted when local men weren't up to scratch."

St. James narrowed his gaze on Ethan, but didn't say a word.

Hardaway lifted a document from the pile and scanned it for information as he spoke. "You're saying that the titled lord who wants your arse on a pike hired this man who is out for your blood after his other men were too gentle with you? That would be amusing if it didn't end in your demise, Ayton."

"You really have a way of getting to the heart of the matter, Hardaway. Thank you for that summary of how dead I will be within the hour, but it's not my life I'm concerned for at the moment."

Thornwood grumbled something Ethan couldn't quite hear.

"You know my thoughts on the matter," St. James cut in before the two men came to blows as they often did.

"I have to agree with St. James," Thornwood offered. "The key to this business is the shopkeeper. What was his name again, Ayton?"

"Sharpe. He's been in my father's employ as long as I can recall. Do you truly think he would hide information such as this? He doesn't seem the sort to be involved with murder."

"There's one way to find out," Hardaway offered, rubbing his hands together and grinning.

"Blast it all, Hardaway, you've already tried to burn the man's shop to the ground, and now you want to beat answers from him?" Ethan asked. He didn't know Sharpe well, but he was fairly sure his father wouldn't want someone in his employ beaten for information.

"It's what I do." Hardaway shrugged. "Sorry, Your Grace. Forget you heard that last bit just as you'll forget you ever heard of the Spare Heirs."

Thornwood nodded in agreement as he examined the back of the necklace.

"It might be a bit suspicious if a carriage piled full of gentlemen pours out onto Bond Street at dusk," Crosby said. "If you don't desire an audience for this interrogation, that is."

"That's why I sent one of the new members for him an hour ago," St. James said, taking a sip of his tea.

Ethan cringed at the thought of one of the family's men being clubbed over the head and stuffed into a carriage. His father would not be pleased. At some point, Ethan would have to return to Ormesby Place and explain some of this, though if he had his druthers, none of the events of the past few weeks would ever come up. Ethan sighed and had just settled back in his chair when the door crashed open and a man with a bag over his head was pushed into the room.

"Sharpe," Ethan said, standing and crossing the room to the man, while motioning for the covering to be removed from his head.

"What is this place?" Sharpe asked, with a wild look in his eyes like a trapped animal, surveying his possible escape route. "Ayton? Who are these gentlemen? What are you doing here?"

"We have some questions for you," Ethan replied as the other gentlemen joined them in the center of the room, surrounding Sharpe and preventing his escape.

The shopkeeper tried to back in two different directions before giving up and standing overly still. "I don't know your interest in me, but I'm not saying a word. I don't know anything."

"Rather on edge for someone who has nothing to hide, don't you agree, Ayton?" Thornwood asked.

"I do," Ethan said, taking a step forward. "I'm guessing he does know something. Come now, Sharpe. We know there has been a theft."

"People snatch things from time to time, but I've done my best to serve your family for years, Lord Ayton."

"This was no small theft," St. James cut in, holding up the necklace. "Perhaps this will help your recollection."

"I can help his recollection too, if you'd like, Ayton." Hardaway had a menacing gleam in his eye as he made a show of clenching his fist.

"That's the piece you took from the shop last week," Sharpe pleaded, looking at Ethan. "There was no theft. You've already been told there wasn't a theft and to leave it be."

Ethan took the necklace from St. James and turned it over in the palm of his hand, showing it to Sharpe. "This piece I got from the shop—my family's shop—is marked with the W. B. Exports emblem. That warehouse at the harbor is full of stolen jet, isn't it?"

"No, I…"

"How long has this been going on, Sharpe? Years? That's quite a large amount of stolen goods. Trevor learned of it, didn't he? He discovered your theft, and you killed him to keep your secret safe." Ethan said the words with as little emotion as he could manage.

"I didn't kill your brother, my lord."

"But you know who did," St. James stated before turning to Ethan. "Who told you there hasn't been a theft, Ayton? This man knows more than he's willing to share."

"I've only discussed this investigation with those

here, Lady Roselyn, and"—Ethan shifted to look at Sharpe—"Cladhart. He discouraged me from my investigation. Determined to protect me, he insisted that if there was any wrongdoing, he would see to it. But it couldn't be him."

"Cladhart. Who is that?" St. James asked.

"Lord Cladhart is my father's business associate," Ethan supplied, feeling rather ill at the direction this was turning. All the pieces were falling into place. Then the swift anger of betrayal swept through him and he turned back to Sharpe. "Sharpe, did you know I've killed a man with a single hit? Your jaw would break quite easily, you know. Do you have a lady in your life? I'm sure she's fond of your face the way it is."

"I had nothing to do with it. Just doing as I was told," Sharpe said, his eyes wide with panic.

"What were you told?" Ethan probed.

When his question was met with silence, Ethan bellowed, "*What were you told?*"

"I knew those Spanish men were no good from the start. 'Keep matters local,' I said. But he doesn't listen to me."

"Who?" Ethan stepped forward, needing to hear confirmation of the truth he already knew.

"It's a much longer story than I wish to tell," Sharpe replied with a twisted look of unease on his face.

"If you're trying to preserve your employ, I can assure you it isn't working." His father's approval didn't matter anymore; if this man had something to do with Trevor's death, Ethan would see him hang.

"I can't tell you any more than I already have," Sharpe stated with more than a little fear in his voice.

Ethan turned and took a few paces away, bracing his hands on the back of a chair. This didn't prove any plot on Cladhart's part. There was always another clue, another place to go, another document to search. When would he find answers? He'd been poring over the pages spread on the table at headquarters for the better part of the season now, and the situation had only gotten worse. Now Roselyn was being threatened and he was no closer than he had been a week ago. He could forget this plan and attempt to gather the funds Santino was after. It would solve nothing, but it would buy him time.

"Ayton, it seems this man would like to call upon your Lord Cladhart, and I think we should allow it," St. James cut in. "It's after the proper time of day, but I'm sure exceptions can be made. Can't they, Sharpe?"

The man didn't answer, only glancing at the door before his gaze fell to the floor before him.

"Looks as if we're taking an outing for tea with this fellow Cladhart," Hardaway said with a teasing air of excitement about him.

"I don't think I've ever looked forward to a social call before," Thornwood mused.

Ethan turned back to the gathered group of gentlemen. "Cladhart is behind this? How could I have been so blind? He was the one who advised me that he would have someone look into the theft. He tried to convince me not to look too deeply into my brother's murder."

"How convenient," St. James remarked. "You never told me of this until tonight."

"You've had your hands rather full as of late, St.

James. I needed answers," Ethan tried to explain because his friend seemed to be upset at the slight. "Cladhart has always been like an uncle, perhaps even a father, to me."

"Is he still?" Thornwood asked with a raised brow.

Ethan didn't reply. There was no need.

"Social call it is! Just a moment while I go retrieve my favorite pistol," Hardaway said as he left the room.

"If we're to do this, someone will need to go straight to the mews and prevent an unwanted escape," St. James said. "Distract his grooms, hide the tack for the horses, things of that sort…"

"Distraction and subterfuge are my specialties," Crosby said, stepping forward. "I'll take that job."

"I'll alert the authorities," Thornwood tossed out. "If Santino is there, I'll see that he's on a ship back to his own country by daybreak. And I know who to contact so as not to make this the latest talk in town. I'll take my carriage and meet you there." He nodded and turned to leave them.

"How far is Cladhart's home?" St. James asked Ethan.

"Not nearly close enough. I want this mess to be dealt with." As long as this situation lingered unmanaged, Roselyn was in danger. Cladhart's home—though on the other side of the city—was reachable tonight, Ethan told himself. He had until tomorrow. Roselyn was safe at her home until then.

"We can leave as soon as the carriage is readied."

"That will take too long," Ethan replied. "We can go by horseback."

St. James raised a brow. "With a hostage?"

"Very well. Go see to the carriage. I'll stay here with Sharpe."

Ethan looked at Sharpe, studying him for a moment. The man could confirm everything Ethan suspected if he wished to do so. Yet he only stared at the rug at his feet. "Did Cladhart have Trevor killed?" But only silence met his ears.

With a nod, Ethan punched the man in the nose, then began pacing the floor. That carriage couldn't be readied fast enough.

❧

Voices of men sounded around her as Roselyn struggled into wakefulness. What had happened? She'd come downstairs to greet a caller and…that's the last she remembered. She swallowed. She needed water. So thirsty. Where was she? She tried to move, but her hands and ankles were bound together.

*Trouble. Terrible trouble.*

Whoever had done this would expect her to be asleep. Safer, then, if she pretended just that. She cracked her eyes open to mere slits. Books lined the walls and a desk stood in front of a row of windows. She turned her head as much as she dared. A fire burned in the grate. Two men stood near it, discussing something—her fate?

What interest did they have in her? Why was she here?

"You stole her from a ducal residence? I thought you said she would be easy to acquire."

"She was," a man replied with broken English. "We drug her and bring her here."

"I don't need this sort of complication. Not now."

"You said you want her dead along with the fighter. You said it could not wait for tomorrow. It is today."

*The fighter*, Roselyn repeated to herself. Ethan! Ethan would come and save her. If only he knew where she was. And there was no hope of him discovering her absence because she'd sent him away. She tried the binding at her hands again, pulling at the thin rope, but it was no use. She was trapped.

"...kill her, and it will be as if she was never here."

*No!* Roselyn tried to pull her ankles apart. She had to run.

"And her body?"

"Let me take care of that. I have skill at such things."

Roselyn squirmed on the thick rug where she'd been tossed, no longer able to stay still and pretend slumber. How could anyone, when men were talking about the best way to kill her as casually as if they were discussing the weather?

With her eyes now fully opened, she could see she was inside someone's library. The Spanish man was the one Ethan had told her of—Santino—but the other man... He was dressed well enough to be a lord. Could he be Trevor's killer? And if so, wasn't Ethan supposed to be here to watch his trap close?

But he wasn't here. She'd sent him away. And now, as she listened to plans of her demise, he was the one person she wished to see.

But she wouldn't lie about waiting to die. She had to escape. There was only the one door on the far wall and the row of windows behind the desk. With her hands and feet bound she couldn't make it to the windows, let alone open one and jump to freedom. But she had to try. She raised her hands to her mouth and began biting at the knot in the rope. By now someone would have raised the alarm at home, wouldn't they? But how would anyone know where she'd been taken?

She was alone in this. *Alone*—sorrow washed over her again at the thought. If only her relationship with Ethan had been real. The Ethan of her dreams would rush in and start throwing punches, but that wasn't going to happen. It was up to her to find a way out of this mess on her own.

The twine bit into her skin as she nipped at the knot with her teeth. Mice made this sort of thing look easy, but it wasn't. Fibers poked at her lips as she worked and the taste was dreadful. If she ever made it from this place, she wanted an entire bottle of wine to herself and a long, undisturbed bath. But those wishes didn't seem likely to occur. The man who wasn't Santino strode calmly toward her with a knife. She rested her hands on the floor beside her face, hoping he hadn't noticed her attempt at escape.

"Pity you have to die, my lady," he said, kneeling over her.

"I don't," she rasped, eyeing the knife in his hand. "You could release me. I'll never speak of it."

"It's too late for that. You've seen too much, and I would have the weight of a dukedom upon me if anyone knew your whereabouts." He frowned as he looked at her. "No, no, no, that wouldn't do."

"I'll speak to my brother," she implored. "He'll give you anything you ask."

"Tempting. Sadly, you witnessed a terrible accident. Didn't you, my lady?"

Trevor's death. Something hardened inside her. This man had hurt Ethan and destroyed any hope any of them had at happiness. She wouldn't beg him for a thing, not even her own life. "That was no accident," she accused.

"So loyal to the Moore family," he mused, but then his mouth curled up into a grin that sent shivers down her spine. "I don't have the same inclination."

"He was my fiancé," Roselyn bit out.

He rested the hand holding the knife on his knee and cocked a brow at her in question. "You moved on rather quickly, didn't you? Perhaps I'm not the only one who feigns loyalty."

"I would have been a loyal wife to Trevor. But he's dead now, and you're to blame."

"Would you have? Ethan has always been a particular favorite of mine, you know. Impetuous boy—as a child he was always the first to try something new. Now that he's grown, he rushes in and takes what he wants without thought. He clearly wanted you, yet you were set to marry his brother. I did him a favor with Trevor, really."

"Is that why you killed Trevor? To help Ethan?"

"No, but it was a lovely added benefit. It's too bad Ethan kept digging about in things long buried or the two of you could have been quite happy together."

"I don't think that was ever our future," Roselyn stated, her heart breaking a bit further with her words.

"Too bad. Ethan's love for you was the only thing prolonging your life this evening. But I suppose there's no sense stretching this out any longer." He flexed the arm holding the blade.

She pulled back from him, but there was no place to go, no escaping this terrible fate. This was the end. And she would not die while shrinking away from danger or pleading with this killer for her life. "Go ahead and kill me then, if that's what you mean to do. Just know that my father was mad, my brother is mad, and so am I. I will haunt you until your last day."

"An unfortunate risk I must take," he mused as he pulled a cloth from his pocket and tied it around her face, covering her mouth to muffle her screams. She tossed her head about but it did nothing to slow the clock. Her time had run out. He raised the knife in his hand just as a deafening bang split the air.

# *Twenty*

ETHAN CHARGED INSIDE, WOOD SPLINTERS SCATTERING around him.

"Cladhart and Santino," he said as he rounded the door to the library. He should have known. Ethan stepped forward into the room, his gaze fixed on the two men. "It seems you were correct in advising me to seek answers elsewhere," he offered to Sharpe in a low growl.

The man behind him groaned in response, and Hardaway pushed him through the door into the library. How could Cladhart have betrayed him so? He was kneeling before the fire with Santino at his back. The surprised look on his face at the sight of Ethan appeared almost pleased. Did the man not know his schemes had come to an end? Ethan curled his fingers into a fist, ready, just as he did before each match.

"It seems our party grows, Santino. Ethan, won't you come in?"

"I believe I invited myself," Ethan replied. "St. James, will you see to Santino?"

"With pleasure," his friend said as he set off across the room, his eyes darkening on Cladhart for a moment before turning his attention back to Santino. St. James ducked a powerful blow and shoved the man to the ground while he was off balance. They disappeared behind the table that backed a sofa on the far side of the room, but thuds and grunts of pain made every movement evident. A moment later all was silent and St. James stood, shaking the wrinkles from his coat.

"Ha!" Cladhart let out a bark of laughter. "My help has once again failed me. Just as well. I've been fighting this battle for many years." He stood from behind the small table set between chairs, pulling something from the floor with him, something that looked like a cascade of soft fabric and curling dark hair.

Ethan's heart stopped. "Roselyn!" He surged forward. "What have you done to her?"

"Stay where you are," Cladhart said, raising his knife to her throat.

Roselyn's eyes were wide as she stared at Ethan above the blade. She was only a few paces away, and yet he couldn't reach her in time.

"Release her," Ethan warned. "She has nothing to do with this."

"She knows too much already," Cladhart replied, shifting the blade in his hand.

"As do I. Let Roselyn go. This is between us. So help me, if you do her any further harm, you'll suffer beyond your worst nightmares," Ethan snarled. "She's done nothing to deserve this."

"Such anger over your demise, my lady. It's as I was saying earlier…"

A gunshot shattered the moment, the thundering crack followed by a loud ringing in Ethan's ears.

He spun around to see Hardaway holding a smoking pistol in his hand. "Did I hit him?" he yelled over the loud ringing that filled the room.

"You're unsure?" Ethan accused him, spinning back to Roselyn. The blasted idiot could have hit her! He was already kicking over a chair between them to reach her when Cladhart crumpled to the ground.

"Are you hurt?" Ethan asked, pulling the gag from her mouth. He ran his hands over her shoulders, checking for damage before holding her at arm's length to look at her. He was shaking as he pulled her into his arms. *She's alive. She's alive.*

Smoke still hung in the air and Cladhart writhed on the floor at his feet, but all Ethan knew was Roselyn. Except that only hours ago, she had wanted nothing to do with him. Loosening his grip, he released her, meaning to back away to a safe distance. But there were a hundred questions in her eyes, not relief or hate.

On the floor, Cladhart was groaning and clutching his leg. The wound matched a hole blown straight through Roselyn's skirts. "Is your leg injured?"

"No," she muttered. "But I would like to sit." She collapsed into the chair behind her and bent to retrieve the fallen knife from the floor, setting to work on her bindings. She looked down and didn't spare him another glance. He put the hurt of it from his mind and turned to deal with Cladhart.

"It was you all along? How could you?"

"How could I not?" Cladhart sneered, propping himself against the base of his desk.

Ethan didn't understand, but God help him, he

would. Or Cladhart would pay with far more than
a wounded leg. He took a step forward but wasn't
fast enough. Cladhart pulled a pistol from under his
desk, pointing it at Ethan. "Damn you for making
me do this!"

"I've yet to make you do anything. Cladhart, this
is madness. If you put the pistol down, we can discuss
matters." He stood stone still between Cladhart and
Roselyn. "No one needs to die today."

"That's where you're wrong, Ethan. You're first
and your lady friend is next. I told you not to dig up
the past." He lifted the pistol higher, pointing it at
Ethan's head. "I told you it would end like this."

"You told me no such thing or I would have
guessed where your loyalties lay weeks ago. How
could you do this to our family? You claim Father as
a friend, yet kill his sons?"

"Your father is no friend of mine. Do you think
I've done all of this for him?"

"You've worked together my entire life," Ethan
said. "Side by side…"

"You weren't there!" The pistol shook in
Cladhart's hands.

"Where?"

"She was so beautiful that first season, every eye
was upon her." Cladhart had a faraway look in his eyes
even though he looked straight at Ethan. "Auburn
hair, eyes that glowed like emeralds…"

"Katie?" Ethan asked. "So help me, if you've laid a
finger on my sister…"

"I'm not speaking of your blasted sister. I've only
loved one lady, and your father stole her from me."

"Mother? You and my *mother*?"

"Herold," Roselyn rasped from the chair at his back.

"Your mother didn't know what was best for her. She didn't know I was the one who cared for her. Charles only wanted to secure his legacy, produce an heir. But then he was the one with the entailed estate, the funds to provide for a wife. Not all gentlemen are so fortunate."

"My mother married my father for money? No. That wasn't her."

"Ladies are only interested in such things. Haven't you noticed this one's taste for finery?" Cladhart waved the pistol in Roselyn's direction.

Roselyn shifted in the chair and Ethan dared a glance at her. She'd cut the ropes that bound her wrists but she hadn't moved from the chair where he'd left her.

"Don't touch her," Ethan warned, stepping to the side to better block the pistol's aim.

"She's just like the rest of them. I'm saving you heartache by killing her. Do you know what I went through to gain enough wealth to draw Katherine to my side? The toil of collecting jet beneath your father's watchful eyes, the effort of arranging sales accounts overseas, the struggle of hiding the scheme from him for so many years."

"I'm sure your efforts had some reward," Ethan growled.

"Don't you see? I had to steal from your father. I had to have enough funds. It was all for Katherine. I wanted her to have everything she desired."

All at once the devastating truth settled upon him. "You're the reason I never found her in France. Where is she? Is she here?"

"It was your father's fault. She belonged with me. I loved her!" Cladhart bellowed.

"What did you do?" Ethan bellowed back.

"I had everything prepared. She would have rooms in my new home. Anything she wanted would be hers. She would finally abandon your father. We could be together at last."

"She would never choose you," Ethan said.

"Your father poisoned her mind against me. She was supposed to be mine. I sacrificed for years for her. And all I received in return from her was a blasted letter asking me to stop seeking her out. She liked our encounters."

Ethan stepped forward, his blood boiling and nothing in his view but red. "You bastard. You forced yourself on my mother, didn't you?"

"She loved me! She was just confused when she said she would go to Charles and tell him everything. After all of my pain, all of my efforts, I couldn't have him win—not again."

"You killed her." Ethan noticed St. James moving in slowly from the side of the room but didn't let on.

"Charles turned her against me. He took her from me. But she spent her last moments with me, so I won in the end. My sweet Katherine."

"She wasn't yours. She was never yours," Ethan spat the words out as he eyed the pistol pointed at his chest. St. James was closing in on Cladhart but not fast enough. "You took a wife from her husband, a mother from her children. That isn't love."

"What do you know of love? Do you think you love this chit?" He tilted the pistol toward Roselyn again.

Ethan moved to block the potential shot. "No! Leave Roselyn out of this."

"Do you hear that, my lady? He doesn't love you. Just as well for you, since you'll both be dead in a few minutes. You won't have to suffer as I have."

"You haven't suffered nearly enough. You killed my mother!" Ethan yelled. "You killed her and then you killed Trevor. And now you dare try to kill Roselyn."

Ethan had to get to that pistol. Clearly Roselyn had the same thought since a second later a vase flew past his head and crashed into the desk beside Cladhart. It wasn't perfect aim, but it worked to draw Cladhart's attention for the one crucial moment that was needed.

Before Ethan could move, St. James lunged for the weapon, the tips of his fingers grazing their target. Cladhart's grip loosened and the barrel of the weapon pointed to the ceiling as he tried to shove St. James away. A fraction of a second, that's all he had to gain the upper hand.

Like an opening in defenses in a fight, Ethan saw his opportunity and dove for the pistol. Ripping the weapon from Cladhart's hands, he slid it across the floor to Hardaway who was still restraining Sharpe. Then Ethan rounded on the man who'd taken everything from him, who'd intended to take Roselyn away as well.

"You killed my mother." He punched Cladhart in the jaw.

"You killed my brother." Another blow broke his nose.

"You stole from my family." He lifted the man from the floor by his shirt and slammed him back against the wooden surface of his desk.

His fist was raised to deliver another hit, this one because he'd dared touch Roselyn, when the warmth of a small hand gripped his shoulder. "Ethan, your mother deserves justice, but she wouldn't want you to kill in her name."

His body vibrated with anger as blood rushed in his ears.

"Ethan!"

He tightened his fist, ready.

"Ethan, your mother wouldn't want this. You're a good man. You're better than him," Roselyn pleaded.

He lowered his hand, his blood still pounding in his ears.

Roselyn was right. She was always right. His mother wouldn't have wanted more violence to come from her death. He exhaled a harsh breath. Her death—she was gone. She'd died before he fought with his father at nineteen. She'd been dead when he went to France to search for her at twenty, and she was gone now.

Ethan was shaking as he dropped Cladhart to the floor and rose to his feet. The room was oddly quiet after such chaos. A chair was knocked over and a table was broken from Santino's struggles, but the man must be unconscious since James was now moving to the grate to stoke the dying fire.

Hardaway shoved Sharpe hard into a chair, clearly irritated that he hadn't been allowed to throw a punch. "I'm keeping the pistol," he announced before turning back to glare at his charge.

And then there was Roselyn. She stood before Ethan, rumpled but alive. He lifted his hands to her shoulders but stopped short of touching her, letting his arms fall back to his sides. He had no right to touch her—not anymore. He had to respect her wishes. It was the least he could do after what he'd put her through. "Are you all right?" he asked.

"I think I am, in light of the circumstances."

"I'm sorry. None of this was…"

"I'm fine, Ethan. Truly, I am."

He nodded and folded his hands across his chest to keep from reaching for her, but that didn't keep his gaze from connecting with hers. She said nothing further, but her lips were pursed as she looked up at him. So much had happened in the past few hours, so much had been said. And yet Cladhart's claims of love were what rang in his ears. "About what Cladhart said…"

"He said quite a few things."

"That he did."

"Ethan, you don't have to explain anything," she offered. "You've been through a great ordeal tonight. Both of us have."

"That's true. But I need to say this." He chose his words carefully. "The part when he said I didn't love you. That wasn't true."

"Oh. That's…" Her voice trailed off as she looked at him.

"I do love you, Roselyn. I always have," he stated clearly, not caring if his friends heard him. As long as she heard him, that was all that mattered.

There was something in her eyes that he wanted to bottle and keep in his pocket forever, yet she said nothing.

"I know forgiveness is too much to ask for. And I'm not going to ask you to find a way to look past my mistakes, but for my part, I want a future with you. The danger that followed me is gone now. I'll need someone to help me find my footing on the estate, and I want it to be you. That place has never felt as if it's my home, but when you're with me, that's my home."

"Ethan, this is all so sudden, so reckless. You've only just…" She looked up at him as if trying to unravel a great mystery. "This isn't rational."

*So that's it, then.* No pronouncement of mutual love. No plans to be his wife now that the threat to her life was lifted. "You're correct, of course," he said through an ever-tightening throat. "Nothing further needs to be said."

Just then Thornwood entered the room with the authorities and Ethan's one shining moment of conversation with Roselyn was over. She didn't wish him to say anything on this subject or, it seemed, any other. It was over—his time with her, the investigation, all of it. And now it was time to let her walk away.

❧

"My lord, you have a caller," the Spares' butler said from the door.

"Send him away," Ethan responded, not looking up from his intense study of the whiskey glass in his hand. He wasn't sure how long he'd been sitting at the table in the corner of the room. He wasn't sure where he was going to go when he finally rose to his feet. But he was damn sure he didn't wish to entertain a guest, nor was he dressed to do so.

"It's a *lady* caller, my lord," the butler replied in a hushed tone.

Ethan was on his feet and pushing the older man from his path before his glass had clanked to a rest on the table. He moved toward the door. A lady. *Please let it be Roselyn.* If he could see her once more before he left town, he could... He shook his head, slowing his pace. There was nothing left to do. He resided in a place beyond her forgiveness, a place she had no interest in visiting.

So, why did he hope now? He hardened his heart, preparing to see some acquaintance from a ball or a grandmother in need of a title for the next generation of her family.

He came in sight of the open door and stopped, his feet rooted to the polished oak floor. His heart sped as he silenced the hope that sang through his limbs and made his fingers twitch with anticipation.

"Roselyn," he whispered, afraid that if he said her name too loudly, she would vanish like a waking dream. He forced himself to move, to take a step closer to her. His boots echoed in the overly quiet room, punctuating his movements. "What are you doing here?"

"I...I'm here to... This is where you live?" Her words were as rushed as her eyes seemed to be as her gaze darted around the room. She only looked at him for a moment before looking away again.

He watched her. Why wouldn't she look at him? Did she hate him to that degree, and if so, why call on him? "I have rooms here," he said, forcing his mind to remain on the conversation.

She cleared her throat and clutched a shawl in

her hands, crushing the fabric into a tight wad. "My brother told me where to find you."

He took three more steps forward, cutting the large expanse of space between them in half.

"It's interesting," she hedged, eyeing the drawing room and makeshift headquarters over his shoulder.

"Ladies don't usually call." He took another step, blocking her from the curious stares of the other gentlemen.

"I would imagine not." With her eyes narrowed on two gentlemen talking over drinks and her voice lowered, she asked, "Ethan, is this a house of ill repute?"

He couldn't contain the bellow of laughter that burst forth from him, shaking loose the nerves that jangled through his body at the sight of her. "No, nothing so depraved as that." He glanced down at her hand, the fingers he would have clasped within his own only a few days ago. Now, however, there was an impassable wall between them. If he touched her, would he frighten her away? He settled for barely touching her elbow to guide her back into the hall where they would have privacy.

She moved away from him to the far side to the room and looked up at the mural of plump little cherubs that covered the ceiling of the hall. He pretended not to notice her desire to stand as far from him as possible. He, at least, was more aware of the distance between them than ever.

"What is this place?" she finally asked as her hand grazed the edge of a cluttered table piled high with men's hats and anything else he and the other gentlemen had in their pockets when they walked in the door.

"Why are you here?" he countered as he closed the drawing room doors. He knew the question was like a punch to the gut, but it needed to be asked. Sometimes it was best to throw the ugly hits early in the match to end the beating that much faster. Against this opponent, however, he could never win. He would be licking his wounds for years to come.

"I asked first," she blurted out, a blush creeping up her neck.

"It's a gentlemen's club." There. Now she must answer his question, because for the life of him, he couldn't guess at her intentions this afternoon.

She paced to the side, peering up the stairs as if looking for spies holding clandestine meetings on the landing. "A secret club? I saw no sign outside."

"We enjoy anonymity." Why had she come here? She certainly hadn't sought him out to question him about his club membership. She was searching for a change of conversation. He knew because he'd lost count of the times he'd done the same while speaking with his father. Whatever she needed to discuss with him must be terrible in her eyes to warrant so many diverting questions. His heart hardened a bit further at the thought.

"Is there a name for your club?" she asked, pacing back to the table with the hats. Her voice was tight as she spoke, and she'd yet to meet his gaze since they entered the hall. "Do you have a special sign you show one another? I've always wondered…"

"Princess, why did you come here?"

She might not have heard him except for the small, gasping breath of air that betrayed her. "It's curious to me. I would imagine there's at least a hand gesture that proves your membership."

"It's the Spare Heirs Society. We have no signs, gestures, or creed we mutter to one another on street corners. Now, why are you here, Roselyn?"

"I…" Her gaze lifted to meet his for the first time since her arrival.

He waited, not daring to cross the room to her or speak when he didn't know her mind. She'd already pushed him away countless times. He couldn't attempt it again.

"I always have a plan," she finally said, leaning back against the far wall as she spoke. "For years now I've sought to have order in my life. I always thought it was from too much time spent surrounded by people believed to be mad. But my mother says I changed when my father left. Perhaps she's correct, but that isn't the point." She heaved a great sigh. "I've been under the impression that I could find success in life by striking through items on a list. I thought that if everything was secure, and all elements of my life were in place and certain, I would be fine… And then I met you."

"And I destroyed your future. You've mentioned as much before."

She held up her hand to stop him. "I've lived my life as if I could be happy by following a great map, and now I'm here. None of this was planned. It isn't logical." She paused, watching him. "I walked out of my door today and left all direction behind, every thought, every plan. I suppose I'm a bit lost, truth be told." A hint of a wry grin tugged at the corner of her lips as she spoke,

"No matter where I go, all of the roads seem to lead in this direction. Do you understand what I'm saying?"

"Not precisely."

"I don't know why I'm here, and I don't know what to do," she stated. Her eyes seemed to plead for him to understand her complicated thoughts.

"What to do about what?"

"You. You are the problem I can't work through in my mind."

"Me," he repeated, and the heart he'd thought he guarded began to sink. He should have guessed at her intentions today. "Will I forever be the cause of trouble in your life? Roselyn, I've caused you pain and I'm sorry for that, but surely I'm not the only problem in your life."

"Perhaps 'problem' was the wrong word to use." She looked down at her hands. The room seemed to grow colder without her eyes on him. "Yesterday when I said what I did… Well, things ended rather abruptly after that. I was wondering if perhaps… I thought I would ask if you…"

"If I what?" he asked a bit too quickly.

"If you would like to dance with me at the next ball, or if that doesn't sound appealing, we could take a stroll, or…"

"You're willing to be near me and risk your toes for a dance?" His heart was pounding, blinding him to all rational thought.

"I'm here." She attempted a grin, as she lifted her arms out a fraction before allowing them to drop back to her sides.

He shouldn't hope, but he couldn't stop himself

from doing so any more than he could knock five men to their backs with one blow. "Roselyn, I shouldn't have risked your life and your reputation as I did. What I did was wrong, and for that I should be taken away in chains."

She took a small step, closing the great divide between them. "I think the proper villain has been punished for his crimes. Perhaps that's why I'm here. I followed my heart, as irrational as that may sound, and my heart wishes things had ended differently. I know my response last night wasn't what you'd hoped to hear. But I've known you all my life, Ethan. It was reckless. I still believe that. What you were insinuating with talk of your estate when we'd just had our lives threatened... It defied logic. But you're my friend and I don't want to lose that."

"You've come to make amends...and secure a dance for the next ball?" His jaw tightened around the words. "That's all you want from me." He exhaled a sharp breath. Of course that was all she wanted from him. He was foolish to wish otherwise. At least she no longer hated him. He could go on with his life, knowing she at least had peace about their dealings.

Only how was he supposed to go on with his life as if nothing happened between them? He would always love her. And he couldn't let her walk away with the promise of his friendship. That would be a lie, and he couldn't lie to her.

"I didn't want you to leave town without speaking to you first," she finally said. "I appreciate your friend-ship and..."

"If it's friendship you seek today, I'll have to

disappoint you." He delivered the words like a strong
left hook, but he couldn't allow her to place him as a
*friend* in her mind. He couldn't stand by and be *friendly*
while she went on with her life. The devastation
would strangle him.

"Oh, I see." She nodded. "I suppose I should leave
then." Her eyes grew wide as she looked at the door
across the large hall, but she made no move to walk
toward it. "I thought…" Her voice cracked and she
broke off.

That was when Ethan saw the tear spill down
her cheek.

He was crossing the hall to her before he could
stop himself. Damn keeping his distance. Damn the
friendship she wanted from him. Damn that dance.
Damn not trying once more to scale her walls, and
damn watching her walk away. She was crying. "You
shouldn't have come here without a maid. It's a bachelor residence, you know."

"I know that now." She sniffed, looking down to
hide her face.

He reached up and brushed away the tear that
spilled down her cheek. "I've already destroyed your
reputation once. I can't allow that to happen again."

"You needn't worry over me."

He lifted her chin until they were eye to eye.
"Princess, thoughts of you fill my mind every second
of every day. And you believe I will allow you to
walk out of that door without a care? That I'll stand
idle as your *friend* while you live your life with someone else? That dance at the next ball is mine, as are
all others."

"Then you really do love me? I thought it was a reaction to having a pistol pointed at your heart."

"You didn't believe me?" His hands fell away from her as he turned and stalked to the other side of the room. He was done adhering to her itineraries and plans. She had come to find him, and she could follow his lead for a change.

Pivoting on his heel, he prowled back to her. "I want you to be my wife!" His deep voice echoed off the cherubs on the ceiling high above their heads. "It was all for you, Roselyn. I came to London so that I might see you once more. I tracked down my brother's killer so that you might have peace. I admit I endangered your life in the process, but that was never my intention. I've been at your heels ever since you slung mud at my face."

"Oh."

"I love you. I want you to marry me. I can't settle for friendship, not now. I want to wait the weeks necessary to have the banns read. I want to wed you properly. I want to return to Ormesby Place with you at my side. I want children who look up at me with your eyes, and I want to grow old together. You may not have had a plan when you arrived here, but I have the path on the map laid out quite clearly and it leads to a happy place. And damn it all, it leads to happiness with you!" He was yelling at her but he couldn't seem to calm himself. Offers of marriage probably shouldn't be shouted, but he didn't care. He would scream it from the nearest London rooftop. He loved Roselyn and wanted her to be his wife.

As loud as he was, she was equally quiet. The

silence pushed in on him as he waited for her to speak. After what seemed an eternity of shifting feet and parted lips on almost answers, her mouth curved up in the smile that was only for him. "I'm certain this is madness, but I can't imagine a future without you at my side. I love you, Ethan. And if that makes me irrational, illogical, and wild, so be it. I'll be all of those things with you because you make me happy. I'll scream my madness for all of London to hear as long as I get to do so with you."

He reached for her, dragging her into his embrace. "You have my word that you can be as wild as you want to be. We'll scream of our mad love for all to hear—together."

Leaning back to look up at him with a grin, she said, "We'll be shocking."

"No, we'll be infamous." And he couldn't imagine anything he'd rather be.

He moved his hands up her spine, pulling her close. He needed to convince himself that she was real, that she'd truly said she loved him and had agreed to be his wife. He'd loved her for so long already, and when he kissed her, it was with the promise of a lifetime of love ahead.

# *Twenty-one*

WHAT HAD SEEMED LIKE AN IMPASSABLE DIVIDE between them only moments ago disappeared as he backed her gently to the wall.

"Roselyn," he whispered as he looked down at her.

Wrapping his hands around her waist, he lifted her from the ground, holding her there with his thigh. He pressed his hips into hers, drawing a pleading noise from her throat. His eyes were dark and greedy as he drove against her again. His movements were those of a beast, his hands running over her body, his gaze steady, never leaving hers. She'd somehow unleashed the wild animal he kept contained within, and she had no wish to tame it. His hands came up to frame her face, tangling in her hair and pulling part of a braid loose. Her fingers dug into his shoulders in an attempt to claw her way to more, more of him, more of this.

Roselyn tried to catch her breath but lost the battle as his mouth descended on hers in a desperate kiss. She opened to him, tasting him again as if for the first time. This time he was hers. He deepened the kiss, fighting for more of her. Hunger, need surged through her veins as well. She pressed her breasts against his chest, lamenting the few layers of clothing between them, yet determined to have more of him.

"Good God, Ayton. Take it to your suite if you must," one of the gentlemen from last night said as he entered the home and tossed his hat onto the table.

"Leave him to his entertainment," another gentleman said as they passed in the hall. A moment later, the drawing room door opened and closed again beside them.

"St. James is correct," Ethan murmured against her lips as he kissed her again. "We're in the hall." He ground his hips against her as he pulled her closer still, making her limbs weak with want. "Your reputation," he managed as he ravaged her mouth once more.

"Hang my reputation," she said breathlessly as she slid her hands up his thickly muscled neck and into his hair.

"Fairly sure that's what we're doing," he said as he drew her legs up around his waist and ran his hands over her thighs and hips.

"Then you'll have to marry me quickly," she countered. She pulled his head back down to hers and kissed him once more.

"We could elope," he offered, pulling back from her to look into her eyes. "This is what you want?"

"I want you." She bit at his lip, forcing a growl from deep within his chest. She smiled at the power she sensed she held over him and brushed her lips across his.

"You're going to be my wife." His words were hollow, as if he couldn't quite believe the truth behind them. Then a slow grin appeared on his face like the sun rising in the morning, sure and bright.

A second later he was ascending the stairs with her wrapped around his body. He moved quickly and she watched over his shoulder at the main hall disappeared below. The cherubs on the ceiling would certainly have something to discuss this evening. She bit her lip and lowered her face to Ethan's neck where she'd apparently stretched his shirt beyond salvation. His warm skin was too enticing to be ignored. She placed a kiss on his muscular shoulder, lifting her lips from him just enough to ask, "How far are your rooms?"

"Too far," he practically growled as she slid her mouth around his neck until his hair tickled her nose.

She laughed and wrapped her legs tighter around him, leaning back to look him in the eye. One hand dipped to the vee of his shirt as she ran her fingers along the edge of the fabric. He hadn't been wearing a cravat or coat when she found him and she couldn't be more thankful. "I want to see you, all of you."

"I would have to agree with you on that score, princess." He kicked open a door and stepped inside.

Unwrapping her legs from about his body, she slid down his chest until her feet met a thick rug.

She ran her hands down his arms and squeezed his fingers before turning away to see where he'd taken her. "This is a rented room? I'd always imagined such places to be rather like servants' quarters. But this isn't small and dank at all."

"Thank you?" He chuckled as he followed her across the room. "These have been my rooms since I left home years ago. Thankfully they were kept for me while I was away."

She stopped at the side of his large poster bed.

Staring down the dark bedclothes like a foe in a dark alley, she imagined what they would share here this afternoon. She didn't move until he wrapped his hand around hers. That one touch was a light in the darkness, promising to lead her into their next adventure. The heat of his body was at her back, but he still wasn't close enough. She wanted more. The memory of their night in the ballroom alcove flooded her mind. Ethan must have felt her shiver, because in the next moment he pulled his hand free of hers and turned her to face him.

He left his hands resting on her hips, his thumbs rubbing slow circles over her body. "Are you sure you want to be my wife? You'll have a lifetime of this."

"As will you. I've been told I'm trouble," she murmured.

He let out a wry laugh as he said, "Trust me, Princess. I'm looking forward to the sort of trouble you bring into my life."

She smiled. This was her first opportunity to be truly alone with Ethan. They were free to touch each other, to be together without the scrutiny of society. There wasn't a ballroom of people just beyond a curtain, or someone who might intrude in the dining room. There were only the two of them—together forever.

*Trust me*, he'd said and she did. She rose to her toes and slipped her hands across his chest, dragging his shirt with her as she moved. Clearly anxious for more, he ripped the shirt over his head and gathered her in his arms, kissing a line across her jaw. He was pressed close to her, but not close enough. She reached for more, her hands gripping his thick arms. He trailed his lips down her neck in an intoxicating mix of soft kisses and rough scratches from the stubble of his beard.

Her head fell back in a silent plea for more. How would that mixture of soft and rough feel against the rest of her body? The private areas? He'd touched her there before. Today promised much more than what had taken place in the alcove. Heat rose through her at the thought, making her shiver with anticipation.

"I won't hurt you." He whispered the promise against her skin before brushing his lips against her flushed neck.

She considered correcting his misunderstanding of her shiver, but her words were lost as he pushed her dress from her shoulder and palmed one breast. His mouth found hers again as he kneaded her flesh, callused fingers grazing her smooth skin. A small whimper escaped her throat at the contact, but she wanted more. Her dress seemed unbearably tight and binding against her body. She wanted to be free, to be touched. She wanted his life-roughened hands all over her body and all at once. "Ethan," she begged, hoping he understood her meaning because she couldn't think of the proper words to say at the moment.

He spun her around and unbraided her hair with deft movements, combing his fingers though it until it hung down her back. She reached back at her sides to keep from tipping sideways, her hands landing on his thighs. His muscles tensed beneath her fingers and his pace increased. Her dress hit the floor at her feet in an instant, followed by her stays and shift. She turned, wanting to rip his clothes from him in a more ruthless manner than what he'd used on her. She grabbed the waist of his breeches, about to rip the placket away regardless of buttons, when he covered her hand with his, stilling her movements.

Glancing up at him, she saw that the ravenous animal she'd unleashed in the hall downstairs had returned. But instead of diving at her as he had before, he stepped back, holding her hands to each side within his. It was then she realized she was only wearing her stockings and shoes. She tried to pull her hands to her, but he held her there.

"Roselyn," he murmured in reverent admiration before he lifted her and tossed her onto the bed, bending to remove her shoes. He climbed up after her a moment later, still tossing clothing off his body. Moving over her to brace his arms on either side of her, he slowed, watching her. She was staring. He was a feast for the eyes and she was starving. She should have felt shame at being caught in such gluttony, but she couldn't find it anywhere inside. Lifting a hand to his chest, she splayed her fingers across the patch of hair that grew there. She looked at her small hand on his broad chest with fascination before glancing up to his face.

At the hint of his crooked grin, she continued, letting her hands drift lower. Corded muscle rippled beneath her fingers as she learned his body, beginning with what was within reach. His stomach, like the rest of him, was all hard planes and rigid lines that tapered down to his hips. Her gaze dipped to see the remainder of him and her breath caught. Everything in the alcove at the ball had happened so fast that she hadn't had time to truly appreciate the sight of him. She jerked her face back up in time to witness his amusement before it faded to something darker, something that echoed in her soul.

He shifted his weight to recline at her side. The length of his body pressed against her. Her breasts rose and fell with her quickened breaths, brushing against his chest and making her heart pound that much faster. She leaned into him, longing for something more, something he apparently understood without words. He turned, pulling her onto his chest. "Sit up," he said, his voice rough with desire.

She pushed to her knees at his side, looking down on him in confusion.

He just grinned. "Not over there, princess."

"Oh," she muttered, then blinked in surprise as he settled her across his stomach. Her legs straddled him. All at once she was exposed, both utterly vulnerable and in control of this beast of a man. At the hint of his crooked grin, she continued, letting her hands drift lower. Corded muscle rippled beneath her fingers.

His hands skated over her skin as if he was attempting to memorize her by touch alone. Her breasts, her waist, her thighs—she shook with the effort to remain still under his attention, finally losing the battle with herself and arching into his touch. Her hips rocked forward against him as she leaned into the heat of his hands. Searching his face to see if she'd done something she wasn't supposed to do, she saw only desire. "You're rather skilled at this," he said as he drew a line down her body with the backs of his knuckles.

"Is there skill involved in sitting atop a gentleman while he—" Her voice cracked and disappeared on a single note of desire as he stroked her core with his fingers.

"There is," he said playfully. "And I look forward to witnessing it. Later. For now…" He broke off as he flipped her to her back, moving with her as one.

With her mind still curiously circling his promise of later, she bit her lip, realizing he now had her pinned to the bed as he lay between her legs. If she had known this could happen when she stood looking at his large bed, it might have frightened her further, but now…Ethan's weight was comfortable bearing down on her. There was an easy confidence to his movements that told her even if she didn't have a plan for the moment, he did.

His head dipped as he traveled down her stomach, kissing her, tasting her skin. When his tongue dipped into her belly button, she reached for him. She dug her fingernails into his shoulders as his deep chuckle rippled through her body. He glanced up at her with twinkling dark eyes, holding her gaze as he moved lower over her body. He dragged his mouth up the inside of her thigh as if he had read her wicked thoughts before. Soft abrasion assailed her senses as her leg fell to the side.

Reading her body like the open pages of a book, he pressed his mouth to her, drawing a cry from her lips. She slipped her fingers into his hair as she grasped for purchase. His tongue, his mouth, she didn't know what he was doing to her but she didn't want it to end. She arched into him. Her body screamed for more as he pulled her apart with every flick of his tongue. Every tug from his lips pulled her deeper into a heated swirl of need until she screamed his name out into the quiet of the room.

He moved over her as she lay sprawled across his bed. His breathing was labored as he knelt between her knees. His hair was mussed from her fingers, adding to his wild look. He'd brought her so much pleasure, yet there was a look of some inner agony on his face. His hands slid up the outsides of her thighs and rested on her hips. Perhaps if she touched him as he had done her, that pained look would ease in his eyes. She reached for the one place she'd yet to touch skin to skin with no boundaries, her hand wrapping around him. She blinked in surprise at the smooth heat beneath her fingers. He moaned and covered her hand with his.

Had she hurt him? "Sorry," she tried to say as she looked up into his dark eyes, but wasn't sure if she'd managed it. Neither dared look away. He moved toward her then, with a gentleness no man of his size should possess. Her hand was still wrapped beneath his when she realized he was poised at her entrance and she'd helped guide him there. Her heart pounded in her chest. He pulled her hand free with a tug of her wrist and tangled his fingers with hers, sliding her arm to the side.

He leaned forward, brushing the hair from her face as he watched her. Her body hummed with anticipation. They would become one and he would be hers. Strands of poetry streamed disjointedly through her mind. Everything in her life thus far came down to this moment, to this beautiful moment when they would join together. He thrust into her in one fluid movement. She braced for the same brief pain she'd experienced only a few nights ago but was surprised when there was no pain—only a delicious fullness that promised great pleasure to come. He paused for a second before retreating from her, only to drive into her again. She arched her hips into him, inviting more.

"Ethan," she murmured as she ran her hands over his arms, his chest, his sides, anything she could touch.

He answered her with more of him, somehow reaching deeper within her, touching a small guarded part of her soul. Claiming her. For once in her life, she embraced the loss of control and reveled in the freedom she found with him. He pushed into her again and again and she met him, challenging him.

Together they journeyed toward the unknown. He drove her higher with every movement, the force of his need for her expressed in the tension of his muscles, the dark gleam in his eyes, the thrust of his body. Her limbs twitched with her own need for him. Arching higher, aching for more, she fought for purchase, grasping at his muscled back. Her world spun as she soared into some great abyss. Something bright shone just before her, and she reached for it, the promise of pure joy. Digging her fingers into his sides, she felt her head fall back as she dove headlong into the abyss, pulling Ethan with her.

His deep guttural outcry echoed through her body as he pushed into her one last time. Her trembling body relaxed into languid satiation as he held her close beneath him. He kissed her temple and her hair before pulling back enough to look into her eyes. She released her hold on him, realizing too late she'd left nail marks on his skin. She soothed the injury with her fingertips.

He withdrew from her and fell to his back at her side, bringing her with him to sprawl across his chest. They lay together in a heap of racing heartbeats, spent muscles, and blissful enjoyment of the moment. She ran her hand over the hair on his chest. "Well, no trees fell on us, but I suppose there are some advantages to a bed," she mused with a smile.

"Quite a few. And I get to show you every single one." He ran his rough fingers up and down her spine in thoughtless lines of delight, making her squirm closer into his embrace. "You were a virgin until that tree-filled room," he stated, slicing through her thoughts.

She twisted in his arms to rest her chin on the hand that draped across his torso, meeting his gaze. "Did you think otherwise?"

"I wasn't certain either way. You were engaged to my brother. If you were mine, I'd scarcely have been able to keep my hands from you."

"I *am* yours."

His hands tightened around her at the proclamation. "*Now* you are, but there was a time…"

This didn't seem the time to introduce the subject of his brother, but if it must be discussed, then so be it. She took a breath, considering her words. "Trevor and I had a certain understanding. He required a wife and sons. I desired a home of my own, security, and predictability."

"But surely he found you desirable as well. How could he not?"

"Ethan, you're as different from your brother as night and day. He was more concerned with his days than my nights. I was to fulfill a need to provide him heirs and nothing more. My decision to marry him was a choice of the easiest path." She didn't have to explain her choices to him, but he needed to understand. She wanted him to understand. "I never loved your brother. I know that now. He was an honorable gentleman and a good choice, but it was no love match."

"Yet you were prepared to marry him. You grieved his loss. Not that I mind the black undergarments," he added with a grin.

"I did mourn him. He was to be my husband. But he didn't… He wasn't…" She wasn't sure how to explain herself without insulting his deceased brother by comparison. "I'm happy here—with you."

"Do you consider this a *good match*?"

"Of course I do."

"I want to be your love match. Is it wrong of me to want more? More than what my brother had?"

"Ethan, you already are my perfect match. Your brother never had my love. He never had me, not really anyway. I think I've always been yours. I was simply waiting for you to come home to me."

He pulled her close, burying his fingers in her hair, and enveloped her entire body within his arms. His muscles relaxed around her and his chest fell as he breathed out. And yet he didn't release her, holding her like a child would hold a beloved doll. "I didn't think this would ever be possible."

She squirmed in his arms until she could see his face. "You know a love match isn't possible without a partner. What do you say? Will you battle with me until death us do part?"

"Will you prance about in those breeches again?" he asked with a chuckle as he brushed her hair from her face. "I love you, Roselyn Grey, and my rather enjoyable battle will be to prove that love to you every day until death us do part."

"Ethan?"

"Yes?"

"Might we have another round in our love match now?"

He tossed her onto the bed at his side and covered her with his body. "Anything for you, my princess. Let's begin this match of ours on the proper footing," he said against her neck as he trailed kisses down to her shoulder. "All challenges of this sort should begin with learning about your opponent, and I look forward to a lifelong education—beginning right now."

# Epilogue

*Dearest Ethan,*

*I'm writing to you from Seville, Spain. It's beautiful, but you already know that. The fountain outside the window of our rooms at the inn is splashing water, and it's the most delightful sound. But the whitewashed buildings dotting the countryside aren't what make this place so perfect—you are. These past few months of marriage to you have been the happiest of my life. When I look back on the great joys of my life, I realize you were always there. When you chased me across the moors and climbed trees with me when we were children, and now when you hold me in your arms and whisper that you love me—these are the best moments of my life. And it's all because of you, my love, my husband. I will cherish every day spent at your side, and I look forward to the day when we return to Ormesby Place to build our lives together.*

*I'm smiling right now because you think I'm writing to your sister while you arrange for our supper to be sent up for us. But this note is for you, just for you. I thought since I ripped the last note to pieces, you could have this one instead. I love you, Ethan, with all my heart. Now, put down this note and come find me in our bedchamber.*

*Yours forever,*
*Roselyn*

Ethan looked up with a grin from the note he'd found in the middle of the floor. He was already moving toward the bedchamber to find his wife. When he reached the door, he found her sitting at the small dressing table with her back to him. She was wearing one of his black shirts—and *only* the shirt. Crossing the room, he smiled over the note before laying it on a table as he neared her.

"Roselyn," he murmured into her ear as he leaned over her with his arms braced on the dressing table. He placed a kiss on Roselyn's shoulder where the large, black shirt had slipped aside, exposing her skin. She was beautiful—and not just the parts wrapped within his own loose clothing. She was even more beautiful deep inside in that place that believed that adventure was best achieved if one dressed for the occasion and the world would be a better place with a bit of organization amid the chaos of life. His wife. He smiled and kissed her shoulder again.

"I see you got my note."

Ethan slipped his fingers into the hair at the back of her neck with a gentle caress. "I'll treasure it always. I think I like this one even better than the last. Although the first note had its uses. It urged me to chase after you, something I've been doing every day since."

Roselyn stood, turning to face him with her arms draped around his waist. "And now that I'm good and caught, what will you do?"

Pulling one of her hands from about him, he placed it on his chest. Tracing the band of metal on her finger, he asked, "You think this means you're caught?"

"Doesn't it?"

She was watching him twist the ring on her finger back and forth where it was pressed against his chest. "I learned long ago never to underestimate my opponent, and you are my most challenging adversary yet."

She lifted her gaze and grinned as she said, "I do throw a nice punch."

"You do, princess. Right in the heart." He pressed her hand to his heart, wanting her to feel the pounding rhythm that beat there only for her.

Rising to her toes she snaked her arm up around his neck. "I'm no princess," she said against his lips as she kissed him. "Did no one teach you about titles in our fair country?"

"You're Lady Ayton, and that makes you my princess." He smiled as he pressed his forehead to hers. "And I shall bow to your wishes for the rest of my days."

"I think I may enjoy this new title," she said, a challenging gleam entering her eyes. "My first command involves all of this black in your wardrobe."

"Not a chance, princess. I like my black ensembles."

"Really?" she asked as she pulled his shirt up over his chest with a grin. "I think I like you more without them."

He ripped the shirt off over his head and lifted her from the floor, tossing her onto their bed. "Who am I to deny my princess what she wishes?"

"You're Lord Ayton, my husband, my love, and the man who is about to lose this match."

"With pleasure," he said against her lips. He would happily lose every match to her, if it meant keeping her at his side, for the rest of their days.

Keep reading for a sneak peek at the next
book in the Spare Heirs series

# *The Rebel Heir*

*Spring, 1817*

"ANY CHANCE YOU CAN PAINT A BIT FASTER THERE,
Stapleton?" Ash leaned out the carriage window to
ask. If the young man hunched outside his carriage
door didn't increase his pace, they would be in chains
by sundown.

"Depends," he muttered. Stapleton didn't pause
to speak or cease his work with the small paintbrush
he kept with him for such occasions. "Do you mind
if the lions you asked for have the general look of
large dogs?"

Ash leaned back against velvet cushions and propped
his boots on the opposite seat, crossing his feet at the
ankle. It was true, they were in somewhat of a rush
with the angry mob chasing them and all, but a lord's
seal and emblem said a great deal about his personal
attributes. "Lions do give the impression of strength,"
he mused, staring up at the tufted fabric on the ceiling.
"Lord Crosby should be a strong fellow."

"Crosby now, is it?"

Ash nodded in response. "Rather rolls off the tongue, don't you agree?"

"As long as you're paying, I'm agreeing."

He ignored the comment, knowing his friend Stapleton wasn't truly interested in coin beyond what he needed to live, nor was he prone to keeping his more disagreeable opinions to himself. No, Stapleton was in this for the grand adventure of it all and always had been—unlike Ash. His own reasons were a bit more complicated.

Ash inhaled the scent of smoke and sausages wafting from inside the inn. If he'd realized Stapleton would take so long with the blasted paint, he could have gone inside for a bit of food. He hadn't had a bite since that dry cake yesterday at the tea where everything had begun to fall to pieces.

The part of the entire debacle that Ash found most troubling was that he could have twisted the truth to escape more easily. He could have stayed a few more days, perhaps gained a bit more coin for his efforts, but he'd allowed his situation to disintegrate. Ash pulled out the calling card he kept in his pocket since it had been given to him last year and read it again.

*Fallon St. James*
*The Spare Heirs Society*

He'd been invited to join the secretive club while passing through London last year. As the fourth son in a newly titled family, he certainly met the qualifications. Even if he never used his true name of Ashley Claughbane, it could serve some purpose. And, if the London job was to be a success, he would need more assistance than Stapleton could provide. He narrowed his eyes on the calling card as if it held the answers to his questions.

St. James posed an interesting offer, but was he ready for it? Was it finally time? He'd been working toward this goal since his school days. A lifetime of preparation came down to this moment of rushed thought behind an old inn.

"Where am I taking the much esteemed Lord Crosby?" Stapleton asked, interrupting his thoughts.

Where to next? Ash stuffed the card back in his pocket and looked out the window. There was no turning back toward Cornwall or Devon now—the men trailing them would see to that much. Ash and Stapleton had moved on through the night, only stopping to change horses—until now.

It was midmorning judging by the building's shadow cast on the ground outside the carriage window. They'd stopped when Stapleton had spotted the cover of the inn. Paying a groom for his silence, they'd slipped behind the stables to make an adjustment to his carriage. The men giving them chase would be gaining ground the longer they stayed here, but a change of identity was necessary.

Ash had worked his way through Wales where news of his existence was less likely to reach his brothers' ears. He moved from town to town, never staying anywhere overlong and never allowing anyone to become too close. It was a surprisingly lucrative and exciting life he'd carved for himself. Some may call it dishonest work, but he sold people hope and there was nothing shameful in hope.

When Ash didn't answer right away, Stapleton continued, "It's north from here to Oxford and south to Hampshire. Hampshire would be nice this time of year. Wouldn't mind finding a house there and staying through the summer. We could find some women…"

"We only have two rules, mate. You know staying would be breaking one of them."

"Aye. I do." Stapleton paused his work with the brush, looking up at Ash. "But, I also know I can lose a tail when leaving a town faster than anyone in the business."

"And you think a sedate summer in Hampshire would suit the likes of us? What will we do for entertainment? Take strolls and enjoy the scenery?" Ash laughed at the thought of the two of them on holiday together like a pair of matronly aunts.

"You heard my mention of women," Stapleton replied with a grin.

He couldn't be serious. Ash shook his head. "Hampshire is filled with widows—and not the amusing kind. The old and bitter kind."

"Had a run in with a widow there, did you?" Stapleton asked with a chuckle. "Oxford then?"

"Or it could finally be time," Ash said, testing the waters of possibility. St. James's card filled his pocket and his thoughts.

"Time," Stapleton repeated. "You can't be serious, Claughbane. London?"

"You want amusement for the summer. I want…" Ash broke off at a sound from the front yard of the inn. Craning around to see through the sliver of space between the buildings, he saw Lord Braxton dismounting from his horse and surveying the inn. The men from Bath had arrived. That was the problem with losing someone on the road—they didn't stay lost for long.

"Forget the lions. I find I'm quite fond of dogs." He was also rather fond of his own head. The men hadn't spotted them yet, but it wouldn't be long. If they slipped away now, they might escape for good.

Stapleton nodded and stood, dusting his hands on his breeches. "You're lucky I'm as skilled with a brush as I am the reins of your carriage."

"Indeed. You might want to take up those reins soon if we're to leave this inn free men."

Stapleton paused, looking up at Ash through the carriage window. "London, then. You're certain?"

The gravity of the moment was reflected in his friend's eyes. They both know what this meant.

"London."

∼

Thank goodness the quadrille offered one room to breathe, because a waltz with this particular gentleman might have led to her untimely death.

Evangeline circled Lord Winfield with practiced steps and offered him her hand, ignoring the overpowering scent of his cologne. Truly, had he taken a swim in the vile brew before attending the ball tonight? She took the smallest breath she dared, focusing on her steps.

The arch of her wrist was in exact accordance with the dancing instruction her mother had insisted upon after last season. She stepped forward, pointing the toe of her beaded slipper until it just peeked out from beneath her ball gown. Everything was going to plan.

Her mother had this season organized down to the second, and at this second she was executing the perfect quadrille in spite of a distinct lack of air around her dance partner. She tilted her chin to a pleasing angle and tossed a smile at his lordship. Moving back toward him, she placed her hand on his arm with a featherlight touch. Two more smiles and this dance would be over.

It was true, most ladies allowed the music to dictate dance length, but to Evangeline dances were a matter of many practiced steps, two elegant curtsies, no more than one allotted lingering hand on a gentleman's arm, and five smiles.

If she made every step as rehearsed, she would find a match her family would approve of. Whoever he may be didn't matter—even his lordship of the cologne. If Evangeline Green could do anything well, it was dressing a part and playing it without flaw. The role of wife would be no different from daughter, sister, cousin, and friend. She was quite skilled at pleasing those around her and a husband would be no different. She would wear the proper gowns, offer the perfect response to those who would call upon her, and always have a warm smile for her husband.

What more could he want? For that matter, what more could she want?

There had been a time last season when she'd thought she desired a different path, but she'd been wrong. Her mother had been correct after all—she couldn't be trusted to choose her own future.

"I do so enjoy the quadrille, Lord Winfield."

"The pleasure is mine, Lady Evangeline. I must admit though, I find the glass ceiling of the Dillsworths' ballroom to be a bit concerning." He glanced up as he spoke, sneering at the elegant roof of glass where the candles danced in merry dots of light. "All those candles suspended from such a small amount of roof seems dangerous."

Her mother's list of rules for conversation circled through her mind. *Never offer an opposing view,* and *Always honor your hosts* collided into a gray area with his last comment. She took a breath, considering the appropriate response. "I suppose some might say it adds a bit of excitement to the average dance. I'm pleased we survived."

"Excitement isn't an ideal I hold in much regard. Predictability gives one comfort for years to come," he intoned as he led her from the floor.

"I too enjoy knowing what is to come." She supposed in a sense that was true. She did enjoy knowing that in a moment she would be away from Lord Winfield's excessive scent. And she enjoyed knowing her next dance was free and she would have a few minutes to chat with her cousins. Of course, her twin cousins were anything but predictable.

She focused on the conversation so as not to make a misstep after executing such a perfect dance. "What if summer couldn't be trusted to be warm or winter cold? It would be quite the mess to be getting on with."

"Winter warm as if it's summer. Such fanciful thoughts, my lady." He chuckled and shook his blond head. "I believe I prefer the seasons as they are."

"As do I, my lord. As you said, some things should be able to be relied upon."

"May I rely on the promise of a dance with you at the next ball?" He leaned in a fraction to ask, invading her senses with his overwhelming use of cologne.

She resisted the urge to pull away to breathe clean air. Instead, smiling the final smile of the encounter, she allowed her hand to trail over his arm in the one allotted lingering touch to make him remember her before letting it fall back to her side. "One in which we will remain quite safe from falling ceilings, I hope."

"Lady Evangeline," he offered in farewell as he bowed and took his leave.

Evangeline was still taking breaths to keep from coughing when her cousins joined her, pulling her back toward the wall of the ballroom where they couldn't be overheard. It was a precaution deemed necessary after the end of last season when Lady Smeltings had heard Victoria's rather loud opinion that her new style of hair made her look like an angry bee about to move in for the sting.

Her mother appeared none too thrilled by the move, but she was thankfully locked in conversation with two other ladies and wouldn't be able to berate Evangeline until later. That didn't stop her narrow-eyed glare, however. Busy overlooking her mother scowl, she took a glass of lemonade from a passing footman.

Evangeline would no doubt pay a high price for her behavior on the carriage ride home, but her two cousins were worth the browbeating. The three of them had become quite close over the two years since Victoria and Isabelle's father inherited his title and estate. Evangeline mourned the lost years between them when she and her older sister, Sue, hadn't been allowed to visit *such common gentry* even if they were family. But, at least she'd had Sue…until last season.

The only correspondence she'd received from her sister in the past year were small sketches of sights Sue must have seen while on her wedding trip with Lord Steelings. There were no messages or locations given. Evangeline understood Sue's reasons for such distance, but it made her heart ache all the same. She drowned the maudlin thoughts of her presumably happily married sister in a large swallow of lemonade. She had her cousins for company now, as well as her new friend Roselyn, and she would not muck that up as she had things with her sister last season.

"Who's next?" Victoria asked, grabbing the card from her wrist and squinting at the names written there with a wince. "You'll want to watch your toes for the remainder of the evening. Not a single good dancer—or interesting conversation for that matter—in that lot."

"Victoria," Evangeline admonished through teeth clenched in a polite smile. "Even standing here, someone could hear you."

"I'd be doing them and all the other ladies here a kindness. Someone should tell them they dance a dull waltz and equivalent discussion on London life. Have you heard Lord Herring drone on about his crop rotations? I almost drifted off to sleep there on the floor mid-twirl."

"Victoria does have a fair point, Evie," Isabelle mused as she investigated her cousin's dance card with a frown on her pouty lips. "You seem to have selected your dance partners based on one's ability to nod off while conversing over tea."

Evangeline pulled her wrist away from her cousins' inspection. The gentlemen in question were selected based on rank, wealth and standing in good society. Her mother would consider no other factors in the equation of with whom she would spend her time. "Really, Isabelle. I expected you to understand. Exceptions must be made in regard to dancing abilities and…conversational skills." She hid a grimace behind her glass of lemonade. "Such things matter little in the game of marriage."

"In the game of marriage, even I place no bets," Victoria said with a shake of her blond head.

"We're expected to play a hand or two at least. Show some effort, Victoria."

"I don't care for the odds." If Victoria was anything, it was sure of her own opinions on everything around her. Evangeline admired her strength. Of course, there was no place for such talk in her own life, but her cousin's words always made her smile.

"I, on the other hand, want to play this game forever. Isn't it wonderfully romantic here tonight? The candlelight, the roses, all the gowns and dashing gentlemen…" Isabelle broke off on a sigh, looking out across the ballroom as if soaking in a particularly beautiful sunset.

"You would find the romance in being paraded about town like a cow at the local harvest festival. I'm sure you'll get the winning ribbon this year, worry not, Isabelle."

Isabelle huffed and turned her back on her sister, her perfect blond ringlets bouncing as she moved.

"A cow at the local harvest festival? Really, Victoria." Evangeline shook her head. Although they bickered, her cousins truly did adore each other. Evangeline thought it was the comfort of their relationship that gave them the ability to say such things to one another. They could say what they wished, but she'd seen them laugh and cry together over the last two years, revealing their true nature.

Victoria chuckled, as unrepentant as always for her words, enjoying the situation even more when Isabelle shot her a look of death over her shoulder.

Evangeline watched the gentleman she was to dance with next move past, trouncing on a lady's toes when she came too close. Leaning toward Victoria, she whispered, "Perhaps you were right about my next dance partner."

"Of course I was. What you need to survive the remainder of this evening is champagne. What you were thinking with that lemonade, I have no idea."

"I was thinking that I had a thirst," Evangeline replied as she sat her lemonade glass on the tray of a passing footman.

Isabelle turned. "Are we going in search of champagne? I believe there's a parlor with refreshments nearby."

But when Evangeline turned to answer her cousin, the crowd parted and there he was.

She blinked, not trusting her own eyes. It couldn't be. She craned her neck to see through the crush of people to the main entrance to the ballroom. He looked into the room, his eyes sweeping the room before he turned and moved away into the hall.

He was here. He'd left her with empty promises a year ago and now he was back. She was already moving in his direction. "Will you excuse me? My gown is in need of repair," she murmured without taking her eyes from the door.

"Your gown is fine, Evie. You always fuss so. Let us go and find some champagne so you'll be fortified before your next dance."

"I really must go repair my gown." Evangeline was crossing the room before Victoria could reply.

Perhaps her eyes were bewitched. She thought she would never see him again. And yet, she never stopped looking for him. She found herself searching crowds for his face. Her mother had accused her of madness when she'd abandoned their shopping last month to follow someone down Bond Street. That gentleman had turned out to be Lord Wellsly, to her everlasting embarrassment. Evangeline gave a mental shudder at the memory. But this time was different. This time it wasn't simply the similar tall, lean build of a man or the coal color of his hair—this time she'd seen his face.

This time she'd seen *him*.

# *Acknowledgments*

What lengths are you willing to go to for your jewelry? In the 1800s, jet jewelry rose to the height of its popularity even though the acquisition of jet was difficult, if not deadly. Intrigued? I know I was.

I began researching the history of jet mining after spending the summer in Northern England years ago. I didn't know then that I would one day write this story, but I did know when the black-clad, black sheep of his family Ethan Moore appeared on the page that he would have ties to the dangerously acquired dark stones. Jet is a semiprecious stone formed from a fossilized tree similar to today's monkey puzzle tree, and was mined in the North Yorkshire Moors. The first jet workshop opened in Whitby, England, in 1808. But due to its popularity in jewelry at the time, by 1850 there were fifty such shops. What's so dangerous about these black stone necklaces, bracelets, and such? The jet mining trade.

Jet mining led to many deaths since the shale-covered mines were inherently unstable. Men were lowered by rope harnesses into the earth to extract the stones, but many did not survive due to the collapse of the rock roofs. One such mine was located at Roseberry Topping, where this story begins. Today it's a place for hiking, mountain biking, and enjoying the scenic views of the moors; but I find its history far more intriguing than a walk on a hillside. Of course, many things can happen while on a walk at Roseberry Topping…

Thank you to my family for making this book possible. I couldn't have done this without your sacrifices every day that allow me time to write. I appreciate it more than you know. Thanks to the Bad Girlz at www.badgirlzwrite.com for the unending friendship and more mimosas than I can count. A huge thank-you must go to Michelle Grajkowski for her support throughout this process. To Mary Altman, thank you for shaping this story into what it is today. To the Sourcebooks team, thank you for all that you do. And to my readers, you are amazing! I'm honored that you chose this book to read when so many beautiful stories grace the shelves of bookstores and libraries. I appreciate each and every one of you.

Hugs to all!
E. Michels

# About the Author

Elizabeth Michels is the award-winning author of the Tricks of the Ton and Spare Heirs series. She grew up on a small Christmas tree farm in South Carolina. After tiptoeing her way through school with her focus on ballet steps and her nose in a book, she met a boy and followed him a thousand miles away from home to Kansas City, Missouri. They spent their summers visiting his family in Middlesbrough, England, soaking up culture, history, and a few pints along the way. Elizabeth attended Park University, where she graduated magna cum laude with a BA in interior design.

Elizabeth now spends her days creating plots and concocting characters at her home in a small lakeside town in North Carolina. When she is not typing as fast as human movement will allow, she is caring for her husband and little boy. Elizabeth Michels is a lover of happily-ever-afters; whether in her writing life or in her home life, she spends her days with one word on her lips——love. She invites you to read her stories, get lost, and enjoy. Elizabeth loves to hear from her readers. Please visit www.elizabethmichels.com for more information.